*Acclaim for Charles Baxter's*

# Gryphon

"Baxter shines [a] bright light on his characters, so bright that the landscape around them, in almost every story, shimmers like a mirage in extreme heat." —*Los Angeles Times*

"Baxter is a genius. . . . [*Gryphon*] keeps us mesmerized to the end. Baxter brings to his masterful stories a quirky slant born of the straight-faced humor of the Midwest." —Jane Ciabattari, *Books We Like*, NPR

"Baxter's writing is spare, but, like a flash of cat eyes in the night, well-crafted images and wit flit onto the pages." —*The Providence Journal*

"Baxter is always engaged in a kind of chemistry experiment, closely monitoring what will ensue when two or more disparate elements are—often impulsively—combined. The results, always complex, can be surprising: and, like Miss Ferenczi in 'Gryphon,' they can bring us wonders we had not known we might see."
—*The New York Review of Books*

"Baxter is a writer who plainly enjoys writing, who revels in it, which is rarer than you might think—not the enjoyment, necessarily, but the palpability of the pleasure. . . . Keen and playful." —*The Boston Globe*

"What a treasure this volume is! . . . Dazzles us with the full brilliance of this writer's vision." —Andrea Barrett, author of *The Air We Breathe*

"Elegant. . . . Baxter is a melancholy expert craftsman." —*The New Yorker*

"[Baxter] truly excels at the short form. He observes Chekhov's admonition not to bore people by telling them everything. And yet his delicately carved slices of life contain a surprising amount of detail and depth."
—*The Miami Herald*

# Charles Baxter

# Gryphon

---

Charles Baxter is the author of the novels *The Feast of Love* (nominated for the National Book Award), *The Soul Thief*, *Saul and Patsy*, *Shadow Play*, and *First Light*, and the collections *Believers*, *A Relative Stranger*, *Through the Safety Net*, and *Harmony of the World*. He lives in Minneapolis and teaches at the University of Minnesota and in the M.F.A. Program for Writers at Warren Wilson College.

www.charlesbaxter.com

# Gryphon

# Gryphon

*New and Selected Stories*

———◆———

Charles Baxter

*Vintage Contemporaries*
VINTAGE BOOKS
A DIVISION OF RANDOM HOUSE, INC.
NEW YORK

FIRST VINTAGE CONTEMPORARIES EDITION, JANUARY 2012

Owing to limitations of space, all acknowledgments for permission to reprint previously
published material may be found at the end of this volume.

The following stories originally appeared in book form: "Harmony of the World,"
"Horace and Margaret's Fifty-second," and "The Would-be Father" in *Harmony of the
World* (University of Missouri Press, 1984, and subsequently published by Vintage Books
in 1997); "The Eleventh Floor," "Gryphon," "Surprised by Joy," and "Winter Journey" in
*Through the Safety Net* (Viking, 1985, and subsequently published by Vintage Books in
1998); and "The Cures for Love," "Flood Snow," "Kiss Away," and "The Next Building I
Plan to Bomb," in *Believers* (Pantheon Books, 1997).

Some stories were previously published in the following: "The Old Murder" and
"Royal Blue" in *The American Scholar*; "Poor Devil" in *The Atlantic*; "Ghosts" and "Mr.
Scary" in *Ploughshares*; and "The Cousins" and "The Winner" in *Tin House*.

The Library of Congress has cataloged the Pantheon edition as follows:
Baxter, Charles, [date]
Gryphon: new and selected stories / Charles Baxter.
p. cm.
I. Title.
PS3552.A854G79 2011
813'.54—dc22
2010013785

**Vintage ISBN: 978-0-307-73952-0**

*Book design by M. Kristen Bearse*

www.vintagebooks.com

Printed in the United States of America
10  9  8  7  6  5  4  3  2

FOR DAN FRANK

AND IN MEMORY OF MICHAEL STEINBERG

# Contents

# Gryphon

# The Would-be Father

WIPING OFF THE kitchen counter after dinner, Burrage happened to glance at the window over the sink and saw a woman's face outside, peering in. The face had an inquisitive but friendly expression. It belonged to Mrs. Schultz from across the street, who tended to wander around the Heritage Condominium complex in the early evening while under the influence of powerful medications prescribed for her after-dinner and bedtime pains.

"Hi, Mrs. Schultz," Burrage said, waving a sponge. "Are you all right? Do you know where you are?"

"I think so," she said, waving back. Her gray hair was bundled at the top of her head, and the lines around her mouth rose when she smiled. "I think I know where I am, if I'm across the street and if you are who I think you are. I wanted to see that boy of yours. Also, I'm thirsty. Can you pass a glass of water to me through this window?"

"I can't, Mrs. Schultz," Burrage said. Looking boyish and preoccupied, as was usual for him, he pointed at the window. "Screens. And Gregory's already in his pajamas. See how late it's getting?" Mrs. Schultz glanced up, but it was still too early for stars. All the same, she nodded. "Let me take you home." He dried his hands, poured a glass of water, and glanced down the hall. Gregory's door was closed, but Burrage could hear him singing. He carried the water outside to where the old lady stood near the arborvitae, slowly moving her left hand back and forth in the air. Burrage realized that she was trying to brush away gnats. "Here," he said, putting the glass in her other hand. She sipped it, thanked him, and gave it back. Then she took his arm, and together they crossed the street. It was spring: he could hear children playing softball in the distance.

"You said it was late," she said, "but I don't see any stars."

They walked up the sidewalk to her front door, which was wide open, and Burrage turned her around so that they faced his house. He could

smell onions, or something acidic, coming from the inside of her condominium, a permanent smell and a sign that she had lost the knack of
effective housekeeping.

"The days are longer now, Mrs. Schultz. Daylight savings time. Look
over the roof of my garage at the sky. What do you see? Do you see
anything?"

"I see a dot," she said.

"That's Mars," Burrage told her, letting out a breath with the word.
"The red planet. So you see? It *is* getting dark. I'm leaving you here,
okay? You should do yourself a favor and go inside now. Try to get some
rest. Will you be all right?" Mrs. Schultz stared at his shirt buttons. "You
should try to be all right," he said.

"Oh, it's you I'm worried about, not me," she said. "What a man in
your position does, after all. And that dot, Mars. It's right over your
house, isn't it? It's not over my house." She looked at him with her I'm-
not-so-dumb face. "Thank you anyway. I'll go in now. Say good night to
that little boy of yours."

"I will."

She turned once more and went in. Burrage watched her trudge down
the hall toward the living-room chair in front of the perpetually blaring
television set. He reached inside her door to make sure the lock was set
and then closed it before going back.


Gregory was kneeling at the side of his bed, his arms stretched out over
the patchwork quilt, his fingers clasped tightly together. The only illumination in the room came from the Scotty dog night-light, which cast a
pale glow on the bed and dresser and made them look like toy furniture
used in a circus act. Gregory, who was five years old, was praying to
Santa Claus. With his face buried in the quilt, his words broke out with
difficulty, a mumble of wishes.

On the opposite side of the room was a narrow rocking chair, next to
a low table on which was placed a windup double-decker bus and an ashtray. Above them was a wall poster of Paddington Bear, a poster the boy
had outgrown. Burrage's routine was to go into the room, kiss Gregory
good night, light up a cigar, and turn on the boy's cassette recorder,
which would play the same selection of tunes as always, Glenn Miller's
greatest hits, starting with "Moonlight Serenade." When Burrage had

been a boy himself, suffering from asthma and unable to sleep, his mother would play Glenn Miller on the phonograph. In this way he became accustomed to falling asleep to the big-band sound.

His prayers finished, the boy climbed into bed and waited for Burrage to tuck him in. He was used to Burrage's cigars and now liked the smell at bedtime. After Burrage entered, he kissed Gregory and, as usual, sat down to be close to the ashtray, before tapping the button on the recorder.

"Where were you?" Gregory asked.

"Mrs. Schultz was over here. I had to help her back across the street." He waited a moment. "Did you say your prayers?"

"Yeah," the boy said. He picked up his stuffed dragon and made a sound.

"Was that a roar," Burrage asked, "or a yawn?"

"He's sleepy," the boy said. "Tell me a story. Tell me a story with me in it. Tell me my horoscope." As always, he tripped over the word. "What's happening tomorrow?"

"Don't you want to hear a bunny story or something?"

"No. My horoscope."

"Okay." Burrage took a deep breath. "The planets are in a good position for you tomorrow, especially Mercury and Venus. They'll take good care of you, just like today. The stars are really interested in what will happen to you at school tomorrow, and they want to know how you're doing. They want to know if you've learned the alphabet and if you're getting along better with Rosemary."

"I don't like her," the boy said. "She kicks people and steals cookies from my lunch."

"The stars will take care of you," Burrage said softly. "When you see Rosemary, just get out of her way and do something else. She just acts funny sometimes. I know from your horoscope that you'll find plenty of crayons and clay to play with."

"A train," the boy said sleepily.

"You will find a train," Burrage said, blowing out cigar smoke, "and you can play with the train if you share it. Rosemary won't bother you. Anyhow, it'll be a fine day. The planets and the stars have decided that it'll be sunny tomorrow morning, and you'll also be playing outside in the sandbox or on the jungle gym. You'll laugh a lot and there's a good chance you'll play hide-and-seek. I have a feeling that there'll be peanut-butter sandwiches in your lunchbox tomorrow. Now go to sleep. Sleep tight." Half asleep, the boy made roaring-dragon sounds. Burrage leaned back in the rocking chair to finish his cigar and listen to Glenn Miller.

Burrage is Gregory's uncle, in actual fact. Burrage's brother Cecil, Gregory's father, and Cecil's wife, Virginia, were on their way back from seeing a movie when they were hit head-on in a residential area of Ann Arbor by a kid who was testing the potential of his father's Corvette. At the time, Burrage was living with a red-haired woman named Leslie who was about to move out anyway: her company had relocated her in Seattle. Very little of what happened to Burrage in this period of his life entered his permanent memory. The phone rang all the time, and he had to talk to lawyers whose names he could never remember. He had to go to the Hall of Justice by himself and sign documents. Cecil and Virginia's will said quite explicitly that Burrage was to be the guardian of Gregory should anything happen to them; Burrage had known about this will but had thought it would never be unlocked from the safety deposit box where it had been stored against the day.

He took a leave from the bank and stayed with his mother in Grosse Pointe Shores for two weeks, where he tried to get used to the shock of his brother's and sister-in-law's deaths and to having Gregory around all the time. Burrage was terrified by every minute of his entire future earthly life. For his part, Gregory went back to sucking his thumb and sat slumped in front of the television set all day, crying in the evening when the children's programming ended. At times he fell asleep during *Mr. Rogers' Neighborhood* and emitted tiny snores. After Burrage had finally taken all of his nephew's toys over to his condominium in Ann Arbor, he moved Gregory out of his mother's home and into his. Six months later Burrage's mother sold her house and moved to Arizona, obviously dazed but not yet incompetent.

After a few weeks, Gregory stopped asking when his mommy and daddy were coming back, but he became more interested in television than ever, especially cartoons and broadcasts of church services. He explained to Burrage that people prayed on television, and he wanted to know how it was done. This request was the first one he had made to

Burrage that did not have to do with getting dressed, going to the bathroom, or eating a meal. Burrage hadn't been brought up in a religious household, didn't know anything about prayers, and said so.

"I want to know how," Gregory said. "They all do it on TV. What do I do?"

"I don't know," Burrage told him. "But try this: kneel beside the bed at night and put your head down and close your eyes. Think of what you're happy about. Then think about the things you want. That's what people usually do when they pray." He stopped and waited. Then he asked, "Why do you want to start doing something like this?"

"It might help," Gregory said.

In this way, Burrage hit on the idea of astrology and horoscopes. He had noticed, at a time when he thought they had nothing in common, that Gregory's birthday and his own were both in May, making them Taureans. One night, while Gregory was curled at his end of the sofa watching television and he himself was reading the paper, he found an astrology column and read the entry for Taureans aloud: "Show greater confidence in yourself and others will pay more attention to your ideas and comments. You cannot handle a project all alone. Share the work—and the glory." At first Gregory said nothing, as if he hadn't heard, but then he turned to Burrage and asked, "What's that?"

Burrage explained that it was his fortune for tomorrow, and that the woman who wrote it was a kind of fortune-teller, and people believed that she could see into the future and tell what was about to happen before it actually happened.

"How?" Gregory asked. "How does she know?"

"It's called astrology," Burrage said. "It's based on the stars and the planets. People think the planets have mysterious forces. They cause things. This says you should share your games at school tomorrow and be nice and not hog everything and not be afraid. Mostly it says not to be afraid."

"I'm not afraid," Gregory said, his eyes on the television.

"I know you're not. But here it says that the stars will help you out not being afraid."

"Okay," Gregory said.

In Ann Arbor, a bookish town, Burrage had no trouble finding a paperback guide to astrology. The one he chose had a bloated, menacing star on the cover, either a red giant or an arcane symbol of some sort. At the cash register he felt quite sheepish, as if he had emotional difficulties that he was trying to cure by himself, but the clerk didn't seem to care very much about what books he bought. He took the book to his car, drove to the nursery school, picked up Gregory, and went home. That night, after Gregory was asleep, he read the book straight through, dismayed by its complexity. Casting Gregory's horoscope would take some time. He took fifteen minutes off from his lunch break at the bank the next day to read relevant sections of the book, which he had brought along in his briefcase, and the next night he began to put Gregory's horoscope together at the kitchen table.

Sun in Taurus: constructive, practical, down-to-earth. Burrage marked down Gregory's Earth sign, appropriate for farmers and others with persistence and domestic virtues. Hitler, the book informed him, had been a Taurus, as was Walt Whitman. Discouraged, he read on. At his birth, Gregory's moon was in Cancer: "You may have a strong bond with your mother. You are good at camouflage. You excel at impersonations." Ascendant or rising sign: Gemini. "Gemini ascending has special problems with bankers and clergymen." Burrage read this sentence again. *"Gemini ascending has special problems with bankers and clergymen."* He continued on. "You may hold several jobs at one time. You may well be divorced. You may lose your children." Burrage could not get Gregory's sign for Mercury; the procedure was too complicated. He paged through the book for Gregory's Venus sign, which was also Gemini. "Venus in Gemini makes you pleasant, sociable, and relaxed." The rest of the description applied only to adults. As for Mars, at Gregory's birth, it had been in Leo: "You are friendly. But you tend to be self-centered and see most events in your own terms. You may have a habit of blowing small things out of proportion."

"What's that?" A voice out of nowhere came from behind Burrage. He turned around and saw Mrs. Schultz looking over his shoulder at the horoscope he was constructing. She was carrying a pair of garden clippers, their blades caked with dirt.

"Mrs. Schultz! This is a horoscope. How did you get in?"

"I was tending to things. I thought this was *my* house. Your front door was unlocked, and so I came in. I get confused in this place because all these damn-fool buildings look alike." She gazed down at the table with an expression of pained amusement. "A horoscope? I thought you were a grown-up."

"I *am* a grown-up. I'm using it for Gregory. He needs it."

The noise Mrs. Schultz made could have been throat-clearing, laughter, or a cough. Burrage decided that he would not ask which one it was. "In that case," she said, "I won't stay. I'm going home, and you don't have to help me this time. I'll find my way by myself, *without* a horoscope. What's that music I hear? Glenn Miller. Well, *that* puts me back into the bloom of youth." She did not shuffle out but picked up her feet ostentatiously. Burrage watched her disappear down the hall and go out the front door, which she left open. He went back to work.

Burrage's composite horoscope for Gregory presented his nephew as a rather shaky and split character with extraordinary requirements for domestic stability. The planetary signs, however, were somewhat obtuse when they were not contradictory, so Burrage decided to change them, to revise the sky. Where there was weakness, Burrage inserted strength. Where he found indecision or calamity, he substituted resolve and good fortune. In place of trauma and loss he wrote down words like "luck" and "intelligence." This, he thought at first, would invalidate the horoscope, but he decided that if the planets had real influence, then they were influencing him now to alter Gregory's life-plan. It was their wish.

He put up Gregory's planetary wheel on the refrigerator door. Above the wheel he wrote down Gregory's virtue-words in blue and yellow crayon. For the next week, he explained the chart to Gregory and told him what the planets said he would be like. He explained what all the words were and what they meant. At first Gregory was silent about all this, but one morning he asked Burrage if he could take his horoscope to school. Given permission, he put the chart in his Lone Ranger lunchbox. That afternoon, when he got into the car, he said that most of the other kids wanted Burrage to make up *their* horoscopes but that the only one he really had to do was Magda Brodsky's.

"Who's Magda Brodsky?" Burrage asked.

"Somebody," Gregory said. "She's in the class."

"Is she your friend?"

"I guess so."

"What does she look like?"

"She's nice."

"I mean, what does she *look* like?"

"I told you. She's nice."

"Is she your friend?"

"I guess. She doesn't say a whole lot."

"When's her birthday?"

"I asked her. She said the fourth of July."

"Is she as old as you are?"

"Yeah."

This time, Burrage did not consult the book, although he pretended to do so whenever Gregory was in the room. He drew the wheel, wrote out the symbols for the signs in the quadrants, and then wrote down Magda Brodsky's virtues in green and orange crayon. It was like making up a calendar that had no relation to real dates or days of the week. Burrage decided that Magda was courageous, businesslike, and articulate. In addition, she was affectionate, physically agile, sensible, and generous. The adjectives came to him easily. Burrage drew a picture of Saturn at the top of the chart, along with several five-pointed stars. He told Gregory to give the chart to Magda, and he explained what all the words were, and what they meant. Gregory took the chart to school the next day.

In the evening, after dinner, Magda's mother called him. Being the assistant manager of a branch bank, Burrage had expected this call and thought he knew how to handle it.

"Hello, Mr. Birmingham? This is Amelia Brodsky." She had a pleasant but resolute voice. "Look, I don't want to disturb you, but Magda brought this sheet of paper home from school today, which she says she got from your boy. I want you to understand that I'm not objecting to it. In fact, it's made a distinct difference in her behavior this afternoon. She's been quite an angel. I just want to know what this thing is. Did you do it? Can you explain it to me?"

"I thought you'd be calling," Burrage said. "Actually, it's her horoscope, but it's not accurate. By that I mean that I made up a horoscope to give my boy some confidence, and he took it to school. When he came home he said his friend Magda wanted one, so I made up that one for her."

"Oh." Mrs. Brodsky sounded discreetly taken aback. "You see," she began, then stopped. She tried again. "You see, it's not that I think this little game is doing any harm." She paused. "What do you mean when you say it's not accurate?"

Burrage smiled and waited a moment. Then he said, "I just drew some symbols on the horoscope and listed a few virtues at the top. It's not accurate because I didn't check an ephemeris, where her planetary signs would be listed. I just wrote down some virtues I thought she might like to have. I've never met your daughter. My boy asked me to do it as a favor to her. Do you mind?"

"Well, no. That is, I don't think so. I'm not sure. I'm not a believer in astrology. Not at all. It's against my discipline. I'm a professional biologist." She said this last sentence as if it were an astounding revelation, with pauses between the words.

"Well," Burrage said, "I don't believe in it either, and I'm a banker."

"If you don't believe in it," she asked, "why did you do it?"

Burrage had had a drink in preparation for this call, which was probably why he said, "I'm trying to learn how to be a parent."

This statement proved to be too much for Mrs. Brodsky, who rapidly thanked Burrage for explaining the whole matter to her before she hung up.

Later in the week, sitting in the dark of Gregory's room, with a cigar in his hand and Glenn Miller playing "Chattanooga Choo-Choo" softly beside him, Burrage began a bunny story. "Once upon a time, there was a bunny who lived with his mommy and daddy bunny in the bunny hole at the edge of the great green wood." All the bunny stories started with that sentence. After it, Burrage was deep in the terror of fictional improvisation. "One day the little bunny went hopping out on the bunny path in the woods when he met his friend the porcupine. The wind was blowing like this." Burrage made a wind sound, and the cigar smoke blew out of his mouth. "Together the bunny and the porcupine walked down the path, gazing at the branches that waved back and forth, when suddenly the little bunny fell into a hole. It was a deep hole that the little bunny hadn't seen, because he had been staring at the branches waving in the wind. 'Help!' he cried. 'Help!' "

"Uncle Burrage," Gregory said.

"What?"

"I don't want to hear any more bunny stories."

"Any of them? Or just this one?"

"Any of them." He brought his stuffed dragon closer to his face. "Tell me my horoscope."

"It will be warm tomorrow," Burrage said, having seen the weather reports. "It will be a fine spring day. Soon it will be summer, and you'll be playing outside." Burrage stopped. "You will learn to swim, and you'll take boat rides."

Gregory's eyes opened. "I want a boat ride."

"When?"

"Right away."

"What kind of boat?"

"I don't care. I want a boat ride. Can Magda come?"

"You want a ride in a rowboat?"

"Sure. Can Magda come?"

"Next Saturday," Burrage said, "if the weather is good. You'll have to remember to invite her."

"Don't worry," Gregory said.


Amelia Brodsky delivered Magda promptly at nine o'clock in the morning ten days later. She kept the pleasantries to a minimum. She couldn't stay to chat, she said, because she was on her way to the farmers' market, where she would have to battle the crowds. She asked which lake they were going to, and when Burrage said Cloverleaf Lake, Mrs. Brodsky nodded and said there *was* a rowboat concession there, with life jackets, and with that she kissed Magda good-bye and left in her station wagon. Burrage had been glad to see her go: she was well over six feet tall and wore a button on her blouse with some slogan on it that he had been unable to read.

Magda was looking at him suspiciously. She was a small girl, even for her age, with tightly curled hair and intelligently watchful brown eyes. She was wearing jeans and a pink sweatshirt that said "Say good things about Detroit" on it, the words printed underneath a rainbow. She and

Gregory climbed into the backseat, whispering to each other but then falling silent. Burrage looked in at them. "Do we have everything?" he asked, feeling shaky himself. "Jackets, caps, snacks, and shoes?" From his list he realized how nervous he was. "Anybody have to go to the bathroom before we leave?" They both shook their heads. "All right," he said. "Here goes." He backed the car out of the driveway into the street, where Mrs. Schultz happened to be standing, a slightly more vacant expression on her face than was usual for her.

"Where are you going?" she asked, through the open window on the driver's side.

"Boating," Burrage said.

Mrs. Schultz's right hand flew to the door handle, clutching it. "Take me along," she said.

"Take her along." It was Gregory. Burrage turned around and stared at him.

"Mrs. Schultz? You want Mrs. Schultz along with us on our boat ride?" Both Gregory and Magda nodded together. "I don't get this," Burrage said aloud, before turning to Mrs. Schultz. "I suppose if you want to come along, you can. Are you dressed for it? Is your house locked up?"

"Doesn't matter." She walked around to the passenger side and got into the front seat, slamming the door fiercely. "Let them steal everything, for all I care. I want to go out in a boat. Let's get going."


On the ten-minute drive to the lake, Magda kept silent, though she would nod if either Burrage or Gregory asked her a question. Meanwhile, in the front seat, Mrs. Schultz was watching the landscape with her eyes wide open, as if she had never ridden in an automobile before. She was offering opinions. "I'm glad it's Saturday," she said. "If this was during the week, I'd be missing my soap operas." They passed a water tower. "Never saw one of those before." Burrage groaned. Mrs. Schultz suddenly turned her gaze on Burrage and asked him, "What does the horoscope say about today, Burrage?"

"It'll be beautiful. It *is* beautiful. Warm. Nothing to worry about."

"No episodes?"

"No. Definitely no episodes."

"Good." She drew in a deep breath. "I'm too old for episodes."

When they reached the lake, Burrage paid to get into the grounds of the state park, which included a beach and boating area. The two children and the old woman did not seem especially pleased about arriving; nobody announced it. They all stepped out of the car in silence as the moist vegetative smell of the lake drifted up to them. "Anybody have to go to the bathroom?" Burrage asked again, being careful to take the snack bag from the backseat. They all shook their heads. "Well, in that case, let's go," he said, and they walked down to the rowboat concession, Mrs. Schultz leading, while Gregory held on to Burrage's hand and Magda held on to Gregory's.

The boy in the concession stand, who was listening to a transistor radio and wearing a Styx T-shirt, tied them all into life jackets, Mrs. Schultz, because of her arthritis, being the hardest to fit. This job finished, he went down to the dock and pulled an aluminum rowboat out to where some steps had been built in the dock's north side. Magda and Gregory went in front, Mrs. Schultz in back, and Burrage sat down in the middle, where he could row. "You got an hour," the boy said, scratching his chest. "If you take longer, it's okay, but you got to pay extra when you get back." Burrage nodded as he lifted the oars. "You know how to row?"

"I know how," Burrage said. "Cast us off." The boy untied the boat and gave it a push.

"Bon voyage," he said, lifting his leg to scratch his ankle.

Burrage watched the dock recede. Mrs. Schultz was observing something in the distance and sniffing the air. Both Magda and Gregory were staring down into the water. "How far do we go?" Burrage asked them all.

"To the middle," Gregory said. "I want to go to the middle."

"Yes, that would be fine," Mrs. Schultz said. "Right to the middle."

"Okay." He felt a slight ache in his shoulders. "If anybody wants a snack," he said, "there are crackers and things in that bag." He stopped rowing with his right hand to point to the bag, and, as he did, the boat turned in the water.

"Come on," Gregory said. "Don't do that. Just row."

"Be nice," Mrs. Schultz said to Gregory. "Always try to be nice."

Like most lakes in the southern part of the state, Cloverleaf was rather shallow and no more than six miles in circumference. All the houses on the shore, most of them summer cabins, were distinctly visible. A slight breeze from the west blew over them. With the sky blue, and the temperature in the low seventies, Burrage, as he rowed, felt his heart loosen in his chest while the mildness of the day crept over him. He could see several families splashing in the water at the public beach. He smiled, and noticed that Mrs. Schultz was doing the same.

"Tell me when we get to the middle of the lake," Burrage said. "Somebody tell me when we're there."

"I'll tell you," Magda said. It was her first complete public sentence of the day.

"Thank you, Magda," Burrage said, turning around to see her. She was doing finger-flicks in the water.

Five minutes later she broke the silence by saying, "We're there." Burrage raised the oars from the water and let the droplets fall one by one before he brought them into the boat. On the south side of the lake an outboard was pulling a water-skier wearing a blue safety vest. Gregory was letting his hand play in the water, humming a song from the Glenn Miller tape, and Magda was now staring down into the water with her nose only four inches or so from its surface. "I see a monster down there," she said. No one seemed surprised. "It's got a long neck and an ugly head."

"A reptile," Mrs. Schultz said, nodding. "Like Loch Ness."

"It could bite," Gregory said. "Watch out."

"Sea monsters," Burrage said, "may not be extinct. Pass me the crackers, please."

"After I have mine," Mrs. Schultz said, her hand in the bag. She was sniffing the air again. "I don't believe I have ever seen a sea monster, not this far inland. I've heard about them, though." She waited. "I like this lake. It's a nice lake."

"There's a bug on me," Magda said, tapping a finger on her sweatshirt. "There. It flew away."

"Pass me a cracker," Gregory said. "Please."

"Look at that water-skier," Burrage said. "He's very good."

The rowboat began to drift, pushed by the breeze. Gregory munched on his cracker, and now Magda was dipping her fingers in the water and experimenting with wave motion. Mrs. Schultz had taken a handkerchief out of her sleeve and put it on her head, apparently to minimize the danger of sunstroke.

"Does anybody want anything?" Burrage asked, feeling regal.

"No," the other three said.

"Don't ask me if I have to go to the bathroom," Mrs. Schultz complained. "Once is enough." She waited. "Do you know," she said, "that my grandfather owned land just north of here? He was Scottish, and, of all things, his life's dream was to build himself a golf course. He was even going to build the hills. But, for some reason, it didn't happen. Instead, he learned how to play the oboe and could play it lying down in a hammock, during the summer. He had the lungs of a seven-year-old boy." She looked at Burrage. "He never smoked cigars."

"What's that?" Magda asked. Her finger was pointing toward shore.

"What's what?"

"That." She was still pointing. "That smoke."

"That's a charcoal grill," Burrage said. "Somebody's cooking hamburgers outside, and that's where all the smoke comes from."

"Cooking with charcoal is bad for you," Mrs. Schultz said. "Too much carbon. Cancer."

"Where's the grill?" Magda asked. "I don't see it."

They all turned to look. Thin strips of smoke rose in the distance behind or near a house. It was hard to tell. The house was a plain white one that seemed to have a screen porch but no other distinguishing features.

"Is that house on fire?" Magda asked.

"No," Burrage said. "It is *not* on fire. *They are just cooking hamburgers.*" He did not want to shout. "It's Saturday. People cook hamburgers on Saturday all the time." Because there was more smoke, he felt he should raise his voice somewhat. "You shouldn't worry."

"Maybe we ought to row toward it," Mrs. Schultz suggested, the handkerchief on her head fluttering as her head shook.

"No," Burrage said. "I don't think so. The children should stay away."

"Look," Gregory said, "they're so small."

"Is there someone inside the house?" Magda asked, and began to cry. "I hope there isn't anyone inside. What if there's someone inside the house?"

"It's not a fire!" Burrage shouted, unable to stop himself. "They're just cooking lunch! You'd see flames if it was a fire!"

While they stared, the boat rocked gently underneath them. A fish jumped behind them and slapped the water. The breeze brought them a scent of smoke. Burrage turned around and glanced at the opposite side of the lake, where the boy in the rowboat concession was sitting with his feet up in the booth. Gregory reached out for Burrage's hand. "You didn't know about this yesterday," Gregory said. "It wasn't in the horoscope. Daddy, Magda's crying."

"I know," Burrage said. "She'll be all right."

"I want to know if someone's in the house," Magda said. Mrs. Schultz was murmuring and muttering. "I want to know," Magda repeated.

Suddenly Mrs. Schultz stared at Burrage. "You said there wouldn't be any episodes," she said, pointing her finger at him. "God damn it, you said nothing would happen to us! And look at what's happening!" She was shouting. "Look at all the smoke and the fire!" Her finger, still pointing, pointed now at Burrage, Magda, and Gregory.

"Mrs. Schultz," Burrage begged, "please don't swear. There are children here."

"It's a fire," she repeated. And then she turned around in the boat, bent down, and cupped her hands in the water. Raising her arms, she doused her head. The water streamed into her gray hair and washed the handkerchief off, so that it dropped onto the gunwales of the rowboat. Again she reached down into the lake and again she scooped a small quantity of water over her head. As the children and Burrage watched, handful by handful the old woman soaked her hair, her skin, and her clothes, as if she were making a formal gesture toward the accidents of life, which in their monotonous regularity had brought her to her present condition.

# Horace and Margaret's
# Fifty-second

A FEW MONTHS AFTER she had put her husband, all memory gone, into the home, she herself woke one morning with an unfamiliar sun shining through a window she hadn't remembered was there. A new window! Pranksters were playing a shabby joke on her. She rose heavily from the bed, a groan bursting by accident out of her throat, and shuffled to the new window they had installed during the night. Through the dusty glass she saw the apartment's ragged backyard of cement and weeds. A puddle had formed in the alley, and a brown bird was flapping in it, making muddy waves as it bathed. Then she looked more closely and saw that the bird was lying on its side.

"I remember this view," she said to herself. "It's not a new window. I just forgot to pull down the shade." She did so now, blocking the sun, which seemed to her more grayish-blue than it had for years. She coughed rhythmically with every other step to the bathroom.

It was Tuesday, and their anniversary. He would forget, as usual. Now, in his vacancy, he had stopped using shaving cream and razor blades. He tore photographs out of their expensive frames, folded them into baskets, and used them as ashtrays. He took cigarette lighters to pieces to see how they worked and left their tiny wet parts scattered all over his nightstand. He refused to read, claiming that what she brought him was dull trash, but she had suspected for a long time that he had forgotten both the meaning of the words and how to read them from left to right across the page. She didn't want to buy him cigarettes (in his dotage, he had secretly and then quite openly taken up smoking again). He lost clothes or put them on backward or declared universal birthdays so he could give everything he owned to strangers. The previous Wednesday, she had asked him what he would want for their upcoming anniversary, their fifty-second. "Lightbulbs," he said, giving her an un-pleasantly sly look.

She glanced at his lamp and saw that the shade was pleated oddly. "They give you plenty of bulbs here," she said. "Ask them."

He shook his head for thirty seconds before he replied. "Wrong bulbs," he said. "It's the special ones I need, with the flames."

"Lightbulbs don't have flames," she said. "It's filaments now."

"Don't argue with me. I know what I want. Lightbulbs."


She was at the breakfast table reading the paper when she remembered that she had dropped an egg into the frypan, where, even at this mo-ment, it must still be frying: hard, angry, and dry. She forgave herself, because she had been thinking about how to get to the First Christian Residence before lunch, and which purple bus she should take. She walked to the little four-burner stove with its cracked oven window, closed her eyes against the smoke, picked up the frypan using a worn potholder with a picture of a cow on it, and dropped her last egg into the wastebasket's brown paper bag. Now she had nothing to eat but toast. She was trying to remember what she had done with the bread when she heard the phone ring and she saw from the kitchen clock that it was ten thirty, two hours later than she had thought.

She picked the receiver angrily off the wall. "Yes," she said. She no longer said "Hello"; she was tired of that.

"Hello?"

"Yes," she said. "Yes, yes, yes, who is it?"

"It's me," the voice said. "Happy anniversary."

Very familiar, this woman's voice. "Thank you," Margaret said. "It's our fifty-second."

"I know," the voice told her. "I just wish I could be there."

"So do I," Margaret said, a thin electrical charge of panic spreading over her. "I wish you could be here to keep me company. How are you?"

"Just fine. Jerry's out of town, but of course David's with me, and last night we roasted marshmallows and made a big bowl of popcorn."

David. Oh, yes: her grandchild. This must be David's mother. "Penny," she said.

"What?"

"I just wanted to say your name."

"Why?"

"Because," Margaret said carelessly. "Because I just thought of it."

"Mother, are you all right?"

"Just fine, dear. I'm going to take the bus to see your father in half an hour's time. I'm going to wish him a happy anniversary. I doubt he'll notice. He won't remember it's our anniversary, I don't think. Maybe he won't remember me. You can never tell." She laughed. "As he says, the moving men just come and take it all away. You can't tell about anything. For example, I thought they put a new window in my room last night, but I'd only forgotten to pull down the window shade." She noticed a list on the refrigerator, a list of things she must do today. It was getting late. "Good-bye, Penny," she said, before hanging up. She took the list off the refrigerator and put it in her pocket. Then she stood in the middle of the room, her mind whirling and utterly blank, while she stared at the faucet on the right-hand side of the sink and, above it, attached to the cabinet, a faded color photograph of a brown-haired girl, looking away from the camera toward a tree. It was probably Penny, when young.

Once Margaret was on the bus, she was sure that everything would be fine. The sun was out, and several children were playing their peculiar games on the sidewalk, smacking each other and rolling over to play dead. Why weren't they in school? She knew better than to ask children to explain their reasons for being in any one spot. If you asked such questions, they always had that look ready.

The bus was practically empty. All the passengers, thank God, seemed to be respectable taxpayers: a gentleman with several strands of attractive gray hair sat two rows in front of her, comforting her with his presence. The sun, now yellow, was shining fiercely on Margaret's side of the bus, its ferocity tempered by tinted glass.

Margaret felt the sun on her face and said, "Sweet sweet sweet sweet sweet tea." This, her one and only phrase to express joy, she had picked up from a newspaper article that had tried to make fun of Gertrude Stein. The article had quoted one of her poems, and Margaret had remembered its first line ever since. "Sweet sweet sweet sweet sweet tea," she said again, gazing out the window at obscurely sinister trees, with far too many leaves, all of them the wrong shape.

Horace, before he had been deposited in the First Christian Residence, had been a great one for trees: after they had bought a house, he had planted them in the backyard, trimmed them, fed them, watered them when droughts dusted their leaves. "Trees," he liked to say, "give back more than they take. Fruit, oxygen, and shade. And for this they expect no gratitude." He would have been happy working in a nursery or a greenhouse. As it was, he worked in a bank, and never talked about exactly what he did there. "It's boring," he would say. "You don't want to hear about it." Margaret agreed; she didn't. Only toward the end had he raged against the nature of his work. But he didn't shout at Margaret; he told the trees. He told them how money had gobbled up his life. He talked about waste and cash, and he wept into his hands. Margaret watched him from the kitchen window. She watched him as he lost his memory and began to give names to the trees: Esther, Jonas, Ezekiel, Isaiah. He told Margaret that trees should have serious, adult names. For eighteen months now, he had confused the names of his trees with the names of his children. He wanted his trees to come visit him in the home. "Bring in Esther," he would say. "I want to see her."

Because of this, Margaret no longer gazed at trunks, branches, or leaves with any special pleasure.

She remembered where to get off the bus and was about to go into the residence when she realized that she had no anniversary present. She stood motionless on the sidewalk. "He won't remember," she said aloud. "What's the difference?" She waited a moment and found that she disagreed with her own assessment. "It does make a difference. He'll think I'm making it up if I don't bring him something." She looked around. At the corner there was a small grocery store with a large red Coca-Cola sign over its door. "I'll go down there," she said.

The store was darker than it should have been and was crowded with confusing teenagers. Margaret found herself looking at peanut-butter labels and long rows of lunch meat. Then she was in front of the cash register, holding two Hershey bars. "I'll buy these," she said to the coarse

girl with the brown ponytail and the pimples. She was already far down
the street when she realized that she hadn't waited for change, or a bag to
put the chocolate in. It was the first time she had given him a present she
hadn't wrapped.

Holding the candy bars and her purse in one hand, she opened the large
front door of the First Christian Residence with the other. This was
the worst moment, because of the smell. Margaret knew that oldsters
couldn't always keep themselves clean and tidy, but their smell offended
her nevertheless. Just inside, a man with wild hair and a bruise on his
forehead, whose eyes were an angelic blue, smiled at her and followed
her in his wheelchair as she walked to the elevator. A yellow Have-a-nice-
day sticker, with a smiley face, was glued to the back of the chair.

"Beautiful day, Margaret. Don't you agree?"

"Yes." This man had been pestering her for months. He was forward,
and looked at her with an old man's dry yearning. "Yes," she repeated,
inside the elevator, as she pressed the button for the third floor, wanting
the door to close. "It is indeed a nice day. You should get outside into the
sunshine for some fresh air and vitamin D, instead of staying in here all
the time."

He wheeled himself onto the elevator and turned around so he was
next to her. "I stayed," he said, "because I was hoping you'd come." The
elevator doors closed, at last. "I can still walk, you know. This chair is a
convenience."

Margaret tried to sound chilly. "I'm going to see Horace, my husband.
I don't have time for you."

"Horace won't miss you. His memory's bad. He remembers the 1945
World Series better than he remembers you. Let's go for a walk."

"No, thank you." She remembered his name. "No, thank you, Mr.
Bartlett."

"It's Jim. Not 'Mr. Bartlett.' Jim." He smiled. She noticed again his
remarkable eyes. The numbers above the doors flashed. It was the slow-
est elevator she'd ever been on, slow to prevent shocks to the elderly.

"This is my stop," she said, backing out into the hallway once the
doors opened. As they closed again, Mr. Bartlett leaned back in his
wheelchair and gave her a bold look.

Horace was in his room, wearing a Wayne State University sweatshirt, gray corduroys, and tennis shoes. He was watching a quiz show and eagerly smoking when Margaret came in. He glanced at her and then went back to the activity of the contestants. On the screen, a woman in uniform was spinning a huge, multicolored wheel, and the studio audience was roaring, but Horace failed to share the excitement and watched the television set indifferently. Margaret picked up a newspaper from the chair by the window and arranged the flowerpots on the sill.

"Good morning, dear," she said. "How did you sleep?"

Horace didn't answer. Perhaps it would be one of those days. Lately he had been retreating into silence. Apparently he found it comforting. Margaret clucked, shook her head, and walked over to the television set, which she turned off.

"It's our anniversary," she said. "I don't want daytime television on our anniversary."

On the table next to Horace was a breakfast roll. A fly walked back and forth on it, as if on sentry duty. Margaret picked up the plate and took it out to the hallway, placing it on the floor next to the wall. When she came back, Horace was still staring at the dark television screen.

She gazed at him for a moment. Then she said brightly, "Do you remember Mrs. Silverman, two floors up in the building, Horace? The apartment building? Where we moved after we sold the house? Mrs. Silverman, whose husband was so terribly bald? I'm sure you do. Well, anyway, several nights ago there was a great commotion, and it seemed that Mrs. Silverman was reading the paper, probably just the want ads, as she did usually, when she had one of those seizures of hers. She knocked over a tall glass of ginger ale. It left a stain on the rug, I think. They came for her and took her to the hospital, but the word in the building is that it may be curtains for Mrs. Silverman."

"The moving men," Horace rasped.

"Yes, Horace, the moving men. Someone in the building called for them. Sometimes they can help and other times they can't. You are looking very scruffy today, Horace," she said. "Where did you get that awful sweatshirt?"

"Someone gave it to me," he said, avoiding eye contact.

"Who?" she asked. "Not that horrid little Mr. List?"

"Maybe." Horace shrugged.

"I'd think you'd be ashamed to be in that sweatshirt. You were never a student at Wayne State. Never. You went to Oberlin."

"It's warm," Horace said. "And it's green."

"Which reminds me," Margaret announced, "that I thought they had put a new window into our bedroom last night. But I just forgot to pull down the shade. Oh. Someone called this morning." She thought for a moment. "Penny." She waited for him to show recognition, but he kept his face turned away from hers. "She called to wish us a happy anniversary. It's our anniversary today, Horace."

"I know that," he said. "I know that very well."

"Well, I'm glad. I brought you something."

"Lightbulbs?"

"No. Not lightbulbs. I explained to you about the lightbulbs. You don't need them. What do you need them for?"

"Bliss," Horace said.

"For bliss? I doubt it. No. Well, what I brought you was this." She handed him the chocolate bars. "Happy anniversary, dear. These were the best I could do. I am sorry. Age has brought us low. I would have presented you with a plant in the old days."

"These *are* the old days," Horace said. He gazed down at the dark brown wrappers. "Thank you. Mr. List likes chocolate. So do I, but Mr. List likes chocolate more than I do." Horace suddenly looked at her, and she flinched. "How's Penny? And where's Isaiah?"

"Penny's fine. She toasted marshmallows with David last night. And Isaiah's lost his leaves because it's late October."

Horace nodded. He appeared to think for a long time. Then he said, "I went out yesterday. I wanted to drop something on the ground the way the trees do. Dead leaves reactivate the soil, you know. They don't rake leaves in the forest, only in the suburbs. It's against nature and foolhardy to rake leaves. I pulled out a strand of my hair and left it in the grass. Why did we get married in October? Tell me again." He smirked at her. "I've forgotten. I've lost my memory."

"It was 1930, Horace. Times were hard. When you finally secured a job at the Farmers' and Mechanics' Bank, I agreed to marry you."

"Yes."

Margaret knew she had made a serious mistake as soon as she saw the tears: she had mentioned the bank.

"When did you stop kissing me?" Horace asked.

"What?"

"After the war. You wouldn't kiss me after the war. Why not?"

"I think this is very unpleasant, Horace. I don't know what you're talking about."

"Of course you do. You wouldn't kiss me after the war. Why?"

"You know very well," she said.

"Tell me again," Horace said. "I've lost my memory."

"I didn't like it," she muttered, standing up to look out of the window.

"What didn't you like?"

"I didn't like the way you kissed me. Too many germs."

"We weren't old yet," Horace said. "It's what adults do. They have passions. You can't fool me about that."

Margaret felt tired and hungry. She wished she hadn't taken the breakfast roll out to the hallway.

"I'm not here to settle old scores," she said. "Do you want to split one of these candy bars?" Outside, a blue convertible with a white canvas roof came to a stop at an intersection and seemed unable to move, and all around it the small pedestrians froze into timeless attitudes, and the sun blinked on and off, as if a boy were flipping a wall switch.

Horace struck a kitchen match on the zipper of his pants and lit up a cigarette. "I love cigarettes," he said. "I get ideas from the smoke. Call me crazy if you want to, but yesterday I was thinking about how few decisions in my life were truly important. I didn't decide about the war and I didn't decide to drop the bomb. They didn't ask me about nuclear generators, or, for that matter, about coal generators. I had opinions. They could have asked me. But they didn't. Mr. List and I were discussing this yesterday. The only thing they ever asked us was what we were going to do on the weekends. That's all. 'What are you doing Saturday night?' That's the only question I can remember."

Margaret tore the brown paper away from the candy bar, then crumpled up the inner wrapper before she snapped off four little squares of the chocolate. Someone seemed to be flicking lights inside the First Christian Residence as well. The taste of the chocolate rushed across her tongue, straight from heaven.

"Want any rum?" Horace asked. "I have some in the closet. Mr. List

brought it for me. On days like this, I take to the rum with a fierce joy."
This line sounded like, and was, one of his favorites.

"Horace, you can't have liquor in here! You'll be expelled!"

Suddenly he appeared not to hear her. His face lost its color, and she could tell he would probably not say another word for the rest of the morning. She took the opportunity to snap off one more piece of the chocolate and to straighten the room, to put smelly ashtrays, pens, shirts, and dulled pencils in their rightful places. There were pencil sketches of trees, which she stacked into a neat pile. In this mess she noticed a photograph of the two of them together, young, sitting under a large chandelier, smiling fixedly. Where was that? Margaret couldn't remember. Another photo showed Natwick, Horace's dog in the 1950s, under a tree, his mouth open and his dirty retriever's teeth prominent. Horace had trained him to smile on cue.

"Someday, Horace," Margaret said, "you'll remember to keep your valuables and to throw away the trash. You've got the whole thing backward." Seeing that he said nothing, she went on. "So often I myself have . . . so often I, too, have found that I have been myself in a place where I have found myself so often in a place where I have found myself." Standing there, squarely in the middle of the room, she felt herself tipping toward Horace's cigarette smoke, falling through it, tumbling as if off a building, end over end, floor after floor. Horace held his hand up. Margaret, whose mind was still plunging, walked toward him. He whirled his hand counterclockwise as an invitation to bring her ear down to his mouth.

"Don't tell me anything," he whispered. "That's for kids. And be quiet. Listen. There's a bird scratching in the tree outside. Hear it?"

She did not. Margaret bent down to kiss his forehead and made her way out of the room, sick with vertigo. The hallway stretched and shrank while she balanced herself like a tightrope walker in a forward progress to the elevator. Three floors down, Mr. Bartlett was waiting for her, wearing a cap and a jacket in his wheelchair, but she tottered past him, out into the sun, which she saw had turned a sickly blue.


There was something wrong with the bus.

She sat near the back. The bus would start, reach twenty-five miles an hour, then stop. Not slow down. Stop. In midair, as it were. When it stopped, so did the world. The trees, pedestrians, and birds froze in midair, the birds glued to the sky. And when this occurred, Margaret grabbed the top of the seat in front of her, pressing it hard with her thumbs, hoping she could restart the world again.

She looked up. In front of her a little girl was kneeling on the plastic seat next to her mother, facing the back, staring at Margaret. The little girl had two pigtails of brown hair, a bright red coat, and round-rimmed glasses too large for her face. As the bus began to move, Margaret stared at the girl, frowning because she wanted the youngster to know that staring is rude, a sign of bad breeding. But as she scowled and frowned, and the bus passengers swayed like a chorus together, she was horrified to feel her own eyes producing tears, which would run partway down her cheeks and then stop, as the bus itself stopped, as time halted. The little girl reminded Margaret of someone, someone she would never exactly remember again.

The girl's mouth opened slightly. Her eyes widened, and now she, too, was crying. Her glasses magnified her tears, which were caught by the rims in tiny pools. Margaret gathered herself together. It was one thing to cry herself for no special reason. It was quite another to make a little girl cry. That was contagion, and a mistake in anyone's part of the world. So Margaret wiped her eyes with her coat sleeve and smiled fiercely at the girl, even laughing now, the laugh sounding like the yip of a small dog. "*Toujours gai, toujours gai,*" she said, louder than necessary, before she realized that little girls on buses don't speak French and would never have heard of archy and mehitabel even if they did. "There's a dance in the old dame yet," Margaret said, to finish the phrase, quietly and to herself. She drew herself up and looked serious, as if she were on her way to someplace. She was not about to be cried at on a public bus in broad daylight.

"What a nice day!" Margaret said aloud, but no one turned toward her. The little girl took off her glasses, wiped her eyes on her mother's coat, and gave Margaret a hostile look before turning around. "The old lady shows her mettle," Margaret continued, editorializing to herself, simultaneously making a mental note not to engage in private conversations where other people could hear her. It takes a minimum of sixty years' experience to recognize how useful and necessary talking to oneself actually is. When you're young, it just seems like a crazy habit. Margaret did not speak these thoughts aloud, as the bus whirled upside down and righted itself; she whispered them.

They went past a world of details. Sidewalks broke into spiderweb patterns. A green squirt gun was in a boy's hand, but the bus was moving too quickly for her to see the rest of the boy. In a tree that she noticed by accident, a brown bird flew out of a nest. Something redbreast. Robin redbreast. The bus driver's head, suddenly in the way of the sun, shone a fine gunmetal blue. On a jungle gym, a boy wearing a green sweatshirt, smaller than Horace's, hung down from a steel bar with only his legs, his knees, holding him there. Margaret stared at him. How was it possible for a human being to hang by his knees from a bar? More important, why would anyone want to do it? Before an answer came, the boy faded out and was replaced by another detail, of a seagull standing proudly in someone's alley, an arrogant look on its face. The seagull cheered Margaret. She admired its pluck. The other details she saw were less invigorating: an old man, very white in all respects, asleep in a doorway; two young people, across the street from the art institute, kissing underneath a tree (the tree and the kissing made her flesh crawl); and now, at last, a cumulating, bright pink, puffing cloud of smoke exploding out of someone's backyard, someone's shed, on fire or dynamited, even the smell reaching her. The bus drove on and Margaret forgot about it.

She remembered her stop, however, and was halfway up the sidewalk when she remembered that she had forgotten to get out at the Safeway to buy groceries. She counted all her canned goods, in her mind's eye. "I'll be all right," she said, "and besides, there are more buses going here and there. It's their fate in life." She trudged on into the building.

Skinny Mr. Fletcher, employee of the United States Postal Service, had already come and gone with his Santa's sack of bills and messages. Margaret unlocked her mailbox, hoping for a free sample of a new soap. Instead, there was a solitary postcard inside, showing on its picture side Buster Keaton walking squarely down the middle of a railroad track. On the other side was a message from Horace, written in his miserable script. Some letters had been crossed out, but he had not given up.

Dear Margaret,
    Happy *51th* aniversery
         today
      from love Horace
        ps remember lightbulbs

Where had he mailed the message? Where, more important, had he found the stamp? How had he remembered the address? It was all very mysterious. The postcard was, of course, simply one of his monstrously large postcard collection, which he had taken with him to the First Christian Residence, over two hundred of them. He had traded a few for cigarettes. Margaret looked at Buster Keaton as she went up the stairs, the stairway extending and shortening, like a human-sized accordion.

She opened her door and stepped into the living room. On the left was her pastel blue sofa, next to her radio and television set, and on the right was her mother's harmonium, underneath a mirror. Behind the sofa were bookshelves, filled with books she and Horace had read to each other: Robert Benchley, Don Marquis, Brooks Atkinson. She could remember their names but not the character of their work. "Feels like I'm walking through gelatin," she meant to say, but no sound could make its way out of her throat.

She stood stranded inside the door, waiting for something to happen. At last the invisible steel wires holding her feet loosened for a moment, and she managed to get as far as the harmonium. Then the movie came to a halt again. She hadn't taken her coat off, nor could she. She was forced to look at more details: the spiral pattern on her white rug; the legs of the harmonium; her own white surprised face in the mirror. "I know where I am," she said. "I'm home." But she didn't remember the mirror. Who had brought it here? Had it been delivered by Mr. Fletcher, from his sack?

"I should go to the kitchen," she said. "Or I should take a nap." Step by step, feeling the great work her progress required, she walked to the kitchen, weighted down by the thousands of details that were in her way. A nick in the floor, a jolly afternoon sun, a cookie crumb in the shape of an elf sleeping on the dinner table. A brown lamp with a tiny dial switch on its base, and hundreds of slits in its metal shade. And on the harmonium, photographs. Photographs of her three daughters, and one of herself, Margaret, and her husband, Horace, sitting down beneath a chandelier somewhere, and smiling. In the chandelier were eight lightbulbs, their glass transparent, shaped from a broad base to a sharp tip, like a flame. "Well, I never noticed," she said. "You can't blame me for that."

In the kitchen, she was drinking water when she looked out the window and saw them. They were dressed in uniforms, and they had big arms and big faces. They had their truck in the alley and were carefully loading chairs, lamps, sofas, and tables into it. She noticed that they didn't joke as they took Mrs. Silverman's furniture away, that it was a solemn event, like running up a flag. Feeling foolish and annoyed, Margaret cranked open the window and began to shout. "Who told you boys to come here? Where do you think you're taking those things?" She noticed a lion painted on the side of the moving van and was momentarily disconcerted. "I hope you boys know what you're doing!" she shouted at last, down to the large, astonished faces. When they finally looked away from her, she lifted the glass of water to them, drank, then spilled out the rest into the sink.

She tried to remember what she had planned to eat for either lunch or dinner and found her way back into the living room, where she sat down in front of the television set. She saw, reflected in the dark screen, herself, in black-and-white, miniaturized. She smiled and laughed at the tricks television could play, whether on or off. And then, behind her, but also in the background of the set, she saw a tree, waiting for her. Horace had left his trees behind when she and he had moved out of the house. She stood up and went to the window again, and with the clatter of furniture being hauled away in the alley serving as a background, she began to stare at the branches and dried leaves of the one tree the management had planted, and then she began to talk. She told the tree about Horace. Then she laughed and said that she and he would probably sit together again, checking on the sun and the other tricks of light shining from odd directions on the open gulf lying radiant and bare between them.

# Harmony of the World

IN THE SMALL Ohio town where I grew up, many homes had parlors that contained pianos, sideboards, and sofas, heavy objects signifying gentility. These pianos were rarely tuned. They went flat in summer around the Fourth of July and sharp in winter at Christmas. Ours was a Story and Clark. On its music stand were copies of Stephen Foster and Ethelbert Nevin favorites, along with one Chopin prelude that my mother would practice for twenty minutes every three years. She had no patience, but since she thought Ohio—all of it, every scrap—made sense, she was happy and did not need to practice anything. Happiness is not infectious, but somehow her happiness infected my father, a pharmacist, and then spread through the rest of the household. My whole family was obstinately cheerful. I think of my two sisters, my brother, and my parents as having artificial, pasted-on smiles, like circus clowns. They apparently thought cheer and good Christian words were universals, respected everywhere. The pianos were part of this cheer. They played for celebrations and moments of pleasant pain. Or rather, someone played them, but not too well, since excellent playing would have been faintly antisocial. "Chopin," my mother said, shaking her head as she stumbled through the prelude. "Why is he famous?"

When I was six, I received my first standing ovation. On the stage of the community auditorium, where the temperature was about ninety-four degrees, sweat fell from my forehead onto the piano keys, making their ivory surfaces slippery. At the conclusion of the piece, when everyone stood up to applaud, I thought they were just being nice. My playing had been mediocre; only my sweating had been extraordinary. Two years later, they stood up again. When I was eleven, they cheered. By that time I was astonishing these small-town audiences with Chopin and Rachmaninoff recital chestnuts. I thought I was a genius and read biographies of Einstein. Already the townspeople were saying that I was the best thing Parkersville had ever seen, *that I would put the place on the map*. Mothers would send their children by to watch me practice. The kids sat with their mouths open while I polished off more classics.

Like many musicians, I cannot remember ever playing badly, in the sense of not knowing what I was doing. In high school, my identity was being sealed shut: my classmates called me "el señor longhair," even though I wore a crew cut, this being the 1950s. Whenever the town needed a demonstration of local genius, it called upon me. There were newspaper articles detailing my accomplishments, and I must have heard the phrase "future concert career" at least two hundred times. My parents smiled and smiled as I collected applause. My senior year I gave a solo recital and was hired for umpteen weddings and funerals. I was good luck. On the Fourth of July the townspeople brought a piano out to the city square so that I could improvise music between explosions at the fireworks display. Just before I left for college, I noticed that our neighbors wanted to come up to me, ostensibly for small talk, but actually to touch me.

In college I made a shocking discovery: other people existed in the world who were as talented as I was. If I sat down to play a Debussy étude, they would sit down and play Beethoven, only faster and louder than I had. I felt their breath on my neck. Apparently there were other small towns. In each one of these small towns there was a genius. Perhaps some geniuses were not actually geniuses. I practiced constantly and began to specialize in the non-Germanic piano repertoire. I kept my eye out for students younger than I was, who might have flashier technique. At my senior recital I played Mozart, Chopin, Ravel, and Debussy, with encore pieces by Scriabin. I managed to get the audience to stand up for the last time.

I was accepted into a large midwestern music school, famous for its high standards. Once there, I discovered that genius, to say nothing of talent, was a common commodity. Since I was only a middling composer, with no interesting musical ideas as such, I would have to make my career as a performer or teacher. But I didn't want to teach, and as a performer I lacked pizzazz. For the first time, it occurred to me that my life might be evolving into something unpleasant, something with the taste of stale bread.

I was beginning to meet performers with more confidence than I had, young musicians to whom doubt was as alien as proper etiquette. Often these people dressed like tramps, smelled, smoked constantly, were gay or sadistic. Whatever their imbalances, they were not genteel. *They did not represent small towns.* I was struck by their eyes. Their eyes seemed to proclaim, "The universe believes in me. It always has."

My piano teacher was a man I will call Luther Stecker. Every year he taught at the music school for six months. For the following six months he toured. He turned me away from the repertoire with which I was familiar and demanded that I learn several pieces by composers whom I had not often played, including Bach, Brahms, and Liszt. Each one of these composers discovered a weak point in me: I had trouble keeping up the consistent frenzy required by Liszt, the mathematical precision required by Bach, the unpianistic fingerings of Brahms.

I saw Stecker every week. While I played, he would doze off. When he woke, he would mumble some inaudible comment. He also coached a trio I participated in, and he spoke no more audibly then than he did during my private lessons.

I couldn't understand why, apart from his reputation, the school had hired him. Then I learned that in every Stecker-student's life, the time came when the Master collected his thoughts, became blunt, and told the student exactly what his future would be. For me, the moment arrived on the third of November 1966. I was playing sections of the Brahms Paganini Variations, a fiendish piece on which I had spent many hours. When I finished, I saw him sit up.

"Very good," he said, squinting at me. "You have talents."

There was a pause. I waited. "Thank you," I said.

"You have a nice house?" he asked.

"A nice house? No."

"You should get a nice house somewhere," he said, taking his handkerchief out of his pocket and waving it at me. "With windows. Windows with a view."

I didn't like the drift of his remarks. "I can't afford a house," I said.

"You will. A nice house. For you and your family."

I resolved to get to the heart of this. "Professor," I asked, "what did you think of my playing?"

"Excellent," he said. "That piece is very difficult."

"Thank you."

"Yes, technically excellent," he said, and my heart began to pound. "Intelligent phrasing. Not much for me to say. Yes. That piece has many notes," he added, enjoying the non sequitur.

I nodded. "Many notes."

"And you hit all of them accurately. Good pedal and good discipline. I like how you hit the notes."

I was dangling on his string, a little puppet.

"Thousands of notes, I suppose," he said, staring at my forehead, which was beginning to get damp, "and you hit all of them. You only forgot one thing."

"What?"

"The passion!" he roared. "You forgot the passion! You always forget it! Where is it? Did you leave it at home? You never bring it with you! Never! I listen to you and think of a robot playing! A smart robot, but a robot! No passion! Never ever ever!" He stopped shouting long enough to sneeze. "You *should* buy a house. You know why?"

"Why?"

"Because the only way you will ever praise God is with a family, that's why! Not with this piano! You are a fine student," he wound up, "but you make me sick! Why do you make me sick?"

He waited for me to answer.

*"Why do you make me sick?"* he shouted. "Answer me!"

"How can I possibly answer you?"

"By articulating words in English! Be courageous! Offer a suggestion! Why do you make me sick?"

I waited for a minute, the longest minute of my life. "Passion," I said at last. "You said there wasn't enough passion. I thought there was. Perhaps not."

He nodded. "No. You are right. No passion. A corruption of music itself. Your playing is gentle, too much good taste. To play the piano like a genius, you must have a bit of the fanatic. Just a bit. But it is essential. You have stubbornness and talent but no fanaticism. You don't have the salt on the rice. Without salt, the rice is inedible, no matter what its quality otherwise." He stood up. "I tell you this because sooner or later someone else will. You will have a life of disappointments if you stay in music. You may find a teacher who likes you. Good, good. *But you will never be taken up! Never!* You should buy a house, young man. With a beautiful view. Move to it. Don't stay here. You are close to success, but it is the difference between leaping the chasm and falling into it, one inch short. You are an inch short. You could come back for more lessons. You *could* graduate from here. But if you are truly intelligent, you will say good-bye. Good-bye." He looked down at the floor and did not offer me his hand.

I stood up and walked out of the room.

Becalmed, I drifted up and down the hallways of the building for half an hour. Then a friend of mine, a student of conducting from Bolivia, a Marxist named Juan Valparaiso, approached and, ignoring my shallow breathing and cold sweat, started talking at once.

"Terrible, furious day!" he said.

"Yes."

"I am conducting *Benvenuto Cellini* overture this morning! All is going well until difficult flute entry. I instruct, with force, flutists. Soon all woodwinds are ignoring me." He raised his eyebrows and stroked his huge gaucho mustache. "Always! Always there are fascists in the woodwinds!"

"Fascists everywhere," I said.

"Horns bad, woodwinds worse. Demands of breath make for insanes. Pedro," he said, "you are appearing irresoluted. Sick?"

"Yes." I nodded. "Sick. I just came from Stecker. My playing makes *him* sick."

"He said that? That you are making him sick?"

"That's right. I play like a robot, he says."

"What will you do?" Juan asked me. "Kill him?"

"No." And then I knew. "I'm leaving the school."

"What? Is impossible!" Tears leaped instantly into Juan's eyes. "Cannot, Pedro. After one whipping? No! Must stick to it." He grabbed me by the shoulders. "Fascists put here on Earth to break our hearts! Must live through. You cannot go." He looked around wildly. "Where could you go anyway?"

"I'm not sure," I said. "He told me I would never amount to anything. I think he's right. But I could do something else." To prove that I could imagine options, I said, "I could work for a newspaper. You know, music criticism."

"Caterpillars!" Juan shouted, his tears falling onto my shirt. "Failures! Pathetic lives! Cannot, cannot! Who would hire you?"

I couldn't tell him for six months, until I was given a job in Knoxville on a part-time trial basis. But by then I was no longer writing letters to my musician friends. I had become anonymous. I worked in Knoxville for two years, then in Louisville—a great city for music—until I moved here, to this city I shall never name, in the middle of New York State, where I bought a house with a beautiful view.

In my hometown, they still wonder what happened to me, but my smiling parents refuse to reveal my whereabouts.


Every newspaper has a command structure. Within that command structure, editors assign certain stories, but the writers must be given some freedom to snoop around and discover newsworthy material themselves. In this anonymous city, I was hired to review all the concerts of the symphony orchestra and to provide some hype articles during the week to boost the ticket sales for Friday's program. Since the owner of the paper was on the symphony board of trustees, writing about the orchestra and its programs was necessarily part of good journalistic citizenship. On my own, though, I initiated certain projects, wrote book reviews for the Sunday section, interviewed famous visiting musicians—some of them my ex-classmates—and during the summer I could fill in on all sorts of assignments, as long as I cleared what I did with the feature editor, Morris Cascadilla.

"You're the first serious musician we've ever had on the staff here," he announced to me when I arrived, suspicion and hope fighting for control on his face. "Just remember this: be clear and concise. Assume they've got intelligence but no information. After that, you're on your own, except that you should clear dicey stuff with me. And never forget the Maple Street angle."

The Maple Street angle was Cascadilla's equivalent to the Nixon administration's "How will it play in Peoria?" No matter what subject I wrote about, I was expected to make it relevant to Maple Street, the newspaper's mythical locus of middle-class values. I could write about electronic, aleatory, or post-Boulez music *if* I suggested that the city's daughters might be corrupted by it. Sometimes I found the Maple Street angle, and sometimes I couldn't. When I failed, Cascadilla would call me in, scowl at my copy, and mutter, "All the Juilliard graduates in town will love this." Nevertheless, the Maple Street angle was a spiritual exercise in humility, and I did my best to find it week after week.

When I first learned that the orchestra was scheduled to play Paul Hindemith's *Harmony of the World* symphony, I didn't think of Hindemith, but of Maple Street, that mythically harmonious place where I actually grew up.

Working on the paper left me some time for other activities. Unfortunately, there was nothing I knew how to do except play the piano and write reviews.

Certain musicians are very practical. Trumpet players (who love valves) tend to be good mechanics, and I have met a few composers who fly airplanes and can restore automobiles. Most performing violinists and pianists, however, are drained by the demands of their instruments and seldom learn how to do anything besides play. In daily life they are helpless and stricken. In midlife the smart ones force themselves to find hobbies. But the less fortunate come home to solitary apartments without pictures or other decorations, warm up their dinners in silence, read whatever books happen to be on the dinner table, and then go to bed.

I am speaking of myself here, of course. As time passed, and the vacuum of my life made it harder to breathe, I required more work. I fancied that I was a tree, putting out additional leaves. I let it be known that I would play as an accompanist for voice students and other recitalists, if their schedules didn't interfere with my commitments for the paper.

One day I received a call at my desk. A quietly controlled female voice asked, "Is this Peter Jenkins?"

"Yes."

"Well," she said, as if she'd forgotten what she meant to tell me, "this is Karen Jensen. That's almost like Jenkins, isn't it?" I waited. "I'm a singer," she said, after a moment. "A soprano. I've just lost my accompanist and I'm planning on giving a recital in three months. They said you were available. Are you? And what do you charge?"

I told her.

"Isn't that kind of steep? That's kind of steep. Well, I suppose . . . I can use somebody else until just before, and then I can use you. They say you're good. And I've read your reviews. I really admire the way you write!"

I thanked her.

"You get so much information into your reviews! Sometimes, when I read you, I imagine what you look like. Sometimes a person can make a mental picture. I just wish the paper would publish a photo or some-thing of you."

"They want to," I said, "but I asked them not to."

"Even your voice sounds like your writing!" she said excitedly. "I can see you in front of me now. Can you play Fauré and Schubert? I mean, is there any composer or style you don't like and won't play?"

"No," I said. "I play anything."

"That's *wonderful!*" she said, as if I had confessed to a remarkable tolerance. "Some accompanists are so picky. 'I won't do this, I won't do that.' Well, *one* I know is like that. Anyhow, could we meet soon? Do you sight-read? Can we meet at the music school downtown? In a prac-tice room? When are you free?"

I set up an appointment.


She was almost beautiful. Her deep eyes were accented by depressed bowls in quarter-moon shadows under them. Though she was only in her late twenties, she seemed slightly scorched by anxiety. She couldn't keep still. Her hands fluttered as they fixed her hair; she scratched ner-vously at her cheeks, and her eyes jumped every few seconds. Soon, how-ever, she calmed down and began to look me in the eye, evaluating me. Then *I* turned away.

She wanted to test me out and had brought along her recital numbers, mostly standard fare: a Handel aria, Mozart, Schubert, and Fauré. The last set of songs, *Nine Epitaphs,* by an American composer I had never heard of, Theodore Chanler, was the only novelty.

"Who is this Chanler?" I asked, looking through the sheet music.

"I . . . I found it in the music library," she said. "I looked him up. He was born in Boston and he died in 1961. There's a recording by Phyllis Curtin. Virgil Thomson says these are maybe the best American art songs ever written."

"Oh."

"They're kind of, you know, lugubrious. I mean, they're all epitaphs written supposedly on tombstones, set to music. They're like portraits. I love them. Is it all right? Do you mind?"

"No, I don't mind."

We started through her program, beginning with Handel's "Un sospiretto d'un labbro pallido" from *Il Pastor fido.* I could immediately see why she was still in central New York State and why she would always be a student. She had a fine voice, clear and distinct, somewhat styled after Victoria de los Angeles (I thought), and her articulation was superb. If these achievements had been the whole story, she might have been a professional. But her pitch wobbled on sustained notes in a maddening way; the effect was not comic and would probably have gone unnoticed by most nonmusicians, but to me the result was harrowing. She could sing perfectly for several measures and then she would miss a note by a semitone, which drove an invisible fingernail into my scalp. It was as though a Gypsy's curse descended every five or six seconds, throwing her off pitch; then she was allowed to be a great singer until the curse descended again. Her loss of pitch was so regularized that I could see it coming and squirmed in anticipation. I felt as though I were in the presence of one of God's more complicated pranks.

Her choice of songs highlighted her failings. Their delicate textures were constantly broken by her lapses. When we arrived at the Chanler pieces, I thought I was accustomed to her, but I found I wasn't. The first song begins with the following verse, written by Walter de la Mare, who had crafted all the poems in archaic epitaph style:

> Here lyeth our infant, Alice Rodd;
> > She were so small
> > Scarce aught at all,
> But a mere breath of Sweetness sent from God.

The vocal line for "She were so small" consists of four notes, the last two rising a half step from the two before them. To work, the passage requires a deadeye accuracy of pitch:

Singing this line, Karen Jensen hit the D-sharp but missed the E and skidded up uncontrollably to F-sharp, which would sound all right to anyone who didn't have the music in front of his nose, as I did. Only a fellow musician could be offended.

Infuriated, I began to feel that I could *not* participate in a recital with this woman. It would be humiliating to perform such lovely songs in this excruciating manner. I stopped playing, turned to her to tell her that I could not continue after all, and then I saw her bracelet.

I am not, on the whole, especially observant, a failing that probably accounts for my having missed the bracelet when we first met. But I saw it now: five silver canaries dangled down quietly from it, and as it slipped back and forth, I saw her wrist and what I suddenly realized *would* be there: the parallel lines of her madness, etched in scar tissue.

The epitaphs finished, she asked me to work with her, and I agreed. When we shook hands, the canaries shook in tiny vibrations, as if pleased with my dutiful kindness, my charity, toward their mad mistress.

Though Paul Hindemith's reputation once equaled Stravinsky's and Bartók's, it suffered after his death in 1963 an almost complete collapse. Only two of his orchestral works, the *Symphonic Metamorphoses on Themes of Weber* and the *Mathis der Maler* symphony, are played with any frequency, thanks in part to their use of borrowed tunes. One hears his woodwind quintets and choral pieces now and then, but the works of which he was most proud—the ballet *Nobilissima Visione, Das Marien-leben* (a song cycle), and the opera *Harmonie der Welt*—have fallen into total obscurity.

The reason for Hindemith's sudden loss of reputation was a mystery to me; I had always considered his craftsmanship if not his inspiration to be first-rate. When I saw that the *Harmony of the World* symphony, almost never played, would be performed in our anonymous city, I told Cascadilla that I wanted to write a story for that week on how fame was gained and lost in the world of music. He thought that subject might be racy enough to interest the tone-deaf citizens of leafy and peaceful Maple Street, where no one is famous, if I made sure the story contained "the human element."

I read up on Hindemith, played his piano music, and listened to the recordings. I slowly found the music to be technically astute but emotionally arid, as if some problem of purely local interest kept the composer's gaze safely below the horizon. Technocratic and oddly timid, his work reminded me of a model train chugging through a tiny town inhabited only by models of people. In fact, Hindemith did have a lifelong obsession with train sets: in Berlin, his collection took up three rooms, and the composer wrote elaborate timetables so that the toys wouldn't collide.

But if Hindemith had a technocrat's intelligence, he also believed in the necessity of universal participation in musical activities. Listening was not enough. Even nonmusical citizens could learn to sing and play, and he wrote music expressly for this purpose. He seemed to have known that passive, drugged listening was a side effect of totalitarian environments and that elitist composers such as Schoenberg were engaged in antisocial Faustian projects that would bewilder and ultimately infuriate most audiences, leaving them isolated and thus eager to be drugged by a musical superman.

As the foremost anti-Nietzschean German composer of his day, therefore, Hindemith left Germany when his works could not be performed, thanks to the Third Reich; wrote textbooks with simple exercises; composed a requiem in memory of Franklin Roosevelt, using a text by Walt Whitman; and taught students, not all of them talented, in Ankara, New Haven, and Buffalo ("this caricature of a town"). As he passed through late middle age, he turned to a project he had contemplated all his life, an opera based on the career of the German astronomer Johannes Kepler, author of *De Harmonice Mundi*. This opera, a summary of Hindemith's ideas, would be called *Harmony of the World*. Hindemith worked out the themes first in a symphony, which bore the same title as the opera, and completed it in 1951. The more I thought about this project, the more it seemed anachronistic. Who believed in world harmony in 1951? Or thereafter? Such a symphony would have to pass beyond technical sophistication into divine inspiration, which Hindemith had never shown any evidence of possessing.

It occurred to me that Hindemith's lifelong sanity had perhaps given way in this case, toppled not by despair (as is conventional) but by faith in harmony.

For the next rehearsal, I drove to Karen Jensen's apartment, where there was, she said, a piano. I'd become curious about the styles of her insanity:

I imagined a hamster cage in the kitchen, a doll-head mobile in the living room, and mottoes written with different-colored inks on memo pads tacked up everywhere on the walls.

She greeted me at the door without her bracelet. When I looked at her wrist, she said, "Hmmm. I see that you noticed. A memento of adolescent despair." She sighed. "But it does frighten people off. Once you've tried to do something like that, people don't really trust you. I don't know why exactly. They don't want your blood on their hands or something. Well, come on in."

I was struck first by her forthrightness and second by her tiny apartment. Its style was much like the style in my house. She owned an attractive but worn-down sofa, a sideboard that supported an antique clock, one chair, a glass-top dinner table, and one nondescript poster on the wall. Trying to keep my advantage, I looked hard for telltale signs of instability but found none. The piano was off in the corner, almost hidden, unlike those in the parlors back home.

"Very nice," I said.

"Well, thanks," she said. "It's not much. I'd like something bigger, but . . . where I work, I'm an administrative assistant, and they don't pay me very much. So that's why I live like a snail here. It's hardly big enough to move around in, right?" She wasn't looking at me. "I mean, I could almost pick it up and carry it away."

I nodded. "You just don't think like a rich person," I said, trying to be hearty. "They like to expand. They need room. Big houses, big cars, fat bodies."

"Oh, I know!" she said, laughing. "My uncle . . . Would *you* like to stay for dinner? You look like you need a good meal. I mean, after the rehearsal. You're just skin and bones, Pet— . . . May I call you Peter?"

"Sure." I sat down on the sofa and tried to think up an excuse. "I really can't stay, Miss Jensen. I have another rehearsal to go to later tonight. I wish I could."

"That's not it, is it?" she asked suddenly, looking down at me. "I don't believe you. I bet it's something else. I bet you're afraid of me."

"Why should I be afraid of you?"

She smiled and shrugged. "That's all right. You don't have to say anything. I know how it goes." She laughed once more, faintly. "I never found a man who could handle it. They want to show you *their* scars, you know? They don't want to see any on you. If they discover any, they just take off." She slapped her right hand on her forehead and then ran her fingers through her hair. "Well, shit, I didn't mean to do this *at all*! I mean, I admire you so much and everything, and here I am running on like this. I guess we should get down to business, right? Since I'm paying you by the hour."

I smiled professionally and went to her piano.

Beneath the high-culture atmosphere that surrounds them, art songs have one subject: love. The permutations of love (lust, solitude, and loss) are present in abundance, of course, but for the most part they are simple vehicles for the expression of that one emotion. I was reminded of this as I played through the piano parts. As much as I concentrated on the music in front of me, I couldn't help but notice that my employer stood next to the piano, singing the words sometimes toward me, sometimes away. She was rather courageously forcing eye contact on me. She kept this up for an hour and a half until we came to the Chanler settings, when at last she turned slightly, singing to the walls.

As before, her voice broke out of control every five seconds, giving isolated words all the wrong shadings. The only way to endure it, I discovered, was to think of her singing as a postmodern phenomenon with its own conventions and rules. As the victim of necessity rather than accident, Karen Jensen was tolerable.

When we were done, she asked, "Sure you won't stay?"

"No, I don't think so."

"You really haven't another engagement, do you?"

"No," I admitted.

"I didn't think so. You were scared of me the moment you walked in the door. You thought I'd be crazy." She waited. "After all, only ugly girls live alone, right? And I'm not ugly."

"No, you aren't," I said. "You're quite attractive."

"Do you think so?" she asked, brightening. "It's so nice to hear that from you, even if you're just paying a compliment. I mean, it still means *something.*" Then she surprised me. As I stood in the doorway, she got down on her knees in front of me and bowed her head in the style of one of her songs. "Please stay," she asked. Immediately she stood up and laughed. "But don't feel obliged to."

"Oh, no," I said, returning to her living room, "I've just changed my mind. Dinner sounds like a good idea."

After she had served and we had started to eat, she looked up at me and said, "You know, I'm not completely good." She paused. "At singing."

"What?" I stopped chewing. "Yes, you are. You're all right."

"Don't lie. I know I'm not. You know I'm not. Come on: let's at least be honest. I think I have certain qualities of musicality, but my pitch is . . . you know. Uneven. You probably think it's awfully vain of me to put on these recitals. With nobody but friends and family coming."

"No, I don't."

"Well, I don't care what you say. It's . . . hmm, I don't know. People encourage me. And it's a discipline. Music's finally a discipline that rewards you. Privately, though. Well, that's what my mother says."

Carefully, I said, "She may be right."

"Who cares if she is?" She laughed, her mouth full of food. "I enjoy doing it. Like I enjoy doing this. Listen, I don't want to seem forward or anything, but are you married?"

"No."

"I didn't think so." She picked up a string bean and eyed it suspiciously. "Why aren't you? You're not ugly. In fact you're all-right looking. You obviously haven't been crazy. Are you gay or something?"

"No."

"No," she agreed, "you don't look gay. You don't even look very happy. You don't look very anything. Why is that?"

"I should be offended by this line of questioning."

"But you're not. You know why? Because I'm interested in you. I hardly know you, but I like you, what I can see. Don't you have any trust?"

"Yes," I said finally.

"So answer my question. Why don't you look very anything?"

"Do you want to hear what my piano teacher once said?" I asked. "He said I wasn't enough of a fanatic. He said that to be one of the great ones you have to be a tiny bit crazy. Touched. And he said I wasn't. And when he said it, I knew all along he was right. I was waiting for someone to say what I already knew, and he was the one. I was too much a good citizen, he said. I wasn't possessed."

She rose, walked around the table to where I was sitting, and stood in front of me, looking down at my face. I knew that whatever she was going to do had been picked up, in attitude, from one of her songs. She touched the back of my arm with two fingers on her right hand. "Well," she said, "maybe you aren't possessed, but what would you think of me as another possession?"

In 1618, at the age of seventy, Katherine Kepler, the mother of Johannes Kepler, was put on trial for witchcraft. The records indicate that her personality was so deranged, so deeply offensive to all, that if she were alive today she would *still* be called a witch. One of Kepler's biographers, Angus Armitage, notes that she was "evil-tempered" and possessed an interest in unnamed "outlandish things." Her trial lasted, on and off, for three years; by 1621, when she was acquitted, her personality had disintegrated completely. She died the following year.

At the age of six, Kepler's son Frederick died of smallpox. A few months later, Kepler's wife, Barbara, died of typhus. Two other children, Henry and Susanna, had died in infancy.

Like many others of his age, Kepler spent much of his adult life cultivating favor from the nobility. He was habitually penniless and was often reduced, as his correspondence shows, to begging for handouts. He was the victim of religious persecution, though luckier in this regard than some.

After he married for a second time, three more children died in infancy, a statistic that in theory carries less emotional weight than one might think, given the accepted levels of infant mortality for that era.

In 1619, despite the facts cited above, Kepler published *De Harmonice Mundi,* a text in which he set out to establish the correspondence between the laws of harmony and the disposition of planets in motion. In brief, Kepler argued that certain intervals, such as the octave, major and minor sixths, and major and minor thirds, were pleasurable, while other intervals were not. History indicated that mankind had always regarded certain intervals as unpleasant. Feeling that this set of universal tastes pointed to immutable laws, Kepler sought to map out the pleasurable intervals geometrically, and then to transfer that geometrical pattern to the order of the planets. The velocity of the planets, rather than their strict placement, constituted the harmony of the spheres. This velocity provided each planet with a note, what Armitage called a "term in a mathematically determined relation."

In fact, each planet performed a short musical scale, set down by Kepler in staff notation. The length of the scale depended upon the eccentricity of the orbit; and its limiting notes could generally be shown to form a concord (except for Venus and the Earth with their nearly circular orbits, whose scales were of very constricted range) . . . at the Creation . . . complete concord prevailed and the morning stars sang together.

We began to eat dinner together. Accustomed to solitude, we did not always engage in conversation. I would read the newspaper or ink in letters on my geometrically patterned crossword puzzles at my end of the table, while Karen would read detective novels or *Time* at hers. If she had cooked, I would clear and wash the dishes. If I had cooked, she did the cleaning. Experience and disappointments had made us methodical. She told me that she had once despised structured experiences governed by timetables, but that after several manic-depressive episodes, she had learned to love regularity. This regularity included taking lithium at the same time—to the minute—each day.

The season being summer, we would pack towels and swimming suits after dinner and drive out to one of several public beaches, where we would swim until darkness came on. On calm evenings, Karen would drop her finger in the water and watch the waves lap outward. I favored immature splashing, or grabbing her by the arm and whirling her around me until I released her and she would spin back and fall into the water, laughing as she sank. One evening, we found a private beach, two hundred feet of sand all to ourselves, on a lake thirty miles out of town. Framed on both sides by woods and well hidden from the highway, this beach had the additional advantage of being unpatrolled. We had no bathhouse in which to change, however, so Karen instructed me not to look as she walked about fifty feet away to a spot where she undressed and put on her suit.

Though we had been intimate for at least a week, I had still not seen her naked: like a good Victorian, she demanded that the shades be drawn, the lights be out, and the covers be pulled discreetly over us. But now, with the same methodical thoroughness, she wanted me to see her, so I looked, despite her warnings. She was bent over, under the tree boughs, the evening light breaking through the leaves and casting broken gold bands on her body. Her arms were delicate, the arms of a schoolgirl, I thought, an impression heightened by the paleness of her skin; but her breasts were full, at first making me think of Rubens's women, then of Renoir's, then of nothing at all. Slowly, knowing I was watching her, she pinned her hair up. Not her breasts or arms, but that expression of vague contentment as she looked out toward the water, away from me: *that* made me feel a tingling below my heart, somewhere in an emotional center near my stomach. I wanted to pick her up and carry her somewhere, but with my knees wobbly it was all I could do to make my way over to where she stood and take her in my arms before she cried out. "Jesus," she said, shivering, "you gave me a surprise." I kissed her, waiting for inspiration to direct me on what to do next: Pick her up? Carry her? Make love to her on the sand? Wade into the water with her and swim out to the center of the bay, where we would drown together in a Lawrentian love-grip? But then we broke the kiss; she put on her swimsuit like a good citizen, and we swam for the usual fifteen minutes in silence. Afterward, we changed back into our clothes and drove home, muttering small talk. Behavior inspired by and demonstrating love embarrassed both of us. When I told her that she was beautiful and that I loved her, she patted me on the cheek and said, "Aw, how nice. You always try to say the right thing."

The Maple Street angle for *Harmony of the World* ran as follows: SYM-PHONY OF FAITH IN A FAITHLESS AGE. Hindemith, I said, wished to confound the skeptics by composing a monument of faith. In an age of organized disharmony, of political chaos, he stood at the barricades defending tonality and traditional musical form. I carefully avoided any specific discussion of the musical materials of the symphony, which in the Schott orchestral score looked overcomplex and melodically ugly. From what I could tell from a sight-reading, Hindemith had employed stunning technique in order to disguise his lack of inspiration, though I did not say so in print. Instead, I wrote that the symphony's failure to win public support was probably the result of Hindemith's refusal to use musical gimmicks on the one hand and sticky-sweet melodies on the other. I wrote that he had not been dismayed by the bad reviews *Harmony of the World* (both the symphony and the opera) had received, which was untrue. I said he was a man of integrity. I did not say that men of integrity are often unable to express joy when the occasion demands. Cascadilla liked my article. "This guy sounds like me," he said, reading my copy. "I respect him." The article ran five days before the concert and was two pages away from the religion-and-faith section. Not long after, the symphony ticket office called me to say that my piece had caused a rush of ticket orders from ordinary folk, nonconcert types, who wanted to hear this "religious symphony." The woman from the business office thanked me for my trouble. "Let's hope they like it," I said.

"Of course they will," she assured me. "You've told them to."

But they didn't. Despite all the oratory in the symphony, it was as spiritually dead as a lampshade. I could see why Hindemith had been shocked by the public reaction. Our audience applauded politely in discouragement, and then I heard an unusual sound for this anonymous city: one man, full of fun and conviction, booing loudly from the balcony. Booing the harmony of the world! He must be a Satanist! Didn't intentions mean anything? So what if the harmony and joy were all counterfeit? The conductor came out for a bow, smiled at the booing man, and very soon the applause died away. I left the hall, feeling responsible. Arriving at the paper, I wrote a review of crushing dullness that reeked of bad faith. God damn Hindemith! Here he was, claiming to have seen God's workings, and they sounded like the workings of a steam engine or a trolley car. A fake symphony, with optimism the composer did not feel! I decided (but did not write) that *Harmony of the World* was just possibly the largest, most misconceived fiasco in modern music's history. It was a symphony that historically could not be written by a man who was constitutionally not equipped to write it. In my review, I kept a civil pen: I said that the performance lacked "luster," "a certain necessary glow."

"I'm worried about the recital tomorrow."

"Aw, don't worry. Here, kiss me. Right here."

"Aren't you listening? I'm worried."

"*I'm* singing. You're just accompanying me. Nobody's going to notice you. Move over a little, would you? Yeah, there. That pillow was forcing my head against the wall."

"Why aren't you worried?"

"Why should I be worried? I don't want to worry. I want to make love. Isn't that better than worrying?"

"Not if *I'm* worried."

"People won't notice you. By the way, have you paid attention to the fact that when I kiss you on the stomach, you get goose bumps?"

"Yes. I think you're taking this pretty lightly. I mean, it's almost unprofessional."

"That's because I'm an amateur. A one hundred percent amateur. Always and totally. Even at this. But that doesn't mean I don't have my moments. Mmmmmm. That's better."

"I thought it would maybe help. But listen. I'm still worried."

"Uhhhh. Oh, wait a minute. Wait a minute. Oh, I get it."

"What?"

"I get it. You aren't worried about yourself. You're worried about me."

Forty people attended her recital, which was sponsored by the city university's music school, in which Karen was a sometime student. Somehow we made our way through the program, but when we came to the Chanler settings, I suddenly wanted Karen to sing them perfectly. I wanted an angel to descend and to take away the Gypsy's curse. But she sang as she always had—off pitch—and when she came to "Ann Poverty," I found myself in that odd region between rage and pity.

> Stranger, here lies
>   Ann Poverty;
> Such was her name
>   And such was she.
> May Jesu pity
>   Poverty.

But I was losing my capacity for pity.

In the green room, her forty friends came back to congratulate her. I met them. They were all very nice. She smiled and laughed: there would be a party in an hour. Would I go? I declined. When we were alone, I said I was going back to my place.

"Why?" she asked. "Shouldn't you come to my party? You're my lover after all. That *is* the word."

"Yes. But I don't want to go with you."

"Why?"

"Because of tonight's concert, that's why."

"What about it?"

"It wasn't very good, was it? I mean, it just wasn't."

"I thought it was all right. A few slips. It was pretty much what I was capable of. All those people said they liked it."

"Those people don't matter!" I said, my eyes watering with anger. "Only the music matters. Only the music is betrayed; they aren't. They don't know about pitch, most of them. I mean, Jesus, they aren't genuine musicians, so how would they know? Do you really think what we did tonight was good? It wasn't! It was a travesty! We ruined those songs! How can you stand to do that?"

"I don't ruin them. I sing them adequately. I project feeling. People get pleasure from them. That's enough."

"It's awful," I said, feeling the ecstatic liftoff into rage. "You're so close to being good, but you *aren't* good. Who cares what those ignoramuses think? They don't know what notes you're *supposed* to hit. It's that god-damn slippery pitch of yours. You're killing those songs. You just *drop* them like watermelons on the stage! It makes me sick! I couldn't have gone on for another day listening to you and your warbling! I'd die first."

She looked at me and nodded, her mouth set in a half moue, half smile of nonsurprise. There may have been tears in her eyes, but I didn't see them. She looked at me as if she were listening hard to a long-distance call. "You're tired of me," she said.

"I'm not tired of you. I'm tired of hearing you sing! Your voice makes my flesh crawl! Do you know why? Can you tell me why you make me sick? Why do you make me sick? Never mind. I'm just glad this is over."

"You don't look glad. You look angry."

"And you look smug. Listen, why don't you go off to your party? Maybe there'll be a talent scout there. Or roses flung riotously at you. But don't give a recital like this again, please, okay? It's a public disgrace. It offends music. It offends *me*."

I turned my back on her and walked out to my car.


After the failure of *Harmony of the World,* Hindemith went on a strenuous tour that included Scandinavia. In Oslo, he was rehearsing the Phil-harmonic when he blinked his bright blue eyes twice, turned to the concertmaster, and said, "I don't know where I am." They took him away to a hospital; he had suffered a nervous breakdown.

I slept until noon, having nothing to do at the paper and no reason to get up. At last, unable to sleep longer, I rose and walked to the kitchen to make coffee. I then took my cup to the picture window and looked down the hill to the trees of the conservation area, the view Stecker had once told me I should have.

The figure of a woman was hanging from one of the trees, a noose around her neck. I dropped my coffee cup and the liquid spilled out over my feet.

I ran out the back door in my pajamas and sprinted painfully down the hill's tall grass toward the tree. I was fifty feet away when I saw that it wasn't Karen, wasn't in fact a woman at all, but an effigy of sorts, with one of Karen's hats, a pillow head, and a dress hanging over a broomstick skeleton. Attached to the effigy was a note:

In the old days, this might have been me. Not anymore. Still, I thought it'd make you think. And I'm not giving up singing, either. By the way, what your playing lacks is not fanaticism, but concentration. You can't seem to keep your mind on one thing for more than a minute at a time. *I* notice things, too. You aren't the only reviewer around here. Take good care of this doll, okay?

XXXXXXX,
Karen

I took the doll up and dropped it in the clothes closet, where it has remained to this hour.

Hindemith's biographer, Geoffrey Skelton, writes, "[On the stage] the episodic scenes from Kepler's life fail to achieve immediate dramatic coherence, and the basic theme remains obscure . . ."

She won't, of course, see me again. She won't talk to me on the phone, and she doesn't answer my letters. I am quite lucidly aware of what I have done. And I go on seeing doubles and reflections and wave motion everywhere. There is symmetry, harmony, after all. I suppose I should have been nice to her. That, too, is a discipline. I always tried to be nice to everyone else.

On Kepler's deathbed, Hindemith has him sing:

*Und muss sehn am End:*
*Die grosse Harmonie, das is der Tod.*
*Absterben is, sie zu bewirken, not.*
*Im Leben hat sie keine Statte.*

Now, at the end, I see it:
The great harmony, it is death.
To find it, we must die.
In life it has no place.

Hindemith's words may be correct. But Dante says that the residents of limbo, having never been baptized, will not see the face of God, despite their having committed no sin, no active fault. In their fated locale, they sigh, which keeps the air "forever trembling." No harmony for them, these guiltless souls. Through eternity, the residents of limbo—where one can imagine oneself if one cannot stand to imagine any part of hell—experience one of the most shocking of all the emotions that Dante names: "duol senza martíri," grief without torment. These sighs are rather like the sounds one hears drifting from front porches in small towns on soft summer nights.

# Winter Journey

HARRELSON, perpetual Ph.D. student, poverty-stricken dissertation nonfinisher, academic man of all work, gourmand, stands in the tiny kitchen cluttered with yellow notepads, a basketball, books, misplaced bookmarks, and boxes of ant killer, staring down at a dented saucepan of cold soup. Harrelson has turned on the burner, but the soup stays cold. At first he thinks that the electric company has at last made good on its promise and turned off the power, yet the bare ceiling bulb continues to shower glare all over everything. The stove is not working. Harrelson grabs the stove on both sides, shaking it, creating lumpy waves in the saucepan. Harrelson's dissertation on the problem of dating Fulke Greville's poetry has not been going well. He has been sipping cheap bourbon all evening. Now, at five minutes past one o'clock, with hunger seizing him and the melancholy of his apartment inflating like a face painted on the side of a balloon, he has opened the can of soup for what his mother used to call "proper nutrition." He lifts the pan, puts his hand over the burner, feels no heat, and transfers the pan to the other burner, twisting the dial to high. He looks out the window. It is snowing a perpetual February snow. Harrelson sees the snow symbolically. Somehow it represents his refusal to sell out. Alone in the kitchen, he says to himself, "Hip hip hooray." He likes to cheer for himself. It is something he has taught himself to do, in secret.

Turning his attention back to the soup, Harrelson notes that it is boiling. As it does, he gazes at the creation of bubbles at the surface of the soup and listens to the liquid hissing on the side of the pan. How long should soup boil before it is ready to eat? He takes the soup can back out of the trash bag, staining his shirtsleeves with catsup as he does so, and reads the directions: DO NOT BOIL. Harrelson turns the heat off, watches the snow fall for a minute, then reaches for a bile-green plastic bowl in the sink. He washes most of the cornflakes out of the bowl and then pours in the soup. Cream of celery, his favorite. As the steam rises, he searches for a clean spoon and at last finds one with Mickey Mouse on the handle, a twenty-year-old souvenir of Disneyland.

Harrelson takes the spoon and the bowl into the living room and sits down at a wobbly desk five feet in front of the television set. In order to make room for the soup, he pushes three books to the side, and by accident one of them falls off the edge of the desk. It is an old book, a critical commentary. When it hits the floor, its binding breaks and several bookmarks fall out of it. The TV set picks up only one station, which is now showing a Charlie Chan movie, *Charlie Chan at the Olympics,* starring Harrelson's favorite Chan, Sidney Toler. Fascinated, Harrelson watches as a world-class track star is discovered to have been murdered. Harrelson drinks the soup and helps himself to the bourbon. Gradually it occurs to him that the phone is ringing. Answering the phone means missing an important clue, but he rises with his eyes still on the television set and backs down the hallway into the bedroom, where the telephone sits inside the bottom drawer of his dresser to minimize the noise of its ringing whenever he has overslept.

He takes the phone out of the drawer and says hello. For a moment he hears nothing and suspects that some sort of prank is being played on him. His friends used to do such things until they found jobs and became respectable. At last a voice rises out of the static clutter and says, "I'm not asking for a favor. I'm demanding it."

"Who is this?" Harrelson asks. He knows that it is a woman's voice and that there is a slight edge of irritation to it.

"This is Meredith," the voice says. She waits. "Meredith. Your fiancée."

"Meredith!" he says delightedly. "It's been a long time. Weeks. I can't remember the last time you called over here. It's great to hear from you! Are we still engaged? What've you been up to, anyway?"

"Cut it out," she says.

"All right." There is a gunshot on the sound track of the movie. Harrelson's foot itches.

"I called because I need help."

"Name it," Harrelson says.

"I'm over here at the Mobil station on Stadium Avenue. My car won't run. Something about the radiator or antifreeze or the water pump. They don't make much sense here. Anyway, I need a ride home."

"I'm drunk," he says.

"How drunk?"

"How drunk what?"

"I mean, how drunk are you?"

"I don't know." He stands up in the bedroom, holding on to the telephone. "I was just having some soup when you called. Celery soup. And there's a Charlie Chan movie on. Something about death and athletics."

"What does that have to do with anything?" Harrelson can hear a cash register clacking in the background of the filling station Meredith is calling from. "Listen," she says. "I'd call a cab, except I didn't bring enough money."

"I will come," Harrelson says.

"Don't come if you're too drunk," Meredith says. "Can you stand?"

"Yes, I can stand. And," he adds, "I can sit."

"Jesus. You *are* drunk. How soon can you be here?"

"The Mobil station?" He thinks. He cannot remember where it is. He makes a guess. "Fifteen minutes."

"Are you sure?"

"It is hard to be sure," Harrelson says, "of anything in this life."

"If you come to get me, promise you won't say anything like that again. Promise?"

"Yes. I promise."

"Now listen," she says. "It's snowing out. You're not sober. You're going to have to be careful. Put on your seat belt. Avoid other cars."

"Okay, okay. Don't worry about me. I'll be there in no time." For some reason he repeats the words "no time" before he hangs up.


He remembers to turn off the range and the television set and the lights, but he forgets to put on overshoes and gloves. When he is walking down the front steps, his feet rush out from under him, and he falls on the middle step. He is unhurt. His hands are in the snow, and when he lifts them up, he is pleased to see an outline of his hands on the step. He can feel the snow falling on his hair. He sticks his tongue out. Snow lands on his tongue's tip like airborne pieces of candy. Now he looks out at the street and sees his car, an ancient Buick, covered with snow, and snow falling in a peaceful rush underneath the streetlight, and more snow accumulating in the street, as if Meredith had thought this through and had wanted a few more difficulties than were absolutely necessary to test his loyalty. Harrelson feels a small quantity of snow working its way into his shoes. "Mr. Nice Guy," he says, still sitting on the step. He puts his hands down in the snow next to the handprints he has already made. He would like to make a snow angel in the front yard, but Meredith is waiting. He stands up, holding on to the buttons of his coat, and walks with great precision and daring to his car.

As he tries to find his car keys, scattered in his pocket, he holds his head up and looks with an expression of vague speculation at his car and the street. There is certainly a great deal of snow all over everything. Some sort of muffled siren howls gently in the distance. Up the street an unclearly outlined figure is shoveling his sidewalk. Harrelson thinks of Meredith waiting for him in the sinister gas station and renews his efforts to find his car keys. He grasps a number of keys, pulls them out, and watches with neutralized dismay as several of them plop into the snow, leaving slots behind that, Charlie Chan–like, Harrelson uses for pursuit and detection. With all the cold, snowy keys gathered up in his hands, he selects the one that unlocks the car door, deposits the rest in his pocket, and gets in.

He says a prayer, turns the key in the ignition, and the engine starts after a few cranks. As it warms up, exhaust fumes begin seeping up from the floor. Harrelson reaches for a fugitive cigarette on the dashboard, left there by some random hitchhiker—he adores hitchhikers and picks them up at every opportunity—and lights up before getting out to clear the windshield. With his bare hands he sweeps the front and side windows, leaving a bit of ice on the glass for the defroster to take care of. When he is back inside the car, he looks in the rearview mirror and observes that he has not cleared the back window. He shrugs to himself and inhales from the cigarette, which brings on a fit of coughing. He opens the window, looks out into the street to see if anything is coming, prays to his guardian angel, puts the car into gear, and steps on the gas.

In any university town there are hundreds of men like Harrelson, out late at night buying pizzas, sitting at bars sipping their beers quietly, or roaming the streets in their old clunkers. They are all afraid of going home, afraid of looking again at the sheets of clean typewriter paper and the notebooks bare of written thought. They are afraid of facing again their sullen wives and lovers, their tattered and noisy children, if they have any. Against the odds, they refuse to succeed, and the wives and lovers know this and understand it as a rebuke to themselves and family life.

"You won't grow up" is Meredith's succinct way of putting it. She has put it to him this way many times, most recently two months ago, in December, the last time they talked. They were sitting in her apartment, its cleanliness a stark contrast to Harrelson's squalor. Meredith is an accountant, a serious worker with a serious income. They have known each other since high school, when their romance took shape. This romance is now, according to Meredith, on its frail last legs. The fireplace in Meredith's apartment supplied potent warmth against the December cold, and she had put out the brandy, a V.S.O.P. Despite the appearances, however, the evening was tense, the screws of pressure twisted by Meredith's contempt for her four-year fiancé. "Look at you," Meredith said. "Look at what you've done with your life. You could have been brilliant. I feel so sorry for you. I don't want to marry a man I feel sorry for."

"I agree with you," Harrelson said. "Pity is a bad foundation for any marriage."

"Honey," she said, "I don't want to break off with you, because I do love you, but I've got other things going for me, and I can't hold them off forever. You know I've been going out with other men."

Harrelson nodded. He was silently praying that she wouldn't continue in this vein.

"And many of them," Meredith continued, "are very nice: very bright, successful, and, uh, you know, handsome. I can't wait forever."

Harrelson thought she had said everything possible to wound him. So he said, "I've made real progress this month. Really, I have. I'm only about fifty pages away from finishing." He smiled. "Fifty pages away from the degree and a good job."

"You're thirty years old," she said. "You're getting too old to hire."

"Oh, no!" This exclamation from Harrelson was more an outcry than a denial.

Meredith leaned forward. Her eyes were glittering. "Honey," she said, "it's just that I don't want to be married to a nerd."

This was more than even Harrelson could take. He put down his brandy, got into his coat, and left. Because he was Harrelson and because he lived according to a consistent style, he did not shout at her or make an accusation in return. He thought his guardian angels were on vacation and had failed to muzzle Meredith. They allowed her to say what shouldn't have been said. What no one else knows is that although he attends no church, Harrelson is in an almost constant state of prayer. He has familiars in the spirit world.

The inside of his car smells of burned electrical wire and popcorn. As he exhales smoke from the hitchhiker's leftover cigarette, a fog appears and frosts visibly on the inside windshield in a pattern of continuous webbing. The car pulls out of its parking spot, its engine making tappet noises that rise to a whine as the back wheels spin on the ice. Fishtailing, the car skids down the street. Harrelson has no snow tires; in fact, the tires are bald. He plans his route in an effort to avoid hills and valleys. Within a minute he has forgotten the route he has planned.

Despite the snow and the streetlights, the street is darker than it should be: a stygian street. Harrelson remembers that one of his headlights has blown out. His hands, gloveless, are aching, numb. And he feels ready to doze off, despite the cold. His drunkenness communicates itself to him as a fanatic desire to crawl into bed and pull the blankets up. He is seeing two of everything: two sets of streetlights, two streets, two steering wheels, two dashboards. And two red lights, both of which he now runs, unable and unwilling to stop the car before entering the intersection. With scholarly interest he observes that he has missed hitting a blue parked car by perhaps two or three feet. For the first time he understands that it might be a moral offense against God and man to be out driving in a snowstorm, drunk. But it is more of an offense before women to be a nerd, a coward, a man *who will not help*. He accelerates.

At high speed, in snow, the houses fan by him on either side, visually glazed and impacted into smears of windows, doors, roofs, unremoved Christmas lights, chimneys, and, again and again, interior lights, the lights of domesticity left on late at night to ward off prowlers and intruders. Where is the street? It has not been plowed. He continues driving. Continuous motion is important. A dog rushes out in front of the car. It is about the size of an enlarged rat and has a narrow snout. It stops in a seizure of panic. Harrelson hears no thump and feels no impact. He opens his window and looks out into the street receding behind him. The dog stands motionless, watching Harrelson's car as Harrelson watches the dog, tire tracks imprinted on either side of it in the snow.

"Run over," Harrelson says aloud, "but not run down." He laughs to himself, feels the need again to doze off as the heater gradually warms up the car, but resists. He decides to recite poetry. " 'Fie, fond desire,' " he quotes from Fulke Greville, " 'think you that love wants glory / Because your shadows do yourself benight? / The hopes and fears of lust may make men sorry, / But love still in herself finds her delight.' " Harrelson hits a parked car. He knows he has hit it from the sound and the impact, but he hasn't seen it because the windows on the right side are coated with snow. After hitting the car, Harrelson's Buick bounces back into the middle of the street and begins to skid toward the other side. It hits another parked car, slides for twenty feet, then stops. Glass and plastic have been heard, breaking. He puts the car into first gear and continues down the street, which now looks darker than ever. "Uh-oh," he says aloud. "I smashed the other headlight."

I'm not funny, I'm a risk, he thinks.

Other cars are around him; some are moving, others are not. The ones that *are* moving honk at him and blink their lights. "I am a hazard to myself," Harrelson says, passing a large building lit up on each floor, as if people are still working. He thinks he sees someone on the third floor looking down at him, an expression of pity on the stranger's face. The thought of a stranger's pity makes Harrelson's eyes smart. Studying the dashboard, trying not to cry, Harrelson steps on the gas, hurrying down the street toward an area where the overhead lights are not so apparent. Sudden darkness: the car plunges into it. He passes two garages and a butcher shop with sausages hanging in the window, the glass lightly covered with snow. What if I hit a child, he thinks. What if I do that.

Now, having made a circle, Harrelson is back under lights in the business district, his car out of control, advancing down the street sideways. He grabs the seat, ready for a collision, and feels the foam under his hand. In front of him is a department-store window, moving from right to left, in which a bald dummy sits wearing a blue polyester leisure suit. He turns the wheel in the direction of the skid, and the Buick straightens out. He feels a sudden elation. He *can* control himself, the car, the weather conditions. He slows down, steers the car toward the curb, and shuts off the engine. He is drowsy. He will take a brief nap. He bends his head down on his chest and within thirty seconds falls asleep. Instantly a dream starts up. In the dream he is driving the car through a blizzard on his way to get Meredith. The car skids, hits a tree, and there is a bright flash. But he continues driving, reaches her apartment, gets out, and enters the building. He ascends the stairs and walks into her living room. Her back is to him as she works at the stove. "I'm here," he says. "Hi," she says, turning around. But now she cannot see him. "Honey," she says, "is that you?" Her eyes scan the room. "Where are you?" Her voice rises. "I can't see you."

He wakes up, full of the intuition that his life is a disaster. He is the sort of person other people cite in order to feel that they themselves are well off: they could live the way Harrelson does. They could *be* Harrelson. They could think Harrelson's grubby thoughts. He starts the car. Then, a non-Catholic, he makes the sign of the cross. He has not been arrested. His guardian angel is in the car with him, working overtime. Once in a dream the angel identified himself as Matthew and told Harrelson that he, Harrelson, was under his, Matthew's, protection. Since that dream, Harrelson has been lazier, more slipshod; sometimes he thinks the dream may have been his undoing.

He drives and drives. He is lost. Visibility is poor. He sees no landmarks. He looks at his watch: he has been in the car for twenty minutes. The windshield wipers move slowly, heavily, like Harrelson's eyes.

And just at the moment when Harrelson thinks that he is Kafka's K. and will never reach the Mobil station no matter how long or how hard he tries, there it is. First it appears through the curtain of snow as a glowing patch of light without any solid outlines. Then, second by second, he sees the snowy spotlights, the fluorescent lights over the gas pumps, the aquamarine station itself with its closed garage doors, and now he sees a small old man in a black overcoat filling his car with gas at the self-service pump, and now, closer, he sees an attendant gazing in his direction with something like stupefaction, at Harrelson behind the wheel, in his dark car with no headlights.

The attendant walks over to him. Harrelson's head is bowed and he is muttering. Though the attendant doesn't know it, Harrelson is thanking his familiars, making concrete spiritual promises. The man, who is covered with snow, knocks on the window. Harrelson looks at him and rolls it down.

"You okay, buddy?" the man asks. He is wearing a blue parka and gazes in at Harrelson with friendly curiosity. His mouth is open, and Harrelson can see the huge gap of his mouth and his bad, crisscrossed teeth.

"Yeah, I'm all right."

"Reason I asked is, you got no headlights."

"I know." Harrelson suddenly remembers. "Is there a woman waiting inside the station? She's waiting for me."

"Yeah," the man says, "she's here. What happened to your face, buddy?"

"My face is all right." He looks toward the door and sees Meredith coming out, all smiles, dressed in her warm red winter coat, her brown boots, and black gloves. Harrelson tries to take his hands off the wheel and finds that he is having difficulty uncurling his fingers. Meredith crosses the front of the car and opens the door on the passenger's side.

"You should put new headlights in," the man says, but now Harrelson is closing the window.

He turns toward Meredith, who, instead of smiling, looks horror-struck. "John," she says, "honey, what happened to you?"

He turns to her, his eyes full of gratitude. "Well," he says, "I drove over here."

"No," she says, "I mean this." She takes off her right glove and raises her hand to his face. When she touches his skin, he feels a dull burning on his left cheek. "There's a cut here. A gash. It's been bleeding. What'd you do?"

"I have no idea."

"Did you have an accident coming over here?"

"Two." He holds up two fingers. "I had *two* accidents."

"You must have hit your head against the window or the . . . this." She reaches over and touches the latch for opening the no-draft window. "You may need stitches."

"No," he says. "It doesn't hurt." He smiles. "It's good to see you." Now he feels happy. "I made it! I made it over here!" He looks at her with a private, conspiratorial expression. "The roads were terrible, and I'm not sober."

"I know." She looks at him, top to bottom. "Get out and come over on this side," she says. "I'll drive back to my place. I don't want you driving anymore."

"All right." He does as he is told. Now, with Meredith behind the wheel, he sits back, and the pain in his cheek flares up. She is driving. Harrelson does not know where they are. He feels sleepy. She is saying something, but he is not quite sure that it makes any sense. Then the car is parked and Meredith has helped him out, and he is sitting in her living room, his face washed lightly with a washcloth, his cut covered with antiseptic cream. Meredith's radio is on, and Dietrich Fischer-Dieskau is singing.

> Habe ja doch nichts begangen
> Dass ich Menschen sollte scheu'n—
> Welch' ein törichtes Verlangen
> Treibt mich in die Wüstenei'n?

" 'I've done no wrong,' " Harrelson translates, hoping to impress Meredith, " 'to shun other men, so what is it that sends me out into the wilderness?' "

"That's the song?"

"That's it."

"What is it?"

"I don't know. It's German."

"I know," she says. "Isn't it interesting?"

"I guess so."

"There." She is finished cleaning Harrelson's cheek. "It's a smaller cut than I thought. Aren't you going to take off your jacket?" He nods but does nothing. She unzips it and helps him out of it. He is not really look-ing toward her but toward the stereo radio. "Poor John," she says. "But listen: thanks for getting me."

"You're welcome."

"I didn't realize how drunk you were."

He waves his hand. "That's all right."

"Are you cold?" He nods. "Come in and take a warm bath." She leads him into the bathroom and sits him down while she fills the tub. The warmth in the bathroom makes him sleepy again. He feels her taking his clothes off and helping him into the bathwater. The water's heat is intensely painful on his chilled feet, like ice picks thrust into the skin. She is still talking. He is bent over in the water, looking at the hair on his legs. "I've made a decision," she is saying. "I'm not going to marry you."

Harrelson nods. "I know."

"How did you know? I've only just decided."

"I just knew." He does not look at her.

"I decided a few days ago. I'm sorry."

"It's all right." He puts his hand on the surface of the bathtub water and moves it back and forth, creating waves.

"I need more security than you can give me," she says. "I'm sorry, but that's the way it is."

"Of course." Now he turns his head toward her. "Please don't say any more."

"I won't."

"Thank you." He takes the soap and washes his arms and chest. "You know, I don't feel very good."

"Where?" she asks. "Is it your face?"

He shakes his head. "I don't feel very good anywhere."

She stands up and turns away. She opens the medicine cabinet and examines the bottles. "Want some aspirin?"

"No."

He rises to his feet unsteadily in the tub. Meredith turns around, then takes his hand. With her other hand she reaches for a towel and dries him off. "You need some sleep," she says. "We both need some sleep." They walk together toward the bedroom, and Harrelson slips between the cold sheets. He hears the radio being turned off. In a moment, Meredith is in her nightgown, next to him. "We can still be friends," she says.

"Yes."

She leans over toward him and kisses him lightly. "We can still make love. There's no harm in that." His eyes are closed, but he nods. "Do you want to?"

"No," he whispers. "I don't."

"Maybe next time," she says. "When you haven't had so much to drink." He nods, then reaches his arms around her and rests his hands in their accustomed place below her breasts. As he falls asleep, Harrelson realizes that, after all, they *are* friends. Meredith does not think he will ever be a husband. Probably she is right. He does not have it in him to take care of another human being. It will never happen. As he drifts over, Harrelson has a premonition that he may not live for long. With what resistance he has left, he dismisses the idea as weakness, a bout of self-pity.

As soon as he is asleep, he finds himself in the company of his familiars. The faces that surround him are illuminated from within, and what they say is articulated in the language of angel speech. One of them welcomes him by saying, "What two time fine," and another replies with "And certainly certainly more sunsets provided than last February." These angels have no interest whatever in meaning. They say whatever pops into their heads. But it hardly matters because they gather around him, all smiles, and are pleased to be in his company. Some dispense with words and speak in music. Archaic joy washes over him. One angel detaches himself from the rest and says, "John, you are quite a poor sort," and it is meant as a compliment. Harrelson accepts the compliment. He feels another one of them bend down and kiss him lightly on the head. He is being gathered up.

But no: at once there is a point on the horizon, a point insistent with earthly magnetism, drawing Harrelson away toward the world, the real world that made Plato so unhappy, and he wakes up, hungover, in Meredith's arms, the sun rising orange over a field of snow. It is daytime, and Meredith is kissing him, and telling him he must go home now.

# Surprised by Joy

## 1

BECAUSE THEIR PSYCHIATRIST had recommended it, they both began to keep journals. Jeremy's was Woolworth-stationery drab, and Harriet's was sea-blue with the title "A Blank Book" printed in gold script in the upper right-hand corner. Thinking that pleasant images would relieve the tone of what was to follow, she sketched a wren in flight, a Victorian lamppost, and an ash tree on the first page. Then she changed her mind and blacked the drawings out. There weren't any drawings in the book Jeremy used. His writing was tiny and defiant. His first sentence, which was undated, read: "Benson told us it would help if we wrote down our thoughts, but I don't have any thoughts, and besides, the fact is that I don't feel like writing a goddamn thing." That was the end of the first entry.

One night Jeremy came home and found all the silverware—knives, forks, spoons, gravy bowls, and ladles—lined up according to type on the living-room carpet in front of the Hide-A-Bed sofa. Harriet said she wanted to do an inventory, to make sure the place settings were all present and accounted for. She threatened to count all the dishes, and all the books. A week later when he arrived home she was standing on her head with her legs crossed and her knees positioned against the wall. He put down his briefcase, hung up his coat, and sat in his chair. "So," he said. "What's this?"

"An article I read says it helps." Upside down, she attempted a smile.

"Standing on your head."

"Yeah. Think about it: the brain under stress needs more blood, the cerebral cortex especially. The article says that when you stand up you feel an instant of physical exhilaration." She closed her eyes. "The plumber came out this morning. The faucet's fixed."

"Physical exhilaration." He turned away from her to stare out at the street, where two children were roaring by on their Big Wheels.

"They say you'll feel better."

"Right. What article did you say this was?" He didn't wait for her to answer. "It sounds like *Parade* magazine. How much did the plumber charge? God, I could use a drink. I have the most amazing willpower." He glanced at her. "Did you cry a lot today?"

"No. Not much. Not like last week. I even did two full baskets of laundry. After lunch, when the plumber was gone, that was hard. For about ten minutes I couldn't help it and locked myself in the bathroom and then I wrote in the journal. Gretchen called and invited me into her weaving class. Do you think I should? It seems so dull and womanish. How was your day?" She tumbled backward, stood up, and looked at him with an unsteady, experimental smile.

"Do you feel exhilarated?" She shrugged. He said, "I feel the usual. Carrying around the black box." He rose, went to the kitchen for a beer, and clomped down the stairs to the basement, where he played his clarinet while watching television with the sound off. His music consisted of absentminded riffs in eerie unrelated keys.


They had brought their child home to a plain three-bedroom brick bungalow of the type referred to as a "starter house" for young married couples. Its distinguishing characteristics were those left by the previous owners. Jeremy and Harriet had never had time to redecorate it; as a result, their bedroom was covered with flocked jungle-orange wallpaper, the paint in Harriet's sewing room was oyster-gray, and the child's room had been painted blue, with two planets and four constellations mapped out on the ceiling with phosphorus dots and circles. At the time, their child was too little to notice such things: she gurgled at the trees outside and at the birds that sang in the shrubbery below her windowsill.

This child, Ellen, had been born after many difficulties. Harriet had had a series of ovarian cysts. She ovulated irregularly and only when provoked by certain powerful hormonal medications that left her so forgetful that she had to draw up hourly schedules for the day's tasks. She had the scars to prove that surgical procedures had been used to remove her enlarged ovaries piece by piece. The baby had been in a troublesome position, and Harriet had endured sixteen hours of labor, during which time she thrashed and groaned. Jeremy watched her lying in the hospital gown, his hands pressed against her lower back, while her breathing grew louder, hoarse and rhythmical. Their Lamaze lessons proved to be useless. The lights glared overhead in the prep room and could not be dimmed. In its labors her body heaved as if her reproductive system were choking in its efforts to expel the child. Her obstetrician was out of town on vacation in Puerto Vallarta, so the delivery was finally performed by a resident, a young woman who had a short hairdo and whose purple fingernail polish was visible through her surgical gloves.

The oyster-gray paint and the phosphorus planets in the house suited Ellen, who, when she was old enough to toddle, would point at the stars on the ceiling and wave at them. At this time she could not pronounce her own name and referred to herself as "Ebbo" or, mysteriously, as "Purl." On a spring morning she climbed from the crib onto the windowsill in pursuit of a chickadee singing outside. Cheered by the sun, Harriet had left the window open to let the breeze in. Ellen pushed herself past the sill and managed to tumble out, breaking the screen. She landed on a soft newly tilled flower bed next to a bush. When Harriet found her, she was tugging at flower shoots and looking pleased with herself. She said, "Purl drop." She shrugged her right shoulder and smiled.

They latched the screen onto a stronger frame and rushed around the house looking for hazards. They installed a lock on the basement door so she wouldn't tumble downstairs, and fastened shut the kitchen sink's lower cabinet so she wouldn't eat the dishwasher detergent. She lived one day past her third Christmas, when for the first time she knew what a Christmas tree was and could look forward to it with dazed anticipation. On Christmas Day she was buried up to her waist in presents: a knee-high table complete with cups and saucers, finger puppets, a plastic phonograph, a stuffed brown bear that made wheezing sounds, a Swiss music box, a windup train that went around in a small circle, a yellow toy police car with a lady cop inside, and, in her stocking, pieces of candy, gum, a comb, and a red rubber ball her mother had bought at Kiddie Land for twenty-five cents.

On December 26, Jeremy and Harriet were slumped in the basement, watching Edmund Gwenn in *Miracle on 34th Street* for the eighth or ninth time, while Ellen played upstairs in her room. They went through three commercial breaks before Harriet decided to check on her. She hadn't been worried because she could hear the phonograph playing a Sesame Street record. Harriet went down the hallway and turned the corner into Ellen's room. Her daughter was lying on the floor, on her side, her skin blue. She wasn't breathing. On her forehead was blood next to a bright cut. Harriet's first thought was that Ellen had somehow been knocked unconscious by an intruder. Then she was shouting for Jeremy, and crying, and touching Ellen's face with her fingers. She picked her up, pounded her back, and then felt the lump of the red rubber ball that Ellen had put in her mouth and that had lodged in her throat. She squeezed her chest and the ball came up into the child's mouth.

Jeremy rushed in behind her. He took Ellen away from Harriet and carried her into the living room, her arms hanging down, swinging. He shouted instructions at Harriet. Some made sense; others didn't. He gave Ellen mouth-to-mouth resuscitation and kept putting his hand against her heart, waiting for a pulse.

Later they understood that Ellen had panicked and had run into the edge of the open closet door. What with the movie and the new phonograph, they hadn't heard her. The edge of the door wasn't sharp, but she had run into it so blindly that the collision had dazed her. She had fallen and reached up to her forehead: a small amount of blood had dried on her hands. She had then reached for her stuffed raccoon; her left hand was gripping its leg. She was wearing, for all time, her yellow pajamas. In the living room, waiting for the ambulance, Harriet clutched her own hands. Then she was drinking glass after glass of water in a white waiting room.

Their parents said, oh, they could have another, a child as beautiful as Ellen. Her doctors disagreed. Harriet's ovaries had been cut away until only a part of one of them remained. In any case, they didn't want replacements. The idea made no sense. What they thought of day and night was what had happened upstairs while they were watching television. Their imaginations put the scene on a film loop. Guiltily, they watched it until their mental screens began to wash the rest of the past away.

For the next two months they lived hour to hour. Every day became an epic of endurance, in which Harriet sat in chairs. Harriet's mother called every few days, offering excruciating maternal comfort. There were photographs, snapshots and studio portraits that neither of them could stand to remove. Nature became Harriet's enemy. She grew to hate the sun and its long, lengthening arcs. When living trees broke open into pink and white blossoms in the spring, Harriet wanted to fling herself against them. She couldn't remember what it was about life that had ever interested her. The world began a vast and buzzing commentary to keep her in cramps, preoccupied with Ellen, who had now irresistibly become Purl. The grass no longer grew up from the ground but instead stood as a witless metaphor of continuing life. Dishes and silverware upset her, unaccountably. She couldn't remember who her friends were and did not recognize them on the street. Every night the sky fell conclusively.

Jeremy had his job, but every evening, after seeing about Harriet, he went straight down to the basement where the television set was. He played his clarinet, drank beer, and watched the local news until it was time for dinner. He opened the twist-top beer bottles and drank the beer mechanically, as if acting on orders. After overhearing the music he played, Harriet began to call it "jazz from Mars," and Jeremy said, yes, that was probably where it came from. He paid attention to things at work; his music could afford to be inattentive.

He came upstairs when dinner was ready. This meal consisted of whatever food Harriet could think of buying and preparing. They didn't like to go out. They often ate hot dogs and potato salad, or hamburger, or pizza. Jeremy sometimes fell asleep at the dinner table, his head tilted back at the top of the chair, and his mouth open, sucking in breaths. Harriet would drape one of his arms around her neck and lower him to the floor, so he wouldn't fall off the chair while asleep. They had talked about getting chairs with arms to prevent accidents of this kind; they both assumed they would spend the rest of their lives falling asleep at the table after dinner.

They started seeing Benson, the therapist, because of what happened with the Jehovah's Witnesses. In mid-May, the doorbell rang just after dinner. Jeremy, who this time was still awake, rose from the table to see who it was. Outside the screen door stood a red-haired man and a small red-haired boy, eight or nine years old, dressed in nearly identical gray coats and bow ties. The father was carrying a copy of *Awake!* and *The Watchtower.* The boy held a Bible, a children's edition with a crude painting of Jesus on the cover. Leaving the screen door shut, Jeremy asked them what they wanted.

"My son would like to read to you," the man said, glancing down at the boy. "Do you have time to listen for a minute?"

Jeremy said nothing.

Taking this as a sign of agreement, the man nodded at the boy, who pushed his glasses back, opened the Bible, and said, "Psalm forty-three." He swallowed, looked up at his father, who smiled, then pulled at the red silk bookmark he had inserted at the beginning of the psalm. He cleared his throat. "Give sentence with me, O God," he read, his finger trailing horizontally along the line of type, his voice quavering, "and defend my cause against the ungodly people; O deliver me from the deceitful and wicked man." He stumbled over "deceitful." The boy paused and looked through the screen at Jeremy. Jeremy was watching the boy with the same emptied expression he used when watching television. The boy's father touched his son on the shoulder and told him to continue. A bird was singing nearby. Jeremy looked up. It was a cardinal on a telephone wire.

"For thou art the God of my strength," the boy read. "Why hast thou put me from thee? and why go I so heavily, while the enemy oppresseth me?"

For the first time, Jeremy said something. He said, "I don't believe it. You can't be doing this." The father and the boy, however, didn't hear him. The boy continued.

"O send out thy light and thy truth, that they may lead me, and bring me unto thy holy hill, and to thy dwelling."

Jeremy said, "Who sent you here?" The father heard what he said, but his only reaction was to squint through the screen to see Jeremy better. He gave off a smell of cheap aftershave.

"And that I may go unto the altar of God," the boy read, "even unto the God of my joy and gladness; and upon the harp will I give thanks unto thee, O God, my God."

"You're contemptible," Jeremy said, "to use children. That's a low trick."

This time both the boy and his father stared in at him. Harriet had appeared and was standing behind Jeremy, pulling at his shirt and whispering instructions to him to thank them and send them on their merry way. The father, however, recovered himself, smiled, pointed at the Bible, and then touched his son on the head, as if pressing a button.

"Why art thou so heavy, O my soul?" the boy read, stuttering slightly. "And why art thou so disquieted within me?"

"Stop it!" Jeremy shouted. "Please stop it! Stop it!" He opened the screen door and walked out to the front stoop so that he was just to the right of the father and his boy. Harriet crossed her arms but otherwise could not or did not move. Jeremy reached up and held on to the man's lapel. He didn't grab it but simply put it between his thumb and forefinger. He aimed his words directly into the center of the father's face. "Who sent you here?" he asked, his words thrown out like stones. "This was no accident. Don't tell me this was an accident, because I'd hate to think you were lying to me. Someone sent you here. Right? Who? How'd they ever think of using kids?" The bird was still singing, and when Jeremy stopped he heard it again, but hearing it only intensified his anger. "You want to sell me *The Watchtower*?" he asked, sinking toward inarticulateness. Then he recovered. "You want my money?" He let go of the man's lapel, reached into his pocket, and threw a handful of nickels and dimes to the ground. "Now go away and leave me alone."

The stranger was looking at Jeremy, and his mouth was opening. The boy was clutching his father's coat. One of the dimes was balanced on his left shoe.

"Go home," Jeremy said, "and never say another word about anything and don't ever again knock on my door." Jeremy was a lawyer. When speeches came to him, they came naturally. His face in its rage was as white as paper. He stopped, looked down, and hurriedly kissed the boy on the top of the head. As he straightened up, he said softly, "Don't mind me." Then, mobilized, Harriet rushed out onto the stoop and grabbed Jeremy's hand. She tried smiling.

"You see that my husband's upset," she said, pulling at him. "I think you should go now."

"Yes, all right," the father mumbled, blinking, taking the Bible from his son and closing it. The air thickened with the smell of his aftershave.

"We've had an accident recently," she explained. "We weren't prepared."

The man had his arm around his son's shoulders. They were starting down the walk to the driveway. "The Bible is a great comfort," the man said over his shoulder. "A help ever sure." He stopped to look back. "Trust in God," he said.

Jeremy made a roaring sound, somewhere between a shout and a bark, as Harriet hauled him back inside.

Benson's office was lodged on the twentieth floor of a steel-and-glass professional building called the Kelmer Tower. After passing through Benson's reception area, a space not much larger than a closet, the patient stepped into the main office, where the sessions were actually conducted. It was decorated in therapeutic pastels, mostly off-whites and pale blues. Benson had set up bookshelves, several chairs, and a couch, and had positioned a rubber plant near the window. In front of the chairs was a coffee table on which was placed, not very originally, a small statue of a Minotaur. Benson's trimmed mustache and otherworldly air made him look like a wine steward. He had been recommended to them by their family doctor, who described Benson as a "very able man."

Harriet thought Benson was supposed to look interested; instead, he seemed bored to the point of stupefaction. He gave the appearance of thinking of something else: baseball, perhaps, or his golf game. Several times, when Jeremy was struggling to talk, Benson turned his face away and stared out the window. Harriet was afraid that he was going to start humming Irving Berlin songs. Instead, when Jeremy was finished, Benson looked at him and asked, "So. What are you going to do?"

"Do? Do about what?"

"Those feelings you've just described."

"Well, what am I supposed to do?"

"I don't think there's anything you're supposed to do. It's a choice. If you want me to recommend something, I can recommend several things, among them that you keep a journal, a sort of record. But you don't have to."

"That's good." Jeremy looked down at the floor, where the slats of sunlight through the venetian blinds made a picket fence across his feet.

"If you don't want my help," Benson said, "you don't have to have it."

"At these prices," Jeremy said, "I want something."

"Writing in a journal can help," Benson continued, "because it makes us aware of our minds in a concrete way." Harriet cringed over Benson's use of the paternal first-person plural. She looked over at Jeremy. He was gritting his teeth. His jaw muscles were visible in his cheek. "Crying helps," Benson told them. "And," Benson said slowly, "it helps to get a change of scene. Once you're ready and have the strength and resources to do it, you might try going on a trip."

"Where?" Harriet asked.

"Where?" Benson looked puzzled. "Why, anywhere. Anywhere that doesn't look like this. Try going to someplace where the scenery is different. Nassau. Florida. Colorado."

"How about the Himalayas?" Jeremy asked.

"Yes," Benson said, not bothering to act annoyed. "That would do."


They both agreed that they might be able to handle it if it weren't for the dreams. Ellen appeared in them and insisted on talking. In Jeremy's dreams, she talked about picnics and hot dogs, how she liked the catsup on the opposite side of the wiener from the mustard, and how she insisted on having someone toast the bun. The one sentence Jeremy remembered with total clarity when he woke up was: "Don't *like* soggy hot dogs." He wouldn't have remembered it if it hadn't sounded like her.

She was wearing a flannel shirt and jeans in Jeremy's dream; in Harriet's she had on a pink jumper that Harriet had bought for her second birthday. Harriet saw that she was outgrowing it. With a corkscrew feeling she saw that Ellen was wearing a small ivory cameo with her own—Harriet's—profile on it. She was also wearing a rain hat that Harriet couldn't remember from anywhere, and she was carrying a Polaroid photograph of her parents. Harriet wondered vaguely how dead children get their hands on such pictures. In this dream Harriet was standing on a street corner in a depopulated European city where the shutters were all closed tight over the windows. Near her, overhead in the intersection, the traffic light hanging from a thick cable turned from green to amber to red, red to green, green to amber to red. However, no cars charged through the intersection, and no cars were parked on the street. A rhythmic thud echoed in the streets. Leaves moldered in the gutters. Harriet knew that it was a bad city for tourists. In this place Ellen scampered toward her down the sidewalk, wearing the pink jumper and the rain hat, the photograph in her hand, the cameo pinned near her collar. She smiled. Harriet stumbled toward her, but Ellen held out her hand and said, "Can't hug." Harriet asked her about the hat, and Ellen said, "Going to rain." She looked up at the bleary sky, and, following her lead, so did Harriet. Flocks of birds flew from left to right across it in no special pattern, wing streaks of indecision. Clouds. Harriet gazed down at Ellen. "Are you okay?" Harriet asked. "Who's taking care of you?" Ellen was picking her nose. "Lots of people," she said, wiping her finger on her pant leg. "They're nice." "Are you all right?" Harriet asked again. Ellen lifted her right shoulder. "Yeah," she said. She looked up. "Miss you, Mommy," she said, and, against directions, Harriet bent down to kiss her, wanting the touch of her skin against her lips, but when she reached Ellen's face, Ellen giggled, looked around quickly as if she were being watched from behind the shuttered windows, reached both hands up to cover her mouth, and disappeared, leaving behind a faint odor of flowers.

"Such dreams are common," Benson said. "Very very common."

"Tell me something else," Harriet said.

"What do you want me to tell you?"

"Something worth all the money we're paying you."

"You sound like Jeremy. What *would* be worth all the money you're paying me?"

"I have the feeling," Harriet said, "that you're playing a very elaborate game with us. And you have more practice at it than we do."

"If it's a game," Benson said, "then I do have more practice. But if it's not a game, I don't." He waited. Harriet stared at the giant leaves of the rubber plant, standing in the early-summer light, torpid and happy. Jeremy hadn't come with her this time. The Minotaur on the coffee table looked inquisitive. "What is the dream telling you about Ellen, do you think?"

"That she's all right?"

"Yes." Benson breathed out. "And what do you have to worry about?"

"Not Ellen."

"No, not Ellen. The dream doesn't say to worry about her. So what do you have to worry about?"

"Jeremy. I don't see him. And I have to worry about getting out of that city."

"Why should you worry about Jeremy?"

"I don't know," Harriet said. "He's hiding somewhere. I want to get us both out of that city. It gives me the creeps."

"Yes. And how are you going to get out of that city?"

"Run?" Harriet looked at Benson. "Can I run out of it?"

"If you want to." Benson thought for a moment. "If you want to, you will run out of it." He smoothed his tie. "But you can't run and pull Jeremy at the same time."

After Jeremy's dream, she no longer served hot dogs for dinner. That night she was serving pork chops, and when Jeremy came in, still in his vest but with his coat over his shoulder, she was seated at the table, looking through a set of brochures she had picked up at a travel agency down the block from Benson's office. After Jeremy had showered and changed his clothes, he was about to take a six-pack out of the refrigerator when he looked over at Harriet studying a glossy photograph of tourists riding mules on Molokai. "It says here," Harriet announced, "in this brochure, that Molokai is the flattest of all the islands and the one with the most agricultural activity."

"Are you going on a quiz show? Is that it?"

She stood up, walked around the dining-room table, then sat down on the other side. She had a fountain pen in her hand. "Now this," she said, pointing with the pen to another brochure, "this one is about New Mexico. I've never been to New Mexico. You haven't, either, right?"

"No," Jeremy said. "Honey, what's this all about?"

"This," she said, "is all about what we're going to do during your two weeks off. I'll be damned if I'm going to sit here. Want to go to Santa Fe?"

Jeremy seemed itchy, as if he needed to go downstairs and play a few measures of jazz from Mars. "Sure, sure," he said. He rubbed his eyes suddenly. "Isn't it sort of hot that time of year?"

She shook her head. "It says here that the elevation's too high. You can stay in the mountains, and it's cool at night."

"Oh." Then, as an afterthought, he said, "Good."

She looked up at him. She stood and put her hand on his face, rubbing her thumb against his cheek. "How's the black box?" she asked. She had recently started to wear glasses and took them off now.

"How's the sky?" he asked. He turned around. "The black box is just fine. I move around it, but it's always there, right in front of me. It's hard to move with that damn thing in your head. I could write a book about it: how to live with a box and be a zombie." He reached for a beer and carried it to the basement. She could hear the television set being clicked on and the exhalation of the beer bottle when he opened it.

# 2

The flight to Albuquerque took four hours. Lunch was served halfway through: chicken in sauce. The flight attendants seemed proud of the meal and handed out the plastic trays with smug smiles. Jeremy had a copy of *BusinessWeek* in his lap, which he dropped to the floor when the food arrived. For much of the four hours he sat back and dozed. Harriet was closer to the window and dutifully looked out whenever the captain announced that they were flying over a landmark.

In Albuquerque they rented a car and drove north toward Taos, the destination Harriet had decided upon, following the advice of the travel agent. They stopped at a motel in Santa Fe for dinner. Appalled by the congestion and traffic, they set out after breakfast the next morning. As they approached the mountains, Jeremy, who was driving, said, "So this is the broom that sweeps the cobwebs away." He said it softly and with enough irony to make Harriet wince and pull at her eyebrow, a recent nervous tic. The trip, it was now understood, had been her idea. She was responsible. She offered him a stick of gum and turned on the radio. They listened to country-western until the mountains began to interfere with the reception.

In Taos they drove through the city until they found the Best Western motel, pale yellow and built in quasi-adobe style. They took showers and then strolled toward the center of town, holding hands. The light was brilliant and the air seemingly without the humidity and torpor of the Midwest, but this atmosphere also had a kind of emptiness that Jeremy said he wasn't used to. In the vertical sun they could both feel their hair heating up. Harriet said she wanted a hat, and Jeremy nodded. He sniffed the air. They passed the Kit Carson museum, and Jeremy laughed to himself. "What is it?" Harriet asked, but he only shook his head. At the central square, the streets narrowed and the traffic backed up with motoring tourists. "Lots of art stores here," Harriet said, in a tone that suggested that Jeremy ought to be interested. She was gazing into a display window at a painting of what appeared to be a stick-figure man with a skull face dancing in a metallic, vulcanized landscape. She saw Jeremy's reflection in the window. He was peering at the stones on the sidewalk. Then she looked at herself: she was standing halfway in front of Jeremy, partially blocking his view.

They walked through the plaza, and Harriet went into a dime store to buy a hat. Jeremy sat outside on a bench in the square, opposite a hotel that advertised a display of the paintings of D. H. Lawrence, banned in England, so it was claimed. He turned away. An old man, an Indian with shoulder-length gray hair, was crossing the plaza in front of him, murmuring an atonal chant. The tourists stepped aside to let the man pass. Jeremy glanced at the tree overhead, in whose shade he was sitting. He could not identify it. He exhaled and examined his watch angrily. He gazed down at the second hand circling the dial face once, then twice. He knew Harriet was approaching when he saw out of the corner of his eye her white cotton pants and her feet in their sandals.

"Do you like it?" she asked. He looked up. She had bought a yellow cap with a visor and the word "Taos" sewn into it. She was smiling, modeling for him.

"Very nice," he said. She sat down next to him and squeezed his arm. "What do people do in this town?" he asked. "Look at vapor trails all day?"

"They walk around," she said. "They buy things." She saw a couple dragging a protesting child into an art gallery. "They bully their kids." She paused, then went on, "They eat." She pointed to a restaurant on the east side of the square with a balcony that looked down at the commerce below. "Hungry?" He shrugged. "I sure am," she said. She took his hand and led him across the square into the archway underneath the restaurant. There she stopped, turned, and put her arms around him, leaning against him. She felt the sweat of his back against her palms. "I'm so sorry," she said. Then they went up the stairs and had lunch, two margaritas each and enchiladas in hot sauce. Sweating and drowsy, they strolled back to the motel, not speaking.

They left the curtains of the front window open an inch or so when they made love that afternoon. From the bed they could see occasionally a thin strip of someone walking past. They made love to fill time, with an air of detachment, while the television set stayed on, showing a Lana Turner movie in which everyone's face was green at the edges and pink at the center. Jeremy and Harriet touched with the pleasure of being close to one familiar object in a setting crowded with strangers. Harriet reached her orgasm with her usual spasms of trembling, and when she cried out he lowered his head to the pillow on her right side, where he wouldn't see her face.

Thus began the pattern of the next three days: desultory shopping for knickknacks in the morning, followed by lunch, lovemaking, and naps through the afternoon, during which time it usually rained for an hour or so. During their shopping trips they didn't buy very much: Jeremy said the art was mythic and lugubrious, and Harriet didn't like pottery. Jeremy bought a flashlight, in case, he said, the power went out, and Harriet purchased a key chain. All three days they went into the same restaurant at the same time and ordered the same meal, explaining to themselves that they didn't care to experiment with exotic regional food. On the third afternoon of this they woke up from their naps at about the same time with the totally clear unspoken understanding that they could not spend another day—or perhaps even another hour—in this manner.

Jeremy announced the problem by asking, "What do we do to-morrow?"

Harriet kicked her way out of bed and walked over to the television, on top of which she had placed a guide to the Southwest. "Well," she said, opening it up, "there *are* sights around here. We haven't been into the mountains north of here. There's a Kiowa Indian pueblo just a mile away. There's a place called Arroyo Seco near here and—"

"What's that?"

"It means Dry Gulch." She waited. "There's the Taos Gorge Bridge." Jeremy shook his head quickly. "The D. H. Lawrence shrine is thirty minutes from here, and so is the Millicent A. Rogers Memorial Museum. There are, it says here, some trout streams. If it were winter, we could go skiing."

"It's summer," Jeremy said, closing his eyes and pulling the sheet up. "We can't ski. What about this shrine?"

She put the book on the bed near Jeremy and read the entry. "It says that Lawrence lived for eighteen months up there, and they've preserved his ranch. When he died, they brought his ashes back and there's a shrine or something. They *call* it a shrine. I'm only telling you what the book says."

"D. H. Lawrence?" Jeremy asked sleepily.

"You know," Harriet said. *"Lady Chatterley's Lover."*

"Yes, I know." He smiled. "It wasn't the books I was asking about, it was the *quality* of the books, and therefore the necessity of making the trip."

"All I know is that it's visitable," she said, "and it's off State Highway Three, and it's something to do."

"Okay. I don't care what damn highway it's on," Jeremy said, reaching for the book and throwing it across the room. "Let's at least get into the car and go somewhere."


After breakfast they drove in the rental car out of town toward the Taos ski valley. They reached it after driving up fifteen miles of winding road through the mountains, following a stream of snow runoff, along which they counted a dozen fishermen. When they reached the valley, they admired the Sangre de Cristo Mountains but agreed it was summer and there was nothing to do in such a place. Neither blamed the other for acting upon an unproductive idea. They returned to the car and retraced their steps to the highway, which they followed for another fifteen miles until they reached the turn for the D. H. Lawrence shrine on Kiowa Ranch Road. Jeremy stopped the car on the shoulder. "Well?" he asked.

"Why do we have to *decide* about everything?" Harriet said, looking straight ahead. "Why can't we just *do* it?"

He accelerated up the unpaved road, which climbed toward a plateau hidden in the mountains. They passed several farms where cattle were grazing on the thin grasses. The light made the land look varnished; even with sunglasses, Harriet squinted at the shimmering heat waves rising from the gravel.

Jeremy said, "What's here?"

"I told you. Anyhow, the description isn't much good. We'll find out. Maybe they'll have a tour of his inner sanctum or have his Nobel Prize up in a frame. The book says they have his actual typewriter."

Jeremy coughed. "He never won the Nobel Prize." Harriet looked over at him and noticed that his face was losing its internal structure and becoming puffy. Grief had added five years to his appearance. She saw, with disbelief, a new crease on his neck. Turning away, she glanced up at the sky: a hawk, cirrus clouds. The air conditioner was blowing a stream of cool air on her knees. Her gums ached.

"Only two more miles," Jeremy said, beginning now to hunch over the wheel slightly.

"I don't like this draft," she said, reaching over to snap off the air conditioner. She cranked down the window and let the breeze tangle her hair. They were still going uphill and had reached, a sign said, an elevation of nine thousand feet. Jeremy hummed Martian jazz as he drove, tapping the steering wheel. The little dirt road went past an open gate, then cut in two, one fork going toward a conference center indicated by a road marker, the other toward the house and shrine. They came to a clearing. In front of them stood a two-story house looking a bit like an English country cottage, surrounded by a white picket fence, with a tire swing in the backyard, beyond which two horses were grazing. They were alone: there were no other cars in sight. Jeremy went up to the door of the house and knocked. A dog began barking angrily from inside, as if the knocks had interrupted its nap. "Look at this," Harriet said.

She had walked a few steps and was looking in the direction they had come from; in the clear air they could see down the mountain and across the valley for a distance of fifty miles or so. "It's beautiful," she said. Jeremy appeared from behind her, shielding his eyes although the sun was behind him. "What're you doing that for?" she asked.

"You have dark glasses. I don't."

"Where's the shrine?" she asked. "I don't see it anywhere."

"You have to turn around. Look." He pointed to the picket fence. At its north corner there was a sign that Harriet had missed.

## SHRINE ☞

"That's very quaint," she said. "And what's this?" She walked toward the fence and picked a child's mitten off one of the posts. Mickey

Mouse's face was printed on the front of the mitten, and one of his arms reached up over the thumb. She began laughing. "It doesn't say anything about Mickey Mouse in *Fodor's*. Do you think he's part of the shrine?"

Jeremy didn't answer. He had already started out ahead of her on a path indicated by the black pointing finger. Harriet followed him, panting from the altitude and the blistering heat, feeling her back begin to sweat as the light rained down on it. She felt the light on her legs and inside her head, on her eardrums. The path turned to the right and began a series of narrowing zigzags going up the side of a hill at the top of which stood the shrine, a small white boxlike building that, as they approached it, resembled a chapel, a mausoleum, or both. A granite phoenix glowered at the apex of the roof.

"The door's open," Jeremy said, twenty feet ahead of her, "and nobody's here." He was wearing heavy jeans, and his blue shirt was soaked with two wings of sweat. Harriet could hear the rhythmic pant of his breathing.

"Are there snakes out here?" she asked. "I hate snakes."

"Not in the shrine," he said. "I don't see any."

"What do you see?"

"A visitors' register." He had reached the door and had stepped inside. Then he came back out.

She was still ten feet away. "There must be more. You can't have a shrine without something in it."

"Well, there's this white thing outside," he said breathlessly. "Looks like a burial stone." She was now standing next to him. "Yes. This is where his wife is buried." They both looked at it. A small picture of Frieda was bolted into the stone.

"Well," Jeremy said, "now for the shrine." They shuffled inside. At the back was a small stained-glass window, a representation of the sun, thick literalized rays burning out from its center. To their left the visitors' register lay open on a high desk, and above it in a display case three graying documents asserted that the ashes stored here were authentically those of D. H. Lawrence, the author. The chapel's interior smelled of sage and cement. At the far side of the shrine, six feet away, was a roped-off area, and at the back an approximation of an altar, at whose base was a granite block with the letters DHL carved on it. "This is it?" Jeremy asked. "No wonder no one's here."

Harriet felt giddy from the altitude. "Should we pray?" she asked, but before Jeremy could answer, she said, "Well, good for him. He got him-self a fine shrine. Maybe he deserves it. God damn, it's hot in here." She turned around and walked outside, still laughing in a broken series of almost inaudible chuckles. When she was back in the sun, she pointed her finger the way the sign had indicated and said, "Shrine."

Jeremy stepped close to her, and they both looked again at the moun-tains in the west. "I used to read him in college," Harriet said, "and in high school I had a copy of *The Rainbow* I hid under my pillow where my mother wouldn't find it. Jesus, it must be ninety-five degrees." She looked suddenly at Jeremy, sweat dripping into her eyes. "I used to have a lot of fantasies when I was a teenager," she said. He was wiping his face with a handkerchief. "Do you see anyone?" she asked.

"Do I see anybody? No. We would've heard a car coming up the road. Why?"

"Because I'm hot. I feel like doing something," Harriet said. "I mean, here we are at the D. H. Lawrence shrine." She was unbuttoning her blouse. "I just thought of this," she said, beginning to laugh again. She put her blouse on the ground and quickly unhooked her bra, dropping it on top of the blouse. "There," she said, sighing. "Now that's better." She turned to face the mountains. When Jeremy didn't say anything, she swung around to look at him. He was staring at her, at the brown circles of her nipples, and his face seemed stricken. She reached over and took his hand. "Oh, Jay, sweetie," she said, "no one will see us. Honey. What is it? Do you want me to get dressed?"

"That's not it." He was staring at her, as if she were not his wife.

"What? What is it?"

"You're free of it." He wiped his forehead.

"What?"

"You're free of it. You're leaving me alone here."

"Alone? Alone in what?"

"You know perfectly damn well," he said. "I'm alone back here." He tapped his head. "I don't know how you did it, but you did it. You broke free. You're gone." He bent down. "You don't know what I'm talking about."

"Yes, I do." She put her bra and blouse back on and turned toward him again. His face was a mixture of agony and rage, but in the huge sunlight these emotions diminished to small vestigial puffs of feeling.

"It's a path," she said. "And then you're surprised. You get out. It'll happen to you. You'll see. Honestly."

She could see his legs shaking. His face was a barren but expressive landscape. "Okay," he said. "Talk all you want. I was just thinking . . ." He didn't finish the sentence.

"You'll be all right," she said, stroking his back.

"I don't *want* to be all right!" he said, his voice rising, a horrible smile appearing on his face: it was a devil's face, Harriet saw, and it was radiant and calm. Sweat poured off his forehead, and his skin had started to flush pink. "It's my pleasure not to be all right. Do you see that? My *pleasure.*"

She wiped her hands on her cotton pants. A stain appeared, then vanished. "You want that? You want to be back there by yourself?"

"Yeah." He nodded. "You bet. I feel like an explorer. I feel like a fucking pioneer." He gave each one of the words a separate emphasis. Meanwhile, he had separated himself from her and was now tilting his head up toward the sky, letting the sun shine on his closed eyelids.

She looked at him. In the midst of the sunlight he was hugging his darkness. She stepped down the zigzag path to the car, leaving him there, but he followed her. Once they were both in the car, the dog inside the ranch house began its frantic barking, but it stopped after a few seconds. She took Jeremy's hand and scanned the clouds in the west, the Sangre de Cristo Mountains to the east, trying to see the sky, the beckoning clouds, the way he did, but she couldn't. All she could see was the land stretched out in front of her, and, far in the distance, fifty miles away, a few thunderheads and a narrow curtain of rain, so thin that the light passed straight through it.

# The Eleventh Floor

CAREFULLY DRUNK, Mr. Bradbury sat on his patio-balcony in the bland morning sunshine, sipping vodka-and-something. He was waiting for his son to visit. This son, Eric, had called and said he would arrive shortly, and that was an hour ago. It was Saturday: vodka day. He peered down from the eleventh floor at the sidewalk trees, where the sparrows were making a racket. Below the sparrows, Mr. Bradbury could see the velvet-brown dot of the doorman's hat. He thought he could smell crab-apple blossoms and something more subtle, like dust.

In shivering glassy clarity, he observed a rusting blue subcompact move into a space in front of a fireplug. That would be Eric, who had a collection of parking tickets, little marks of risk and daring. Watching him lock his car, his father mashed out his cigarette in a blue pottery ash-tray balanced on the balcony railing. He coughed, putting his hand in front of his mouth. Eric had stopped to talk to the doorman, George. George and Eric, two human dots. Eric's pinpoint face turned, tilted, and stared up at the rows of balconies, finding his father on the eleventh. He did not wave.

Standing up, Mr. Bradbury tested his reflexes. He bent his knees and thought of a line from Byron: "From the dull palace to the dirty hovel, something something something novel." The problem with poetry was that you were always having to look it up. He couldn't recall which poem contained the dull palace, nor did he care. He stepped out of the sunlight into the living room and sank into the sofa, trying not to groan. Elena, the Peruvian housekeeper, was preparing lunch, probably one of her crude ethnic casseroles. She didn't inform him of her plans in advance. He reached over to the coffee table and pressed the MUTE button on the remote control to silence the CNN announcer. His neck hurt. He rubbed it, and to his own fingers the skin felt scaly. At least no swellings or lumps. He let his right arm drop down onto the side table. His thumb landed in the engraved silver scallop-shell ashtray and emerged from it with a gray coating of ash. He bent over and was rubbing the thumb on the carpet just as his son knocked.

The boy had a key; the knock was some kind of ritual announcement of estrangement. He heaved himself up to his feet and, remembering to stand straight, made his way past the bookshelves and the paintings to the foyer.

"Eric," he said, opening the door and seeing his son in a blast of sentimental pride. "I'm glad you came." The flaring of his love made him shy, so that he drew back his body even as he extended his hand. Eric shook his hand, gazed down at his father's face with an examining look, and sniffed twice. Mr. Bradbury could tell that Eric was trying to catch the scent of his breath. "Come in, come in," he said. "Don't loiter out there in the hall. Why didn't you just let yourself in with your key?"

"I lost it," Eric said. "I lost all my keys."

"Where?"

"I don't know. A party. Yeah, that's right. A party."

Eric stood in the center of the living room, checking out the familial furniture. Then he tossed his jacket on a chair and bent down to unlace his shoes. For some reason his father noticed that his son was wearing thick white cotton socks. Then Eric straightened up, pleased to be on display, his thumbs hooked in the back pockets of his jeans.

"You're getting sizable. Is it the swimming?"

"Not this season," Eric said. "It's track. They had us on a training program."

"I always forget what a big kid you are. I don't remember anyone in the family being your size except your mother's uncle Gus, who worked in the Water Department. He had the worst halitosis I've ever encountered in an adult human being. Your mother used to say that he smelled like a Labrador with stomach lesions." He smiled as his son walked toward the open porch door and the balcony. It was an athletic, pantherish walk. "You let your hair grow," his father said. "You have a beard. You look like a Renaissance aide-de-camp."

Eric reached over for the ashtray on the railing and fastidiously put it down on the deck. Without turning around, he said, "I thought I'd try it out." Mr. Bradbury saw him glance at his drink, measuring it, counting the ice cubes.

"Try what? Oh. The beard. You should. Absolutely."

Eric lifted himself easily and sat on the railing, facing his father. He hooked his feet around the bars. He squinted toward the living room, where his father stood. "Did it surprise you?"

"What?" The beard: he meant the beard. "Oh, a bit, maybe. But I'm in a state of virtually constant surprise. George surprises me with tales of his riotous family, you surprise me with your sudden visits, and Elena out there in the kitchen surprises me every time she manages to serve me a meal. Your old dad lives in a state of paralyzed amazement. So. How's college life? You've been kind of short on the letters."

"It's only across town, Dad."

"I know how far away it is. You could call. You could put your finger on the old rugged dial."

"I forget. And so do you." Eric put his arms out and leaned his head back to catch the rays of the sun. If he fell, he'd fall eleven floors.

"In that sunlight," his father said, "your skin looks shellacked."

Eric eyed his father, then the patio deck, where the glass of vodka and fruit juice made a small festive group with the ashtray, a lighter, and an FM transistor radio. "Shellacked?"

Mr. Bradbury put his hands in his pockets. He took three steps forward. "I only meant that you look like you've already had some sun this year. That's all I meant." He laughed, one rushed chuckle. "I will not have my vocabulary questioned." He stepped onto the balcony and sat down in a canvas chair, next to the drink and the cigarettes. "Do you ever write your sister?"

"I call her. She's okay. She asks about you. Your health and things like that." Mr. Bradbury was shading his eyes. "How's your breathing?"

"My breathing?" Mr. Bradbury took his hand away from his eyes. "Fine. Why do you ask?"

"It seems sort of shallow or something."

"You were never much for tact, were you, kid?" His father leaned back. "I don't have emphysema yet, if that's the question. But I still smoke. Oh, yes." He smiled oddly. "Cigarettes," he said, "are my friends. They have the faith."

Eric hopped down, so that he was no longer looking at his father, and turned to survey the city park two blocks west. "How's business?"

His father waved his hand in a gesture that wasn't meant to express anything. "Good. Business is good. I'm doing commercials for a bank owned by a cartel of international slime, and I also have a breakfast-food account now, aimed at kids. Crispy Snax. The demographics are a challenge. We're using animated cartoons and we've invented this character, Colonel Crisp, who orders the kids to eat the cereal. He raises a sword and the product appears in a sort of animated blizzard of sugar. We're going for the Napoleonic touch. It's coercive, of course, but it's funny if you're positioned behind the joke instead of in front of it. We're getting angry letters from mothers. We must be doing something right." He stared at his son's back. "Of course, I get tired sometimes."

"Tired?"

He waited, then said, "I don't know. I should take a vacation." He looked past his son at the other buildings across the street with their floors of patio-balconies, some with hanging plants, others with bicycles. "So I could recollect sensations sweet in hours of weariness 'mid the din of towns and cities. Listen, you want a drink? You know where it is."

Eric turned and stared at his father. "Eleven thirty in the morning?" He lifted himself on the railing again.

Mr. Bradbury shrugged. "It's all right. It's Saturday. It warms up the mental permafrost. On weekends it's okay to drink before lunch. I've got a book here that says so."

"You *wrote* that book, Pop."

"Well, maybe I did." He sat up. "Damn it, stop worrying about me. *I* don't worry about *you*. You're too young to be worrying about me, and besides, I'm making out like a bandit."

Eric said nothing. He was looking away from his father into the living room, at a Lichtenstein print above the sofa. It showed a comic-book woman passionately kissing a comic-book man.

"You won't mind if I do?"

"What?" Eric said. "Have a drink? No, I won't mind."

Mr. Bradbury stood up and walked to the kitchen, remembering to aim himself and to keep his shoulders thrown back. "Your semester must be about done," he said, his voice raised above the sound of ice cubes clattering out of the tray. "How much longer?"

"Two weeks."

"You taking that lifeguarding job again this summer?"

"That's part of what I came to talk to you about."

"Oh." In a moment he returned with what was identifiably a screwdriver. "Cheers," he said, raising it. "I knew there must be some reason." He settled down into the chair, reached over for the ashtray and lighter, and lit a cigarette. "How's your love life? How's the bad Penny?"

"Penny and I split."

"You and Penny split up? I wasn't informed." He took a sip of the drink, inhaled from the cigarette, then laughed. Smoke came out his mouth as he did. "I'm going to miss that girl, wandering around here in her flower-pattern pajamas, her little feet sinking into the carpet, and asking me in broken French my opinions of Proust. '*Monsieur Bradbury, aimez-vous Proust?*' '*Oh, oui, Penny. Proust, c'est un écrivain très diligent.*' " He waited, but his son didn't smile. "Was she an inattentive lover?"

"Jesus Christ, Dad." Eric picked at something beneath the hair on his right forearm. "You can't ask about that."

"Sure I can. You asked about my breathing. So what was the problem? Wasn't she assiduous enough for you?"

"Assiduous?" Eric thought for a moment. "Yeah, yeah. She was assiduous enough. She was good in bed. Is that what you want to know? She was fine. That's not why we split."

Eric's father was brushing the top of his head with the palm of his hand. "You know, Eric, I envy you. I suffer from *Glückschmerz:* the envy we feel upon hearing of the good fortune of others."

Eric nodded. "I know it, Pop." He jumped down from the railing a second time and sat next to his father, so that they would both be looking at the building across the street and the rest of the city's skyline, not at each other. "I have this other girl now. I think I love her."

Mr. Bradbury watched an airplane off in the distance and began to hum "In a Sentimental Mood."

"Did you hear me? I said I was in love."

"I heard you." He took another sip of his drink and then reached for the cigarette. "Sure, I heard you. I've been hearing about all the women you've fallen in love with since you were sixteen. No, fifteen. Almost six years now. That's the price I pay for an amorous son. What's her name this time?"

"Lorraine."

"Lorraine." He smiled. "Ah, sweet Lorraine. The Cross of Lorraine. Alsace-Lorraine. You two aren't married, are you?"

"No, we aren't married. Why?"

"To what," his father asked, "do I owe the honor of this visit?"

"Oh, come on, Pop." Mr. Bradbury felt his son's hand on his knee. The gesture made him feel ninety-two years old. "It's not that. I'm going to be asking you for money."

"Oh, and when will that be?"

"In about thirty minutes." His son waited. "It'd be impolite to ask before that."

"You do know how to close a deal. Wait until the old man is in his cups. So it's not bad news after all."

"No, Dad, it's not bad news. It's—"

He stopped when Elena called them to the table. It was not an ethnic casserole. She'd prepared ham with salad and asparagus in hollandaise sauce. Eric's father carried his drink and his cigarettes over to the table and placed them carefully next to his engraved silver napkin ring. "Putting on the ritz for you here today," he said. "Isn't Elena a swell woman?" he asked loudly, so that she'd hear. "You'll love this meal!" he almost shouted.

"Cut out the shit, Pop," Eric said, whispering. "I can't stand it."

"Okeydoke." He sat back and with one eye shut examined the wine bottle Elena had put on the table. "Château Smith, '69. An obscure California wine, heh heh. I think you'll like it." He swallowed part of his drink, put the glass aside, then picked up his fork and pushed a slice of ham around on the plate. "So. What's the money for? I thought you *had* some money. I hope to God you aren't one of these young goddamn entrepreneurs. I'd hate that." He took a bite. "I wouldn't join the bourgeois circus a minute before I had to."

"I'm not. This is for getting away."

"Getting away from what?" He chewed. "There's no getting away from anything."

"Yes, there is. I want to live up north in the woods near Ely for a year."

"You want to do *what?*" Eric's father put down his fork and stared at his son, an astonished smile breaking across his face. "I don't believe it. Is *that* what you came here to tell me? You want to go off into the woods and live like a rustic?" He threw back his head and laughed. "Oh my God," he said. "Rousseau lives." He sat chuckling, then turned to Eric again. "Let me guess. You want to discover yourself. You want to discover *who you are.* You and this Lorraine have been having deep sinister whispered talks far into the night, and she thinks you need to find your authentic blah blah blah blah blah. Am I right so far?"

Eric scowled at his father, holding himself silent. His big hands fidgeted with the silverware. Then he said, "Lorraine just suggested it. What I want is to get away from college and the city . . . and this." He swept his hand to indicate his father's dinner table, apartment, and the view outside the eleventh floor. "Lorraine's family has a cabin up north, and I want to live there this winter and work close by, if I can find a job. That's what I want for a year." He was staring intently at his fork.

"I see. You don't want to end up middle-aged and red-eyed."

Eric pretended not to hear. "Lorraine's staying down here in the city. Her family's letting me use their place. It's for myself."

Eric's father took his lower lip in his teeth as he smiled. Then he said, "I didn't think your generation indulged in such hefty idealism. I thought they were all designing computers and snorting the profits gram by gram. But this, a rustication, living in cabins and searching the soul, why, it's positively Russian. With that beard, you even look slightly Russian. Who've you been reading, Thoreausky?"

"I've read Thoreau," Eric said, looking out the window.

"I bet you have," his father said. "Look, kid, I'm very pleased. No kidding. Just make one promise. While you're up there, read some Chekhov. If you're going to be a Russian, that's the kind of Russian to be. Skip the other claptrap. You promise?"

"Sure. If you want me to."

"Yup," his father said. "I do." He paused. His arms and shoulders ached. Every time he ate, he felt a hard lump in his stomach. He furtively touched his neck, then glanced at Eric, shoveling in the food, and said, "If your mother were still alive, I'd be getting all riled up and telling you to get settled down and finish your studies and all that sort of thing. Mothers don't like it when their sons go off sulking into the woods. She'd've been worried. But you can handle yourself. And frankly I think it's a great idea." He leaned back. " 'Season of mists and mellow fruitfulness,' " he said. "Keats. I once used it in an ad for the Wisconsin State Board of Tourism. It's the wrong season, but the thought's right. Go north before you get tired."

"Tired?"

Mr. Bradbury wiped his mouth with his napkin and stared vaguely at the television set next to the sideboard. It, too, was tuned to CNN. He could no longer resist alcoholic gloom. "You'll get tired someday," he said. "Like a damaged mainspring. You'll get home at night and stand in front of the window as the sun sets. You'll always know what time it is without looking at your watch. You'll see odd mists you can't identify coming up from the pond in the park. There's a pattern in those mists, but you won't find it. Then the fraud police knock on your door. Those bastards won't leave a man alone."

"Pop, you drink too much."

Mr. Bradbury's face reddened. "If we weren't pals," he said, "I'd sock you in the nose. Listen, kid. When I'm sober I don't mortify people with the known facts of life. But you're family." He rose from the table and walked unsteadily across the thick carpeting of the living room. In five minutes he returned, carrying a check and waving it in the air as if to dry the ink. "A huge sum," he said. "The damaged fruits of a sedentary life. If you don't find work right away, you can read and bum around in the woods with the other unemployed animals on the dole. If you *do* find a job, which I doubt, since it's a depressed area, you can refund the unused portion. Someday you can pay this back. That's the convention between fathers and sons."

"I'll try to come down at Christmas."

"Wouldn't that be nice." Mr. Bradbury cut a spear of his asparagus into small pieces and worried the tip with his fork. The check was in the middle of the table, and Eric reached out and picked it up, folding it into his trouser pocket.

"Good," his father said. "You didn't lunge." He didn't look up. "You have a picture of this Lorraine?"

"No. Sorry. Are you seeing anybody yourself?"

His father shrugged. "There's a woman in Chicago I visit every month or so. Or she comes here. Someone I met through business. A small affair. Morgan, her name is. Her children are grown up, same age as you. She has a pretty laugh. The thought of that laugh has gotten me through many a desperate week. We're thinking of embarking on a short cruise together in the Caribbean this winter." He stopped. "But it's all quite pointless." He rubbed his forehead. "On the other hand, maybe it isn't. I'll be damned if I know what it is."

After lunch they made small talk, then went into the living room. Just before Eric left, his father said, "You snob, you never call. You always wait for me to do it. It's beggarly and humiliating. You never invite me over to your sordid lair. It irritates me." He was staring at the television screen, where a man was applying shaving cream to a bathroom mirror. "I don't like to be the one who calls all the damn time." He sneezed. "Still collecting parking tickets?"

"Still doing it. Dad, I gotta go. Lorraine's expecting me later this afternoon. I'll be in touch."

"Right." He started to extend his hand, thought better of it, and stood up. He held out his arms and embraced his son. He was four inches shorter than Eric, and when they drew together, his son's thick beard brushed against his face. "Be sure to call," he said. Eric nodded, turned around, and hurried toward the door. "Don't you dare hold me in contempt," he said inaudibly, under his breath.

With his hand on the doorknob, Eric shouted backward, "Thanks for the money, Dad. Thanks for everything."

Then he was gone.

Mr. Bradbury stood in the same position until he heard the elevator doors close. Then he backed into the living room and stood for a moment watching the television screen. He turned off the set. In his study, he bent down at the desk and subtracted two thousand dollars from the balance in his checking account. He glanced at the bookshelves above his desk, reached for a copy of Chekhov's stories and another volume, Keats's poems, put them on the desk, then walked down the hallway to the front closet. He put on a sweater and told Elena he was stepping out for a few minutes.

He crossed the street and headed for the park. In the center of this park was a pond, and on the far side of the water was a rowboat concession. He counted the rowboats in the pond: twelve. Feeling the onset of hangover, he strolled past some benches, reaching into his shirt pocket for a breadstick he had stashed there for the ducks. As he walked, he broke up the bread and threw it into the water, but the water was littered with bread and the ducks didn't notice him.

When he reached the rowboat concession, he paid a twenty-five-dollar deposit and left his driver's license as security, then let the skinny acned attendant fit him for an orange life jacket. He carried the two oars in either hand and eased himself into the blue rowboat he'd been assigned. He tried breathing the air for the scent but could smell nothing but his own soured breath. Taking the oars off the dock, panting, he fit them into the oarlocks. Then, with his back to the prow of the boat, he rowed, the joints squeaking, out to the middle of the lake.

Once there, he lifted the oars and brought them over the gunwales. He listened. The city traffic was reduced to vague honks and hums; the loudest sounds came from the other boaters and from their radios. Taking a cigarette out of his sweater pocket, he gazed at his building, counting the floors until he could see his bedroom window. There I am, he thought. A rowboat went by to his right, with a young man sitting in front, and his girlfriend pulling at the oars. He watched them until they were several boat lengths away, and then he cursed them quietly. He flicked his cigarette into the water.

As he gazed at the west side of the pond, he noticed that the apple blossoms floating on the water had collected into a kind of clump. The water lapped against the boat. He bent over and with his right index finger began absentmindedly to write his name on the pond's pale green surface. When he realized what he was doing, he started to laugh.

Eric called in September, November, and twice in December. In a remote and indistinct voice he said he wasn't having an easy time of it, living by himself. Two weeks before Christmas he announced that he had moved out of the cabin and was living in a rented room in Ely, where he worked as a stock boy at the supermarket. He thought he would give the experiment another month and then call it quits. He said—as if it were incidental—that he had met another woman.

"What about Lorraine?" his father asked.

"That's over."

"It's a good thing you fall out of love as fast as you fall in. Who's the new one?"

"You'll meet her."

"I hope so."

In February, after a heavy snowstorm, Eric called again to say that he'd be down the following Saturday and would bring Darlene with him. "Darlene?" his father asked. "I knew a Darlene once. She ran a bowling alley."

"You should talk," his son said. "Wilford."

"All right, all right. I see your point. So you'll be here on Saturday. Looking forward to it. How long'll you stay?"

"How should I know?" his son said.


George buzzed the apartment to let him know that his son and his son's new girlfriend had just come in. Mr. Bradbury was waiting at the door when he heard the elevator slide open, and he went on waiting there, under the foyer's chandelier, while in the hallway Eric and Darlene worked out a plan. The only remark he could catch was his son's "Don't let him tell you . . ." He couldn't hear the rest of it. What to do, or what to think, or something of the sort.

After they knocked, he waited thirty seconds, timing it by his Rolex. When his son knocked a second time, harder and faster, he said, "I'm coming, I'm coming."

He opened the door and saw them: a surprised young couple. His son had shaved his beard and cut his hair short; the effect was to make him seem exposed and small-townish. He looked past his father into the apartment with the roving gaze of a narcotics agent. "Hi, Dad," he said. The woman next to him looked at Eric, then at his father, waiting for them to shake hands or embrace; when they did neither, she said, "Hi, Mr. Bradbury," and thrust out her hand. "Darlene Spinney." The hand was rough and chapped. She glanced into the apartment. "Pleased to meet you."

"Likewise," Eric's father said, moving aside so that they could step into the foyer. "Come in and warm up." Eric slipped off his parka, draped it over a chair, groaned, and immediately walked down the hall-way to the bathroom. Mr. Bradbury helped Darlene with her coat, noting from the label that she had purchased it at Sears. The woman's figure was substantial, north-woods robust: capable of lifting canoes. "I wonder where that son of mine went to?"

"Eric?" She glanced down the hall. "He's in the bathroom. I'll tell you something, Mr. Bradbury: you make your son real nervous. He's as jumpy as a cat. What I think it is, he's got diarrhea, bringing me here and seeing you. That's two strikes. One more strike and the boy'll be out cold."

He looked at her with some interest. "Come into the living room, Miss Spinney," he said. "Care for a drink?"

"I don't know. Maybe a beer?"

"Sure." He leaned toward her. "I suppose my son has warned you about my drinking."

"What he said was you sometimes have hard stuff before lunch."

"That is correct." He went to the refrigerator, took out a Heineken, and poured it into a glass. "That is what I do. But only on weekends. You can think of it as my hobby. Did he tell you anything else?"

"Oh, I asked, all right. Nothing much but mumbles."

"What'd you ask?"

"Well, for instance, did you get mean."

"When I drank."

"Right."

"Why'd you want to know?" He came out of the kitchen and handed the glass to her. They both walked toward the front window.

"Do you know mean drinkers, Mr. Bradbury? I don't guess so. *I* know a few. In my family, this is. It's not nice conversation and I won't go through all the details, about being hit and everything. This," she said, looking out the window, "is different. I sort of figured you were a man who doesn't have to hit things."

"I never learned," he said, giving the words a resentful torque. "I hired people. Now where did you and Eric meet? I can't imagine."

"At the supermarket. He was working in produce, and I was up there at the checkout. I'd never seen him in town before he started working in the back. Well, I mean"—she looked for a place to set down her beer, hesitated, and held on to it—"I thought, oh, what a nice face. Two glances and you don't have to think about it. So we ate our lunches together. Traded cookies and carrots. He's nice. He gave me a parking ticket. He said it was an old joke? Anyway, we talked. He wasn't like the local boys."

"No?"

"No. He can sit by himself. When he works, he listens to the boss, Mr. Glusac, giving him orders, and he has this so-what look on his face. He's sweet. Like he's always making plans. He's a dreamer. Can't fix a car."

"I don't think he ever learned."

"That's the truth. Doesn't know what gaskets are, says he never learned to use a socket wrench. That car of his was hard-starting and dieseling, and I told him to tune it, you know, with a timing light, and he tells me he's never removed a spark plug in his life. 'We didn't do that,' he says. Jesus, it's a long way down." She was gazing at the frozen pond in the park.

"Eleven floors," Mr. Bradbury said. "You can't hear the harlot's cry from street to street up here, more's the pity. I look down on it all from a great height. I have an eleventh-floor view of things."

She said, "I can see a man walking a dog. Eric says you write commercials." She sat down on the sofa and glanced at the muted newscaster on the television set. He noticed that her fingernails were painted bright red, and that the back of one hand was scarred. "Is it hard, writing commercials?"

"Not if your whole life prepares you to do it. And of course there are the anodynes. If it weren't for them, my heart wouldn't be in it."

"Anodynes."

"I'm sorry. Painkillers. Things that come in bottles and tubes."

"I only had a year of community college before I had to go to work," Darlene said, and just as Mr. Bradbury understood what her remark was supposed to explain, she said, "I'm always afraid I'm boring people. Eric says I don't bore him. Do you know your TV set is on?"

"Yes."

"Why's it on if you aren't listening to it?"

"I like to have someone in the room with me, in case I get a call from the fraud police. Ah, hey, here's the kid."

Eric had reappeared silently. His father turned to look at him; he might have been standing in the hallway, out of sight, listening to them both for the last five minutes. Eric sat down next to Darlene on the sofa, putting his arm around her shoulders. She snuggled close to him, and Mr. Bradbury resisted the impulse to close his eyes. He sat down in his Barcelona chair. "So," he began, with effort, "here you are. Give me a report. How was nature?"

"Nature was fine." With his free hand Eric brutally rubbed his nose. The nose was running, and he wiped his hand on the sofa.

"Fine? Did the flora and fauna suit you? I want a report. Did you discover yourself? Let's hear something about the pastoral panorama." Darlene, he noticed, was staring at his mouth.

"It was fine," Eric said, staring, without subtlety, at the ceiling.

"I hate it when you look at the ceiling. A world without objects is a sensible emptiness. Come on, Eric, let's have a few details. Did you from outward forms win the passion and the life, whose fountains are within?"

"My dad is a quoter," Eric said. He glanced at Darlene. "He quotes." He saw his father looking at him. "It was fine," he repeated, facing his father.

"He won't talk about that time alone in that cabin, Mr. Bradbury, so you might as well not ask. Lord knows I've tried."

"Just between him and his psyche, eh?"

" 'Psyche,' " Eric said, shaking his head. "Jesus Christ."

"There you go, criticizing my vocabulary again. When *will* I be allowed to use the six-dollar words they taught us at college? Never, it appears." He smiled at Darlene. "Pay no attention to me. I inflict my irony on everybody."

A long pause followed. Eric's father had begun counting the seconds in groups of two when Darlene said, "You wouldn't believe all the city people who come up north to commune with nature. Like that woman Lorraine, *her* family. We see them all summer. They buy designer backpacks and dehydrated foods they don't eat. Then they sleep on the ground for two weeks, complain of colds, and whiz home in their station wagons. Me, I'm lucky if I can sleep in a bed."

"Darlene has insomnia," Eric explained.

"Right. I do. That's why I don't understand people sleeping on the ground. Who wants that when you can shower in a bathroom and sleep in a bed and look out from the eleventh floor? Not me."

"Insomnia," Mr. Bradbury said. "How interesting. Ever tried pills?"

"You have insomnia?" she asked. "Try bananas. Or turkey. They have an enzyme, tryptophan, and that's what you need. Unless you're hardcore, like me. I have to run, eat bananas, skip coffee, but it usually doesn't make any difference."

"We jog together," Eric said.

They were cuddling there, Darlene and Eric, Mr. Bradbury decided, to test his powers of detachment. Before this was over he would be a Zen saint. He thought longingly of the vodka bottle in the kitchen cupboard, whose cap he had not, *not,* removed once today: his hands were folded in his lap, as he watched Darlene place her hand on Eric's leg. The truth, he thought, raising one hand to scratch his ear, is an insufferable test of a man's resources. Tilting his head imperceptibly, he glanced for relief at the Lichtenstein above the sofa. "Bananas?" he said.

"Eric says you wrote those Colonel Crisp commercials." Her voice was egging him on into the kitchen: glass, ice cubes, and the tender care of the liquor.

"Yes." He would not stand it. He *could* not stand it, and began to get up.

Darlene twisted around, so that Eric's hand fell off her shoulders onto the sofa, to look at the wall behind her. "What's that?" she asked.

"That? Oh, that's a Lichtenstein." He sat down again.

"Is it valuable?"

"Yes. I suppose so. Yes."

She was looking at it closely, probably, Mr. Bradbury thought, counting the dots in the woman's face. "Do you write radio commercials, too?"

"Oh, yes. I once wrote a spot for a lightbulb company with a Janáček fanfare in the background. *That* made them sit up."

"Jesus!" Eric stood suddenly. "I can't *stand* this!" He went down the hallway, and they both heard a door slam. Just then Elena came into the living room to announce that lunch was ready.

"It's a hard life up here on the eleventh floor," Mr. Bradbury mused. "Maybe he went to get a banana." He waited. "Or some white meat."

"I'll get him," Darlene said, rising. "His moods've never bothered me. Did you know," she began, then stopped. She apparently decided to plunge ahead, because she said, "He talks a lot about his mother."

"Not to me. She died of cancer, you know."

"Yeah. He said so. He remembers all of it. He *likes* you, Mr. Bradbury. Don't get him wrong. He's crazy about you. I shouldn't say this."

"Oh, please say it. Crazy about me?"

"Oh sure. Didn't you know?" She looked surprised.

Mortified and pleased, he watched her disappear down the hall.


After lunch, whose terrain was crossed by Mr. Bradbury's painfully constructed comic anecdotes about daily work in an advertising agency, he suggested that they all go out for a walk in the park. Eric and Darlene agreed with an odd fervor. After bundling themselves up, they took the elevator down, Darlene checking her face, making moues, in the elevator's polished mirror.

Outside the temperature was ten degrees above zero, with no wind, and a sunny sky. When they reached the park, Darlene ran out ahead of them onto the pond, where the park authorities had cleared a rink for skating. A loudspeaker was playing Waldteufel.

"Don't lecture me," Eric said. "Don't tell me what I should or shouldn't be doing."

"Who, me?" Darlene was now out of earshot. "That's for suckers. Can you tell me yet how long you're staying?"

"Why do you keep asking? A few days. Then we're going north again. I'm going to be up there for the rest of the winter and then re-enroll next fall and graduate in the spring."

"I don't suppose she's going with you."

"I don't know." He waited. "She's interested in our money. *The* money."

"A good woman's failing. I kind of like her," Mr. Bradbury said. "Diamond in the rough and all that. At first I thought she was queen of the roller derby. Didn't know if she was playing with a full deck."

"I almost proposed to her," Eric said. "Almost."

"Oh Christ." His father stomped his right foot in the snow. "You, with all your, well, call it potential, and you want to marry a girl who counts out change?"

She was far ahead of them on the ice, pulling two children on skates around in a circle. The children yelled with pleasure.

"She's . . . different, Pop. With her, everything's simpler. They don't have women like her around here, I don't think. You don't get what I mean at all."

"Oh, I get it. You went up north looking for nature, and you found it, and you brought it back, and there it, I mean she, is. Overbite, straight hair, chapped hands, whopping tits, and all."

"You wouldn't believe," Eric said, watching her, "how comforting she is."

"What?" He stopped and waited. "Well, I might."

"When I wake up, she's always awake. She has a way of touching that makes me feel wonderful. Generous." Now they were both watching her. "It's like love comes easily to her."

"God, you're romantic," his father said. "It must be your age."

"Want to hear about how wonderful she is? In bed?"

"No. No, I don't think so."

"You *used* to want to hear."

"I shouldn't've asked. That was a mistake. *Glückschmerz.* Besides, couples don't live in bed. You can't insult a waiter or cash a check in bed. As a paradigm for life, it's inadequate."

Eric was showing an unsteady smile. "I want to throw myself at her feet," he said. "We're the king and queen of lovers. Love. God, I just lap it up. We can go and go. I don't want life. I want love. And so does she."

"Have we always talked this way?" his father asked. "It's deplorable."

"We started getting a little raw about two years ago. That was when you began asking me about my girlfriends. Some pretty raw questions, things you shouldn't have been asking. I mean, we all know *why,* right?"

"Just looking out for my boy." In the cold, he could feel his eyelid twitching.

"You could mind your own business, Pop. You could try that." He said this with equanimity. Darlene was running back toward them. She ran awkwardly, with her upper torso leaning forward and her arms flailing. Three children were following her. As she panted, her breath was visible in the cold air.

"Sometimes I think I lead a strange life," Eric's father said. "Sometimes I think that none of this is real."

"Yeah, Chekhov," Eric said. "I read him, just like you told me to." Darlene ran straight up to Eric and put her blue mittens, which had bullet-sized balls of snow stuck to them, up to both sides of his face. She exposed all her teeth when she smiled. She took Eric's left hand. Then she reached down with her other hand and grasped Mr. Bradbury's doeskin glove. Standing between them, she said, "I love winter. I love the cold."

"Yes," Mr. Bradbury said. "The bitterness invigorates."

Not letting go of either of their hands, she walked between them back to the apartment building.

They sat around for the rest of the afternoon; Darlene tried to take a nap, and Eric and his father watched a basketball game, DePaul against Marquette. When the game was half over, Eric turned to his father and asked, "Where are your cigarettes, Pop?"

"My little friends? I evicted them."

"How come?"

"I quit in December. I woke up in the middle of the night and thought I was fixing to die. The outlines of my heart were all but visible under the skin, it hurt so much. I felt like a corpse ready for the anatomy lesson. So: I stopped. Imagine this. I threw my gold Dunhill lighter, the one your mother gave me, down the building's trash shaft, along with all the cigarettes in the house. I heard the lighter whine and clatter all the way to the heap at the bottom. What a scarifying loss was there. And how I miss the nicotine. But I wasn't about to go. I may look like Samuel Gompers, but I'm only fifty-two. I figured there must be more to life than patient despair, right?"

Sitting on the floor, leaning against the sofa on which his father was sitting, Eric held his hand up in the air behind him. "Congratulations," he said. The two of them shook hands. "That took real guts."

"Thank you." He checked his fingers, still yellow from nicotine stains. "Yes, it did. I agree." He thumped his chest. "Guts."

At dinner Darlene was gulping her wine. "I don't get to drink this much at home. And furthermore, I shouldn't. Wine keeps you awake. Did you know that? What is this, French?" She peered at the label. "Romanian. Well. That was my next guess."

"A nice table wine," Mr. Bradbury said. "And when it turns, you can use it as salad dressing."

She looked at Eric. Eric shook his head, shrugged, and continued eating.

"He never says much at dinner," Darlene said, pointing at Eric. Mr. Bradbury nodded. After a pause, she said, "I don't think I ever told you about the time I met Bill Cosby."

At one o'clock Mr. Bradbury found himself lying awake, staring at the curtains. His back itched, and as he rubbed his neck he thought he felt a swelling. The damnable Romanian wine had given him a headache. Sitting up, he lowered his feet to the floor and put on his slippers. Then, shuffling across the bedroom, he opened the door that led out to the hallway.

He was halfway to the kitchen when he stopped outside Eric's bedroom door. He heard whispering. He stood and listened. It wasn't whispering so much as a drone from his son. " 'The only completely stationary object in the room,' " he was saying, " 'was an enormous couch on which two young women were buoyed up as though upon an anchored balloon.' " As Eric went on—Daisy and Tom and Jordan Baker undramatically droned into existence—his voice, indifferent to the story, spread out its soporific waves of narration. His father turned around and padded back into his own bedroom.

Three hours later, still feeling sleepless, Mr. Bradbury rose again out of bed and again advanced down the hall. All the lights were blazing. Halfway to the kitchen, he looked toward the refrigerator and saw the two of them huddled together side by side at the dining-room table, Darlene in her bathrobe, Eric in a nightshirt. Randomly he noticed the width of his son's shoulders, the fullness of Darlene's breasts. Her head was in her hands. Unobserved, Mr. Bradbury watched his son butter the bread, apply the mayonnaise, add the sandwich meat and the lettuce, close the sandwich, cut it in half, remove the crusts, and then hand it on its plate to her. "Thank you," she said. She began to eat. She chewed with her mouth open. She said, "You're so sweet. I love you." She kissed the air in his direction. Mr. Bradbury moved back, stood still, then turned toward his bedroom.

He closed the door and clicked on the bedside lamp. From far down on the other side of the hallway, he heard Darlene's loud laugh. He started to slip in under the covers, thought better of it, and went to his window to part the curtains. Getting back into bed, he switched off the bulb; then, with his head on the pillow, he gazed at the city skyline, half consciously counting the few apartments in the high-rise across the street that still had all their lights burning.

# Gryphon

ON WEDNESDAY AFTERNOON, between the geography lesson on ancient Egypt's hand-operated irrigation system and an art project that
involved drawing a model city next to a mountain, our fourth-grade
teacher, Mr. Hibler, developed a cough. This cough began with a series of
muffled throat-clearings and progressed to propulsive noises contained
within Mr. Hibler's closed mouth. "Listen to him," Carol Peterson whispered to me. "He's gonna blow up." Mr. Hibler's laughter—dazed and
infrequent—sounded a bit like his cough, but as we worked on our
model cities we would look up, thinking he was enjoying a joke, and see
his face turning red, his cheeks puffed out. This was not laughter. Twice
he bent over, and his loose tie, like a plumb line, hung down straight
from his neck as he exploded himself into a Kleenex. He would excuse
himself, then go on coughing. "I'll bet you a dime," Carol Peterson whispered, "we get a substitute tomorrow."

Carol sat at the desk in front of mine and was a bad person—when
she thought no one was looking she would blow her nose on notebook
paper, then crumple it up and throw it into the wastebasket—but at
times of crisis she spoke the truth. I knew I'd lose the dime.

"No deal," I said.

When Mr. Hibler stood us in formation at the door just prior to the
final bell, he was almost incapable of speech. "I'm sorry, boys and girls,"
he said. "I seem to be coming down with something."

"I hope you feel better tomorrow, Mr. Hibler," Bobby Kryzanowicz,
the faultless brownnoser, said, and I heard Carol Peterson's evil giggle.
Then Mr. Hibler opened the door and we walked out to the buses, a
clique of us starting noisily to hawk and raugh as soon as we thought we
were a few feet beyond Mr. Hibler's earshot.

Since Five Oaks was a rural community, and in Michigan, the supply of substitute teachers was limited to the town's unemployed community college graduates, a pool of about four mothers. These ladies fluttered, provided easeful class days, and nervously covered material we had mastered weeks earlier. Therefore it was a surprise when a woman we had never seen came into the class the next day, carrying a purple purse, a checkerboard lunchbox, and a few books. She put the books on one side of Mr. Hibler's desk and the lunchbox on the other, next to the Voice of Music phonograph. Three of us in the back of the room were playing with Heever, the chameleon that lived in a terrarium and on one of the plastic drapes, when she walked in.

She clapped her hands at us. "Little boys," she said, "why are you bent over together like that?" She didn't wait for us to answer. "Are you tormenting an animal? Put it back. Please sit down at your desks. I want no cabals this time of the day." We just stared at her. "Boys," she repeated, "I asked you to sit down."

I put the chameleon in his terrarium and felt my way to my desk, never taking my eyes off the woman. With white and green chalk, she had started to draw a tree on the left side of the blackboard. She didn't look usual. Furthermore, her tree was outsized, disproportionate, for some reason.

"This room needs a tree," she said, with one line drawing the suggestion of a leaf. "A large, leafy, shady, deciduous . . . oak."

Her fine, light hair had been done up in what I would learn years later was called a chignon, and she wore gold-rimmed glasses whose lenses seemed to have the faintest blue tint. Harold Knardahl, who sat across from me, whispered, "Mars," and I nodded slowly, savoring the imminent weirdness of the day. The substitute drew another branch with an extravagant arm gesture, then turned around and said, "Good morning. I don't believe I said good morning to all of you yet."

Facing us, she was no special age—an adult is an adult—but her face had two prominent lines, descending vertically from the sides of her mouth to her chin. I knew where I had seen those lines before: *Pinocchio*. They were marionette lines. "You may stare at me," she said to us, as a few more kids from the last bus came into the room, their eyes fixed on her, "for a few more seconds, until the bell rings. Then I will permit no more staring. Looking I will permit. Staring, no. It is impolite to stare, and a sign of bad breeding. You cannot make a social effort while staring."

Harold Knardahl did not glance at me, or nudge, but I heard him whisper "Mars" again, trying to get more mileage out of his single joke with the kids who had just come in.

When everyone was seated, the substitute teacher finished her tree, put down her chalk fastidiously on the phonograph, brushed her hands, and faced us. "Good morning," she said. "I am Miss Ferenczi, your teacher for the day. I am fairly new to your community, and I don't believe any of you know me. I will therefore start by telling you a story about myself."

While we settled back, she launched into her tale. She said her grandfather had been a Hungarian prince; her mother had been born in some place called Flanders, had been a pianist, and had played concerts for people Miss Ferenczi referred to as "crowned heads." She gave us a knowing look. "Grieg," she said, "the Norwegian master, wrote a concerto for piano that was . . ."—she paused—"my mother's triumph at her debut concert in London." Her eyes searched the ceiling. Our eyes followed. Nothing up there but ceiling tile. "For reasons that I shall not go into, my family's fortunes took us to Detroit, then north to dreadful Saginaw, and now here I am in Five Oaks, as your substitute teacher, for today, Thursday, October the eleventh. I believe it will be a good day: all the forecasts coincide. We shall start with your reading lesson. Take out your reading book. I believe it is called *Broad Horizons,* or something along those lines."

Jeannie Vermeesch raised her hand. Miss Ferenczi nodded at her. "Mr. Hibler always starts the day with the Pledge of Allegiance," Jeannie whined.

"Oh, does he? In that case," Miss Ferenczi said, "you must know it *very* well by now, and we certainly need not spend our time on it. No, no allegiance pledging on the premises today, by my reckoning. Not with so much sunlight coming into the room. A pledge does not suit my mood." She glanced at her watch. "Time *is* flying. Take out *Broad Horizons.*"

She disappointed us by giving us an ordinary lesson, complete with vocabulary and drills, comprehension questions, and recitation. She didn't seem to care for the material, however. She sighed every few minutes and rubbed her glasses with a frilly handkerchief that she withdrew, magician-style, from her left sleeve.

After reading we moved on to arithmetic. It was my favorite time of the morning, when the lazy autumn sunlight dazzled its way through ribbons of clouds past the windows on the east side of the classroom and crept across the linoleum floor. On the playground the first group of children, the kindergartners, were running on the quack grass just beyond the monkey bars. We were doing multiplication tables. Miss Ferenczi had made John Wazny stand up at his desk in the front row. He was supposed to go through the tables of six. From where I was sitting, I could smell the hair tonic soaked into John's plastered hair. He was doing fine until he came to six times eleven and six times twelve. "Six times eleven," he said, "is sixty-eight. Six times twelve is . . ." He put his fingers to his head, quickly and secretly sniffed his fingertips, and said, ". . . seventy-two." Then he sat down.

"Fine," Miss Ferenczi said. "Well, now. That was very good."

"Miss Ferenczi!" One of the Eddy twins was waving her hand desperately in the air. "Miss Ferenczi! Miss Ferenczi!"

"Yes?"

"John said that six times eleven is sixty-eight and you said he was right!"

"*Did* I?" She gazed at the class with a jolly look breaking across her marionette's face. "Did I say that? Well, what *is* six times eleven?"

"It's sixty-six!"

She nodded. "Yes. So it is. But, and I know some people will not entirely agree with me, at some times it is sixty-eight."

"When? When is it sixty-eight?"

We were all waiting.

"In higher mathematics, which you children do not yet understand, six times eleven can be considered to be sixty-eight." She laughed through her nose. "In higher mathematics numbers are . . . more fluid. The only thing a number does is contain a certain amount of something. Think of water. A cup is not the only way to measure a certain amount of water, is it?" We were staring, shaking our heads. "You could use saucepans or thimbles. In either case, the water *would be the same.* Perhaps," she started again, "it would be better for you to think that six times eleven is sixty-eight only when I am in the room."

"Why is it sixty-eight," Mark Poole asked, "when you're in the room?"

"Because it's more interesting that way," she said, smiling very rapidly behind her blue-tinted glasses. "Besides, I'm your substitute teacher, am

I not?" We all nodded. "Well, then, think of six times eleven equals sixty-eight as a substitute fact."

"A substitute fact?"

"Yes." Then she looked at us carefully. "Do you think," she asked, "that anyone is going to be hurt by a substitute fact?"

We looked back at her.

"Will the plants on the windowsill be hurt?" We glanced at them. There were sensitive plants thriving in a green plastic tray, and several wilted ferns in small clay pots. "Your dogs and cats, or your moms and dads?" She waited. "So," she concluded, "what's the problem?"

"But it's wrong," Janice Weber said, "isn't it?"

"What's your name, young lady?"

"Janice Weber."

"And you think it's wrong, Janice?"

"I was just asking."

"Well, all right. You were just asking. I think we've spent enough time on this matter by now, don't you, class? You are free to think what you like. When your teacher, Mr. Hibler, returns, six times eleven will be sixty-six again, you can rest assured. And it will be that for the rest of your lives in Five Oaks. Too bad, eh?" She raised her eyebrows and glinted herself at us. "But for now, it wasn't. So much for that. Let us go on to your assigned problems for today, as painstakingly outlined, I see, in Mr. Hibler's lesson plan. Take out a sheet of paper and write your names on the upper left-hand corner."

For the next half hour we did the rest of our arithmetic problems. We handed them in and then went on to spelling, my worst subject. Spelling always came before lunch. We were taking spelling dictation and looking at the clock. "Thorough," Miss Ferenczi said. "Boundary." She walked in the aisles between the desks, holding the spelling book open and looking down at our papers. "Balcony." I clutched my pencil. Somehow, the way she said those words, they seemed foreign, mis-voweled and mis-consonanted. I stared down at what I had spelled. *Balconie.* I turned the pencil upside down and erased my mistake. *Balconey.* That looked better, but still incorrect. I cursed the world of spelling and tried erasing it again and saw the paper beginning to wear away. *Balkony.* Suddenly I felt a hand on my shoulder.

"I don't like that word, either," Miss Ferenczi whispered, bent over, her mouth near my ear. "It's ugly. My feeling is, if you don't like a word, you don't have to use it." She straightened up, leaving behind a slight odor of Clorets.

At lunchtime we went out to get our trays of sloppy joes, peaches in heavy syrup, coconut cookies, and milk, and brought them back to the classroom, where Miss Ferenczi was sitting at the desk, eating a brown sticky thing she had unwrapped from tightly rubber-banded waxed paper. "Miss Ferenczi," I said, raising my hand, "you don't have to eat with us. You can eat with the other teachers. There's a teachers' lounge," I ended up, "next to the principal's office."

"No, thank you," she said. "I prefer it here."

"We've got a room monitor," I said. "Mrs. Eddy." I pointed to where Mrs. Eddy, Joyce and Judy's mother, sat silently at the back of the room, doing her knitting.

"That's fine," Miss Ferenczi said. "But I shall continue to eat here, with you children. I prefer it," she repeated.

"How come?" Wayne Razmer asked without raising his hand.

"I talked to the other teachers before class this morning," Miss Ferenczi said, biting into her brown food. "There was a great rattling of the words for the fewness of the ideas. I didn't care for their brand of hilarity. I don't like ditto-machine jokes."

"Oh," Wayne said.

"What's that you're eating?" Maxine Sylvester asked, twitching her nose. "Is it food?"

"It most certainly *is* food. It's a stuffed fig. I had to drive almost down to Detroit to get it. I also brought some smoked sturgeon. And this," she said, lifting some green leaves out of her lunchbox, "is raw spinach, cleaned this morning."

"Why're you eating raw spinach?" Maxine asked.

"It's good for you," Miss Ferenczi said. "More stimulating than soda pop or smelling salts." I bit into my sloppy joe and stared blankly out the window. An almost invisible moon was faintly silvered in the daytime autumn sky. "As far as food is concerned," Miss Ferenczi was saying, "you have to shuffle the pack. Mix it up. Too many people eat . . . well, never mind."

"Miss Ferenczi," Carol Peterson said, "what are we going to do this afternoon?"

"Well," she said, looking down at Mr. Hibler's lesson plan, "I see that your teacher, Mr. Hibler, has you scheduled for a unit on the Egyptians."

Carol groaned. "Yessss," Miss Ferenczi continued, "that is what we will do: the Egyptians. A remarkable people. Almost as remarkable as the Americans. But not quite." She lowered her head, did her quick smile, and went back to eating her spinach.

After noon recess we came back into the classroom and saw that Miss Ferenczi had drawn a pyramid on the blackboard close to her oak tree. Some of us who had been playing baseball were messing around in the back of the room, dropping the bats and gloves into the playground box, and Ray Schontzeler had just slugged me when I heard Miss Ferenczi's high-pitched voice, quavering with emotion. "Boys," she said, "come to order right this minute and take your seats. I do not wish to waste a minute of class time. Take out your geography books." We trudged to our desks and, still sweating, pulled out *Distant Lands and Their People.* "Turn to page forty-two." She waited for thirty seconds, then looked over at Kelly Munger. "Young man," she said, "why are you still fossicking in your desk?"

Kelly looked as if his foot had been stepped on. "Why am I what?"

"Why are you . . . burrowing in your desk like that?"

"I'm lookin' for the book, Miss Ferenczi."

Bobby Kryzanowicz, the faultless brownnoser who sat in the first row by choice, softly said, "His name is Kelly Munger. He can't ever find his stuff. He always does that."

"I don't care what his name is, especially after lunch," Miss Ferenczi said. "*Where is your book?*"

"I just found it." Kelly was peering into his desk and with both hands pulled at the book, shoveling along in front of it several pencils and crayons, which fell into his lap and then to the floor.

"I hate a mess," Miss Ferenczi said. "I hate a mess in a desk or a mind. It's . . . unsanitary. You wouldn't want your house at home to look like your desk at school, now, would you?" She didn't wait for an answer. "I should think not. A house at home should be as neat as human hands can make it. What were we talking about? Egypt. Page forty-two. I note from Mr. Hibler's lesson plan that you have been discussing the modes of Egyptian irrigation. Interesting, in my view, but not so interesting as what we are about to cover. The pyramids, and Egyptian slave labor. A plus on one side, a minus on the other." We had our books open to page forty-two, where there was a picture of a pyramid, but Miss Ferenczi wasn't looking at the book. Instead, she was staring at some object just outside the window.

"Pyramids," Miss Ferenczi said, still looking past the window. "I want you to think about pyramids. And what was inside. The bodies of the pharaohs, of course, and their attendant treasures. Scrolls. Perhaps," Miss Ferenczi said, her face gleeful but unsmiling, "these scrolls were novels for the pharaohs, helping them to pass the time in their long voyage through the centuries. But then, I am joking." I was looking at the lines on Miss Ferenczi's skin. "Pyramids," Miss Ferenczi went on, "were the repositories of special cosmic powers. The nature of a pyramid is to guide cosmic energy forces into a concentrated point. The Egyptians knew that; we have generally forgotten it. Did you know," she asked, walking to the side of the room so that she was standing by the coat closet, "that George Washington had Egyptian blood, from his grandmother? Certain features of the Constitution of the United States are notable for their Egyptian ideas."

Without glancing down at the book, she began to talk about the movement of souls in Egyptian religion. She said that when people die, their souls return to Earth in the form of carpenter ants or walnut trees, depending on how they behaved—"well or ill"—in life. She said that the Egyptians believed that people act the way they do because of magnetism produced by tidal forces in the solar system, forces produced by the sun and by its "planetary ally," Jupiter. Jupiter, she said, was a planet, as we had been told, but had "certain properties of stars." She was speaking very fast. She said that the Egyptians were great explorers and conquerors. She said that the greatest of all the conquerors, Genghis Khan, had had forty horses and forty young women killed on the site of his grave. We listened. No one tried to stop her. "I myself have been in Egypt," she said, "and have witnessed much dust and many brutalities." She said that an old man in Egypt who worked for a circus had personally shown her an animal in a cage, a monster, half bird and half lion. She said that this monster was called a gryphon and that she had heard about them but never seen them until she traveled to the outskirts of Cairo. She wrote the word out on the blackboard in large capital letters: "GRYPHON." She said that Egyptian astronomers had discovered the planet Saturn but had not seen its rings. She said that the

Egyptians were the first to discover that dogs, when they are ill, will not drink from rivers, but wait for rain, and hold their jaws open to catch it.

"She lies."

We were on the school bus home. I was sitting next to Carl Whiteside, who had bad breath and a huge collection of marbles. We were arguing. Carl thought she was lying. I said she wasn't, probably.

"I didn't believe that stuff about the bird," Carl said, "and what she told us about the pyramids? I didn't believe that, either. She didn't know what she was talking about."

"Oh yeah?" I had liked her. She was strange. I thought I could nail him. "If she was lying," I said, "what'd she say that was a lie?"

"Six times eleven isn't sixty-eight. It isn't ever. It's sixty-six. I know for a fact."

"She said so. She admitted it. What else did she lie about?"

"I don't know," he said. "Stuff."

"What stuff?"

"Well." He swung his legs back and forth. "You ever see an animal that was half lion and half bird?" He crossed his arms. "It sounded real fakey to me."

"It could happen," I said. I had to improvise, to outrage him. "I read in this newspaper my mom bought in the supermarket about this scientist, this mad scientist in the Swiss Alps, and he's been putting genes and chromosomes and stuff together in test tubes, and he combined a human being and a hamster." I waited, for effect. "It's called a humster."

"You never." Carl was staring at me, his mouth open, his terrible bad breath making its way toward me. "What newspaper was it?"

"The *National Enquirer*," I said, "that they sell next to the cash registers." When I saw his look of recognition, I knew I had him. "And this mad scientist," I said, "his name was, um, Dr. Frankenbush." I realized belatedly that this name was a mistake and waited for Carl to notice its resemblance to the name of the other famous mad master of permutations, but he only sat there.

"A man and a hamster?" He was staring at me, squinting, his mouth opening in distaste. "Jeez. What'd it look like?"

When the bus reached my stop, I took off down our dirt road and ran up through the backyard, kicking the tire swing for good luck. I dropped my books on the back steps so I could hug and kiss our dog, Mr. Selby. Then I hurried inside. I could smell brussels sprouts cooking, my unfavorite vegetable. My mother was washing other vegetables in the kitchen sink, and my baby brother was hollering in his yellow playpen on the kitchen floor.

"Hi, Mom," I said, hopping around the playpen to kiss her. "Guess what?"

"I have no idea."

"We had this substitute today, Miss Ferenczi, and I'd never seen her before, and she had all these stories and ideas and stuff."

"Well. That's good." My mother looked out the window in front of the sink, her eyes on the pine woods west of our house. That time of the afternoon her skin always looked so white to me. Strangers always said my mother looked like Betty Crocker, framed by the giant spoon on the side of the Bisquick box. "Listen, Tommy," she said. "Would you please go upstairs and pick your clothes off the floor in the bathroom, and then go outside to the shed and put the shovel and ax away that your father left outside this morning?"

"She said that six times eleven was sometimes sixty-eight!" I said. "And she said she once saw a monster that was half lion and half bird." I waited. "In Egypt."

"Did you hear me?" my mother asked, raising her arm to wipe her forehead with the back of her hand. "You have chores to do."

"I know," I said. "I was just telling you about the substitute."

"It's very interesting," my mother said, quickly glancing down at me, "and we can talk about it later when your father gets home. But right now you have some work to do."

"Okay, Mom." I took a cookie out of the jar on the counter and was about to go outside when I had a thought. I ran into the living room, pulled out a dictionary next to the TV stand, and opened it to the G's. After five minutes I found it. *Gryphon:* variant of "griffin." *Griffin:* "a fabulous beast with the head and wings of an eagle and the body of a lion." Fabulous was right. I shouted with triumph and ran outside to put my father's tools in their proper places.

Miss Ferenczi was back the next day, slightly altered. She had pulled her hair down and twisted it into pigtails, with red rubber bands holding them tight one inch from the ends. She was wearing a green blouse and a pink scarf, making her difficult to look at for a full class day. This time there was no pretense of doing a reading lesson or moving on to arithmetic. As soon as the bell rang, she simply began to talk.

She talked for forty minutes straight. There seemed to be less connection between her ideas, but the ideas themselves were, as the dictionary would say, fabulous. She said she had heard of a huge jewel, in what she called the antipodes, that was so brilliant that when light shone into it at a certain angle it would blind whoever was looking at its center. She said the biggest diamond in the world was cursed and had killed everyone who owned it, and that by a trick of fate it was called the Hope Diamond. Diamonds are magic, she said, and this is why women wear them on their fingers, as a sign of the magic of womanhood. Men have strength, Miss Ferenczi said, but no true magic. That is why men fall in love with women but women do not fall in love with men: they just love being loved. George Washington had died because of a mistake he made about a diamond. Washington was not the first *true* president, but she didn't say who was. In some places in the world, she said, men and women still live in the trees and eat monkeys for breakfast. Their doctors are magicians. At the bottom of the sea are creatures thin as pancakes that have never been studied by scientists because when you take them up to air, the fish explode.

There was not a sound in the classroom, except for Miss Ferenczi's voice, and Donna DeShano's coughing. No one even went to the bathroom.

Beethoven, she said, had not been deaf; it was a trick to make himself famous, and it worked. As she talked, Miss Ferenczi's pigtails swung back and forth. There are trees in the world, she said, that eat meat: their leaves are sticky and close up on bugs like hands. She lifted her hands and brought them together, palm to palm. Venus, which most people think is the next closest planet to the sun, is not always closer, and, besides, it is the planet of greatest mystery because of its thick cloud cover. "I know what lies underneath those clouds," Miss Ferenczi said, and waited. After the silence, she said, "Angels. Angels live under those clouds." She said that angels were not invisible to everyone and were in fact smarter than most people. They did not dress in robes as was often claimed but instead wore formal evening clothes, as if they were about to attend a concert. Often angels *do* attend concerts and sit in the aisles, where, she said, most people pay no attention to them. She said the most terrible angel had the shape of the Sphinx. "There is no running away from that one," she said. She said that unquenchable fires burn just under the surface of the earth in Ohio, and that the baby Mozart fainted dead away in his cradle when he first heard the sound of a trumpet. She said that someone named Narzim al Harrardim was the greatest writer who ever lived. She said that planets control behavior, and anyone conceived during a solar eclipse would be born with webbed feet.

"I know you children like to hear these things," she said, "these secrets, and that is why I am telling you all this." We nodded. It was better than doing comprehension questions for the readings in *Broad Horizons.*

"I will tell you one more story," she said, "and then we will have to do arithmetic." She leaned over, and her voice grew soft. "There is no death," she said. "You must never be afraid. Never. That which is, cannot die. It will change into different earthly and unearthly elements, but I know this as sure as I stand here in front of you, and I swear it: you must not be afraid. I have seen this truth with these eyes. I know it because in a dream God kissed me. Here." And she pointed with her right index finger to the side of her head, below the mouth where the vertical lines were carved into her skin.

Absentmindedly we all did our arithmetic problems. At recess the class was out on the playground, but no one was playing. We were all standing in small groups, talking about Miss Ferenczi. We didn't know if she was crazy, or what. I looked out beyond the playground, at the rusted cars piled in a small heap behind a clump of sumac, and I wanted to see shapes there, approaching me.

On the way home, Carl sat next to me again. He didn't say much, and I didn't, either. At last he turned to me. "You know what she said about the leaves that close up on bugs?"

"Huh?"

"The leaves," Carl insisted. "The meat-eating plants. I know it's true. I saw it on television. The leaves have this icky glue that the plants have got smeared all over them and the insects can't get off 'cause they're stuck. I saw it." He seemed demoralized. "She's tellin' the truth."

"Yeah."

"You think she's seen all those angels?"

I shrugged.

"I don't think she has," Carl informed me. "I think she made that part up."

"There's a tree," I suddenly said. I was looking out the window at the farms along County Road H. I knew every barn, every broken windmill, every fence, every anhydrous ammonia tank, by heart. "There's a tree that's . . . that I've seen . . ."

"Don't you try to do it," Carl said. "You'll just sound like a jerk."


I kissed my mother. She was standing in front of the stove. "How was your day?" she asked.

"Fine."

"Did you have Miss Ferenczi again?"

"Yeah."

"Well?"

"She was fine. Mom," I asked, "can I go to my room?"

"No," she said, "not until you've gone out to the vegetable garden and picked me a few tomatoes." She glanced at the sky. "I think it's going to rain. Skedaddle and do it now. Then you come back inside and watch your brother for a few minutes while I go upstairs. I need to clean up before dinner." She looked down at me. "You're looking a little pale, Tommy." She touched the back of her hand to my forehead and I felt her diamond ring against my skin. "Do you feel all right?"

"I'm fine," I said, and went out to pick the tomatoes.


Coughing mutedly, Mr. Hibler was back the next day, slipping lozenges into his mouth when his back was turned at forty-five-minute intervals and asking us how much of his prepared lesson plan Miss Ferenczi had followed. Edith Atwater took the responsibility for the class of explaining to Mr. Hibler that the substitute hadn't always done exactly what he, Mr. Hibler, would have done, but we had worked hard even though she talked a lot. About what? he asked. All kinds of things, Edith said. I sort of forgot. To our relief, Mr. Hibler seemed not at all interested in what Miss Ferenczi had said to fill the day. He probably thought it was woman's talk: unserious and not suited for school. It was enough that he had a pile of arithmetic problems from us to correct.

For the next month, the sumac turned a distracting red in the field, and the sun traveled toward the southern sky, so that its rays reached Mr. Hibler's Halloween display on the bulletin board in the back of the room, fading the pumpkin-head scarecrow from orange to tan. Every three days I measured how much farther the sun had moved toward the southern horizon by making small marks with my black Crayola on the north wall, ant-sized marks only I knew were there.

And then in early December, four days after the first permanent snowfall, she appeared again in our classroom. The minute she came in the door, I felt my heart begin to pound. Once again, she was different: this time, her hair hung straight down and seemed hardly to have been combed. She hadn't brought her lunchbox with her, but she was carrying what seemed to be a small box. She greeted all of us and talked about the weather. Donna DeShano had to remind her to take her overcoat off.

When the bell to start the day finally rang, Miss Ferenczi looked out at all of us and said, "Children, I have enjoyed your company in the past, and today I am going to reward you." She held up the small box. "Do you know what this is?" She waited. "Of course you don't. It is a Tarot pack."

Edith Atwater raised her hand. "What's a Tarot pack, Miss Ferenczi?"

"It is used to tell fortunes," she said. "And that is what I shall do this morning. I shall tell your fortunes, as I have been taught to do."

"What's fortune?" Bobby Kryzanowicz asked.

"The future, young man. I shall tell you what your future will be. I can't do your whole future, of course. I shall have to limit myself to the five-card system, the wands, cups, swords, pentacles, and the higher arcanes. Now who wants to be first?"

There was a long silence. Then Carol Peterson raised her hand.

"All right," Miss Ferenczi said. She divided the pack into five smaller packs and walked back to Carol's desk, in front of mine. "Pick one card from each one of these packs," she said. I saw that Carol had a four of cups and a six of swords, but I couldn't see the other cards. Miss Ferenczi studied the cards on Carol's desk for a minute. "Not bad," she said. "I do not see much higher education. Probably an early marriage. Many children. There's something bleak and dreary here, but I can't tell what. Perhaps just the tasks of a housewife life. I think you'll do very well, for the most part." She smiled at Carol, a smile with a certain lack of interest. "Who wants to be next?"

Carl Whiteside raised his hand slowly.

"Yes," Miss Ferenczi said, "let's do a boy." She walked over to where Carl sat. After he picked his five cards, she gazed at them for a long time. "Travel," she said. "Much distant travel. You might go into the army. Not too much romantic interest here. A late marriage, if at all. But the Sun in your major arcana, that's a very good card." She giggled. "You'll have a happy life."

Next I raised my hand. She told me my future. She did the same with Bobby Kryzanowicz, Kelly Munger, Edith Atwater, and Kim Foor. Then she came to Wayne Razmer. He picked his five cards, and I could see that the Death card was one of them.

"What's your name?" Miss Ferenczi asked.

"Wayne."

"Well, Wayne," she said, "you will undergo a great metamorphosis, a change, before you become an adult. Your earthly element will no doubt leap higher, because you seem to be a sweet boy. This card, this nine of swords, tells me of suffering and desolation. And this ten of wands, well, that's a heavy load."

"What about this one?" Wayne pointed at the Death card.

"It means, my sweet, that you will die." She gathered up the cards. We were all looking at Wayne. "But do not fear," she said. "It is not really death. Just change. Out of your earthly shape." She put the cards on Mr. Hibler's desk. "And now, let's do some arithmetic."

At lunchtime Wayne went to Mr. Faegre, the principal, and informed him of what Miss Ferenczi had done. During the noon recess, we saw Miss Ferenczi drive out of the parking lot in her rusting green Rambler American. I stood under the slide, listening to the other kids coasting down and landing in the little depressive bowls at the bottom. I was kicking stones and tugging at my hair right up to the moment when I saw Wayne come out to the playground. He smiled, the dead fool, and with the fingers of his right hand he was showing everyone how he had told on Miss Ferenczi.

I made my way toward Wayne, pushing myself past two girls from another class. He was watching me with his little pinhead eyes.

"You told," I shouted at him. "She was just kidding."

"She shouldn't have," he shouted back. "We were supposed to be doing arithmetic."

"She just scared you," I said. "You're a chicken. You're a chicken, Wayne. You are. Scared of a little card," I singsonged.

Wayne fell at me, his two fists hammering down on my nose. I gave him a good one in the stomach and then I tried for his head. Aiming my fist, I saw that he was crying. I slugged him.

"She was right," I yelled. "She was always right! She told the truth!" Other kids were whooping. "You were just scared, that's all!"

And then large hands pulled at us, and it was my turn to speak to Mr. Faegre.

In the afternoon Miss Ferenczi was gone, and my nose was stuffed with cotton clotted with blood, and my lip had swelled, and our class had been combined with Mrs. Mantei's sixth-grade class for a crowded afternoon science unit on insect life in ditches and swamps. I knew where Mrs. Mantei lived: she had a new house trailer just down the road from us, at the Clearwater Park. She was no mystery. Somehow she and Mr. Bodine, the other fourth-grade teacher, had managed to fit forty-five desks into the room. Kelly Munger asked if Miss Ferenczi had been arrested, and Mrs. Mantei said no, of course not. All that afternoon, until the buses came to pick us up, we learned about field crickets and two-striped grasshoppers, water bugs, cicadas, mosquitoes, flies, and moths. We learned about insects' hard outer shell, the exoskeleton, and the usual parts of the mouth, including the labrum, mandible, maxilla, and glossa. We learned about compound eyes, and the four-stage metamorphosis from egg to larva to pupa to adult. We learned something, but not much, about mating. Mrs. Mantei drew, very skillfully, the internal anatomy of the grasshopper on the blackboard. We learned about the dance of the honeybee, directing other bees in the hive to pollen. We found out about which insects were pests to man, and which were not. On lined white pieces of paper we made lists of insects we might actually see, then a list of insects too small to be clearly visible, such as fleas; Mrs. Mantei said that our assignment would be to memorize these lists for the next day, when Mr. Hibler would certainly return and test us on our knowledge.

# Fenstad's Mother

ON SUNDAY MORNING after communion Fenstad drove across town to visit his mother. Behind the wheel, he exhaled with his hand flat in front of his mouth to determine whether the wine on his breath could be detected. He didn't think so. Fenstad's mother was a lifelong social progressive who was amused by her son's churchgoing, and, wine or no wine, she could guess where he had been. She had spent her life in the company of rebels and deviationists, and she recognized all their styles.

Passing a frozen pond in the city park, Fenstad slowed down to watch the skaters, many of whom he knew by name and skating style. From a distance they were dots of color ready for flight, frictionless. To express grief on skates seemed almost impossible, and Fenstad liked that. He parked his car on a residential block and took out his skates from the backseat, where he kept them all winter. With his fingertips he touched the wooden blade guards, thinking of the time. He checked his watch; he had fifteen minutes.

Out on the ice, still wearing his churchy Sunday-morning suit, tie, and overcoat, but now circling the outside edge of the pond with his bare hands in his overcoat pockets, Fenstad admired the overcast sky and luxuriated in the brittle cold. He was active and alert in winter but felt sleepy throughout the summer. He passed a little girl in a pink jacket, pushing a tiny chair over the ice. He waved to his friend Ann, an off-duty cop, practicing her twirls. He waved to other friends. Without exception they waved back. As usual, he was impressed by the way skates improved human character.

Twenty minutes later, in the doorway of his mother's apartment, she said, "Your cheeks are red." She glanced down at his trousers, damp with melted snow. "You've been skating." She kissed him on the cheek and turned to walk into her living room. "Skating after church? Isn't that some sort of doctrinal error?"

"It's just happiness," Fenstad said. Quickly he checked her apartment for any signs of memory loss or depression. He found none and immediately felt relief. The apartment smelled of soap and Lysol, the signs of an old woman who wouldn't tolerate nonsense. Out on her coffee table, as usual, were the letters she was writing to her congressman and to political dictators around the globe. Fenstad's mother pleaded for enlightened behavior and berated the dictators for their bad political habits.

She grasped the arm of the sofa and let herself down slowly. Only then did she smile. "How's your soul, Harry?" she asked. "What's the news?"

He smiled back and smoothed his hair. Martin Luther King's eyes locked onto his from the framed picture on the wall opposite him. In the picture King was shaking hands with Fenstad's mother, the two of them surrounded by smiling faces. "My soul's okay, Ma," he said. "It's a hard project. I'm always working on it." He reached down for a chocolate-chunk cookie from a box on top of the television. "Who brought you these?"

"Your daughter Sharon. She came to see me on Friday." Fenstad's mother tilted her head at him. "You *want* to be a good person, but she's the real article. Goodness comes to her without any effort at all. She says you have a new girlfriend. A pharmacist this time. Susan, is it?" Fenstad nodded. "Harry, why does your generation always have to find the right person? Why can't you learn to live with the wrong person? Sooner or later everyone's wrong. Love isn't the most important thing, Harry, far from it. Why can't you see that? I still don't comprehend why you couldn't live with Eleanor." Eleanor was Fenstad's ex-wife. They had been divorced for a decade, but Fenstad's mother hoped for a reconciliation.

"Come on, Ma," Fenstad said. "Over and done with, gone and gone." He took another cookie.

"You live with somebody so that you're living with *somebody,* and then you go out and do the work of the world. I don't understand all this pickiness about lovers. In a pinch anybody'll do, Harry, believe me."

On the side table was a picture of her late husband, Fenstad's mild, middle-of-the-road father. Fenstad glanced at the picture and let the silence hang between them before asking, "How are you, Ma?"

"I'm all right." She leaned back in the sofa, whose springs made a strange, almost human groan. "I want to get out. I spend too much time in this place in January. You should expand my horizons. Take me somewhere."

"Come to my composition class," Fenstad said. "I'll pick you up at dinnertime on Tuesday. Eat early."

"They'll notice me," she said, squinting. "I'm too old."

"I'll introduce you," her son said. "You'll fit right in."

Fenstad wrote brochures in the publicity department of a computer company during the day, and taught an extension English-composition class at the downtown campus of the state university two nights a week. He didn't need the money; he taught the class because he liked teaching strangers and because he enjoyed the sense of hope that classrooms held for him. This hopefulness and didacticism he had picked up from his mother.

On Tuesday night she was standing at the door of the retirement apartment building, dressed in a dark blue overcoat—her best. Her stylishness was belied slightly by a pair of old fuzzy red earmuffs. Inside the car Fenstad noticed that she had put on perfume, unusual for her. Leaning back, she gazed out contentedly at the nighttime lights.

"Who's in this group of students?" she asked. "Working-class people, I hope. Those are the ones you should be teaching. Anything else is just a career."

"Oh, they work, all right." He looked at his mother and saw, as they passed under a streetlight, a combination of sadness and delicacy in her face. Her usual mask of tough optimism seemed to be deserting her. He braked at a red light and said, "I have a hairdresser and a garage mechanic and a housewife, a Mrs. Nelson, and three guys who're sanitation workers. Plenty of others. One guy you'll really like is a young black man with glasses who sits in the back row and reads *Workers' Vanguard* and Bakunin during class. He's brilliant. I don't know why he didn't test out of this class. His name's York Follette, and he's—"

"I want to meet him," she said quickly. She scowled at the moonlit snow. "A man with ideas. People like that have gone out of my life." She looked over at her son. "What I hate about being my age is how *nice* everyone tries to be. I was never nice, but now everybody is pelting me with sugar cubes." She opened her window an inch and let the cold air blow over her, ruffling her stiff gray hair.

When they arrived at the school, snow had started to fall, and at the other end of the parking lot a police car's flashing light beamed long crimson rays through the dense flakes. Fenstad's mother walked deliberately toward the door, shaking her head mistrustfully at the building and the police. Approaching the steps, she took her son's hand. "I liked the columns on the old buildings," she said. "The old university buildings, I mean. I liked Greek Revival better than this Modernist-bunker stuff." Inside, she blinked in the light at the smooth, waxed linoleum floors and cement-block walls. She held up her hand to shade her eyes. Fenstad took her elbow to guide her over the snow melting in puddles in the entryway. "I never asked you what you're teaching tonight."

"Logic," Fenstad said.

"Ah." She smiled and nodded. "Dialectics!"

"Not quite. Just logic."

She shrugged. She was looking at the clumps of students standing in the glare of the hallway, drinking coffee from paper cups and smoking cigarettes in the general conversational din. She wasn't used to such noise: she stopped in the middle of the corridor underneath a wall clock and stared happily in no particular direction. With her eyes shut she breathed in the close air, smelling of wet overcoats and smoke, and Fenstad remembered how much his mother had always liked smoke-filled rooms, where ideas fought each other, and where some of those ideas died.

"Come on," he said, taking her hand again. Inside Fenstad's classroom six people sat in the angular postures of pre-boredom. York Follette was already in the back row, his copy of *Workers' Vanguard* shielding his face. Fenstad's mother headed straight for him and sat down in the desk next to his. Fenstad saw them shake hands, and in two minutes they were talking in low, rushed murmurs. He saw York Follette laugh quietly and nod. What was it that blacks saw and appreciated in his mother? They had always liked her—written to her, called her, checked up on her—and Fenstad wondered if they recognized something in his mother that he himself had never been able to see.

At seven thirty-five most of the students had arrived and were talking to each other vigorously, as if they didn't want Fenstad to start and thought they could delay him. He stared at them, and when they wouldn't quiet down, he made himself rigid and said, "Good evening. We have a guest tonight." Immediately the class grew silent. He held his arm out straight, indicating with a flick of his hand the old woman in the back row. "My mother," he said. "Clara Fenstad." For the first time all semester his students appeared to be paying attention: they turned around collectively and looked at Fenstad's mother, who smiled and waved. A few of the students began to applaud; others joined in. The applause was quiet but apparently genuine. Fenstad's mother brought herself slowly to her feet and made a suggestion of a bow. Two of the students sitting in front of her turned around and began to talk to her. At the front of the class Fenstad started his lecture on logic, but his mother wouldn't quiet down. This was a class for adults. They were free to do as they liked.

Lowering his head and facing the blackboard, Fenstad reviewed problems in logic, following point by point the outline set down by the textbook: post hoc fallacies, false authorities, begging the question, circular reasoning, ad hominem arguments, all the rest. Explaining these problems, his back turned, he heard sighs of boredom, boldly expressed. Occasionally he glanced at the back of the room. His mother was watching him carefully, and her face was expressing all the complexity of dismay. Dismay radiated from her. Her disappointment wasn't personal, because his mother didn't think that people as individuals were at fault for what they did. As usual, her disappointed hope was located in history and in the way people agreed with already existing histories.

She was angry with him for collaborating with grammar. She would call it unconsciously installed authority. Then she would find other names for it.

"All right," he said loudly, trying to make eye contact with someone in the room besides his mother, "let's try some examples. Can anyone tell me what, if anything, is wrong with the following sentence? 'I, like most people, have a unique problem.' "

The three sanitation workers, in the third row, began to laugh. Fenstad caught himself glowering and singled out the middle one.

"Yes, it is funny, isn't it?"

The man in the middle smirked and looked at the floor. "I was just thinking of my unique problem."

"Right," Fenstad said. "But what's wrong with saying, 'I, like most people, have a unique problem'?"

"Solving it?" This was Mrs. Nelson, who sat by the window so that she could gaze at the tree outside, lit by a streetlight. All through class she looked at the tree as if it were a lover.

"Solving what?"

"Solving the problem you have. What is the problem?"

"That's actually not what I'm getting at," Fenstad said. "Although it's a good *related* point. I'm asking what might be wrong logically with that sentence."

"It depends," Harold Ronson said. He worked in a service station and sometimes came to class wearing his work shirt with his name tag, HAROLD, stitched into it. "It depends on what your problem is. You haven't told us your problem."

"No," Fenstad said, "my problem is *not* the problem." He thought of Alice in Wonderland and felt, physically, as if he himself were getting small. "Let's try this again. What might be wrong with saying that most people have a unique problem?"

"You shouldn't be so critical," Timothy Melville said. "You should look on the bright side, if possible."

"What?"

"He's right," Mrs. Nelson said. "Most people have unique problems, but many people do their best to help themselves, such as taking night classes or working at meditation."

"No doubt that's true," Fenstad said. "But why can't most people have a unique problem?"

"Oh, I disagree," Mrs. Nelson said, still looking at her tree. Fenstad glanced at it and saw that it was crested with snow. It *was* beautiful. No wonder she looked at it. "I believe that most people do have unique problems. They just shouldn't talk about them all the time."

"Can anyone," Fenstad asked, looking at the back wall and hoping to see something there that was not wall, "can anyone give me an example of a unique problem?"

"Divorce," Barb Kjellerud said. She sat near the door and knitted during class. She answered questions without looking up. "Divorce is unique."

"No, it isn't!" Fenstad said, failing in the crucial moment to control his voice. He and his mother exchanged glances. In his mother's face for a split second was the history of her compassionate, ambivalent attention to him. "Divorce is not unique." He waited to calm himself. "It's everywhere. Now try again. Give me a unique problem."

Silence. "This is a trick question," Arlene Fisher said. "I'm sure it's a trick question."

"Not necessarily. Does anyone know what 'unique' means?"

"One of a kind," York Follette said, gazing at Fenstad with dry amusement. Sometimes he took pity on Fenstad and helped him out of jams. Fenstad's mother smiled and nodded.

"Right," Fenstad crowed, racing toward the blackboard as if he were about to write something. "So let's try again. Give me a unique problem."

"You give *us* a unique problem," one of the sanitation workers said. Fenstad didn't know whether he'd been given a statement or a command. He decided to treat it as a command.

"All right," he said. He stopped and looked down at his shoes. Maybe it *was* a trick question. He thought for ten seconds. Problem after problem presented itself to him. He thought of poverty, of the assaults on the earth, of the awful complexities of love. "I can't think of one," Fenstad said. His hands went into his pockets.

"That's because problems aren't personal," Fenstad's mother said from the back of the room. "They're collective." She waited while several students in the class sat up and nodded. "And people must work together on their solutions." She talked for another two minutes, taking the subject out of logic and putting it neatly in politics, where she knew it belonged.

The snow had stopped by the time the class was over. Fenstad took his mother's arm and escorted her to the car. After easing her down on the passenger side and starting the engine, he began to clear the front windshield. He didn't have a scraper and had forgotten his gloves, so he was using his bare hands. When he brushed the snow away on his mother's side, she looked out at him, surprised, a terribly aged Sleeping Beauty awakened against her will.

Once the car had warmed up, she was in a gruff mood and repositioned herself under the seat belt while making quiet but aggressive remarks. The sight of the new snow didn't seem to calm her. "Logic," she said at last. "That wasn't logic. Those are just rhetorical tactics. It's filler and drudgery."

"I don't want to discuss it now."

"All right. I'm sorry. Let's talk about something more pleasant."

They rode together in silence. Then she began to shake her head. "Don't take me home," she said. "I want to have a spot of tea somewhere before I go back. A nice place where they serve tea, all right?"

He parked outside an all-night restaurant with huge front plate-glass windows; it was called Country Bob's. He held his mother's elbow from the car to the door. At the door, looking back to make sure that he had turned off his headlights, he saw his tracks and his mother's in the snow. His were separate footprints, but hers formed two long lines.

Inside, at the table, she sipped her tea and gazed at her son for a long time. "Thanks for the adventure, Harry. I do appreciate it. What're you doing in class next week? Oh, I remember. How-to papers. That should be interesting."

"Want to come?"

"Very much. I'll keep quiet next time, if you want me to."

Fenstad shook his head. "It's okay. It's fun having you along. You can say whatever you want. The students loved you. I knew you'd be a sensation, and you were. They'd probably rather have you teaching the class than me."

He noticed that his mother was watching something going on behind him, and he turned around in the booth so that he could see what it was. At first all he saw was a woman, a young woman with long hair wet from snow and hanging in clumps, talking in the aisle to two young men, both of whom were nodding at her. Then she moved on to the next table. She spoke softly. Fenstad couldn't hear her words, but he saw the solitary customer to whom she was speaking shake his head once, keeping his eyes down. Then the woman saw Fenstad and his mother. In a moment she was standing in front of them.

She wore two green plaid flannel shirts and a thin torn jacket. Like Fenstad, she wore no gloves. Her jeans were patched, and she gave off a strong smell, something like hay, Fenstad thought, mixed with tar and sweat. He looked down at her feet and saw that she was wearing penny loafers with no socks. Coins, old pennies, were in both shoes; the leather was wet and cracked. He looked in the woman's face. Under a hat that seemed to collapse on either side of her head, her face was thin and chalk-white except for the fatigue lines under her eyes. The eyes themselves were bright blue, beautiful, and crazy. To Fenstad, she looked desperate, percolating slightly with insanity, and he was about to say so to his mother when the woman bent down toward him and said, "Mister, can you spare any money?"

Involuntarily, Fenstad looked toward the kitchen, hoping that the manager would spot this person and take her away. When he looked back again, his mother was taking her blue coat off, wriggling in the booth to free her arms from the sleeves. Stopping and starting again, she appeared to be stuck inside the coat; then she lifted herself up, trying to stand, and with a quick, quiet groan slipped the coat off. She reached down and folded the coat over and held it toward the woman. "Here," she said. "Here's my coat. Take it before my son stops me."

"Mother, you can't." Fenstad reached forward to grab the coat, but his mother pulled it away from him.

When Fenstad looked back at the woman, her mouth was open, showing several gray teeth. Her hands were outstretched, and he understood, after a moment, that this was a posture of refusal, a gesture saying no, and that the woman wasn't used to it and did it awkwardly. Fenstad's mother was standing and trying to push the coat toward the woman, not toward her hands but lower, at waist level, and she was saying, "Here, here, here, here." The sound, like a human birdcall, frightened Fenstad, and he stood up quickly, reached for his wallet, and removed the first two bills he could find, two twenties. He grabbed the woman's chapped, ungloved left hand.

"Take these," he said, putting the two bills in her icy palm, "for the love of God, and please go."

He was close to her face. Tonight he would pray for her. For a moment the woman's expression was vacant. His mother was still pushing the coat at her, and the woman was unsteadily bracing herself. The woman's mouth was open, and her stagnant-water breath washed over him. "I know you," she said. "You're my little baby cousin."

"Go away, please," Fenstad said. He pushed at her. She turned, clutching his money. He reached around to put his hands on his mother's shoulders. "Ma," he said, "she's gone now. Mother, sit down. I gave her money for a coat." His mother fell down on her side of the booth, and her blue coat rolled over on the bench beside her, showing the label and the shiny inner lining. When he looked up, the woman who had been begging had disappeared, though he could still smell her odor, an essence of wretchedness.

"Excuse me, Harry," his mother said. "I have to go to the bathroom."

She rose and walked toward the front of the restaurant, turned a corner, and was out of sight. Fenstad sat and tried to collect himself. When the waiter came, a boy with an earring and red hair in a flattop, Fenstad just shook his head and said, "More tea." He realized that his mother hadn't taken off her earmuffs, and the image of his mother in the ladies' room with her earmuffs on gave him a fit of uneasiness. After getting up from the booth and following the path that his mother had taken, he stood outside the ladies'-room door and, when no one came in or out, he knocked. He waited for a decent interval. Still hearing no answer, he opened the door.

His mother was standing with her arms down on either side of the first sink. She was holding herself there, her eyes following the hot water as it poured from the tap around the bright porcelain sink down into the drain, and she looked furious. Fenstad touched her and she snapped toward him.

"Your logic!" she said.

He opened the door for her and helped her back to the booth. The second cup of tea had been served, and Fenstad's mother sipped it in silence. They did not converse. When she had finished, she said, "All right. I do feel better now. Let's go."

At the curb in front of her apartment building he leaned forward and kissed her on the cheek. "Pick me up next Tuesday," she said. "I want to go back to that class." He nodded. He watched as she made her way past the security guard at the front desk; then he put his car into drive and started home.

That night he skated in the dark for an hour with his friend Susan, the pharmacist. She was an excellent skater; they had met on the ice. She kept late hours and, like Fenstad, enjoyed skating at night. She listened attentively to his story about his mother and the woman in the restaurant. To his great relief she recommended no course of action. She listened. She didn't believe in giving advice, even when asked.

The following Tuesday, Fenstad's mother was again in the back row next to York Follette. One of the fluorescent lights overhead was flickering, which gave the room, Fenstad thought, a sinister quality, like a debtors' prison or a refuge for the homeless. He'd been thinking about such people for the entire week. For seven days now he had caught whiffs of the woman's breath in the air, and one morning, Friday, he thought he caught a touch of the rotten-celery smell on his own breath, after a particularly difficult sales meeting.

Tonight was how-to night. The students were expected to stand at the front of the class and read their papers, instructing their peers and answering questions if necessary. Starting off, and reading her paper in a frightened monotone, Mrs. Nelson told the class how to bake a cheese soufflé. Arlene Fisher's paper was about mushroom hunting. Fenstad was put off by the introduction. "The advantage to mushrooms," Arlene Fisher read, "is that they are delicious. The disadvantage to mushrooms is that they can make you sick, even die." But then she explained how to recognize the common shaggymane by its cylindrical cap and dark tufts; she drew a model on the board. She warned the class against the *Clito-cybe illudens,* the Jack-o'-Lantern. "Never eat a mushroom like this one or *any* mushroom that glows in the dark. Take heed!" she said, fixing her gaze on the class. Fenstad saw his mother taking rapid notes. Harold Ronson, the mechanic, reading his own prose painfully and slowly, told the class how to get rust spots out of their automobiles. Again Fenstad noticed his mother taking notes. York Follette told the class about the proper procedures for laying down attic insulation and how to know when enough was enough, so that a homeowner wouldn't be robbed blind, as he put it, by the salesmen, in whose ranks he had once counted himself.

Barb Kjellerud had brought along a cassette player, and told the class that her hobby was ballroom dancing; she would instruct them in the basic waltz. She pushed the PLAY button on the tape machine, and "Tales from the Vienna Woods" came booming out. To the accompaniment of the music she read her paper, illustrating, as she went, how the steps were to be performed. She danced alone in front of them, doing so with flair. Her blond hair swayed as she danced, Fenstad noticed. She looked a bit like a contestant in a beauty contest who had too much personality to win. She explained to the men the necessity of leading. Someone had to lead, she said, and tradition had given this responsibility to the male. Fenstad heard his mother snicker.

When Barb Kjellerud asked for volunteers, Fenstad's mother raised her hand. She said she knew how to waltz and would help out. At the front of the class she made a counterclockwise motion with her hand, and for the next minute, sitting at the back of the room, Fenstad watched his mother and one of the sanitation workers waltzing under the flickering fluorescent lights.

"What a wonderful class," Fenstad's mother said on the way home. "I hope you're paying attention to what they tell you."

Fenstad nodded. "Tea?" he asked.

She shook her head. "Where're you going after you drop me off?"

"Skating," he said. "I usually go skating. I have a date."

"With the pharmacist? In the dark?"

"We both like it, Ma." As he drove, he made an all-purpose gesture. "The moon and the stars," he said simply.

When he left her off, he felt unsettled. He considered, as a point of courtesy, staying with her a few minutes, but by the time he had this idea he was already away from the building and was headed down the street.

He and Susan were out on the ice together, skating in large circles, when Susan pointed to a solitary figure sitting on a park bench near the lake's edge. The sky had cleared; the moon gave everything a cold, fine-edged clarity. When Fenstad followed the line of Susan's finger, he saw at once that the figure on the bench was his mother. He realized it simply because of the way she sat there, drawn into herself, attentive even in the winter dark. He skated through the uncleared snow over the ice until he was standing close enough to speak to her. "Mother," he said, "what are you doing here?"

She was bundled up, a thick woolen cap drawn over her head and two scarves covering much of her face. He could see little other than the two lenses of her glasses facing him in the dark. "I wanted to see you two," she told him. "I thought you'd look happy, and you did. I like to watch happiness. I always have."

"How can you see us? We're so far away."

"That's how I saw you."

This made no sense to him, so he asked, "How'd you get here?"

"I took a cab. That part was easy."

"Aren't you freezing?"

"I don't know. I don't know if I'm freezing or not."

He and Susan took her back to her apartment as soon as they could get their boots on. In the car Mrs. Fenstad insisted on asking Susan what kind of safety procedures were used to ensure that drugs weren't smuggled out of pharmacies and sold illegally, but she didn't appear to listen to the answer, and by the time they reached her building, she seemed to be falling asleep. They helped her up to her apartment. Susan thought that they should give her a warm bath before putting her into bed, and, together, they did. She did not protest. She didn't even seem to notice them as they guided her in and out of the bathtub.

Fenstad feared that his mother would catch some lung infection, and it turned out to be bronchitis, which kept her in her apartment for the first three weeks of February, until her cough went down. Fenstad came by every other day to see how she was, and one Tuesday, after work, he went up to her floor and heard piano music: an old recording, which sounded much-played, of the brightest and fastest jazz piano he had ever heard—music of superhuman brilliance. He swung open the door to her apartment and saw York Follette sitting near his mother's bed. On the bedside table was a small tape player, from which the music poured into the room.

Fenstad's mother was leaning back against the pillow, smiling, her eyes closed.

Follette turned toward Fenstad. He had been talking softly. He motioned toward the tape machine and said, "Art Tatum. It's a cut called 'Battery Bounce.' Your mother's never heard it."

"Jazz, Harry," Fenstad's mother said, her eyes still closed, not needing to see her son. "York is explaining to me about Art Tatum and jazz. Next week he's going to try something more progressive on me." Now his mother opened her eyes. "Have you ever heard such music before, Harry?"

They were both looking at him. "No," he said, "I never heard anything like it."

"This is my unique problem, Harry." Fenstad's mother coughed and then waited to recover her breath. "I never heard enough jazz." She smiled. "What glimpses!" she said at last.

After she recovered, he often found her listening to the tape machine that York Follette had given her. She liked to hear the Oscar Peterson Trio as the sun set and the lights of evening came on. She now often mentioned glimpses. Back at home, every night, Fenstad spoke about his mother in his prayers of remembrance and thanksgiving, even though he knew she would disapprove.

# Westland

SATURDAY MORNING at the zoo, facing the lions' cage, overcast sky and a light breeze carrying the smell of peanuts and animal dung, the peacocks making their stilted progress across the sidewalks. I was standing in front of the gorge separating the human viewers from the lions. The lions weren't caged, exactly; they just weren't free to go. One male and one female were slumbering on fake rock ledges. Raw meat was nearby. My hands were in my pockets and I was waiting for a moment of energy so I could leave and do my Saturday-morning errands. Then this girl, this teenager, appeared from behind me, hands in *her* pockets, and she stopped a few feet away on my right. In an up-all-night voice, she said, "What would you do if I shot that lion?" She nodded her head: she meant the male, the closer one.

"Shot it?"

"That's right."

"I don't know." Sometimes you have to humor people, pretend as if they're talking about something real. "Do you have a gun?"

"Of course I have a gun." She wore a protective blankness on her thin face. She was fixed on the lion. "I have it here in my pocket."

"I'd report you," I said. "I'd try to stop you. There are guards here. People don't shoot caged animals. You shouldn't even carry a concealed weapon, a girl your age."

"This is Detroit," she explained.

"I know it is," I said. "But people don't shoot caged lions in Detroit or anywhere else."

"It wouldn't be that bad," she said, nodding at the lions again. "You can tell from their faces how much they want to check out."

I said I didn't think so.

She turned to look at me. Her skin was so pale it seemed bleached, and she was wearing a vaudeville-length overcoat and a pair of high-top tennis shoes and jeans with slits at the knees. She looked like a fifteen-year-old bag lady. "It's because you're a disconnected person that you can't see it," she said. She shivered and reached into her pocket and pulled out a crumpled pack of cigarettes. "Lions are so human. Things get to them. They experience everything more than we do. They're romantic." She glanced at her crushed pack of cigarettes, and in a shivering motion she tossed it into the gorge. She swayed back and forth. "They want to kill and feast and feel," she said.

I looked at this girl's bleached skin, that candy-bar-and-cola complexion, and I said, "Are you all right?"

"I slept here last night," she said. She pointed vaguely behind her. "I was sleeping over there. Under those trees. Near the polar bears."

"Why'd you do that?"

"I wasn't alone *all* night." She was answering a question I hadn't asked. "This guy, he came in with me for a while to be nice and amorous but he couldn't see the point in staying. He split around midnight. He said it was righteous coming in here and being solid with the animal world, but he said you had to know when to stop. I told him I wouldn't defend him to his friends if he left, and he left, so as far as I'm concerned, he is over, he is zippo."

She was really shivering now, and she was huddling inside that long overcoat. I don't like to help strangers, but she needed help. "Are you hungry?" I asked. "You want a hamburger?"

"I'll eat it," she said, "but only if you buy it."

I took her to a fast-food restaurant and sat her down and brought her one of their famous giant cheeseburgers. She held it in her hands familiarly as she watched the cars passing on Woodward Avenue. I let my gaze follow hers, and when I looked back, half the cheeseburger was gone. She wasn't even chewing. She didn't look at the food. She ate like a soldier in a foxhole. What was left of her food she gripped in her skinny fingers decorated with flaking pink nail polish. She was pretty in a raw and sloppy way.

"You're looking at me."

"Yes, I am," I admitted.

"How come?"

"A person can look," I said.

"Maybe." Now she looked back. "Are you one of those creeps?"

"Which kind?"

"The kind of old man creep who picks up girls and drives them places, and, like, terrorizes them for days and then dumps them into fields."

"No," I said. "I'm not like that. And I'm not that old."

"Maybe it's the accent," she said. "You don't sound American."

"I was born in England," I told her, "but I've been in this country for thirty years. I'm an American citizen."

"You've got to be born in this country to sound American," she said, sucking at her chocolate shake through her straw. She was still gazing at the traffic. Looking at traffic seemed to restore her peace of mind. "I guess you're okay," she said distantly, "and I'm not worried anyhow, because, like I told you, I've got a gun."

"Oh yeah," I said.

"You're not a real American because you don't *believe*!" Then this child fumbled in her coat pocket and clunked down a small shiny handgun on the table, next to the plastic containers and the french fries. "So there," she said.

"Put it back," I told her. "Jesus, I hope the safety's on."

"I think so." She wiped her hand on a napkin and dropped the thing back into her pocket. "So tell me your name, Mr. Samaritan."

"Warren," I said. "My name's Warren. What's yours?"

"I'm Jaynee. What do you do, Warren? You must do something. You look like someone who does something."

I explained to her about governmental funding for social work and therapy, but her eyes glazed and she cut me off.

"Oh yeah," she said, chewing her french fries with her mouth open so that you could see inside if you wanted to. "One of those professional friends. I've seen people like you."

I drove her home. She admired the tape machine in the car and the carpeting on the floor. She gave me directions on how to get to her house in Westland, one of the suburbs. Detroit has four shopping centers at its cardinal points: Westland, Eastland, Southland, and Northland. A town grew up around Westland, a blue-collar area, and now Westland is the name of both the shopping center and the town.

She took me down fast-food alley and then through a series of right and left ninety-degree turns on streets with bungalows covered by aluminum siding. Few trees, not much green except the lawns, and the half-sun dropped onto those perpendicular lines with nothing to stop it or get in its way. The girl, Jaynee, picked at her knees and nodded, as if any one of the houses would do. The houses all looked exposed to me, with a straight shot at the elements out there on that flat grid.

I was going to drop her off at what she said was her driveway, but there was an old chrome-loaded Pontiac in the way, one of those vintage 1950s cars, its front end up on a hoist and some man working on his back on a rolling dolly underneath it. "That's him," the girl said. "You want to meet him?"

I parked the car and got out. The man pulled himself away from underneath the car and looked over at us. He stood up, wiping his hands on a rag, and scowled at his daughter. He wasn't going to look at me right away. I think he was checking Jaynee for signs of damage.

"What's this?" he asked. "What's this about, Jaynee?"

"This is about nothing," she said. "I spent the night in the zoo and this person found me and brought me home."

"At the zoo. Jesus Christ. At the zoo. Is that what happened?" He was asking me.

"That's where I saw her," I told him. "She looked pretty cold."

He dropped a screwdriver I hadn't noticed he was holding. He was standing there in his driveway next to the Pontiac, looking at his daughter and me and then at the sky. I'd had those moments, too, when nothing made any sense and I didn't know where my responsibilities lay. "Go inside," he told his daughter. "Take a shower. I'm not talking to you here on the driveway. I know that."

We both watched her go into the house. She looked like an overcoat with legs. I felt ashamed of myself for thinking of her that way, but there are some ideas you can't prevent.

We were both watching her, and the man said, "You can't go to the public library and find out how to raise a girl like that." He said something else, but an airplane passed so low above us that I couldn't hear him. We were about three miles from the airport. He ended his speech by saying, "I don't know who's right."

"I don't, either."

"Earl Lampson." He held out his hand. I shook it and took away a feel of bone and grease and flesh. I could see a fading tattoo on his forearm of a rose run through with a sword.

"Warren Banks," I said. "I guess I'll have to be going."

"Wait a minute, Warren. Let me do two things. First, let me thank you for bringing my daughter home. Unhurt." I nodded to show I understood. "Second. A question. You got any kids?"

"Two," I said. "Both boys."

"Then you know about it. You know what a child can do to you. I was awake last night. I didn't know what had happened to her. I didn't know if she had planned it. That was the worst. She makes plans. Jesus Christ. The zoo. The lions?"

I nodded.

"She'll do anything. And it isn't an act with her." He looked up and down the street, as if he were waiting for something to appear, and I had the wild idea that I was going to see a float coming our way, with beauty queens on it, and little men dressed up in costumes.

I told him I had to leave. He shook his head.

"Stay a minute, Warren," he said. "Come into the backyard. I want to show you something."

He turned around and walked through the garage, past a pile of snow tires and two rusted-out bicycles. I followed him, thinking of my boys this morning at their Scout meeting, and of my wife, out shopping or maybe home by now and wondering vaguely where I was. I was supposed to be getting groceries. Here I was in this garage. She would look at the clock, do something else, then look back at the clock.

"Now, how about this?" Earl pointed an index finger toward a wooden construction that stood in the middle of his yard, running from one side to another: a play structure, with monkey bars and a swing set, a high perch like a ship's crow's nest, a set of tunnels to crawl through and climb on, and a little rope bridge between two towers. I had never seen anything like it, so much human effort expended on a backyard toy, this huge contraption.

I whistled. "It must have taken you years."

"Eighteen months," he said. "And she hasn't played on it since she was twelve." He shook his head. "I bought the wood and put it together piece by piece. She was only three years old when I did it, weekends when I wasn't doing overtime at Ford's. She was my assistant. She'd bring me nails. I told her to hold the hammer when I wasn't using it, and she'd stand there, real serious, just holding the hammer. Of course, now she's too old for it. I have the biggest backyard toy in Michigan and a daughter who goes off to the zoo and spends the night there and that's her idea of a good time."

A light rain had started to fall. "What are you going to do with this thing?" I asked.

"Take it apart, I guess." He glanced at the sky. "Warren, you want a beer?"

It was eleven o'clock in the morning. "Sure," I said.


We sat in silence on his cluttered back porch. We sipped our beers and watched the rain fall over things in our line of sight. Neither of us was saying much. It was better being there than being at home, and my morning gloom was on its way out. It wasn't lifting so much as converting into something else, as it does when you're in someone else's house. I didn't want to move as long as I felt that way.

I had been in the zoo that morning because I had been reading the newspaper again, and this time I had read about a uranium plant here in Michigan whose employees were spraying pastureland with a fertilizer recycled from radioactive wastes. They called it treated raffinate. The paper said that in addition to trace amounts of radium and radioactive thorium, this fertilizer spray had at least eighteen poisonous heavy metals in it, including molybdenum, arsenic, and lead. It had been sprayed out into the pastures and was going into the food supply. I was supposed to get up from the table and go out and get the groceries, but I had gone to the zoo instead to stare at the animals. This had been happening more often lately. I couldn't keep my mind on ordinary, daily things. I had come to believe that depression was the realism of the future, and phobias a sign of sanity. I was supposed to know better, but I didn't.

I had felt crazy and helpless, but there, on Earl Lampson's porch, I was feeling a little better. Calm strangers sometimes have that effect on you.

Jaynee came out just then. She'd been in the shower, and I could see why some kid might want to spend a night in the zoo with her. She was in a T-shirt and jeans, and the hot water had perked her up. I stood and excused myself. I couldn't stand to see her just then, breaking my mood. Earl went to a standing position and shook my hand and said he appreciated what I had done for his daughter. I said it was nothing and started to leave when Earl, for no reason that I could see, suddenly said he'd be calling me during the week, if that was all right. I told him that I would be happy to hear from him.

Walking away from there, I decided, on the evidence so far, that Earl had a good heart and didn't know what to do with it, just as he didn't know what to do with that thing in his backyard. He just had it, and it was no use to him.

He called my office on Wednesday. I'd given him the number. There was something new in his voice, of someone wanting help. He repeated his daughter's line about how I was a professional friend, and I said, yes, sometimes that was what I was. He asked me if I ever worked with "bad kids"—that was his phrase—and I said that sometimes I did. Then he asked me if I would help him take apart his daughter's play structure on the following Saturday. He said there'd be plenty of beer. I could see what he was after: a bit of free counseling, but since I hadn't prepared myself for his invitation, I didn't have a good defense ready. I looked around my office cubicle, and I saw myself in Earl's backyard, a screwdriver in one hand and a beer in the other. I said yes.

The day I came over, it was a fair morning, for Michigan. This state is like Holland. Cold, clammy mists mix with freezing rain in autumn, and hard rains in the spring are broken by tropical heat and tornadoes. It's attack weather. The sky covers you with a metallic-blue, watercolor wash over tinfoil. But this day was all right. I worked out there with Earl, pulling the wood apart with our crowbars and screwdrivers, and we had an audience, Jaynee and Earl's new woman. That was how she was introduced to me: Jody. She's the new woman. She didn't seem to have more than about eight or nine years on Jaynee, and she was nearsighted. She had those thick corrective lenses. But she was pretty in the details, and when she looked at Earl, the lenses enlarged those eyes, so that the love was large and naked and obvious.

I was pulling down a support bar for the north end of the structure and observing from time to time the neighboring backyards. My boys had gone off to a Scout meeting again, and my wife was busy, catching up on some office work. No one missed me. I was pulling at the wood, enjoying myself, talking to Earl and Jaynee and Jody about some of the techniques people in my profession use to resolve bad family quarrels; Jaynee and Jody were working at pulling down some of the wood, too. We already had two piles of scrap lumber.

I had heard a little of how Earl raised Jaynee. Her mother had taken off, the way they sometimes do, when Jaynee was three years old. He'd done the parental work. "You've been the dad, haven't you, Earl?" Jody said, bumping her hip at him. She sat down to watch a sparrow. Her hair was in a ponytail, one of those feminine brooms. "Earl doesn't know the first thing about being a woman, and he had to teach it all to Jaynee here." Jody pointed her cigarette at Jaynee. "Well, she learned it from somewhere. There's not much left she doesn't know."

"Where's the mystery?" Jaynee asked. She was pounding a hammer absentmindedly into a piece of wood lying flat on the ground. "It's easier being a woman than a girl. Men treat you better 'cause they want you."

Earl stopped turning his wrench. "Only if you don't go to the zoo anytime some punk asks you."

"That was once," she said.

Earl aimed himself at me. "I was strict with her. She knows about the laws I laid down. Fourteen laws. They're framed in her bedroom. Nobody in this country knows what it is to be decent anymore, but I'm trying. It sure to hell isn't easy."

Jody smiled at me. "Earl restrained himself until I came along." She laughed. Earl turned away so I wouldn't see his face.

"I only spent the night in the zoo *once,*" Jaynee repeated, as if no one had been listening. "And besides, I was protected."

"Protected," Earl repeated, staring at her.

"You know." Jaynee pointed her index finger at her father with her thumb in the air and the other fingers pulled back, and she made an explosive sound in her mouth.

"You took that?" her father said. "You took that to the zoo?"

Jaynee shrugged. At this particular moment, Earl turned to me. "Warren, did you see it?"

I assumed he meant the gun. I looked over toward him from the bolt I was unscrewing, and I nodded. I was so involved in the work of this job that I didn't want my peaceful laboring disturbed.

"You shouldn't have said that," Jody said to Jaynee. Earl had disappeared inside the house. "You know your father well enough by now to know that." Jody stood up and walked to the yard's back fence. "Your father thinks that women and guns are a terrible combination."

"He always said I should watch out for myself," Jaynee said, her back to us. She pulled a cookie out of her pocket and began to eat it.

"Not with a gun," Jody said.

"He showed me how to use it," the daughter said loudly. "I'm not ignorant about firearms." She didn't seem especially interested in the way the conversation was going.

"That was just information," Jody said. "It wasn't for you to use." She was standing and waiting for Earl to reappear. I didn't do work like this, and I didn't hear conversations like this during the rest of the week, and so I was the only person still dismantling the play structure when Earl reappeared in the backyard with the revolver in his right hand. He had his shirtsleeve pulled back so anybody could see the tattoo of the rose run through with the saber on his forearm. Because I didn't know what he was going to do with that gun, I thought I had just better continue to work.

"The ninth law in your bedroom," Earl announced, "says you use violence only in self-defense." He stepped to the fence, then held his arm straight up into the air and fired once. That sound, that shattering, made me drop my wrench. It hit the ground with a clank, three inches from my right foot. Through all the backyards of Westland I heard the blast echoing. The neighborhood dogs set up a barking chain; front and back doors slammed.

Earl was breathing hard and staring at his daughter. We were in a valley, I thought, of distinct silence. "That's all the bullets I own for that weapon," he said. He put the gun on the doorstep. Then he made his way over to where his daughter was sitting. There's a kind of walk, a little stiff, where you know every step has been thought about, every step is a decision. This was like that.

Jaynee was munching the last of her cookie. Her father grabbed her by the shoulders and began to shake her. It was like what you see in movies, someone waking up a sleepwalker. Back and forth her head tossed. "Never never never never never," he said. I started to laugh, but it was too crazed and despairing to be funny. He stopped. I could see he wanted to make a parental speech: his face was tightening up, his flesh stiff, but he didn't know how to start it, the right choice for the first word, and his daughter pushed him away and ran into the house. In that run, something happened to me, and I knew I had to get out of there.

I glanced at Jody, the new woman. She stood with her hands in her blue jeans. She looked bored. She had lived here all her life. What had just happened was a disturbance in the morning's activities. Meanwhile, Earl had picked up a board and was tentatively beating the ground with it. He was staring at the revolver on the steps. "I got to take that gun and throw it into Ford Lake," he said. "First thing I do this afternoon."

"Have to go, Earl," I said. Everything about me was getting just a little bit out of control, and I thought I had better get home.

"You're going?" Earl said, trying to concentrate on me for a moment. "You're going now? You're sure you don't want another beer?"

I said I was sure. The new woman, Jody, went over to Earl and whispered something to him. I couldn't see why, right now, out loud, she couldn't say what she wanted to say. Christ, we were all adults, after all.

"She wants you to take that .22 and throw it," Earl said. He went over to the steps, picked up the gun, and returned to where I was standing. He dropped it into my hand. The barrel was warm, and the whole apparatus smelled of cordite.

"Okay, Earl," I said. I held this heavy object in my hand, and I had the insane idea that my life was just beginning. "You have any particular preference about where I should dispose of it?"

He looked at me, his right eyebrow going up. This kind of diction he hadn't heard from me before. "Particular preference?" He laughed without smiling. "Last I heard," he said, "when you throw a gun out, it doesn't matter where it goes so long as it's gone."

"Gotcha," I said. I was going around to the front of the house. "Be in touch, right?"

Those two were back to themselves again, talking. They would be interested in saying good-bye to me about two hours from now, when they noticed that I wasn't there.

In the story that would end here, I go out to Belle Isle in the city of Detroit and drop Earl's revolver off the Belle Isle Bridge at the exact moment when no one is looking. But this story has a ways to go. That's not what I did. To start with, I drove around with that gun in my car, underneath the front seat, like half the other residents of this area. I drove to work and at the end of the day I drove home, a model bureaucrat, and each time I sat in the car and turned on the ignition, I felt better than I should have because that gun was on the floor. After about a week, the only problem I had was not that the gun was there but that it wasn't loaded. So I went to the ammo store—it's actually called the Michigan Rod and Gun Club—about two miles away from my house and bought some bullets for it. This was all very easy. In fact, the various details were getting easier and easier. I hadn't foreseen this. I've read Freud and Heinz Kohut and D. W. Winnicott, and I can talk to you about psychotic breaks and object-relations and fixation on oedipal grandiosity characterized by the admixture of strong object cathexes and the implicitly disguised presence of castration fears, and, by virtue of my being able to talk about those conditions, I have had some trouble getting into gear and moving when the occasion called for it. But now, with the magic wand under the front seat, I was getting ready for some kind of adventure.

Around the house my character was improving rather than degenerating. Knowing my little secret, I was able to sit with Gary, my younger son, as he practiced the piano, and I complimented him on the Czerny passages he had mastered, and I helped him through the sections he hadn't learned. I was a fiery angel of patience. With Sam, my older boy, I worked on a model train layout. I cooked a few more dinners than I usually did: from honey-mustard chicken, I went on to varieties of stuffed fish and other dishes with sauces that I had only imagined. I was attentive to Ann. The nature of our intimacies improved. We were whispering to each other again. We hadn't whispered in years.

I was front-loading a little fantasy. After all, I had tried intelligence. Intelligence was not working, not with me, not with the world. So it was time to try the other thing.

My only interruption was that I was getting calls from Earl. He called the house. He had the impression that I understood the mind and could make his ideas feel better. I told him that nobody could make his ideas feel better, ideas either feel good or not, but he didn't believe me.

"Do you mind me calling like this?" he asked. It was just before dinner. I was in the study, and the news was on. I pushed the MUTE button on the remote control. While Earl talked, I watched the silent coverage of mayhem.

"No, I don't mind."

"I shouldn't do this, I know, 'cause you get paid to listen, being a professional friend. But I have to ask your advice."

"Don't call me a professional friend. Earl, what's your question?" The pictures in front of me showed a boy being shot in the streets of Beirut.

"Well, I went into Jaynee's room to clean up. You know how teenage girls are. Messy and everything."

"Yes." More Beirut carnage.

"And I found her diary. How was I to know she had a diary? She never told me."

"They often don't, Earl. Was it locked?"

"What?"

"Locked. Sometimes diaries have locks."

"Well," Earl said, "this one didn't."

"Sounds as though you read it." Shots now on the TV of the mayor of New York, then shots of bag ladies in the streets.

Earl was silent. I decided not to get ahead of him again. "I thought that maybe I shouldn't read it, but then I did."

"How much?"

"All of it," he said. "I read all of it."

I waited. He had called *me*. I hadn't called him. I watched the pictures of Gorbachev, then pictures of a girl whose face had been slashed by an ex-boyfriend. "It must be hard, reading your daughter's diary," I said. "And not *right,* if you see what I mean."

"Not the way you think." He took a deep breath. "I don't mind the talk about boys. She's growing up, and you can wish it won't happen, but it does. You know what I'm saying?"

"Yes, I do, Earl." A commercial now, for Toyotas.

"I don't even mind the sex, how she thinks about it. Hey, I was no priest myself when I was that age, and now the women, they want to have the freedom we had, so how am I going to stop it, and maybe why should I?"

"I see what you mean."

"She's very aggressive. *Very* aggressive. The things she does. You sort of wonder if you should believe it."

"Diaries are often fantasies. You probably shouldn't be reading your daughter's diary at all. It's *hers,* Earl. She's writing for herself, not for you."

"She writes about me, sometimes."

"You shouldn't read it, Earl."

Now pictures of a nuclear reactor, and shots of men in white outer-space protective suits with lead shielding, cleaning up some new mess. I felt my anger rising, as usual.

"I can't help reading it," Earl said. "A person starts prying, he can't stop."

"You shouldn't be reading it."

"You haven't heard what I'm about to say," Earl told me. "It's why I'm calling you. It's what she says."

"What's that?" I asked him.

"Not what I expected," he said. "She pities me."

"Well," I said. More shots of the nuclear reactor. I was getting an idea.

"Well is right." He took another breath. "First she says she loves me. That was shock number one. Then she says she feels sorry for me. That was shock number two. Because I work on the line at Ford's and I drink beer and I live in Westland. Where does she get off? That's what I'd like to know. She mentions the play structure. She feels *sorry* for me! My God, I always hated pity. I could never stand it. It weakens you. I never wanted anybody on earth pitying me, and now here's my punk daughter doing it."

"Earl, put that diary away."

"I hear you," he said. "By the way, what did you do with that gun?"

"Threw it off the Belle Isle Bridge," I said.

"Sure you did," he said. "Well, anyway, thanks for listening, Warren." Then he hung up. On the screen in front of me, the newscaster was introducing the last news story of the evening.

Most landscapes, no matter where you are, manage to keep something wild about them, but the land in southern Michigan along the Ohio border has always looked to me as if it had lost its self-respect some time ago. This goes beyond being tamed. This land has been beaten up. The industrial brass knuckles have been applied to wipe out the trees, and the corporate blackjack has stunned the soil, and what grows there—the grasses and brush and scrub pine—grows tentatively. The plant life looks scared and defeated, but all the other earthly powers are busily at work.

Such were my thoughts as I drove down to the nuclear reactor in Holbein, Michigan, on a clear Saturday morning in August, my loaded gun under my seat. I was in a merry mood. Recently activated madcap joy brayed and sang inside my head. I was speeding. My car was trembling because the front end was improperly aligned and I was doing about seventy-five. One false move on the steering wheel and I'd be perma-

nently combined with a telephone pole. I had an eye out for the constables but knew I would not be arrested. A magic shield surrounded my
car, and I was so invincible that Martians could not have stopped me.

Although this was therapy rather than political action, I was taking it
very seriously, especially at the moment when my car rose over the hum-
ble crest of a humiliated grassy hill and I saw the infernal dome and cooling towers of the Holbein reactor a mile or so behind a clutch of hills and
trees ahead and to my left. The power company had surrounded all this
land with high Cyclone fencing, crowned with barbed wire and that new
kind of coiled lacerating razor wire they've invented. I slowed down to
see the place better.

There wasn't much to see because they didn't want you to see anything; they'd built the reactor far back from the road, and in this one case
they had let the trees grow (the usual demoralized silver maples and wil-
lows and jack pines) to hide the view. I drove past the main gate and
noted that a sign outside the guards' office regretted that the company
could not give tours because of the danger of sabotage. Right. I hadn't
expected to get inside. A person doesn't always have to get inside.

About one mile down, the fence took a ninety-degree turn to the left,
and a smaller county road angled off from the highway I was on. I
turned. I followed this road another half mile until there was a break in
the trees and I could get a clear view of the building. I didn't want a window. I wanted a wall. I was sweating like an amateur thief. The back of
my shirt was stuck to the car seat, and the car was jerking because my
foot was trembling with excited shock on the accelerator.

Through the thin trees, I saw the solid wall of the south building,
whatever it held. There's a kind of architecture that makes you ashamed
of human beings, and in my generic rage, my secret craziness that felt
completely sensible, I took the gun and held my arm out of the window.
It felt good to do that. I was John Wayne. I fired four times at that building, once for me, once for Ann, and once for each of my two boys. I
don't know what I hit. I don't care. I probably hit that wall. It was the
only kind of heroism I could imagine, the Don Quixote kind. But I
hadn't fired the gun before and wasn't used to the recoil action, with the
result that after the last shot, I lost control of the car, and it went off the
road. In any other state my car would have flipped, but this is southern
Michigan, where the ditches are shallow, and I was bumped around—in
my excitement I had forgotten to wear my seat belt—until the engine

finally stalled in something that looked like a narrow offroad parking area.

I opened my door, but instead of standing up I fell out. With my head on the ground I opened my eyes, and there in the stones and pebbles in front of me was a shiny penny. I brought myself to a standing position, picked up the penny, a lucky penny, for my purposes, and surveyed the landscape where my car had stopped. I walked around to the other side of the car and saw a small pile of beer cans and a circle of ashes, where some revelers, sometime this summer, had enjoyed their little party of pleasure there in the darkness, close by the inaudible hum of the Holbein reactor. I dropped the penny in my trouser pocket, put the gun underneath the front seat again, and started the car. After two tries I got it out, and before the constables came to check on the gunshots, I had made my escape.

I felt I had done something in the spirit of Westland. I sang, feeling very good and oddly patriotic. On the way back I found myself behind a car with a green bumper sticker.

CAUTION: THIS VEHICLE
EXPLODES UPON IMPACT!

That's me, I said to myself. I am that vehicle.

There was still the matter of the gun, and what to do with it. Fun is fun, but you have to know when the party's over. Halfway home, I pulled off the road into one of those rest stops, and I was going to discard the gun by leaving it on top of a picnic table or by dropping it into a trash can. What I actually did was to throw it into the high grass. Half an hour later, I walked into our suburban kitchen with a smile on my face. I explained the scratch on my cheek as the result of an accident while playing racquetball at the health club. Ann and the boys were delighted by my mood. That evening we went out to a park and, sitting on a blanket, ate our picnic dinner until the darkness came on.

Many of the American stories I was assigned to read in college were about anger, a fact that would not have surprised my mother, who was British, from Brighton. "Warren," she used to say to me, "watch your tongue in front of these people." "These people" always meant "these

Americans." Among them was my father, who had been born in Omaha and who had married her after the war. "Your father," my mother said, "has the temper of a savage." Although it is true that my mind has retained memories of household shouting, what I now find queer is that my mother thought that anger was peculiar to this country.

Earl called me a few more times, in irate puzzlement over his life. The last time was at the end of the summer, on Labor Day. Usually Ann and I and the boys go out on Labor Day to a Metropark and take the last long swim of the summer, but this particular day was cloudy, with a forecast for rain. Ann and I had decided to pitch a tent on the back lawn for the boys, and to grill some hot dogs and hamburgers. We were hoping that the weather would hold until evening. What we got was drizzle, off and on, so that you couldn't determine what kind of day it was. I resolved to go out and cook in the rain anyway. I often took the weather personally. I was standing there, grim-faced and wet, firing up the coals, when Ann called me to the telephone.

It was Earl. He apologized for bringing me to the phone on Labor Day. I said it was okay, that I didn't mind, although I *did* mind, in fact. We waited. I thought he was going to tell me something new about his daughter, and I was straining for him not to say it.

"So," he said, "have you been watching?"

"Watching what? The weather? Yes, I've been watching that."

"No," he said, "not the sky. The Jerry Lewis Telethon."

"Oh, the telethon," I said. "No, I don't watch it."

"It's important, Warren. We need all the money we can get. We're behind this year. You know how it's for Jerry's kids."

"I know it, Earl." Years ago, when I was a bachelor, once or twice I sat inside drinking all weekend and watching the telethon and making drunken pledges of money. I didn't want to remember such entertainment now.

"If we're going to find a cure for this thing, we need for everybody to contribute. It's for the kids."

"Earl," I said, "they won't find a cure. It's a genetic disorder, some scrambling in the genetic code. They might be able to prevent it, but they won't *cure* it."

There was a long silence. "You weren't born in this country, were you?"

"No," I said.

"I didn't think so. You don't sound like it. I can tell you weren't born here. At heart you're still a foreigner. You have a no-can-do attitude. No offense. I'm not criticizing you for it. It's not your fault. You can't help it. I see that now."

"Okay, Earl."

Then his voice brightened up. "What the hell," he said. "Come out anyway. You know where Westland is? Oh, right, you've been here. You know where the shopping center's located?"

"Yes," I said.

"It's the clown races. We're raising money. Even if you don't believe in the cure, you can still come to the clown races. We're giving away balloons, too. Your kids will enjoy it. Bring 'em along. *They'll* love it. It's quite a show. It's all on TV."

"Earl," I said, "this isn't my idea of what a person should be doing on a holiday. I'd rather—"

"I don't want to hear what you'd rather do. Just come out here and bring your money. All right?" He raised his voice after a quick pause. "Are you listening?"

"Yes, Earl," I said. "I'm listening."


Somehow I put out the charcoal fire and managed to convince my two boys and my wife that they should take a quick jaunt to Westland. I told them about Earl, the clown races, but what finally persuaded the boys was that I claimed there'd be a remote TV unit out there, and they might turn up with their faces on Channel 2. Besides, the rain was coming down a little harder, a cool rain, one of those end-of-summer drizzles that make your skin feel the onset of autumn. When you feel like that, it helps to be in a crowd.

They had set up a series of highway detours around the shopping center, but we finally discovered how to get into the north parking lot. They'd produced the balloons, tents, and lights, but they hadn't produced much of a crowd. They had a local TV personality dressed in a LOVE NETWORK raincoat trying to get people to cheer. The idea was, you made a bet for your favorite clown and put your money in his fishbowl. If your clown won, you'd get a certificate for a free cola at a local restaurant. It wasn't much of a prize, I thought; maybe it *was* charity, but I felt that they could do better than that.

Earl was clown number three. We'd brought three umbrellas and were standing off to the side when he came up to us and introduced himself to my wife and the boys. He was wearing an orange wig and a clown nose, and he had painted his face white, the way clowns do, and he was wearing Bozo shoes, the size eighteens, but one of his sleeves was rolled up, and you could see the tattoo of that impaled rose. The white paint was running off his face a bit in the rain, streaking, but he didn't seem to mind. He shook hands with my children and Ann and me very formally. He had less natural ability as a clown than anyone else I've ever met. It would never occur to you to laugh at Earl dressed up in that suit. What you felt would be much more complicated. It was like watching a family member descend into a weakness like alcoholism. Earl caught the look on my face.

"What's the matter, Warren?" he asked. "You okay?"

I shrugged. He had his hand in a big clown glove and was shaking my hand.

"It's all for a good cause," he said, waving his other hand at the four lanes they had painted on the parking lot for the races. "We've made a lot of money already. It's all for the kids, kids who aren't as lucky as ours." He looked down at my boys. "You have to believe," he said.

"You sound like Jaynee," I told him. My wife was looking at Earl. I had tried to explain him to her, but I wasn't sure I had succeeded.

"Believe what?" she asked.

"You've been married to this guy for too long," he said, laughing his big clown laugh. "Maybe your kids can explain it to you, about what the world needs now." There was a whistle. Earl turned around. "Gotta go," he said. He flopped off in those big shoes.

"What's he talking about?" my wife asked.

They lined up the four clowns, including Earl, at the chalk, and those of us who were spectators stood under the tent and registered our bets while the LOVE NETWORK announcer from Channel 2 stood in front of the cameras and held up his starter's gun. I stared for a long time at that gun. Then I placed my bet on Earl.

The other three clowns were all fat middle-aged guys, Shriners or Rotarians, and I thought Earl had a good chance. My gaze went from the gun down to the parking lot, where I saw Jaynee. She was standing in the rain and watching her old man. I heard the gun go off, but instead of watching Earl, I watched her.

Her hair was stuck to the sides of her head in that rain, and her cotton jacket was soaked through. She had her eyes fixed on her father. By God, she looked affectionate. If he wanted his daughter's love, he had it. I watched her clench her fists and start to jump up and down, cheering him on. After twenty seconds I could tell by the way she raised her fist in the air that Earl had clumped his way to victory. Then I saw the new woman, Jody, standing behind Jaynee, her big glasses smeared with rain, grinning.

I looked around the parking lot and thought: Everyone here understands what's going on better than I do. But then I remembered that I had fired shots at a nuclear reactor. All the desperate remedies. And I remembered my mother's first sentence to me when we arrived in New York harbor when I was ten years old. She pointed down from the ship at the pier, at the crowds, and she said, "Warren, look at all those Americans." I felt then that if I looked at that crowd for too long, something inside my body would explode, not metaphorically but literally: it would blow a hole through my skin, through my chest cavity. And it came back to me in that shopping center parking lot, full of those LOVE NETWORK people, that feeling of pressure of American crowds and exuberance.

We collected our free cola certificates, and then I hustled my wife and kids back into the car. I'd had enough. We drove out of the Westland parking lot, then were directed by a detour sign into a service drive that circled the entire shopping center and reentered the lot on the north side, back at the clown races. I saw Jaynee again, still in the rain, hugging her American dad, and Jody holding on to his elbow, looking up at him, pressing her thigh against his. I took another exit out of the lot but somehow made the same mistake I had made before and, once again, found myself back in Westland. Every service drive seemed designed to bring us back to this same scene of father, daughter, and second wife. I gave them credit for who they were and what they were doing—I give them credit now—but I had to get out of there immediately. I don't know how I managed to get out of that place, but on the fourth try I succeeded.

# Shelter

COOPER HAD STOPPED at a red light on his way to work and was adjusting the dial on his radio when he looked up and saw a man in a filthy brown corduroy suit and a three-day growth of beard staring in through the front windshield and picking with his fingernails at Cooper's windshield wiper. Whenever Cooper had seen this man before, on various Ann Arbor street corners, he had felt a wave of uneasiness and unpleasant compassion. Rolling down the window and leaning out, Cooper said, "Wait a minute there. Just wait a minute. If you get out of this intersection and over to that sidewalk, I'll be with you in a minute"—the man stared at him—"*I'll have something for you.*"

Cooper parked his car at a meter two blocks up, and when he returned, the man in the corduroy suit was standing under a silver maple tree, rubbing his back against the bark.

"Didn't think you'd come back," the man said, glancing at Cooper. His hair fell over the top of his head in every direction.

"How do you do?" Cooper held his hand out, but the man—who seemed rather old, close up—didn't take it. "I'm Cooper." The man smelled of everything, a bit like a municipal dump. Cooper tried not to notice it.

"It doesn't matter who I am," the man said, standing unsteadily. "I don't care who I am. It's not worth anybody thinking about it." He looked up at the sky and began to pick at his coat sleeve.

"What's your name?" Cooper asked softly. "Tell me your name, please."

The old man's expression changed. He stared at the blue sky, perfectly empty of clouds, and after a moment said, "My mother used to call me James."

"Good. Well, then, how do you do, James?" The man looked dubiously at his own hand, then reached over and shook. "Would you like something to eat?"

"I like sandwiches," the man said.

"Well, then," Cooper said, "that's what we'll get you."

As they went down the sidewalk, the man stumbled into the side of a bench at a bus stop and almost tripped over a fire hydrant. He had a splay-footed walk, as if one of his legs had once been broken. Cooper began to pilot him by touching him on his back.

"Would you like to hear a bit of the Gospels?" the man asked.

"All right. Sure."

He stopped and held on to a light pole. "This is the fourth book of the Gospels. Jesus is speaking. He says, 'I will not leave you desolate; I will come to you. Yet a little while, and the world will see me no more, but you will see me; because I live, you will live also.' That's from John," the man said. They were outside the Ann Arbor Diner, a neon-and-chrome Art Deco hamburger joint three blocks down from the university campus. "There's more," the old man said, "but I don't remember it."

"Wait here," Cooper said. "I'm going to get you a sandwich."

The man was looking uncertainly at his lapel, fingering a funguslike spot.

"James!" Cooper said loudly. "Promise me you won't go away!"

The man nodded.

When Cooper came out again with a bag of french fries, a carton of milk, and a hamburger, the man had moved down the street and was leaning against the plate-glass window of a seafood restaurant with his hands covering his face. "James!" Cooper said. "Here's your meal." He held out the bag.

"Thank you." When the man removed his hands from his face, Cooper saw in his eyes a moment of complete lucidity and sanity, a glance that took in the street and himself, made a judgment about them all, and quickly withdrew from any engagement with them. He took the hamburger out of its wrapping, studied it for a moment, and then bit into it. As he ate, he gazed toward the horizon.

"I have to go to work now," Cooper said.

The man glanced at him, nodded again, and turned his face away.


"What are we going to do?" Cooper said to his wife. They were lying in bed at sunrise, when they liked to talk. His hand was on her thigh and was caressing it absently and familiarly. "What are we going to do about these characters? They're on the street corners. Every month there are more of them. Kids, men, women, everybody. It's a horde. They're sleeping in the arcade, and they're pushing those terrible grocery carts around with all their worldly belongings, and it makes me nuts to watch them. I don't know what I'm going to do, Christine, but whatever it is, I have to do it." With his other hand, he rubbed his eyes. "I dream about them."

"You're such a good person," she said sleepily. Her hand brushed over him. "I've noticed that about you."

"No, that's wrong," Cooper said. "This has nothing to do with good. Virtue doesn't interest me. What this is about is not feeling crazy when I see those people."

"So what's your plan?"

He rose halfway out of bed and looked out the back window at the tree house he had started for Alexander, their seven-year-old. Dawn was breaking, and the light came in through the slats of the blinds and fell in strips over him.

When he didn't say anything, she said, "I was just thinking. When I first met you, before you dropped out of law school, you always used to have your shirts laundered, with starch, and I remember the neat creases in your trouser legs, from somebody ironing them. You smelled of aftershave in those days. Sexually, you were ambitious. You took notes slowly. Fastidious penmanship. I like you better now."

"I remember," he said. "It was a lecture on proximate cause."

"No," she said. "It was contribution and indemnification."

"Whatever."

He took her hand and led her to the bathroom. Every morning Cooper and his wife showered together. He called it soul-showering. He had picked up the phrase from a previous girlfriend, though he had never told Christine that. Cooper had told his wife that by the time they were thirty they would probably not want to do this anymore, but they were both now thirty-one, and she still seemed to like it.

Under the sputter of the water, Christine brushed some soap out of her eyes and said, "Cooper, were you ever a street person?"

"No."

"Smoke a lot of dope in high school?"

"No."

"I bet you drank a lot once." She was an assistant prosecutor in the district attorney's office and sometimes brought her professional habits home. "You tapped kegs and lay out on the lawns and howled at the sorority girls."

"Sometimes I did that," he said. He was soaping her back. She had wide, flaring shoulders from all the swimming she had done, and the soap and water flowed down toward her waist in a pattern of V's. "I did all those things," he said, "but I never became that kind of person. What's your point?"

She turned around and faced him, the full display of her smile. "I think you're a latent vagrant," she said.

"But I'm not," he said. "I'm here. I have a job. *This* is where I am. I'm a father. How can you say that?"

"Do I love you?" she asked, water pouring over her face. "Stay with me."

"Well, sure," he said. "That's my plan."

The second one he decided to do something about was standing out of the hot summer sun in the shade of a large catalpa tree near a corner newsstand. This one was holding what seemed to be a laundry sack with the words AMERICAN LINEN SUPPLY stenciled on it. She was wearing light summer clothes—a Hawaiian shirt showing a palm tree against a bloody splash of sunset, and a pair of light cotton trousers, and red Converse tennis shoes—and she stood reading a paperback, beads of sweat falling off her face onto the pages.

This time Cooper went first to a fast-food restaurant, bought the hamburger, french fries, and milk, and then came back.

"I brought something for you," Cooper said, walking to the reading woman. "I brought you some lunch." He held out a bag. "I've seen you out here on the streets many times."

"Thank you," the woman said, taking the bag. She opened it, looked inside, and sniffed appreciatively.

"Are you homeless?" Cooper asked.

"They have a place where you can go," the woman said. She put down the bag and looked at Cooper. "My name's Estelle," she said. "But we don't have to talk."

"Oh, that's all right. If you want. Where's this shelter?"

"Over there." The woman gestured with a french fry she had picked out. She lifted the bag and began to eat. Cooper looked down at the book and saw that it was in a foreign language. The cover had fallen off. He asked her about it.

"Oh, that?" she said. She spoke with her mouth full of food, and Cooper felt a moment of superiority about her bad manners. "It's about women—what happens to women in this world. It's in French. I used to be Canadian. My mother taught me French."

Cooper stood uncomfortably. He took a key ring out of his pocket and twirled it around his index finger. "So what happens to women in this world?"

"What *doesn't*?" the woman said. "Everything happens. It's terrible but sometimes it's all right, and, besides, you get used to it."

"You seem so normal," Cooper said. "How come you're out here?"

The woman straightened up and looked at him. "My mind's not quite right," she said, scratching an eyelid. "Mostly it is but sometimes it isn't. They messed up my medication and one thing led to another and here I am. I'm not complaining. I don't have a bad life."

Cooper wanted to say that she *did* have a bad life, but stopped himself.

"If you want to help people," the woman said, "you should go to the shelter. They need volunteers. People to clean up. You could get rid of your guilt over there, mopping the floors."

"What guilt?" he asked.

"All men are guilty," she said. She was chewing but had put her bag of food on the ground and was staring hard and directly into Cooper's face. He turned toward the street. When he looked at the cars, everyone heading somewhere with a kind of fierce intentionality, braking hard at red lights and peeling rubber at the green, he felt as though he had been pushed out of his own life.

"You're still here," the woman said. "What do you want?"

"I was about to leave." He was surprised by how rude she was.

"I don't think you've ever seen the Rocky Mountains or even the Swiss Alps, for that matter," the woman said, bending down to inspect something close to the sidewalk.

"No, you're right. I haven't traveled much."

"We're not going to kiss, if that's what you think," the woman said, still bent over. Now she straightened up again, glanced at him, and looked away.

"No," Cooper said. "I just wanted to give you a meal."

"Yes, thank you," the woman said. "And now you have to go."

"I was . . . I *was* going to go."

"I don't want to talk to you anymore," the woman said. "It's nothing against you personally, but talking to men just tires me out terribly and drains me of all my strength. Thank you very much, and good-bye." She sat down again and opened up her paperback. She took some more french fries out of the sack and began to eat as she read.


"They're polite," Cooper said, lying next to his wife. "They're polite, but they aren't nice."

"Nice? Nice? Jesus, Cooper, I prosecute rapists! Why should they be nice? They'd be crazy to be nice. Who cares about nice except you? This is the 1980s, Cooper. Get real."

He rolled over in bed and put his hand on her hip. "All right," he said.

They lay together for a while, listening to Alexander snoring in his bedroom across the hall.

"I can't sleep, Cooper," she said. "Tell me a story."

"Which one tonight?" Cooper was a good improviser of stories to help his wife relax and doze off. "Hannah, the snoopy cleaning woman?"

"No," Christine said. "I'm tired of Hannah."

"The adventures of Roderick, insurance adjuster?"

"I'm sick of him, too."

"How about another boring day in Paradise?"

"Yeah. Do that."

For the next twenty minutes, Cooper described the beauty and tedium of Paradise—the perfect rainfalls, the parks with roped-off grassy areas, the sideshows and hot-air-balloon rides, the soufflés that never fell—and in twenty minutes, Christine was asleep, her fingers touching him. He was aroused. "Christine?" he whispered. But she was sleeping.


The next morning, as Cooper worked at his baker's bench, rolling chocolate-almond croissants, he decided that he would check out the shelter in the afternoon to see if they needed any help. He looked up from his hands, with a trace of dough and sugar under the fingernails, over toward his boss, Gilbert, who was brewing coffee and humming along to some Coltrane coming out of his old radio perched on top of the mixer. Cooper loved the bakery where he worked. He loved the smell and everything they made there. He had noticed that bread made people unusually happy. Customers closed their eyes when they ate Cooper's doughnuts and croissants and Danishes. He looked up toward the skylight and saw that the sky had turned from pale blue to dark blue, what the Crayola 64 box called blue-indigo. He could tell from the tint of the sky that it was seven o'clock, time to unlock the front doors to let in the first of the customers. After Gilbert turned the key and the mechanics from down the street shuffled in to get their morning doughnuts and coffee in Styrofoam cups, Cooper stood behind the counter in his whites and watched their faces, the slow private smiles that always registered when they first caught the scent of the baked dough and the sugared fruit.


The shelter was in a downtown furniture store that had gone out of business during the recession of '79. To provide some privacy, the first volunteers had covered over the front plate-glass window with long strips of paper from giant rolls, with the result that during the daytime the light inside was colored an unusual tint, somewhere between orange and off-white. As soon as he volunteered, he was asked to do odd jobs. He first went to work in the evening ladling out food—stew, usually, with ice-cream-scoop mounds of mashed potatoes.

The director of the shelter was a brisk and slightly overweight woman named Marilyn Adams, who, though tough and efficient, seemed vaguely annoyed about everything. Cooper liked her officious irritability. He didn't want any baths of feeling in this place.

Around five o'clock on a Thursday afternoon—the bakery closed at four—Cooper was making beds near the front window when he heard a voice from behind him. "Hey," the voice said. "I want to get in here."

Cooper turned around. He saw the reddest person he had ever laid eyes on: the young man's hair was red, his face flamed with sunburn and freckles, and, as if to accentuate his skin and hair tone, he was wearing a bright pink Roxy Music T-shirt. He was standing near the window, with the light behind him, and all Cooper could see of him was a still, flat expression and deeply watchful eyes. When he turned, he had the concentrated otherworldliness of figures in religious paintings.

Cooper told the young man about the shelter's regulations and told him which bed he could have. The young man—he seemed almost a boy—stood listening, his right foot thumping against the floor and his right hand shaking in the air as if he were trying to get water off it. When the young man nodded, his head went up and down too fast, and Cooper thought he was being ironic. "Who are you?" he finally asked. "My name's Cooper."

"Billy Bell," the young man said. "That's a real weird name, isn't it?" He shook his head but didn't look at Cooper or wait for him to agree or disagree. "My mother threw me out last week. Why shouldn't she? She thought I was doing drugs. I wasn't doing drugs. Drugs are so boring. Look at those awful capitalist lizards using them and you'll know what I mean. But I *was* a problem. She was right. She had to get on my case. She decided to throw me away for a while. Trash trash. So I've been sleeping in alleys and benches and I slept for a couple of nights in the Arboretum, but there are too many mosquitoes this time of year for that and I've got bites. I was living with a girl but all my desires left me. You live here, Cooper? You homeless yourself, or what?"

"I'm a volunteer," he said. "I just work here. I've got a home."

"I don't," Billy Bell said. "People should have homes. I don't work now. I lost my job. I'm full of energy but I'm apathetic. Very little appeals to me. I guess I'm going to start some of those greasy minimum-wage things if I can stand them. I'm smart. I'm not a loser. I'm definitely not one of these messed-up ghouls who call this place home."

Cooper stood up and walked toward the kitchen, knowing that the young man would follow him. "They aren't ghouls," he said. "Look around. They're more normal than you are, probably. They're down on their luck."

"Of course they are, of course they are," Billy said, his voice floating a few inches behind Cooper's head. Cooper began to wipe off the kitchen counter, as the young man watched him. Then Billy began waving his right hand again. "My problem, Cooper, my problem is the problem of the month, which is pointlessness and the point of doing anything, which I can't see most of the time. I want to heal people but I can't do that. I'm stalled. What happened was, about a year ago, there was this day. I remember it was sunny, I mean the sun was out, and I heard these wings flapping over my head because I was out in the park with my girlfriend feeding Cheerios to the pigeons. Then this noise: *flap flap flap.* Wings, Cooper, *big* wings, taking my soul away. I didn't want to look behind me because I was afraid they'd taken my shadow, too. It could happen, Cooper, it could happen to anybody. Anyhow, after that, what I knew was, I didn't want what everybody else did, I mean I don't have any desires for anything, and at some times of day I *don't* cast a shadow. My desires just went away like that—poof, poor desires. I'm a saint now but I'm not enjoying it one bit. I can bless people but not heal them. Anybody could lose his soul the way I did. Now all I got is that sad robot feeling. You know, that five-o'clock feeling? But all day, with me."

"You mentioned your mother," Cooper said. He dropped some cleanser into the sink and began to scour. "What about your father?"

"Let me do that." Billy nudged Cooper aside and started to clean the sink with agitated, almost frantic hand motions. "I've done a *lot* of this. My father died last year. I did a lot of housecleaning. I'm a man-maid. My father was in the hospital, but we took him out, and I was trying to be, I don't know, a sophomore in college, which is a pretty dumb thing to aspire to, if you think about it. But I was also sitting by my father's bed and taking care of him—he had pancreatic cancer—and I was reading *Popular Mechanics* to him, the home-improvement section, and feeding him when he could eat, and then when he died, the wings flew over me, though that was later, and there wasn't much I wanted to do. What a sink."

As he talked, Billy's hand accelerated in its motions around the drain.

"Come on," Cooper said. "I'm going to take you somewhere."


His idea was to lift the young man's spirits, but he didn't know quite how to proceed. He took him to his car and drove him down the river road to a park, where Billy got out of the car, took his shoes off, and waded into the water. He bent down, and, as Cooper watched, cupped his hands in the river before splashing it over his face. Cooper thought his face had a strange expression, something between ecstasy and despair. He couldn't think of a word in English for this expression but thought there might be a word in another language for it. German, for example. When Billy was finished washing his face, he looked up into the sky. Pigeons and killdeer were flying overhead. After he had settled back into the front seat of Cooper's car, drops of water from his face dripping onto the seat, Billy said, "That's a good feeling, Cooper. You should try it. You wash your face in the flowing water and then you hear the cries of the birds. I'd like to think it makes me a new man but I know it doesn't. How old are you, Cooper?"

"I'm thirty-one."

"Seven years older than me. And what did you say you did?"

"I'll show you."

He drove Billy to the bakery and parked in the back alley. It was getting close to twilight. After Cooper had unlocked the back door, Billy walked into the dark bakery kitchen and began to sniff. "I like this place," he said. "I like it very much." He shook some invisible water off his hand, then ran his finger along the bench. "What's this made of?"

"Hardrock maple. It's like the wood they use in bowling alleys. Hardest wood there is. You can't dent it or break it. Look up."

Billy twisted backward. "A skylight," he said. "Cooper, your life is on the very top of the eggshell. You have grain from the earth and you have the sky overhead. Ever been broken into?"

"No."

Cooper looked at Billy and saw, returning to him, a steady gaze made out of the watchful and flat expression he had first seen on the young man's face when he had met him a few hours before. "No," he repeated, "never have." He felt, suddenly, that he had embarked all at once on a series of misjudgments. "What did your father do, Billy?"

"He was a surgeon," Billy said. "He did surgery on people."

They stood and studied each other in the dark bakery for a moment.

"We'll go one more place," Cooper said. "I'll get you a beer. Then I have to take you back to the shelter."

Cooper's dog, Hugo, came out through the backyard and jumped up on him as he got out of his car. A load of wash, mostly Alexander's shirts, flapped on the clothesline in the evening breeze. Cooper heard children calling from down the street.

"Here we are," Cooper said. "We'll go in through this door."

Inside the house, Christine was sitting at the dining-room table with two legal pads set up in front of her and a briefcase down by the floor. Behind her, in the living room, Alexander was lying on the floor in front of the TV set, his chin cupped in his hands. He was watching a Detroit

Tigers game. They both looked up when Cooper knocked on the kitchen doorframe and came into the hallway, followed by Billy, whose hands were in his pockets and who nodded as he walked.

"Christine," Cooper said. "This is Billy. I met him at the shelter." Billy walked quickly around the table and shook Christine's hand. "I brought him here for a beer."

Christine did not change her posture. Behind a smile, she gave Billy a hard look. "Hello," she said. "And welcome, I guess."

"Thank you," Billy said. Cooper went out to the kitchen, opened a beer, and brought it back to him. Billy looked at the bottle, then took a long swig from it. After wiping his mouth, he said, "Well, my goodness. I certainly never expected to be here in your home tonight."

"Well, we didn't expect you, either, Mr.—?"

"Bell," Billy said. "Billy Bell."

"We didn't expect you, either, Mr. Bell. You're lucky. My husband never does this." She looked now at Cooper. "He never *never* does this."

Cooper pointed toward the living room. "Billy, that's Alexander over there. He's in the Alan Trammell fan club. I guess you can tell."

Alexander turned around, looked at Billy, and said, "Hi," waving quickly. Billy returned the greeting, but Alexander had already returned to the TV set, now showing a commercial for shaving cream.

"So, Mr. Bell," Christine said. "What brings you to Ann Arbor?"

"Oh, I've always lived here," Billy said. "Graduated from Pioneer High and everything." He began a little jumping motion, then quelled it. "How about you?"

"Oh, not me," Christine said. "I'm from Dayton, Ohio. I came here to law school. That's where I met Cooper."

"I thought he was a baker."

"He is now. He dropped out of law school."

"You didn't drop out?" Billy glanced at Christine's legal pads. "You became a lawyer?"

"I became a prosecutor, yes, that's right. In the district attorney's office. That's what I do."

"Do you like it?" Cooper thought Billy was about to explode in some way; he was getting redder and redder.

"Oh, yes," Christine said. "I like it very much."

"Why?"

"Why?" She touched her face and her smile faded. "I came from a family of bullies, Mr. Bell. Three brothers. They tied me up and played tricks on me, and they did this for years. Little-boy criminals. Every promise they made to me, they broke. Then I discovered the law, when I grew up. It's about limits and enforced regulation and binding agreements. It's a net of words, Mr. Bell. Legal formulas for proscribing behavior. That's what the law is. Now I have a career of putting promise-breakers behind bars. That makes me happy. What makes you happy, Mr. Bell?"

Billy hopped once, then leaned against the counter. "I didn't have any dreams until today," he said, "but now I do, seeing your cute house and your cute family. Here's what I'd like to do. I want to be *just like all of you.* I'd put on a chef's hat and stand outside in my apron like one of those assholes you see in the Sunday magazine section with a spatula in his hand, and, like, I'll be flipping hamburgers and telling my kids to keep their hands out of the chive dip and go run in the sprinkler or do some shit like that. I'll belong to do-good groups like Save the Rainforests, and I'll ask my wife how she likes her meat, rare or well done, and she'll say well done with that pretty smile she has, and that's how I'll do it. A wonderful fucking barbecue, this is, with folding aluminum chairs and paper plates and ketchup all over the goddamn place. Oceans of vodka and floods of beer. Oh, and we've sprayed the yard with that big spray that kills anything that moves, and all the flies and mosquitoes and bunnies are dead at our feet. Talk about the good life. That has got to be it."

Alexander had turned around and was staring at Billy, and Christine's face had become masklike and rigid. "Finish your beer, Mr. Bell," she said. "I think you absolutely have to go now. Don't let's waste another minute. Finish the beer and back you go."

"Yes," he said, nodding and grinning.

"I suppose you think what you just said was funny," Cooper said, from where he was standing in the back of the kitchen.

"No," Billy said. "I can't be funny. I've tried often. It doesn't work. No gift for that."

"Have you been in prison, Mr. Bell?" Christine asked, looking down at her legal pad and writing something there.

"No," Billy said. "I have not."

"Oh good," Christine said. "I was afraid maybe you had been."

"Do you think that's what will become of me?" Billy asked. His voice had lowered from its previous manic delivery and become soft.

"Oh, who knows?" Christine said, running her hand through her hair. "It could happen, or maybe not."

"Because I think my life is out of my hands," Billy said. "I just don't think I have control over it any longer."

"Back you go," Christine said. "Good-bye. Fare thee well."

"Thank you," Billy said. "That was a nice blessing. And thank you for the beer. Good-bye, Alexander. It was nice meeting you."

"Nice to meet you," the boy said from the floor.

"Let's go," Cooper said, picking at Billy's elbow.

"Back I go," Billy said. "Fare thee well, Billy, good-bye and Godspeed. So long, Mr. Human Garbage. Okay, all right, yes, now I'm gone." He did a quick walk through the kitchen and let the screen door slam behind him. Christine gave Cooper a look, which he knew meant that she was preparing a speech for him, and then he followed Billy out to the car.

On the way to the shelter, Billy slouched down on the passenger side. He said nothing for five minutes. Then he said, "I noticed something about your house, Cooper. I noticed that in the kitchen there were all these glasses and cups and jars out on the counter, and the jars weren't labeled, not the way they usually label them, and so I looked inside one of them, one of those jars, and you know what I saw? I suppose you must know, because it's your kitchen."

"What?" Cooper asked.

"Pain," Billy said, looking straight ahead and nodding. "That jar was full of pain. I had to close the lid over it immediately. Now tell me something, because I don't have the answer to it. Why does a man like you, a baker, have a jar full of pain in his kitchen? Can you explain that?"

Out through the front windows, Cooper saw the reassuring lights of the city, the lamplights shining out through the front windows, and the streetlights beginning to go on. A few children were playing on the sidewalks, hopscotch and tag, and in the sky a vapor trail from a jet was beginning to dissolve into orange wisps. What was the price one paid for loving one's own life? He felt a tenderness toward existence and toward his own life, and felt guilty for that.

At the shelter, he let Billy out without saying good night. He watched the young man do his hop-and-skip walk toward the front door; then he put the car into gear and drove home. As he expected, Christine was waiting up for him and gave him a lecture, in bed, about guilty liberalism and bringing the slime element into your own home.

"That's an exaggeration," Cooper said. He was lying on his side of the bed, his hip touching hers. "That's not what he was. I'm not wrong. I'm not." He felt her lips descending over him and remembered how she always thought that his failures in judgment made him sensual.

Two days later he arrived at work before dawn and found Gilbert standing motionless in front of Cooper's own baker's bench. Cooper closed the door behind him and said, "Hey, Gilbert."

"It's all right," Gilbert said. "I already called the cops."

"What?"

Gilbert pointed. On the wood table were hundreds of pieces of broken glass from the scattered skylight in a slice-of-pie pattern, and, over the glass, a circle of dried blood the width of a teacup. Smaller dots of blood, like afterthoughts, were scattered around the bench and led across the floor to the cash register, which had been jimmied open. Cooper felt himself looking up. A bird of a type he couldn't identify was perched on the broken skylight.

"Two hundred dollars," Gilbert said, overpronouncing the words. "Somewhere somebody's all cut up for a lousy two hundred dollars. I'd give the son of a bitch a hundred not to break in, if he'd asked. But you know what I really mind?"

"The blood," Cooper said.

"Bingo." Gilbert nodded, as he coughed. "I hate the idea of this guy's blood in my kitchen, on the floor, on the table and over there in the mixing pans. I really hate it. A bakery. What a fucking stupid place to break into."

"I told you so," Christine said, washing Cooper's face. Then she turned him around and ran the soapy washcloth down his back and over his buttocks.

August. Three days before Christine's birthday. Cooper and his son were walking down Main Street toward a store called the Peaceable Kingdom to get Christine a present, a small stuffed pheasant that Alexander had had his eye on for many months. Alexander's hand was in Cooper's as they crossed at the corner, after waiting for the WALK sign to go on. Alexander had been asking Cooper for an exact definition of trolls, and how they differ from ghouls. And what, he wanted to know, *what exactly* is a goblin, and how are they born? In forests? Can they be born anywhere, like trolls?

Up ahead, squatting against the window of a sporting-goods store, was the man perpetually dressed in the filthy brown corduroy suit: James. His hands were woven together at his forehead, thumbs at temples, to shade his eyes against the sun. As Cooper and his son passed by, James spoke up. He did not ask for money. He said, "Hello, Cooper."

"Hello, James," Cooper said.

"Is this your boy?" He pulled his hands apart and pointed at Alexander.

"Yes."

"Daddy," Alexander said, tugging at his father's hand.

"A fine boy," James said, squinting. "Looks a bit like you." The old man smelled as he had before: like a city dump, like everything.

"Thank you," Cooper said, beaming. "He's a handsome boy, isn't he?"

"Indeed," James said. "Would you like to hear a bit of the Gospels?"

"No, thank you, James," Cooper said. "We're on our way to get this young man's mother a birthday present."

"Well, I won't keep you," the old man said.

As Cooper reached for his wallet, Alexander suddenly spoke: "Daddy, don't."

"What?"

"Don't give him any money," the boy said.

"Why not?"

Alexander couldn't say. He began to shake his head, looking at James, then at his father. He backed away, down the sidewalk, his lower lip beginning to stick out and his eyes starting to grow wet.

"Here, James," Cooper said, watching his son, who had retreated down the block and was hiding in the doorway of a hardware store. He handed the old man five dollars.

"Bless you," James said. "And bless Jesus." He put the money in his pocket, then placed his hands together in front of his chest, lowered himself to his knees, and began to pray.

"Good-bye, James," Cooper said. With his eyes closed, James nodded. Cooper ran down the block to catch up with his son.

After Alexander had finished crying, he told his father that he was afraid—afraid that he was going to bring that dirty man home, the way he did with the red-haired guy, and let him stay, maybe in the basement, in the extra room.

"I wouldn't do that," Cooper said. "Really. I wouldn't do that."

"Wouldn't you?" his wife asked, that night, in bed. "Wouldn't you? I think you might."

"No. Not home. Not again."

But he had been accused, and he rose up and walked down the hall to his son's room. The house was theirs, no one else's; his footsteps were the only audible ones. In Alexander's room, in the dim illumination spread by the Swiss-chalet night-light, Cooper saw his son's model airplanes and the posters of his baseball heroes, but in looking around the room, he felt that something was missing. He glanced again at his son's dresser. The piggy bank, stuffed with pennies, was gone.

He's frightened of my charity, Cooper thought, looking under the bed and seeing the piggy bank there, next to Alexander's favorite softball.

Cooper returned to bed. "He's hidden his money from me," he said.

"They do that, you know," Christine said. "And they go on doing that."

"You can't sleep," Cooper said, touching his wife.

"No," she said. "But it's all right."

"I can't tell you about Paradise," Cooper told her. "I gave you all the stories I knew."

"Well, what *do* you want?" she asked.

He put his hands over hers. "Shelter me," he said.

"Oh, Cooper," she said. "Which way this time? Which way?"

To answer her, he rolled over, and, as quietly as he could, so as not to wake their son in the next room, he took her into his arms and held her there.

# Snow

---

TWELVE YEARS OLD, and I was so bored I was combing my hair just for the hell of it. This particular Saturday afternoon, time was stretching out unpleasantly in front of me. I held the comb under the tap and then stared into the bathroom mirror as I raked the wave at the front of my scalp upward so that it would look casual and sharp and perfect. For inspiration I had my transistor radio, balanced on the doorknob, tuned to an AM Top 40 station. But the music was making me jumpy, and instead of looking casual my hair, soaking wet, had the metallic curve of the rear fins of a De Soto. I looked aerodynamic but not handsome. I dropped the comb into the sink and went down the hallway to my brother's room.

Ben was sitting at his desk, crumpling up papers and tossing them into a wastebasket near the window. He was a great shot, particularly when he was throwing away his homework. His stainless-steel sword, a souvenir of military school, was leaning against the bookcase, and I could see my pencil-thin reflection in it as I stood in his doorway. "Did you hear about the car?" Ben asked, not bothering to look at me. He was gazing through his window at Five Oaks Lake.

"What car?"

"The car that went through the ice two nights ago. Thursday. Look. You can see the pressure ridge near Eagle Island."

I couldn't see any pressure ridge; it was too far away. Cars belonging to ice fishermen were always breaking through the ice, but swallowing up a car was a slow process in January, though not in March or April, and the drivers usually got out safely. The clear lake ice reflected perfectly the flat gray sky this drought winter, and we could still see the spiky brown grass on our back lawn. It crackled and crunched whenever I walked on it.

"I don't see it," I said. "I can't see the hole. Where did you hear about this car? Did Pop tell you?"

"No," Ben said. "Other sources." Ben's sources, his network of friends and enemies, were always calling him on the telephone to tell him things. He basked in information. Now he gave me a quick glance. "Holy smoke," he said. "What did you do to your hair?"

"Nothing," I said. "I was just combing it."

"You look like that guy," he said. "The one in the movies."

"Which guy?"

"That Harvey guy."

"Jimmy Stewart?"

"Of course not," he said. "You know the one I mean. Everybody knows that guy. The Harvey guy." When I looked blank, he said, "Never mind. Let's go down to the lake and look at that car. You'd better tell them we're going." He gestured toward the other end of the house.

In the kitchen I informed my parents that I was headed somewhere with my brother, and my mother, chopping carrots for one of her stews, looked up at me and my hair. "Be back by five," she said. "Where did you say you were off to?"

"We're driving to Navarre," I said. "Ben has to get his skates sharpened."

My stepfather's eyebrows started to go up; he exchanged a glance with my mother—the usual pantomime of skepticism. I turned around and ran out of the kitchen before they could stop me. I put on my boots, overcoat, and gloves, and hurried outside to my brother's car. He was already inside. The motor roared.

The interior of the car smelled of gum, cigarettes, wet wool, analgesic balm, and aftershave. "What'd you tell them?" my brother asked.

"I said you were going to Navarre to get your skates sharpened."

He put the car into first gear, then sighed. "Why'd you do that? I have to explain everything to you. Number one: my skates aren't in the car. What if they ask to see them when we get home? I won't have them. That's a problem, isn't it? Number two: when you lie about being somewhere, you make sure you have a friend who's there who can say you *were* there, even if you weren't. Unfortunately, we don't have any friends in Navarre."

"Then we're safe," I said. "No one will say we *weren't* there."

He shook his head. Then he took off his glasses and examined them as if my odd ideas were visible right there on the frames. I was just doing my job, being his private fool, but I knew he liked me and liked to have me around. My unworldliness amused him; it gave him a chance to lecture me. But now, tired of wasting words on me, he turned on the radio. Pulling out onto the highway, he steered the car in his customary way. He had explained to me that only very old or very sick people actually grip steering wheels. You didn't have to hold the wheel to drive a car. Resting your arm over the top of the wheel gave a better appearance. You dangled your hand down, preferably with a cigarette in it, so that the car, the entire car, responded to the mere pressure of your wrist.

"Hey," I said. "Where are we going? This isn't the way to the lake."

"We're not going there first. We're going there second."

"Where are we going first?"

"We're going to Five Oaks. We're going to get Stephanie. Then we'll see the car."

"How come we're getting her?"

"Because she wants to see it. She's never seen a car underneath the ice before. She'll be impressed."

"Does she know we're coming?"

He gave me that look again. "What do they teach you at that school you go to? Of course she knows. We have a date."

"A date? It's three o'clock in the afternoon," I said. "You can't have a date at three in the afternoon. Besides, I'm along."

"Don't argue," Ben said. "Pay attention."

By the time we reached Five Oaks, the heater in my brother's car was blowing out warm air in tentative gusts. If we were going to get Stephanie, his current girlfriend, it was fine with me. I liked her smile— she had an overbite, the same as I did, but she didn't seem self-conscious about it—and I liked the way she shut her eyes when she laughed. She had listened to my crystal radio set and admired my collection of igneous rocks on one of her two visits to our house. My brother liked to bring his girlfriends over to our house because the house was old and large and, my brother said, they would be impressed by the empty rooms and the long hallways and the laundry chutes that dropped down into nowhere. They'd be snowed. Snowing girls was something I knew better than to ask my brother about. You had to learn about it by watching and listening. That's why he had brought me along.

Ben parked outside Stephanie's house and told me to wait in the car. I had nothing to do but look at houses and telephone poles. Stephanie's front-porch swing had rusted chains, and the paint around her house seemed to have blistered in cobweb patterns. One drab lamp with a low-wattage bulb was on near an upstairs window. I could see the lampshade: birds—I couldn't tell what kind—had been painted on it. I adjusted the dashboard clock. It didn't run, but I liked to have it seem accurate. My brother had said that anyone who invented a clock that would really work in a car would become a multimillionaire. Clocks in cars never work, he said, because the mainsprings can't stand the shock of potholes. I checked my wristwatch and yawned. The inside of the front window began to frost over with my breath. I decided that when I grew up I would invent a new kind of timepiece for cars, without springs or gears. At three twenty I adjusted the clock again. One minute later, my brother came out of the house with Stephanie. She saw me in the car, and she smiled.

I opened the door and got out. "Hi, Steph," I said. "I'll get in the backseat."

"That's okay, Russell," she said, smiling, showing her overbite. "Sit up in front with us."

"Really?"

She nodded. "Yeah. Keep us warm."

She scuttled in next to my brother, and I squeezed in on her right side, with my shoulder against the door. As soon as the car started, she and my brother began to hold hands: he steered with his left wrist over the steering wheel, and she held his right hand. I watched all this, and Stephanie noticed me watching. "Do you want one?" she asked me.

"What?"

"A hand." She gazed at me, perfectly serious. "My other hand."

"Sure," I said.

"Well, take my glove off," she said. "I can't do it by myself."

My brother started chuckling, but she stopped him with a look. I took Stephanie's wrist in my left hand and removed her glove, finger by finger. I hadn't held hands with anyone since second grade. Her hand was not much larger than mine, but holding it gave me an odd sensation, because it was a woman's hand, and where my fingers were bony, hers were soft. She was wearing a bright green cap, and when I glanced up at it she said, "I like your hair, Russell. It's kind of slummy. You're getting to look dangerous. Is there any gum?"

I figured she meant in the car. "There's some up there on the dashboard," Ben said. His car always had gum in it. It was a museum of gum. The ashtrays were full of cigarette butts and gum, mixed together, and the floor was flecked silver from the foil wrappers.

"I can't reach it," Stephanie said. "You two have both my hands tied down."

"Okay," I said. I reached up with my free hand and took a piece of gum and unwrapped it. The gum was light pink, a sunburn color.

"Now what?" I asked.

"What do you think?" She looked down at me, smiled again, then opened her mouth. I suddenly felt shy. "Come on, Russell," she said. "Haven't you ever given gum to a girl before?" I raised my hand with the gum in it. She kept her eyes open and on me. I reached forward, and just as I got the gum close to her mouth she opened wider, and I slid the gum in over her tongue without even brushing it against her lipstick. She closed and began chewing.

"Thank you," she said. Stephanie and my brother nudged each other. Then they broke out in short quick laughs—vacation laughter. I knew that what had happened hinged on my ignorance, but that I wasn't exactly the butt of the joke and could laugh, too, if I wanted. My palm was sweaty, and she could probably feel it. The sky had turned darker, and I wondered whether, if I was still alive fifty years from now, I would remember any of this. I saw an old house on the side of the highway with a cracked upstairs window, and I thought, That's what I'll remember from this whole day when I'm old—that one cracked window.

Stephanie was looking out at the dry winter fields and suddenly said, "The state of Michigan. You know who this state is for? You know who's really happy in this state?"

"No," I said. "Who?"

"Chickens and squirrels," she said. "They love it here."


My brother parked the car on the driveway down by our dock, and we walked out onto the ice on the bay. Stephanie was stepping awkwardly, a high-center-of-gravity shuffle. "Is it safe?" she asked.

"Sure, it's safe," my brother said. "Look." He began to jump up and down. Ben was heavy enough to be a tackle on his high-school football team, and sounds of ice cracking reverberated all through the bay and beyond into the center of the lake, a deep echo. Already, four ice fishermen's houses had been set up on the ice two hundred feet out—four brightly painted shacks, male hideaways—and I could see tire tracks over the thin layer of sprinkled snow. "Clear the snow and look down into it," he said.

After lowering herself to her knees, Stephanie dusted the snow away. She held her hands to the side of her head and looked. "It's real thick," she said. "Looks a foot thick. How come a car went through?"

"It went down in a channel," Ben said, walking ahead of us and calling backward so that his voice seemed to drift in and out of the wind. "It went over a pressure ridge, and that's all she wrote."

"Did anyone drown?"

He didn't answer. She ran ahead to catch up to him, slipping, losing her balance, then recovering it. In fact I knew that no one had drowned. My stepfather had told me that the man driving the car had somehow—I wasn't sure how a person did this—pulled himself out through the window. Apparently the front end dropped through the ice first, but the car had stayed up for a few minutes before it gradually eased itself into the lake. The last two nights had been very cold, with lows around fifteen below zero, and by now the hole the car had gone through had iced over.

Both my brother and Stephanie were quite far ahead of me, and I could see them clutching at each other, Stephanie leaning against him, and my brother trying out his military-school peacock walk. I attempted this walk for a moment, then thought better of it. The late-afternoon January light was getting very raw: the sun came out for a few seconds, lighting and coloring what there was, then disappeared again, closing up and leaving us in a kind of sour grayness. I wondered if my brother and Stephanie actually liked each other or whether they were friends because they had to be.

I ran to catch up to them. "We should have brought our skates," I said, but they weren't listening to me. Ben was pointing at some clear ice, and Stephanie was nodding.

"Quiet down," my brother said. "Quiet down and listen."

All three of us stood still. Some cloud or other was beginning to drop snow on us, and from the ice underneath our feet we heard a continual chinging and barking as it slowly shifted.

"This is exciting," Stephanie said.

My brother nodded, but instead of looking at her he turned slightly to glance at me. Our eyes met, and he smiled.

"It's over there," he said, after a moment. The index finger of his black leather glove pointed toward a spot in the channel between Eagle Island and Crane Island where the ice was ridged and unnaturally clear. "Come on," he said.

We walked. I was ready at any moment to throw myself flat if the ice broke beneath me. I was a good swimmer—Ben had taught me—but I wasn't sure how well I would swim wearing all my clothes. I was absorbent and would probably sink headfirst, like that car.

"Get down," my brother said.

We watched him lowering himself to his hands and knees, and we followed. This was probably something he had learned in military school, this crawling. "We're ambushing this car," Stephanie said, creeping in front of me.

"There it is," he said. He pointed down.

This new ice was so smooth that it reminded me of the thick glass in the Shedd Aquarium, in Chicago. But instead of seeing a loggerhead turtle or a barracuda I looked through the ice and saw this abandoned car, this two-door Impala. It was wonderful to see—white-painted steel filtered by ice and lake water—and I wanted to laugh out of sheer happiness at the craziness of it. Dimly lit but still visible through the murk, it sat down there, its huge trunk and the sloping fins just a bit green in the algae-colored light. This is a joke, I thought, a practical joke meant to confuse the fish. I could see the car well enough to notice its radio antenna, and the windshield wipers halfway up the front window, and I could see the chrome of the front grille reflecting the dull light that ebbed down to it from where we were lying on our stomachs, ten feet above it.

"That is one unhappy automobile," Stephanie said. "Did anyone get caught inside?"

"No," I said, because no one had, and then my brother said, "Maybe."

I looked at him quickly. As usual, he wasn't looking back at me. "They aren't sure yet," he said. "They won't be able to tell until they bring the tow truck out here and pull it up."

Stephanie said, "Well, either they know or they don't. Someone's down there or not, right?"

Ben shook his head. "Maybe they don't know. Maybe there's a dead body in the backseat of that car. Or in the trunk."

"Oh, no," she said. She began to edge backward.

"I was just fooling you," my brother said. "There's nobody down there."

"What?" She was behind the area where the ice was smooth, and she stood up.

"I was just teasing you," Ben said. "The guy that was in the car got out. He got out through the window."

"Why did you lie to me?" Stephanie asked. Her arms were crossed in front of her chest.

"I just wanted to give you a thrill," he said. He stood up and walked over to where she was standing. He put his arm around her.

"I don't mind normal," she said. "Something could be normal and I'd like that, too." She glanced at me. Then she whispered into my brother's ear for about fifteen seconds, which is a long time if you're watching. Ben nodded and bent forward and whispered something in return, but I swiveled and looked around the bay at all the houses on the shore, and the old amusement park in the distance. Lights were beginning to go on, and, as if that weren't enough, it was snowing. As far as I was concerned, all those houses were guilty, both the houses and the people in them. The whole state of Michigan was guilty—all the adults, anyway—and I wanted to see them locked up.

"Wait here," my brother said. He turned and went quickly off toward the shore of the bay.

"Where's he going?" I asked.

"He's going to get his car," she said.

"What for?"

"He's going to bring it out on the ice. Then he's going to drive me home across the lake."

"That's really stupid!" I said. "That's really one of the dumbest things I ever heard! You'll go through the ice, just like that car down there did."

"No, we won't," she said. "I know we won't."

"How do you know?"

"Your brother understands this lake," she said. "He knows where the pressure ridges are and everything. He just *knows*, Russell. You have to trust him. And he can always get off the ice if he thinks it's not safe. He can always find a road."

"Well, I'm not going with you," I said. She nodded. I looked at her, and I wondered if she might be crazed with the bad judgment my parents had told me all teenagers had. Bad judgment of this kind was starting to interest me; it was a powerful antidote for boredom, which seemed worse.

"You don't want to come?"

"No," I said. "I'll walk home." I gazed up the hill, and in the distance I could see the lights of our house, a twenty-minute walk across the bay.

"Okay," Stephanie said. "I didn't think you'd want to come along." We waited. "Russell, do you think your brother is interested in me?"

"I guess so," I said. I wasn't sure what she meant by "interested." Anybody interested him, up to a point. "He says he likes you."

"That's funny, because I feel like something in the Lost and Found," she said, scratching her boot into the ice. "You know, one of those gloves that don't match anything." She put her hand on my shoulder. "One glove. One left-hand glove, with the thumb missing."

I could hear Ben's car starting, and then I saw it heading down Gallagher's boat landing. I was glad he was driving out toward us, because I didn't want to talk to her this way anymore.

Stephanie was now watching my brother's car. His headlights were on. It was odd to see a car with headlights on out on the ice, where there was no road. I saw my brother accelerate and fishtail the car, then slam on the brakes and do a 360-degree spin. He floored it, revving the back wheels, which made a high, whining sound on the ice, like a buzz saw working through wood. He was having a thrill and soon would give Stephanie another thrill by driving her home across ice that might break at any time. Thrills did it, whatever it was. Thrills led to other thrills.

"Would you look at that," I said.

She turned. After a moment she made a little sound in her throat. I remember that sound. When I see her now, she still makes it—a sign of impatience or worry. After all, she didn't go through the ice in my brother's car on the way home. She and my brother didn't drown, together or separately. Stephanie had two marriages and several children. Recently, she and her second husband adopted a Korean baby. She has the complex dignity of many small-town people who do not resort to alcohol until well after night has fallen. She continues to live in Five

Oaks, Michigan, and she works behind the counter at the post office, where I buy stamps from her and gossip, holding up the line, trying to make her smile. She still has an overbite and she still laughs easily, despite the moody expression that comes over her when she relaxes. She has moved back to the same house she grew up in. Even now the exterior paint on that house blisters in cobweb patterns. I keep track of her. She and my brother certainly didn't get married; in fact, they broke up a few weeks after seeing the Chevrolet under ice.

"What are we doing out here?" Stephanie asked. I shook my head. "In the middle of winter, out here on this stupid lake? I'll tell you, Russell, I sure don't know. But I do know that your brother doesn't notice me enough, and I can't love him unless he notices me. You know your brother. You know what he pays attention to. What do I have to do to get him to notice me?"

I was twelve years old. I said, "Take off your shoes."

She stood there, thinking about what I had said, and then, quietly, she bent down and took off her boots, and, putting her hand on my shoulder to balance herself, she took off her brown loafers and her white socks. She stood there in front of me with her bare feet on the ice. I saw in the grayish January light that her toenails were painted. Bare feet with painted toenails on the ice—this was a desperate and beautiful sight, and I shivered and felt my fingers curling inside my gloves.

"How does it feel?" I asked.

"You'll know," she said. "You'll know in a few years."

My brother drove up close to us. He rolled down his window and opened the passenger-side door. He didn't say anything. I watched Stephanie get into the car, carrying her shoes and socks and boots, and then I waved good-bye to them before turning to walk back to our house. I heard the car heading north across the ice. My brother would be looking at Stephanie's bare feet on the floor of his car. He would probably not be saying anything just now.

When I reached our front lawn, I stood out in the dark and looked in through the kitchen window. My mother and stepfather were sitting at the kitchen counter; I couldn't be sure if they were speaking to each other, but then I saw my mother raise her arm in one of her can-you-believe-this gestures. I didn't want to go inside. I wanted to feel cold, so cold that the cold itself became permanently interesting. I took off my overcoat and my gloves. Tilting my head back, I felt some snow fall onto my face. I thought of the word "exposure" and of how once or twice a year deer hunters in the Upper Peninsula died of it, and I bent down and stuck my hand into the snow and frozen grass and held it there. The cold rose from my hand to my elbow, and when I had counted to forty and couldn't stand another second of it, I picked up my coat and gloves and walked into the bright heat of the front hallway.

# The Disappeared

WHAT HE FIRST NOTICED about Detroit and therefore America was the smell. Almost as soon as he walked off the plane, he caught it: an acrid odor of wood ash. The smell seemed to go through his nostrils and take up residence in his head. In Sweden, his own country, he associated this smell with autumn, and the first family fires of winter, the smoke chuffing out of chimneys and settling familiarly over the neighborhood. But here it was midsummer, and he couldn't see anything burning.

On the way in from the airport, with the windows of the cab open and hot stony summer air blowing over his face, he asked the driver about it.

"You're smelling Detroit," the driver said.

Anders, who spoke very precise school English, thought that perhaps he hadn't made himself understood. "No," he said. "I am sorry. I mean the burning smell. What is it?"

The cabdriver glanced in the rearview mirror. He was wearing a knitted beret, and his dreadlocks flapped in the breeze. "Where you from?"

"Sweden."

The driver nodded to himself. "Explains why," he said. The cab took a sharp right turn on the freeway and entered the Detroit city limits. The driver gestured with his left hand toward an electronic signboard, a small windowless factory at its base, and a clustered group of cramped clapboard houses nearby. When he gestured, the cab wobbled on the freeway. "Fires here most all the time," he said. "Day in and day out. You get so you don't notice. Or maybe you get so you do notice and you like it."

"I don't see any fires," Anders said.

"That's right."

Feeling that he was missing the point somehow, Anders decided to change the subject. "I see a saxophone and a baseball bat next to you," he said, in his best English. "Do you like to play baseball?"

"Not in this cab, I don't," the driver said quietly. "It's no game then, you understand?"

The young man sat back, feeling that he had been defeated by the American idiom in his first native encounter with it. An engineer, he was in Detroit to discuss his work in metal alloys that resist oxidation. The company that had invited him had suggested that he might agree to become a consultant on an exclusive contract, for what seemed to him an enormous, American-sized fee. But the money meant little to him. It was America he was curious about, attracted by, especially its colorful disorderliness.

Disorder, of which there was very little in Sweden, seemed sexy to him: the disorder of a disheveled woman who has rushed down two flights of stairs to offer a last long kiss. Anders was single, and before he left the country he hoped to sleep with an American woman in an American bed. It was his ambition. He wondered if the experience would have any distinction. He had an idea that he might be able to go home and tell one or two friends about it.

At the hotel, he was met by a representative of the automobile company, a gray-haired man with thick glasses who, to Anders's surprise, spoke rather good Swedish. Later that afternoon, and for the next two days, he was taken down silent carpeted hallways and shown into plush windowless rooms with recessed lighting. He showed them his slides and metal samples, cited chemical formulas, and made cost projections; he looked at the faces looking back at him. They were interested, friendly, but oddly blank, like faces he had seen in the military. He saw corridor after corridor. The building seemed more expressive than the people in it. The lighting was both bright and diffuse, and a low-frequency hum of power and secrecy seemed to flow out from the ventilators. Everyone complimented him on his English. A tall woman in a tailored suit, flashing him a secretive smile, asked him if he intended to stay in this country for long. Anders smiled, said that his plans on that particular point were open, and managed to work the name of his hotel into his conversation.

At the end of the third day, the division head once again shook Anders's hand in the foyer of the hotel lobby and said they'd be getting in touch with him very soon. Finally free, Anders stepped outside the hotel and sniffed the air. All the rooms he had been in since he had arrived had

had no windows, or windows so blocked by drapes or blinds that he couldn't see out.

He felt restless and excited, with three days free for sightseeing in a wide-open American city, not quite in the Wild West but close enough to it to suit him. He returned to his room and changed into a pair of jeans, a light cotton shirt, and a pair of running shoes. In the mirror, he thought he looked relaxed and handsome. His vanity amused him, but he felt lucky to look the way he did. Back out on the sidewalk, he asked the doorman which direction he would recommend for a walk.

The doorman, who had curly gray hair and sagging pouches under his eyes, removed his cap and rubbed his forehead. He did not look back at Anders. "You want my recommendation? Don't walk anywhere. I would not recommend a walk. Sit in the bar and watch the soaps." The doorman stared at a fire hydrant as he spoke.

"What about running?"

The doorman suddenly glanced at Anders, sizing him up. "It's a chance. You might be okay. But to be safe, stay inside. There's movies on the cable, you want them."

"Is there a park here?"

"Sure, there's parks. There's always parks. There's Belle Isle. You could go there. People do. I don't recommend it. Still and all you might enjoy it if you run fast enough. What're you planning to do?"

Anders shrugged. "Relax. See your city."

"You're seeing it," the doorman said. "Ain't nobody relaxed, seeing this place. Buy some postcards, you want sights. This place ain't built for tourists and amateurs."

Anders thought that perhaps he had misunderstood again and took a cab out to Belle Isle; as soon as he had entered the park, he saw a large municipal fountain and asked the cabbie to drop him off in front of it. On its rim, children were shouting and dangling their legs in the water. The ornamentation of the stone lions was both solemn and whimsical and reminded him of the forced humor of Danish public sculpture. Behind the fountain he saw families grouped in evening picnics on the grass, and many citizens, of various apparent ethnic types, running, bicycling, and walking. Anders liked the way Americans walked, a sort of busyness in their step, as if, having no particular goal, they still had an unconscious urgency to get somewhere, to seem purposeful.

He began to jog, and found himself passing a yacht club of some sort, and then a small zoo, and more landscaped areas where solitaries and couples sat on the grass listening to the evening baseball game on their radios. Other couples were stretched out by themselves, self-absorbed. The light had a bluish-gold quality. It looked like almost any city park to him, placid and decorative, a bit hushed.

He found his way to an old building with a concession stand inside. After admiring the building's fake Corinthian architecture, he bought a hot dog and a cola. Thinking himself disguised as a native—America was full of foreigners anyway—he walked to the west windows of the dining area to check on the unattached women. He wanted to praise, to an American, this evening, and this park.

There were several couples on this side of the room, and what seemed to be several unattached men and women standing near the open window and listening to their various earphones. One of these women, with her hair partially pinned up, was sipping a lemonade. She had just the right faraway look. Anders thought he recognized this look. It meant that she was in a kind of suspension, between engagements.

He put himself in her line of sight and said, in his heaviest accent, "A nice evening!"

"What?" She removed the earphones and looked at him. "What did you say?"

"I said the evening was beautiful." He tried to sound as foreign as he could, the way Germans in Sweden did. "I am a visitor here," he added quickly, "and not familiar with any of this." He motioned his arm to indicate the park.

"Not familiar?" she asked. "Not familiar with what?"

"Well, with this park. With the sky here. The people."

"Parks are the same everywhere," the woman said, leaning her hip against the wall. She looked at him with a vague interest. "The sky is the same. Only the people are different."

"Yes? How?"

"Where are you from?"

He explained, and she looked out the window toward the Canadian side of the Detroit River, at the city of Windsor. "That's Canada, you know," she said, pointing a finger at the river. "They make Canadian whiskey right over there." She pointed at some high buildings and what seemed to be a grain elevator. "I've never drunk the whiskey. They say it tastes of acid rain. I've never been to Canada. I mean, I've seen it, but I've never been there. If I can see it from here, why should I go there?"

"To be in Canada," Anders suggested. "Another country."

"But I'm *here*," she said suddenly, turning to him and looking at him directly. Her eyes were so dark they were almost colorless. "Why should I be anywhere else? Why are *you* here?"

"I came to Detroit for business," he said. "Now I'm sightseeing."

"Sightseeing?" She laughed out loud, and Anders saw her arch her back. Her breasts seemed to flare in front of him. Her body had distinct athletic lines. "No one sightsees here. Didn't anyone tell you?"

"Yes. The doorman at the hotel. He told me not to come."

"But you did. How did you get here?"

"I came by taxi."

"You're joking," she said. Then she reached out and put her hand momentarily on his shoulder. "You took a taxi to this park? How do you expect to get back to your hotel?"

"I suppose"—he shrugged—"I will get another taxi."

"Oh no you won't," she said, and Anders felt himself pleased that things were working out so well. He noticed again her pinned-up hair and its intense black. Her skin was deeply tanned or naturally dark, and he thought that she herself might be black or Hispanic, he didn't know which, being unpracticed in making such distinctions. Outside he saw fireflies. No one had ever mentioned fireflies in Detroit. Night was coming on. He gazed up at the sky. Same stars, same moon.

"You're here *alone*?" she asked. "In America? And in this city?"

"Yes," he said. "Why not?"

"People shouldn't be left alone in this country," she said, leaning toward him with a kind of vehemence. "They shouldn't have left you here. It can get kind of weird, what happens to people. Didn't they tell you?"

He smiled and said that they hadn't told him anything to that effect.

"Well, they should have." She dropped her cup into a trash can, and he thought he saw the beginning of a scar, a white line, traveling up the underside of her arm toward her shoulder.

"Who do you mean?" he asked. "You said 'they.' Who is 'they'?"

"Any they at all," she said. "Your guardians." She sighed. "All right.

Come on. Follow me." She went outside and broke into a run. For a moment he thought that she was running away from him, then realized that he was expected to run *with* her; it was what people did now, instead of holding hands, to get acquainted. He sprinted up next to her, and as she ran, she asked him, "Who are you?"

Being careful not to tire—she wouldn't like it if his endurance was poor—he told her his name, his professional interests, and he patched together a narrative about his mother, father, two sisters, and his aunt Ingrid. Running past a slower couple, he told her that his aunt was eccentric and broke china by throwing it on the floor on Fridays, which she called "the devil's day."

"Years ago, they would have branded her a witch," Anders said. "But she isn't a witch. She's just moody."

He watched her reactions and noticed that she didn't seem at all interested in his family, or any sort of background. "Do you run a lot?" she asked. "You look as if you're in pretty good shape."

He admitted that, yes, he ran, but that people in Sweden didn't do this as much as they did in America.

"You look a little like that tennis star, that Swede," she said. "By the way, I'm Lauren." Still running, she held out her hand, and, still running, he shook it. "Which god do you believe in?"

"Excuse me?"

"Which god?" she asked. "Which god do you think is in control?"

"I had not thought about it."

"You'd better," she said. "Because one of them is." She stopped suddenly and put her hands on her hips and walked in a small circle. She put her hand to her neck and took her pulse, timing it on her wristwatch. Then she placed her fingers on Anders's neck and took his pulse. "One hundred fourteen," she said. "Pretty good." Again she walked away from him and again he found himself following her. In the growing darkness he noticed other men, standing in the parking lot, watching her, this American with pinned-up hair, dressed in a running outfit. He thought she was pretty, but maybe Americans had other standards so that here, in fact, she wasn't pretty, and it was some kind of optical illusion.

When he caught up with her, she was unlocking the door of a blue Chevrolet rusting near the hubcaps. He gazed down at the rust with professional interest—it had the characteristic blister pattern of rust caused by salt. She slipped inside the car and reached across to unlock the passenger side, and when he got in—he hadn't been invited to get in, but he thought it was all right—he sat down on several small plastic tape cassette cases. He picked them out from underneath him and tried to read their labels. She was taking off her shoes. Debussy, Bach, 10,000 Maniacs, Screamin' Jay Hawkins.

"Where are we going?" he asked. He glanced down at her bare foot on the accelerator. She put the car into reverse. "Wait a minute," he said. "Stop this car." She put on the brake and turned off the ignition. "I just want to look at you," he said.

"Okay, look." She turned on the interior light and kept her face turned so that he was looking at her in profile. Something about her suggested a lovely disorder, a ragged brightness toward the back of her face.

"Are we going to do things?" he asked, touching her on the arm.

"Of course," she said. "Strangers should always do things."

She said that she would drop him off at his hotel, that he must change clothes. This was important. She would then pick him up. On the way over, he saw almost no one downtown. For some reason, it was quite empty of shoppers, strollers, or pedestrians of any kind. "I'm going to tell you some things you should know," she said. He settled back. He was used to this kind of talk on dates: everyone, everywhere, liked to reveal intimate details. It was an international convention.

They were slowing for a red light. "God is love," she said, downshifting, her bare left foot on the clutch. "At least I think so. It's my hope. In the world we have left, only love matters. Do you understand? I'm one of the Last Ones. Maybe you've heard of us."

"No, I have not. What do you do?"

"We do what everyone else does. We work and we go home and have dinner and go to bed. There is only one thing we do that is special."

"What is that?" he asked.

"We don't make plans," she said. "No big plans at all."

"That is not so unusual," he said, trying to normalize what she was saying. "Many people don't like to make—"

"It's not liking," she said. "It doesn't have anything to do with liking or not liking. It's a faith. Look at those buildings." She pointed toward several abandoned multistoried buildings with broken or vacant windows. "What face is moving behind all that? Something is. I live and work here. I'm not blind. *Anyone* can see what's taking place here. You're not blind, either. Our church is over on the east side, off Van Dyke Avenue. It's not a good part of town, but we want to be near where the face is doing its work."

"Your church?"

"The Church of the Millennium," she said. "Where they preach the Gospel of Last Things." They were now on the freeway, heading up toward the General Motors Building and his hotel. "Do you understand me?"

"Of course," he said. He had heard of American cult religions but thought they were all in California. He didn't mind her talk of religion. It was like talk of the sunset or childhood; it kept things going. "Of course I have been listening."

"Because I won't sleep with you unless you listen to me," she said. "It's the one thing I care about, that people listen. It's so damn rare, listening I mean, that you might as well care about it. I don't sleep with strangers too often. Almost never." She turned to look at him. "Anders," she said, "what do you pray to?"

He laughed. "I don't."

"Okay, then, what do you plan for?"

"A few things," he said.

"Like what?"

"My dinner every night. My job. My friends."

"You don't let accidents happen? You should. Things reveal themselves in accidents."

"Are there many people like you?" he asked.

"What do you think?" He looked again at her face, taken over by the darkness in the car but dimly lit by the dashboard lights and the oncoming flare of traffic. "Do you think there are many people like me?"

"Not very many," he said. "But maybe more than there used to be."

"Any of us in Sweden?"

"I don't think so. It's not a religion over there. People don't . . . They didn't tell us in Sweden about American girls who listen to Debussy and 10,000 Maniacs in their automobiles and who believe in gods and accidents."

"They don't say 'girls' here," she told him. "They say 'women.' "

She dropped him off at the hotel and said that she would pick him up in forty-five minutes. In his room, as he chose a clean shirt and a sport coat and a pair of trousers, he found himself laughing happily. He felt giddy. It was all happening so fast; he could hardly believe his luck. I am a very lucky man, he thought.

He looked out his hotel window at the streetlights. They had an amber glow, the color of gemstones. This city, this American city, was unlike any he had ever seen. A downtown area emptied of people; a river with huge ships going by silently; a park with girls who believe in the millennium. No, not girls: women. He had learned his lesson.

He wanted to open the hotel window to smell the air, but the casement frames were welded shut.

After walking down the stairs to the lobby, he stood out in front of the hotel doorway. He felt a warm breeze against his face. He told the doorman, Luis, that he had met a woman on Belle Isle who was going to pick him up in a few minutes. She was going to take him dancing. The doorman nodded, rubbing his chin with his hand. Anders said that she was friendly and wanted to show him, a foreigner, things. The doorman nodded. "Yes, I agree," Luis said. "Dancing. Make sure that this is what you do."

"What?"

"Dancing," Luis said, "yes. Go dancing. You know this woman?"

"I just met her."

"Ah," Luis said, and stepped back to observe Anders, as if to remember his face. "Dangerous fun." When her car appeared in front of the hotel, she was wearing a light summer dress, and when she smiled, she looked like the melancholy baby he had heard about in an American song. As they pulled away from the hotel, he looked back at Luis, who was watching them closely, and then Anders realized that Luis was reading the numbers on Lauren's license plate. To break the mood, he leaned over to kiss her on the cheek. She smelled of cigarettes and something else—soap or cut flowers.

She took him uptown to a club where a trio played soft rock and some jazz. Some of this music was slow enough to dance to, in the slow way he wanted to dance. Her hand in his felt bony and muscular; physically, she was direct and immediate. He wondered, now, looking at her face, whether she might be an American Indian, and again he was frustrated because he couldn't tell one race in this country from another. He knew it was improper to ask. When he sat at the table, holding hands with her and sipping from his drink, he began to feel as if he had known her for a long time and was related to her in some obscure way.

Suddenly he asked her, "Why are you so interested in me?"

"Interested?" She laughed, and her long black hair, no longer pinned up, shook in quick thick waves. "Well, all right. I have an interest. I like it that you're so foreign that you take cabs to the park. I like the way you look. You're kind of cute. And the other thing is, your soul is so raw and new, Anders, it's like an oyster."

"What?" He looked at her near him at the table. Their drinks were half finished. "My soul?"

"Yeah, your soul. I can almost see it."

"Where is it?"

She leaned forward, friendly and sexual and now slightly elegant. "You want me to show you?"

"Yes," Anders said. "Sure."

"It's in two places," she said. "One part is up here." She released his hand and put her thumb on his forehead. "And the other part is down here." She touched him in the middle of his stomach. "Right there. And they're connected."

"What are they like?" he asked, playing along.

"Yours? Raw and shiny, just like I said."

"And what about your soul?" he asked.

She looked at him. "My soul is radioactive," she said. "It's like plutonium. Don't say you weren't warned."

He thought that this was another American idiom he hadn't heard before, and he decided not to spoil things by asking her about it. In Sweden, people didn't talk much about the soul, at least not in conjunction with oysters or plutonium. It was probably some local metaphor he had never heard in Sweden.

In the dark he couldn't make out much about her building, except that it was several floors high and at least fifty years old. Her living-room window looked out distantly at the river—once upstairs, he could see the lights of another passing freighter—and through the left side of the window he could see an electrical billboard. The name of the product was made out of hundreds of small incandescent bulbs, which went on and off from left to right. One of the letters was missing.

It's today's CHEVR LET!

All around her living-room walls were brightly framed watercolors, almost celebratory and Matisse-like, but in vague shapes. She went down the hallway, tapped on one of the doors, and said, "I'm home." Then she returned to the living room and kicked off her shoes. "My grandmother," she said. "She has her own room."

"Are these your pictures?" he asked. "Did you draw them?"

"Yes."

"I can't tell what they are. What are they?"

"They're abstract. You use wet paper to get that effect. They're abstract because God has gotten abstract. God used to have a form but now He's dissolving into pure light. That's what you see in those pictures. They're pictures of the trails that God leaves behind."

"Like the vapor trails"—he smiled—"behind jets."

"Yes," she said. "Like that."

He went over to her in the dark and drew her to him and kissed her. Her breath was layered with smoke, apparently from cigarettes. Immediately he felt an unusual physical sensation inside his skin, like something heating up in a frypan.

She drew back. He heard another siren go by on the street outside. He wondered whether they should talk some more in the living room—share a few more verbal intimacies—to be really civilized about this and decided, no, it was not necessary, not when strangers make love, as they do, sometimes, in strange cities, away from home. They went into her bedroom and undressed each other. Her body, by the light of a dim bedside lamp, was as beautiful and as exotic as he had hoped it would be, darker than his own skin in the dark room, native somehow to this continent. She had the flared shoulders and hips of a dancer. She bent down and snapped off the bedside light, and as he approached her, she was lit from behind by the billboard. Her skin felt vaguely electrical to him.

They stood in the middle of her bedroom, arms around each other, swaying, and he knew, in his arousal, that something odd was about to occur: he had no words for it in either his own language or English.

They moved over and under each other, changing positions to stay in the breeze created by the window fan. They were both lively and attentive, and at first he thought it would be just the usual fun, this time with an almost anonymous American woman. He looked at her in the bed and saw her dark leg alongside his own, and he saw that same scar line running up her arm to her shoulder, where it disappeared.

"Where did you get that?" he asked.

"That?" She looked at it. "That was an accident that was done to me."

Half an hour later, resting with her, his hands on her back, he felt a wave of happiness; he felt it was a wave of color traveling through his body, surging from his forehead down to his stomach. It took him over again, and then a third time, with such force that he almost sat up.

"What is it?" she asked.

"I don't know. It is like . . . I felt a color moving through my body."

"Oh that?" She smiled at him in the dark. "It's your soul, Anders. That's all. That's all it is. Never felt it before, huh?"

"I must be very drunk," he said.

She put her hand up into his hair. "Call it anything you want to. Didn't you feel it before? Our souls were curled together."

"You're crazy," he said. "You are a crazy woman."

"Oh yeah?" she whispered. "Is that what you think? Watch. Watch what happens now. You think this is all physical. Guess what. You're the crazy one. Watch. Watch."

She went to work on him, and at first it was pleasurable, but as she moved over him it became a succession of waves that had specific colorations, even when he turned her and thought he was taking charge. Soon he felt some substance, some glossy blue possession entangled in the air above him.

"I bet you're going to say that you're imagining all this," she said, her hand skidding across him.

"Who are you?" he said. "Who in the world are you?"

"I warned you," she whispered, her mouth directly over his ear. "I warned you. You people with your things, your rusty things, you suffer so bad when you come into where *we* live. Did they tell you we were all soulless here? Did they say that?"

He put his hands on her. "This is not love, but it—"

"Of course not," she said. "It's something else. Do you know the word? Do you know the word for something that opens your soul at once? Like that?" She snapped her fingers on the pillow. Her tongue was touching his ear. "Do you?" The words were almost inaudible.

"No."

"Addiction." She waited. "Do you understand?"

"Yes."


In the middle of the night he rose up and went to the window. He felt like a stump, amputated from the physical body of the woman. At the window he looked down, to the right of the billboard, and saw another apartment building with heavy decorations with human forms near the roof's edge, and on the third floor he saw a man at the window, as naked as he himself was but almost completely in shadow, gazing out at the street. There were so far away from each other that being unclothed didn't matter. It was vague and small and impersonal.

"Do you always stand at the window without clothes on?" she asked, from the bed.

"Not in Sweden," he said. He turned around. "This is odd," he said. "At night no one walks out on the streets. But there, over on that block, there's a man like me, at the window, and he is looking out, too. Do people stand everywhere at the windows here?"

"Come to bed."

"When I was in the army, the Swedish army," he said, still looking out, "they taught us to think that we could *decide* to do anything. They talked about the will. Your word 'willpower.' All Sweden believes this—choice, will, willpower. Maybe not so much now. I wonder if they talk about it here."

"You're funny," she said. She had moved up from behind him and embraced him.


In the morning he watched her as she dressed. His eyes hurt from sleeplessness. "I have to go," she said. "I'm already late." She was putting on a light blue skirt. As she did, she smiled. "You're a lovely lover," she said. "I like your body very much."

"What are we going to do?" he asked.

"We? There is no 'we,' Anders. There's you and then there's me. We're not a couple. I'm going to work. You're going back to your country soon. What are you planning to do?"

"May I stay here?"

"For an hour," she said, "and then you should go back to your hotel. I don't think you should stay. You don't live here."

"May I take you to dinner tonight?" he asked, trying not to watch her as he watched her. "What can we do tonight?"

"There's that 'we' again. Well, maybe. You can teach me a few words of Swedish. Why don't you hang around at your hotel and maybe I'll come by around six and get you, but don't call me if I don't come by, because if I don't, I don't."

"I can't call you," he said. "I don't know your last name."

"Oh, that's right," she said. "Well, listen. I'll probably come at six." She looked at him lying in the bed. "I don't believe this," she said.

"What?"

"You think you're in love, don't you?"

"No," he said. "Not exactly." He waited. "Oh, I don't know."

"I get the point," she said. "Well, you'd better get used to it. Welcome to our town. We're not always good at love but we are good at that." She bent to kiss him and then was gone. Happiness and agony simultaneously reached down and pressed against his chest. They, too, were like colors, but when you mixed the two together, you got something greenish-pink, excruciating.

He stood up, put on his trousers, and began looking into her dresser drawers. He expected to find trinkets and whatnot, but all she had were folded clothes, and, in the corner of the top drawer, a small turquoise heart for a charm bracelet. He put it into his pocket.

In the bathroom, he examined the labels on her medicines and facial creams before washing his face. He wanted evidence but didn't know for what. He looked, to himself, like a slightly different version of what he had once been. In the mirror his face had a puffy look and a passive expression, as if he had been assaulted during the night.

After he had dressed and entered the living room, he saw Lauren's grandmother sitting at a small dining-room table. She was eating a piece of toast and looking out of the window toward the river. The apartment, in daylight, had an aggressively scrubbed and mopped look. On the kitchen counter a small black-and-white television was blaring, but the old woman wasn't watching it. Her black hair was streaked with gray, and she wore a ragged pink bathrobe decorated with pictures of orchids. She was very frail. Her skin was as dark as her granddaughter's. Looking at her, Anders was once again unable to guess what race she was. She might be Arabic, or a Native American, or Hispanic, or black. Because he couldn't tell, he didn't care.

Without even looking at him, she motioned at him to sit down.

"Want anything?" she asked. She had a high, distant voice, as if it had come into the room over wires. "There are bananas over there." She made no gesture. "And grapefruit, I think, in the refrigerator."

"That's all right." He sat down on the other side of the table and folded his hands together, studying his fingers. The sound of traffic came up from the street outside.

"You're from somewhere," she said. "Scandinavia?"

"Yes," he said. "How can you tell?" Talking had become a terrible effort.

"Vowels," she said. "You sound like one of those Finns up north of here. When will you go back? To your country?"

"I don't know," he said. "Perhaps a few days. Perhaps not. My name is Anders." He held out his hand.

"Nice to meet you." She touched but did not shake his hand. "Why don't you know when you're going back?" She turned to look at him at last. It was a face on which curiosity still registered. She observed him as if he were an example of a certain kind of human being in whom she still had an interest.

"I don't know . . . I am not sure. Last night, I . . ."

"You don't finish your sentences," the old woman said.

"I am trying to. I don't want to leave your granddaughter," he said. "She is"—he tried to think of the right adjective—"amazing to me."

"Yes, she is." The old woman peered at him. "You don't think you're in love, do you?"

"I don't know."

"Well, don't be. She won't ever be married, so there's no point in being in love with her. There's no point in being married *here*. I see them, you know."

"Who?"

"All the young men. Well, there aren't many. A few. Every so often. They come and sleep here with her and then in the morning they come out for breakfast with me and then they go away. We sit and talk. They're usually very pleasant. Men are, in the morning. They should be. She's a beautiful girl."

"Yes, she is."

"But there's no future in her, you know," the old woman said. "Sure you don't want a grapefruit? You should eat something."

"No, thank you. What do you mean, 'no future'?"

"Well, the young men usually understand that." The old woman looked at the television set, scowled, and shifted her eyes to the window. She rubbed her hands together. "You can't invest in her. You can't do that at all. She won't let you. I know. I know how she thinks."

"We have women like that in my country," Anders said. "They are—"

"Oh no you don't," the old woman said. "Sooner or later they want to get married, don't they?"

"I suppose most of them."

She glanced out the window toward the Detroit River and the city of Windsor on the opposite shore. Just when he thought that she had forgotten all about him, he felt her hand, dry as a winter leaf, taking hold of his own. Another siren went by outside. He felt a weight descending in his stomach. The touch of the old woman's hand made him feel worse than before, and he stood up quickly, looking around the room as if there were some object nearby he had to pick up and take away immediately. Her hand dropped away from his.

"No plans," she said. "Didn't she tell you?" the old woman asked. "It's what she believes." She shrugged. "It makes her happy."

"I am not sure I understand."

The old woman lifted her right hand and made a dismissive wave in his direction. She pursed her mouth; he knew she had stopped speaking to him. He called a cab, and in half an hour he was back in his hotel room. In the shower he realized that he had forgotten to write down her address or phone number.


He felt itchy: he went out running, returned to his room, and took another shower. He did thirty push-ups and jogged in place. He groaned and shouted, knowing that no one would hear. How would he explain this to anyone? He was feeling passionate puzzlement. He went down to the hotel's dining room for lunch and ordered Dover sole and white wine but found himself unable to eat much of anything. He stared at his plate and at the other men and women consuming their meals calmly, and he was suddenly filled with wonder at ordinary life.

He couldn't stand to be by himself, and after lunch he had the doorman hail a cab. He gave the cabdriver a fifty and asked him to drive him around the city until all the money was used up.

"You want to see the nice parts?" the cabbie asked.

"No."

"What is it you want to see then?"

"The city."

"You tryin' to score, man? That it?"

Anders didn't know what he meant. He was certain that no sport was intended. He decided to play it safe. "No," he said.

The cabdriver shook his head and whistled. They drove east and then south; Anders watched the water-ball compass stuck to the front window. Along Jefferson Avenue they went past the shells of apartment buildings, and then, heading north, they passed block after block of vacated or boarded-up properties. One old building with Doric columns was draped with a banner.

PROGRESS! THE OLD MUST MAKE WAY
FOR THE NEW
Acme Wrecking Company

The banner was worn and tattered. Anders noticed broken beer bottles, sharp brown glass, on sidewalks and vacant lots, and the glass, in the sun, seemed perversely beautiful. Men were sleeping on sidewalks and in front stairwells; one man, wearing a hat, urinated against the corner of a burned-out building. He saw other men—there were very few women out here in the light of day—in groups gazing at him with cold slow deadly expressions. In his state of mind, he understood it all; he identified with it. All of it, the ruins and the remnants, made perfect sense.

At six o'clock she picked him up and took him to a Greek restaurant. All the way over, he watched her. He examined her with the puzzled curiosity of someone who wants to know how another person who looks rather attractive but also rather ordinary could have such power. Her physical features didn't explain anything.

"Did you miss me today?" she asked, half jokingly.

"Yes," he said. He started to say more but didn't know how to begin. "It was hard to breathe," he said at last.

"I know," she said. "It's the air."

"No, it isn't. Not the air."

"Well, what then?"

He looked at her.

"Oh, come on, Anders. We're just two blind people who staggered into each other and we're about to stagger off in different directions. That's all."

Sentences struggled in his mind, then vanished before he could say them. He watched the pavement pass underneath the car.

In the restaurant, a crowded and lively place smelling of beer and roasted meat and cigars, they sat in a booth and ordered an antipasto plate. He leaned over and took her hands. "Tell me, please, who and what you are."

She seemed surprised that he had asked. "I've explained," she said. She waited, then started up again. "When I was younger I had an idea that I wanted to be a dancer. I had to give that up. My timing was off." She smiled. "Onstage, I looked like a memory of what had already happened. The other girls would do something and then *I'd* do it. I come in late on a lot of things. That's good for me. I've told you where I work. I live with my grandmother. I go with her into the parks in the fall and we watch for birds. And you know what else I believe." He gazed at the gold hoops of her earrings. "What else do you want to know?"

"I feel happy and terrible," he said. "Is it you? Did you do this?"

"I guess I did," she said, smiling faintly. "Tell me some words in Swedish."

"Which ones?"

"House."

*"Hus."*

"Pain."

*"Smärta."*

She leaned back. "Face."

*"Ansikte."*

"Light."

*"Ljus."*

"Never."

*"Aldrig."*

"I don't like it," she said. "I don't like the sound of those words at all. They're too cold. They're cold-weather words."

"Cold? Try another one."

"Soul."

*"Själ."*

"No, I don't like it." She raised her hand to the top of his head, grabbed a bit of his hair, and laughed. "Too bad."

"Do you do this to everyone?" he asked. "I feel such confusion."

He saw her stiffen. "You want to know too much. You're too messed up. Too messed up with plans. You and your rust. All that isn't important. Not here. We don't do all that explaining. I've told you *everything* about me. We're just supposed to be enjoying ourselves. Nobody has to explain. That's freedom, Anders. Never telling why." She leaned over toward him so that her shoulders touched his, and with a sense of shock and desperation, he felt himself becoming aroused. She kissed him, and her lips tasted slightly of garlic. "Just say hi to the New World," she said.

"You feel like a drug to me," he said. "You feel experimental."

"We don't use that word that way," she said. Then she said, "Oh," as if she had understood something, or remembered another engagement. "Okay. I'll explain all this in a minute. Excuse me." She rose and disappeared behind a corner of the restaurant, and Anders looked out the window at a Catholic church the color of sandstone, on whose front steps a group of boys sat, eating Popsicles. One of the boys got up and began to ask passersby for money; this went on until a policeman came and sent the boys away. Anders looked at his watch. Ten minutes had gone by since she had left. He looked up. He knew without thinking about it that she wasn't coming back.

He put a ten-dollar bill on the table and left the restaurant, jogging into the parking structure where she had left the car. Although he wasn't particularly surprised to see that it wasn't there, he sat down on the concrete and felt the floor of the structure shaking. He ran his hands through his hair, where she had grabbed at it. He waited as long as he could stand to do so, then returned to the hotel.

Luis was back on duty. Anders told him what had happened.

"Ah," Luis said. "She is disappeared."

"Yes. Do you think I should call the police?"

"No," Luis said. "I do not think so. They have too many disappeared already."

"Too many disappeared?"

"Yes. All over this city. Many many disappeared. For how many times do you take this lady out?"

"Once. No, twice."

"And this time is the time she leave you?"

Anders nodded.

"I have done that," Luis said. "When I get sick of a woman, I, too, have disappeared. Maybe," he said suddenly, "she will reappear. Sometimes they do."

"I don't think she will." He sat down on the sidewalk in front of the hotel and cupped his chin in his hands.

"No, no," Luis said. "You cannot do that in front of the hotel. This looks very bad. Please stand up." He felt Luis reaching around his shoulders and pulling him to his feet. "What you are acting is impossible after one night," Luis said. "Be like everyone else. Have another night." He took off his doorman's cap and combed his hair with precision. "Many men and women also disappear from each other. It is one thing to do. You had a good time?"

Anders nodded.

"Have another good time," Luis suggested, "with someone else. Beer, pizza, go to bed. Women who have not disappeared will talk to you, I am sure."

"I think I'll call the police," Anders said.

"Myself, no, I would not do that."

He dialed a number he found in the telephone book for a local precinct station. As soon as the station officer understood what Anders was saying to him, he became angry, said it wasn't a police matter, and hung up on him. Anders sat for a moment in the phone booth, then looked up the Church of the Millennium in the directory. He wrote down its address. Someone there would know about her, and explain.

The cab let him out in front. It was like no other church he had ever seen before. Even the smallest places of worship in his own country had vaulted roofs, steeples, and stained glass. This building seemed to be someone's remodeled house. On either side of it, two lots down, were two skeletal homes, one of which had been burned and which now stood with charcoal windows and a charcoal portal where the front door had once been. The other house was boarded up; in the evening wind, sheets of newspaper were stuck to its south wall. Across the street was an almost deserted playground. The saddles had been removed from the swing set, and the chains hung down from the upper bar and moved slightly in the wind. Four men stood together under a basketball hoop, talking. One of the men bounced a basketball occasionally.

A signboard had been planted into the ground in front of the church, but so many letters had been removed from it that Anders couldn't make out what it was supposed to say.

Ch r ch of  e Mill  n i m
Rev. H r old T.  oodst th, Pas or
Everyo e  elco e!
"Love on  other, lest ye f ll to  d  t le for  r le m!"

On the steps leading up to the front door, he turned around and saw, to the south, the lights of the office buildings of downtown Detroit suspended like enlarged stars in the darkness. After hearing what he thought was some sound in the bushes, he opened the front doors of the church and went inside.

Over a bare wood floor, folding chairs were lined up in five straight rows, facing toward a front chest intended as an altar, and everywhere there was a smell of incense, of ashy pine. Above the chest, and nailed to the far wall where a crucifix might be located in a Protestant church, was a polished brass circle with a nimbus of rays projecting out from its top. The rays were extended along the wall for a distance of about four feet. One spotlight from a corner behind him lit up the brass circle, which in the gloom looked like either a deity-sun or some kind of explosion. The bare walls had been painted with flames: buildings of the city, some he had already seen, painted in flames, the earth in flames. There was an open Bible on the chest, and on one of the folding chairs a deck of playing cards. Otherwise, the room was completely empty. Glancing at a side door, he decided that he had never seen a church so small, or one that filled him with a greater sense of desolation. Behind him, near the door, was a bench. He had the feeling that the bench was filled with the disappeared. He sat down on it, and as he looked at the folding chairs it occurred to him that the disappeared were in fact here now, in front of him, sitting or standing or kneeling.

He composed himself and went back out onto the street, thinking that perhaps a cab would go by, but he saw neither cabs nor cars, not even pedestrians. After deciding that he had better begin walking toward the downtown area, he made his way down two blocks, past a boarded-up grocery store and a vacated apartment building, when he heard what he thought was the sound of footsteps behind him.

He felt the blow at the back of his head; it came to him not as a sensation of pain but as an instant crashing explosion of light in his brain, a bursting circle with a shooting aura irradiating from it. As he turned to fall, he felt hands touching his chest and his trousers; they moved with speed and almost with tenderness, until they found what they were looking for and took it away from him.

He lay on the sidewalk in a state somewhere between consciousness and unconsciousness, hearing the wind through the trees overhead and feeling some blood trickling out of the back of his scalp, until he felt the hands again, perhaps the same hands, lifting him up, putting him into something, taking him somewhere. Inside the darkness he now inhabited, he found that at some level he could still think: Someone hit me and I've been robbed. At another, later point, he understood that he could open his eyes; he had that kind of permission. He was sitting in a wheelchair in what was clearly a hospital emergency room. It felt as though someone were pushing him toward a planetary corridor. They asked him questions, which he answered in Swedish. "*Det gör ont,*" he said, puzzled that they didn't understand him. "*Var är jag?*" he asked. They didn't know. English was what they wanted. He tried to give them some.

They X-rayed him and examined his cut; he would need four stitches, they said. He found that he could walk. They told him he was lucky, that he had not been badly hurt. A doctor, and then a nurse, and then another nurse told him that he might have been killed—shot or knifed—and that victims of this type, strangers who wandered into the wrong parts of the city, were not unknown. He mentioned the disappeared. They were polite, but said that there was no such phrase in English. When he mentioned the name of his hotel, they said, once again, that he was lucky: it was only a few blocks away, walking distance. They smiled. You're a lucky man, they said, grinning oddly. They knew something but weren't saying it.

As the smaller debris of consciousness returned to him, he found himself sitting in a brightly lit room, like a waiting room, near the entryway for emergency medicine. From where he sat, he could see, through his fluent tidal headache, the patients arriving, directed to the Triage Desk, where their conditions were judged.

They brought in a man on a gurney, who was hoarsely shouting. They rushed him through. He was bleeding, and they were holding him down as his feet kicked sideways.

They brought in someone else, a girl, who was stumbling, held up on both sides by friends. Anders heard something that sounded like "Odie." Who was Odie? Her boyfriend? "Odie," she screamed. "Get me Odie."

Anders stood up, unable to watch any more. He shuffled through two doorways and found himself standing near an elevator. From a side window, he saw light from the sun rising. He hadn't realized that it was day. The sun made the inside of his head shriek. To escape the light, he stepped on the elevator and pressed the button for the fifth floor.

As the elevator rose, he felt his knees weakening. In order to clear his head, he began to count the other people on the elevator: seven. They seemed normal to him. The signs of this were coats and ties on the men, white frocks and a stethoscope on one of the women, and blouses and jeans on the other women. None of them looked like her. From now on, none of them ever would.

He felt that he must get home to Sweden quickly, before he became a very different person, unrecognizable even to himself.

At the fifth floor the doors opened and he stepped out. Close to the elevators was a nurses' station, and beyond it a long hallway leading to an alcove. He walked down this hallway, turned the corner, and heard small squalling sounds ahead. At the same time, he saw the windows in the hallway and understood that he had wandered onto the maternity floor. He made his way to the viewing window and looked inside. He counted twenty-five newborns, each one in its own clear plastic crib. He stared down at the babies, hearing, through the glass, the cries of those who were awake.

He was about to turn around and go back to his hotel when one of the nurses saw him. She raised her eyebrows quizzically and spread her hands over the children. He shook his head to indicate no. Still she persisted. She pointed to a baby with white skin and a head of already-blond hair. He shook his head no once again. He would need to get back to the hotel, call his bank in Sweden, get money for the return trip. He touched his pants pocket and found that the wallet was still there. What had they taken? The nurse, smiling, nodded as if she understood, and motioned toward the newborns with darker skin, the Hispanics and light-skinned blacks and all the others, babies of a kind he never saw in Sweden.

Well, he thought, why not? Now that they had done this to him.


His right arm rose. He pointed at a baby whose skin was the color of clay, the color of polished bronze. Now the nurse was wheeling the baby he had pointed to closer to the window. When it was directly in front of him, she left it there, returning to the back of the nursery. Standing on the other side of the glass, staring down at the sleeping infant, he tapped on the panel twice and waved, as he thought fathers should. The baby did not awaken. Anders put his hand in his pocket, then pressed his forehead against the glass of the window and recovered himself. He stood for what seemed to him a long time, before taking the elevator down to the ground floor and stepping out onto the front sidewalk, and to the air, which smelled as it always had, of powerful combustible materials and their traces, fire and ash.

# Kiss Away

THE HOUSE had an upstairs sleeping porch, and she first saw the young man from up there, limping through the alley and carrying a torn orange-and-yellow Chinese kite. He had a dog with him, and both the dog and the man had an air of scruffy unseriousness. From the look of it, no project these two got involved with could last longer than ten minutes. That was the first thing she liked about them.

Midmorning, midweek, midsummer: even teenagers were working, and in this flat July heat no one with any sense was trying to fly kites. No one but a fool would fly a kite in this weather.

The young man threw the ball of string and the ripped cloth into the alley's trash bin while the dog watched him. Then the dog sat down and with an expression of pained concentration scratched violently behind its ear. It looked around for something else to be interested in, barked at a cat on a window ledge, then gave up the effort and scratched its ear again.

From the upstairs sleeping porch, the young man looked exactly like the fool in the tarot pack—shaggy and loose-limbed, a songster at the edge of cliffs—and the dog was the image of the fool's dog, a frisky yellow mutt. Dogs tended to like fools. They had an affinity. Fools always gave dogs plenty to do. Considering this, the woman near the window felt her heart pound twice. Her heart was precise. It was like a doorbell.

She was unemployed. She had been out of college for a year, hadn't been able to find a job she could tolerate for more than a few days, and with the last of her savings had rented the second floor of this house in Minneapolis, which included an old-fashioned sleeping porch facing east. She slept out here, and then in the mornings she sat in a hard-backed chair reading books from the library, drinking coffee, and listening to classical music on the public radio station. Right now they were playing the *Goyescas* of Enrique Granados. She was running out of money and trying to stay calm about it, and the music helped her. The music seemed to say that she could sit like this all morning, and no one would punish her. It was very Spanish.

She put on her shoes and threw her keys into the pocket of her jeans. She raised the slatted blinds. "Hey!" she yelled down into the alley.

"Hey, yourself," the young man yelled back. He smiled at her and squinted. Apparently he couldn't see her clearly. That was the second thing she liked about him.

"You can't throw that kite in there," she said. "That Dumpster's only for people who live in this building." She shaded her eyes against the sun to see him better. The guy's dog was now standing and wagging its tail.

"Okay," he said. "I'll take it out," and when she told him not to and that she'd be down in a second and he should just wait there, she knew he would do what she asked. What she hadn't expected was that he would smile enormously at her and, when she appeared, give her a hug—they were strangers after all—right out of the blue. She pushed him away but could not manage to get angry at him. Then she felt the dog's tongue slurping on her fingers, as if she'd spilled sauce on them and they needed some cleaning.


He offered to buy her coffee, and he explained himself as they walked. He had once had good prospects, he said, and a future about which he could boast. He had been accepted into medical school eighteen months ago but had come down with a combination of mononucleosis and bacterial pneumonia, and after recuperating, he had lost all his interest in great plans. The two illnesses—one virus and one bacteria—had taken the starch out of him, he said. He actually used expressions like that. He had a handsome face when you saw him up close, but as soon as you walked a few feet away something went wrong with his appearance; it degenerated somehow.

His name was Walton Tyner Ross, but he liked to be called Glaze because of his taste for doughnuts and his habitual faraway expression. She didn't think someone whose nickname was Glaze was ever going to become a successful practitioner of medicine, but in a certain light in the morning he was the finest thing she had seen in some time, especially when viewed from a few inches away, as they walked down Hennepin Avenue for breakfast.

Stopping under a tree that gave them both a moment of shade, he told her that if she wanted him to, he would show up regularly in the morning from now on. He needed motivation. Maybe she did, too. They would project themselves into the world, he said. She agreed, and on the next few mornings he appeared in the alley with his dog, Einstein, a few feet behind him. He called up to her, and the dog barked in chorus. She didn't think it was very gallant, his yelling up at her like that, but she had had her phone disconnected, and his passion for her company pleased and moved her.

They would walk down Hennepin Avenue past what he called the Church of the Holy Oil Can—because of its unbecoming disproportionate spire—to one of several greasy smoky restaurants with plate-glass front windows and red-and-white-checkered café curtains and front counters with stools. They always sat at the stools because Walton liked to watch the grill. The first time he bought Jodie a breakfast of scrambled eggs and a biscuit and orange juice. As the breakfast went on, he became more assertive. Outside, Einstein sat near a lamppost and watched the passing pedestrians.

Walton Tyner Ross—looking very much like a fool as he spilled his breakfast on his shirt—was a Roman candle of theories and ideas. Jodie admired his idea that unemployment was like a virus. This virus was spreading and was contagious. The middle class was developing a positive taste for sloth. One person's unemployment could infect anyone else. "Take you," he said. "Take us." He wolfed down his toast slathered with jam. "We shouldn't feel guilty over not working. It's like a flu we've both got. We're infected with indifference. We didn't ask to get it. We inhaled it, or someone sneezed it on us."

"I don't know," she said. In front of her, the fry cook, a skinny African-American kid with half-steamed glasses, was sweating and wiping his brow on his shirtsleeve. The restaurant had the smell of morning ambition and resolution: coffee and cigarette smoke and maple syrup and cheap aftershave and hair spray. "Maybe you're right," she said. "But maybe we're both just kind of lazy. My sister says *I'm* lazy. I think it's more complicated than that. I once had plans, too," Jodie said, indicating with a flick of her wrist the small importance of these plans.

"Like what? What sort of plans?"

She was watching the fry cook and could hardly remember. "Oh," she said. "What I wanted was an office job. Keeping accounts and books.

Something modest, a job that would leave the rest of my life alone and not eat up my resources." She waited a moment and touched her cheek with her finger. "In those days—I mean, a few months ago—my big project was love. I always wanted big love. Like that game, Careers, where you decide what you want out of life? I wanted a small job and huge love, like a big *event*. An event so big you couldn't say when it would ever stop."

He nodded. "But so far all the love you've gotten has been small."

She looked at him and shrugged. "Maybe it's the times. Maybe I'm not pretty enough."

He leaned back and grinned at her to dispute this.

"No, I mean it," she said. "I can say all this to you because we don't know each other. Anyway, I was once almost engaged. The guy was nice, and I guess he meant well, and my parents liked him. They didn't mind that he was kind of ragged, but almost as soon as he became serious about me, he was taking everything for granted. It's hard to explain," she said, pushing her scrambled eggs around on the plate and eyeing the ketchup bottle. "It wasn't his fault, exactly. He couldn't do it. He couldn't play me." She gave up and poured some ketchup on her eggs. "You don't have to play me all the time, but if you're going to get married, you should be played *sometimes*. You should play him, he should play you. With him, there was no tune coming out of me. Just prose. You know, Walton," she said suddenly, "you sometimes look like the fool illustration on the tarot pack. No offense. You just do."

"Sure, I do," he said, and when he turned, she could see that his ears were pierced, two crease incisions on each lobe. "Okay, look. Here's what's going to happen. You and me, we're going to go out together in the morning and look for work. Then in the afternoon we'll drive around, I don't know, a treasure hunt, something that doesn't cost anything. Then I don't know what we're going to do in the evening. You can decide that." He explained that good fortune had put them together but that maybe they should at least try to fight the virus of sloth.

She noticed a fat balding man on Walton's other side, with hideous yellow-green eyes, staring at her. "Okay," she said. "I'll think about it."


The next day, he was there in the hot dusty alley with his morning paper and his dog and his limp, and she came down to him without his having to call up to her. She wasn't totally presentable—she was wearing the same jeans as the day before, and a hand-me-down shirt from her sister—but she had put on a silver bracelet for him. As they walked to the restaurant he complimented her on her pleasant sexiness. He told her that in the moments when she had descended the back steps, his heart had been stirred. "Your heart. Yeah, right," she said.

Walking with her toward the café, Einstein trotting behind them and snapping at flies, he said that today they would scan the want ads and would calculate their prospects. In the late morning they would go to his apartment—he had a phone—and make a few calls. They would be active and brisk and aggressive. They would pretend that adulthood—getting a job—made sense. Matching his stride, enjoying his optimism, Jodie felt a passing impulse to take Walton's arm. He was gazing straight ahead, not glazed at all, and his shirtsleeves were rolled up, and she briefly admired his arms and the light on his skin.

In the restaurant, at the counter spotted with dried jam and brown gravy, where the waitress said, "Hiya, Glaze," and poured him his coffee without being asked, Jodie felt a pleasant shiver of jealousy. So many people seemed to know and to like this unremarkable but handsome guy; he, or something about him, was infectious. The thought occurred to her that he might change her life. By the time her Belgian waffle arrived, Jodie had circled six want ads for temp secretaries with extensive computer experience. She knew and understood computers backward and forward and hated them all, but they were like family members and she could work with them if she had to. She didn't really want the jobs—she wanted to sit on the sleeping porch with her feet up on the windowsill and listen to the piano music of Granados and watch things go by in the alley—but the atmosphere of early-morning ambition in the café was beginning to move her to action. She had even brought along a pen.

She felt a nudge in her ribs.

She turned to her left and saw sitting next to her the same fat balding man with horrible yellow-green eyes whom she had seen the day before. His breath smelled of gin and graham crackers. He was smiling at her unpleasantly. He was quite a package. "'Scuse me, miss," he said. "Hate to bother you. I'm short bus fare. You got seventy-five cents?" His speech wore the clothes of an obscure untraceable Eastern European accent.

"Sure," she said without thinking. She fished out three quarters from her pocket and gave the money to him. "Here." She turned back to the want ads.

"Oboy," he said, scooping it up. "Are you lucky."

"Am I?" she asked.

"You got that right," he said. He rose unsteadily and his yellow-green eyes leered at her, and for a moment Jodie thought that he might topple over, like a collapsed circus tent, covering her underneath his untucked shirt and soiled beltless trousers. "I," he announced to the restaurant, although no one was paying any attention to him, "am the Genie of the Magic Lamp."

No one even looked up.

The fat man bent down toward her. "Come back tomorrow," he said in a ghoulish whisper. Now he smelled of fireplace ash. "You get your prize." After a moment, he staggered out of the restaurant in a series of forward and sideways lurching motions, almost knocking over on the way a stainless-steel coatrack. The waitress behind the counter watched him leave with an expression on her face of irritated indifference made more explicit by her hand on her hip and a pink bubble almost the color of blood expanding from her lips. Bubble gum was shockingly effective at expressing contempt, Jodie thought. All the great waitresses chewed gum.

"Who was that?" she asked Walton.

He shook his head like a spring-loaded toy on the back shelf of a car. As usual, he smiled before answering. "I don't know," he said. "Some guy. Tad or Tadeusz or like that. He always asks people for money. Usually people ignore him. Nobody's given him any money in a long time. Come on. We're going to my place to make some phone calls. Then we'll go on a treasure hunt."

When they came out to the sidewalk, Einstein cried and shivered with happiness to see them, barking twice as a greeting. Walton loosened her from a bicycle stand to which she had been tethered, while Jodie breathed in the hot summer air and said, "By the way, Walton, where did you get that thing in your walk? Is it, like, arthritis?"

He turned and smiled at her. Her heart started thumping again. She couldn't imagine why men didn't smile more often than they did. It was the most effective action they knew how to take, but they were always amateurs at it. Jodie thought that maybe she hadn't been smiled upon that much in her life. Perhaps that was it.

"Fascists," Walton said, getting up. "My dog and I fought the fascists."

Walton's apartment was upstairs from an ice-cream parlor, and it smelled of fudge and heavy cream. Although the apartment had a small study area with bookshelves and a desk, and a bedroom where the bed was neatly made and where even the dog's rubber squeak toys were kept in the corner, the effect of neatness was offset by a quality of gloom characteristic of places where sunlight had never penetrated. It was like Bluebeard's castle. The only unobstructed windows faced north. All the other windows faced brick or stone walls so that no matter what time of day it was, the lamps had to be kept on.

They went through the circled want ads, made some telephone calls, and arranged for two interviews, one for Jodie as a receptionist at a discount brokerage house and one for Walton as a shipping clerk.

Having finished that task, Jodie dropped herself onto one of the floor pillows and examined a photograph on the wall over the desk showing a young couple, both smiling. Wearing a flowery summer dress, the woman sat on a swing, and the man stood behind her, about to give her a push.

"That's my father," Walton said, standing behind Jodie.

"It's your mother, too."

"I know it. I know it's my mother, too. But it's mostly my father. He always liked to meet my girlfriends."

"I'm not your girlfriend, Walton," she said. "I hardly know you."

He was quiet for a moment. "Want a beer?" he asked. "For lunch?"

He said unemployed people should always seek out castoffs and that was what they would do during the afternoon, but just as they were about to go out to his car, he fell asleep in his chair, his dog at his feet, her front paws crossed.

Jodie sat where she was for a moment, painfully resisting the impulse to go rummaging through Walton's medicine cabinet and desk and dresser drawers. Instead, she brought a chair over next to him, sat down in it, and studied his face. Although it wasn't an unusual face, at this distance certain features about it were certainly noteworthy. The line where the beard began on his cheek—he was cleanshaven—was so straight that it seemed to have been implanted there with a ruler. He had two tiny, almost microscopic pieces of dandruff in his eyebrows. His lashes were rather long, for a man. His lower lip was also rather full, but his upper lip was so small and flat at the bottom that you might not notice it unless you looked carefully. When he exhaled, his breath came in two puffs: It sounded like *hurr hurr*. He had a thin nose, and his left cheek appeared to have the remnant of an acne scar, a little blossom of reddening just beneath the skin like a truffle. With his head leaning forward, his hair in back fell halfway to his shoulders; these shoulders seemed to her to be about average width for a man of his height and weight. Even in sleep, his forehead was creased as if in thought. His hair had a wavy back-and-forth directionality, and it reminded Jodie of corrugated tin roofing. She found wavy hair mysterious; her own was quite straight. She reached up to touch his hair, being careful not to touch his scalp. That would wake him. She liked the feeling of his hair in her fingers. It was like managing a small profit after two quarters of losses.

She was sitting again on the floor pillow when he woke up five minutes later. He shook his head and rubbed his face with his hands. He looked over to where Jodie was sitting. "Hi," he said.

"Here's 'hi' comin' back at you," she said. She waved all the fingers of her right hand at him.


That evening she went to a pay telephone and called her older sister, the married and employed success story. Her older sister told Jodie to take her time, to buy some nice clothes, to be careful not to lend him her credit card, and to watch and wait to see what would happen. Be careful; he might be a psychopath. Sit tight, she said. Jodie thought the advice was ironic because that kind of sitting was the only sort her sister knew how to do. She told Jodie to have her phone reconnected; it wouldn't cost that much, and after all, telephones were a necessity for a working girl in whom a man was taking an interest. She asked if Jodie needed a loan, and Jodie said no.

Her best friend gave Jodie the same advice, except with more happy laughter and enthusiasm. Wait and see, go for it, she said. What's the difference? It'll be fun either way. Come over. Let's talk.

Soon, Jodie said. We'll see each other soon.


Her dreams that night were packs of lies, lies piled on lies, an exhibit of lies. Mayhem, penises on parade, angels in seersucker suits, that sort of thing. She woke up on the sleeping porch ashamed of her unconscious life. She hated the vulgarity and silliness of her own dreams, their subtle unstated untruths.

Her job interview was scheduled for eleven o'clock the following morning, and after Walton had called up to her and taken her to the café, she stared down into her third cup of coffee and considered how she might make the best impression on her potential employers. She had worn a rather formal white ruffled blouse with the palm tree pin and a dark blue skirt, and she had a semi-matching blue purse, at the sight of which Walton had announced that Jodie had "starchy ideas of elegance," a phrase he didn't care to explain. He told her that at the interview she should be eager and honest and self-possessed. "It's a brokerage house," he said. "They like possession in places like that, especially self-possession. Be polite. Don't call them motherfuckers. They don't like that. But be honest. If you're straightforward, they'll notice and take to you right away. Just be yourself, you know, whatever that is."

But she wasn't convinced. At the moment, the idea of drifting like a broken twig on the surface of a muddy river was much more appealing. All through college she had worked at a clothing store as a checkout clerk, and the experience had filled her with bitter wisdom about the compromises of tedium and the hard bloody edge of necessity. She had had a gun pointed at her during a holdup her fourth day on the job. On two other occasions, the assistant manager had propositioned her in the stockroom. When she turned him down, she expected to be fired, but for some reason she had been kept on.

"There you are." A voice: her left ear: a phlegm rumble.

Jodie turned on her stool and saw the fat man with yellow-green eyes staring at her. "Yes," she said.

"I hadda get things in order," he said, grinning and snorting. He pulled out a handkerchief speckled with excretions and blew his nose into it. "I hadda get my ducks in a row. So. Here we are again. What's your three wishes?"

"Excuse me?"

"Just ignore the guy," Walton said, pouring some cream into his coffee. "Just ignore the guy."

"If I was you," the fat man said, "I'd ignore *him*. They don't call him Glaze for nothing. So what's your three wishes? I am the Genie of the Magic Lamp, like I said. You did me a favor, I do you a favor." Jodie noticed that the fat man's voice was hollow, as if it had emerged out of an echo chamber. Also, she had the momentary perception that the fat man's limbs were attached to the rest of his body with safety pins.

"I don't have three wishes," Jodie said, studying her coffee cup.

"Everybody's got three wishes," the fat man said. "Don't bullshit the Genie. There's nobody on Earth that doesn't have three wishes. The three wishes," he proclaimed, "are universal."

"Listen, Tad," Walton said, turning himself toward the fat man and spreading himself a bit wider at the shoulders. He was beginning, Jodie noticed, a slow, threatening, male dancelike sway back and forth, the formal prelude to a fight. "Leave the lady alone."

"All I'm asking her for is three wishes," the fat man said. "That's not much." He ran his dirty fingers through his thinning hair. "You can whisper them if you want," he said. "There's some people that prefer that."

"All right, all right," Jodie said. She leaned toward him and lowered her voice toward the Genie of the Magic Lamp so that only he could hear. She just wanted to be left alone with Walton. She wanted to finish her coffee. Her needs were small. "I want a job," she said softly, "and I'd like that guy sitting next to me to love me, and I'd like a better radio when I listen to music in the morning."

"*That's it?*" The fat man stood up, a look of storybook outrage on his face. "I give you three wishes and you kiss them away like that? What's the matter with you? Give an American three wishes, and what do they do? Kiss them away! That's the trouble with this country. *No imagination when it comes to wishes!* All right, my pretty, you got it." And he dropped his dirty handkerchief in her lap. When she picked it up to remove it, she felt something travel up her arm—the electricity of disgust. The fat man rose and waddled out of the restaurant. She let go of the handkerchief and it drifted toward the floor.

"What was that?" Jodie asked. "What just happened?" She was shaking.

"That," Walton told her, "was a typical incident at Clara's Country Kitchen Café. The last time Tad gave someone three wishes, it was because the guy'd bought him a cup of coffee, and a tornado hit the guy's garage a couple of weeks later. Fat guys have really funny delusions, have you noticed that?" He waited. "You're shaking," he said, and put his hand on her shoulder. "What'd you ask for, Jodie?"

She turned to look out the front window and saw Walton's dog gazing straight back at her in an eerie manner.

"I asked for a job, and a better radio, and a million dollars."

"Then what was all that stuff about 'kiss away'?"

"Oh, I don't know. Walton, can we go, please? Can we pay our bill and leave?"

"I just remembered," Walton said. "It's that Rolling Stones tune. It's on one of those antique albums, I think." He raised his head to sing.

Love, sister, is just a kiss away,
Kiss away, kiss away, kiss away.

"I don't think that's what he meant," Jodie said.

Walton leaned forward and gave her a little harmless peck on the cheek. "Who knows?" he said. "Maybe it was. Anyhow, just think of him as an overweight placebo-person. He doesn't grant you the wish because, after all, he's just a fat psycho, but he *could* put you in the right frame of mind. We've got to think positively here."

"I like how you defended me," Jodie said. "Getting all male and everything."

"No problem," Walton said, holding up his fist for inspection. "I like fights."

She thought that she had interviewed well, but she wasn't offered the job she had applied for that day. They called her a week later—she had finally had a phone installed—and told her that they had given the position to someone else but that they had been impressed by her qualities and might call her again soon if another position opened up.

She and Walton continued their job-and-castoffs hunt, and it was Walton who found a job first, at the loading dock of a retailer in the suburbs, a twenty-four-hour discount store known internationally for shoddy merchandise. The job went from midnight to eight a.m.

She thought he wasn't quite physically robust enough for such work, but he claimed that he was stronger than he appeared. "It's all down here," he said, pointing to his lower back. "This is where you need it."

She didn't ask him what he was referring to—the muscles or the vertebrae or the cartilage. She had never seen his lower back. However, she was beginning to want to. On the passenger side of his car, she considered the swinging fuzzy dice and the intricately woven twigs of a bird's nest tossed on the top of the dashboard as he drove her to her various job interviews. His conversation was sprinkled with references to local geology and puzzles in medicine and biology. He was interested in most observable phenomena, and the pileup of souvenirs in the car reflected him. She liked this car. She had become accustomed to its ratty disarray and to the happy panting of Einstein, who always sat in the backseat, monitoring other dogs in other cars at intersections.

At one job interview, in a glass building so sterile she thought she should wear surgery-room snoods over her shoes, she was asked about her computer skills; at another, about what hobbies she liked to fill her spare time. She didn't think that the personnel director had any business asking her such questions. These days she filled her spare time daydreaming about sex with Walton. She didn't say so and didn't get the job. But at a wholesale supplier of office furniture and stationery, she was offered a position on the spot by a man whose suit was so wrinkled that it was prideful and emblematic. He was a gaudy slob. He owned the business. She was being asked to help them work on a program for inventory control. She would have other tasks. She sighed—those fucking computers were in her future again, they were unavoidable—but she took what they offered her. If she hadn't met Walton, if Walton and Einstein hadn't escorted her to the interview, she wouldn't have.

To celebrate, she and Walton decided to escape the August heat by hiking down Minnehaha Creek to its mouth at the Mississippi River across from Saint Paul. He didn't have to be at work for another four hours. He had brought his fishing pole and tackle box, and while he cast his line into the water, his dog sat behind him in the shade of a gnarled cottonwood and Jodie walked downriver, looking, but not looking for anything, exactly, just looking without a goal, for which she felt she had a talent. She found a bowling ball in usable condition and one bruised and broken point-and-shoot camera that she left under a bush.

She walked back along the river to Walton, carrying the bowling ball. On her face she had constructed an expression of delight. She was feeling hot and extremely beautiful.

"See what I've found?" She hoisted the ball.

"Hey, great," he said, casting her a smile. "See what I've caught?" He held up an imaginary line of invisible fish.

"Good for you," she said. His eyes were steady on her. He had been gazing at her for the last few days in a prolonged way; she'd been watching him do it. She could feel his presence now in her stomach and her knees. She heard the double blast of a boat horn. Another boat passed, pulling a water-skier with a strangely unhappy look on her face. The clock stopped; the moment paused: when he said he wanted to make love to her, that he almost couldn't wait, that he had lost his appetite lately just thinking about her and couldn't sleep, she didn't quite hear him saying it, she was so happy. She threw the bowling ball out as far as she could into the river. She didn't notice whether it splashed. She took her time getting into his arms, and when he kissed her, first at the base of her neck and then, lifting her up, all over her exposed skin, she put her hands in his hair. Suddenly she liked kissing in public. She wanted people to see them together. "Walton," she said, "make love to me. Right here."

"Let's go to your place," he said. "Let's go there, okay?"

"Happy days," she said in agreement, putting her fingers down inside his loose beltless jeans.

He was a slow-motion lover. She had made him some iced tea, but instead of drinking from it, he raised the cold glass to her forehead. Einstein had found a corner where she was panting with her eyes closed.

Jodie had taken him by the hand and had led him out to the sleeping porch. You couldn't have known it from the way he looked in his street clothes, but his body was lean and muscular, and he made love shyly at first and didn't really become easy and wild over her until he saw how she was responding to him. She was embarrassed by how quickly and how effortlessly he made her come. She put her arms up above her head and just gave in.

Maybe fools made the best lovers. They were devotees of passing pleasures, connoisseurs of them, and this, being the best of the passing pleasures, was the one at which they were most adept. His fire didn't burn away. He wasn't ashamed of any impulse he had, so he kept having them. He couldn't stop bringing himself into her. "Look at me," she said, as she was about to come again, and he looked at her with a slow grin on his face, pleased with himself and pleased with her. When she looked back at him, she let him see into her soul, all the way down, where she'd never allowed anyone to own her nakedness before.


"So. Happy ever after?"

Walton was asleep after a night's work, and Jodie had gone down to Clara's Country Kitchen Café by herself. This morning the fat man with yellow-green eyes was full of mirthless merriment, and he seemed to be spilling over the counter stool on all sides. If anything, he was twice as big as before. He was like a balloon filled with gravy. Jodie had been in the middle of her second cup of coffee and her scrambled eggs with ketchup when he sat down next to her. It was hard to imagine someone who could be more deliberately disgusting than this gentleman. He had a rare talent, Jodie thought, for inspiring revulsion. The possible images of the Family of Humankind did not somehow include him. He sat there shoveling an omelet and sausages into his mouth. Only occasionally did he chew.

"Happy enough," she said.

He nodded and snorted. " 'Happy enough,' " he quoted back to her. Sounds of swallowing and digestion erupted from him. "I give you a wish and you ask for a radio. There you have it." His accent was even more obscure and curious this morning.

"Where are you from?" Jodie asked. She had to angle her left leg away from his because his took up so much space under the counter. "You're not from here."

"No," he said. "I'm not really from anywhere. I was imported from Venice. A beautiful city, Venice. You ever been there?"

"Yes," she said, although she had not been. But she did love to read histories. "Lagoons, the Bridge of Sighs, and typhoid. Yeah, I've been there." She put her money down on the counter, and when she stood up, she felt a faint throbbing, almost a soreness but not quite that, Walton's desire, its trace, still inside her. "I have to go."

He resumed eating. "You didn't even thank me," the fat man said. "You smell of love and you didn't even thank me."

"All right. Thank you." She was hurrying out.

When she saw him in the mirror behind the cash register, he tipped an imaginary hat. She had seen something in his eyes: malice, she thought. As soon as she was out on the sidewalk, under the café's faded orange awning, her thoughts returned to Walton. She wanted to see him immediately and touch him. She headed for the crosswalk, all thoughts of the fat man dispersing and vanishing like smoke.

On the way back, she saw a thimble in the gutter. She deposited it in her purse. A fountain pen on the brick ledge of a storefront income-tax service gleamed at her in the cottony hazy heat, and she took that, too. Walton had given her the habit of appreciating foundlings. When she walked onto the sleeping porch, she took off her shoes. She still felt ceremonial with him. She showed him the thimble and the fountain pen. Then they were making love, their bodies slippery with sweat, and this time she stopped him for a moment and said, "I saw that fat man again," but he covered her mouth, and she sucked on his fingers. Afterward, she showered and dressed and caught the bus to work. Einstein groaned in her sleep as Jodie passed her in the hallway. The dog, Jodie thought, was probably jealous.

On the bus, Jodie hummed and smiled privately. She hadn't known about all these resources of pleasure in the world. It was a great secret. She looked at the other passengers with politeness but no special interest. Her love was a power that could attract and charm. She was radiantly burning with it. Everyone could see it.

Through the window she spotted a flock of geese in a V pattern flying east and then veering south.

From time to time, at work—where she was bringing people rapidly into her orbit thanks to her aura of good fortune—she would think of her happiness and try to hide it. She remembered not to speak of it, good luck having a tendency to turn to its opposite when mentioned.

She called her sister and her mother, both of whom wanted to meet Walton as soon as possible. Jodie tried to be dryly objective about him, but she couldn't keep it up for long; with her sister, she began giggling and weeping with happiness. Her best friend, Marge, came over one stormy afternoon in a visit of planned spontaneity and was so impressed by Walton that she took off her glasses and sang for him, thunder and lightning crashing outside and the electric lights flickering. She'd once been the vocalist in a band called Leaping Salmon, which had failed because of the insipid legato prettiness of their songs; when they changed their name to Toxic Waste and went for a grunge sound, the other band members had ousted her. Singing in Leaping Salmon had been her only life adventure, and she always mentioned it in conversations to people she had just met and wanted to impress, but while she was singing in her high, honeyed soprano, Walton walked over to Jodie, sat down next to her, and put his hand on the inside of her thigh. So that was that.

I have a lover, Jodie thought. Most people have lovers without paying any attention to what they have. They think pleasure is a birthright. They don't even know what luck they have when they have it.

At the end of the day she couldn't wait to see him. Every time she came into the room, his face seemed alert, relaxed, and sensual. Sometimes, thinking about him, she could feel a tightening, a prickling, all over her body. She was so in love and her skin so sensitive that she had to wear soft fabrics, cottons repeatedly washed. Her bras began to feel confining and priggish; on some days, she wouldn't wear them. The whole enterprise of love was old-fashioned and retrograde, she knew, but so what? Sometimes she thought, What's happening to me? She felt a certain evangelical enthusiasm and piety about sex, and pity for those who were unlucky in love.

Her soul became absentminded.

On some nights when Walton didn't have to go to the loading dock, she lay awake, with him draped around her. After lovemaking, his breath smelled of almonds. She would detach herself from him limb by limb and tiptoe into the kitchen. There, naked under the overhead light, she would remove her tarot pack from the coupon drawer and lay out the cards on the table.

Using the Celtic method of divination in the book of instructions, she would set down the cards.

This covers me.

This crosses me.

This crowns me, this is beneath me, this is behind me, this is before me, this is myself.

*These are my hopes and fears.*

The cards kept turning up in a peculiar manner. Instead of the cards promising blessings and fruitfulness, she found herself staring at the autumn and winter cards, the coins and the swords. This is before me:

the nine of swords, whose illustration is that of a woman waking at night with her face in her hands.

She had also been unnerved by the repeated appearance of the Chariot in reverse, a sign described in the guidebooks as "failure in carrying out a project, riot, litigation."

Propped up in her living-room chair, she had been dozing after dinner when the phone rang. She answered it in a stupor. She barely managed a whispered "hello."

She could make out the voice, but it seemed to come from the tomb, it was so faint. It belonged to a woman and it had some business to transact, but Jodie couldn't make out what the business was. "What?" she asked. "What did you say?"

"I said we should talk," the woman told her in a voice barely above a whisper, but still rich in wounded private authority. "We could meet. I know I shouldn't intrude like this, but I feel that I could tell you things. About Glaze. I know that you know him."

"Who are you? Are you seeing him?"

"Oh no no no," the woman said. "It isn't that." Then she said her name was Glynnis or Glenna—something odd and possibly resistant to spelling. "You don't know anything about him, do you?" The woman waited a moment. "His past, I mean."

"I guess I don't know that much," Jodie admitted. "Who are you?"

"I can fill you in. Look," she said, "I hate to do this, I hate sounding like this and I hate being like this, but I just think there are some facts you should know. These are facts I have. I'm just . . . I don't know what I am. Maybe I'm just trying to help."

"All right," Jodie said. She uncrossed her legs and put her feet on the floor and tried to clear her mind. "I get off work at five. The office is near downtown." She named a bar where her friends sometimes went in the late afternoons.

"Oh, there?" the woman asked, her voice rising with disappointment. "Do you really like that place?" When Jodie didn't respond, the woman said, "The *smoke* in there makes me *cough*. I have allergies. Quite a few allergies." She suggested another restaurant, an expensive Italian place with lazily stylish wrought-iron furniture on the terrace and its name above the door in leaded glass. Jodie remembered the decor—she hadn't liked it. However, she didn't want to prolong these negotiations for another minute. "And *don't* tell Glaze I called," the woman said. Her speech was full of italics.

When Jodie hung up, she began to chew her thumbnail. She glanced up and saw her reflection in a window. She pulled her thumb away quickly; then she tried to smile at herself.

She was seated in what she considered a good spot near a window in the nonsmoking section when the woman entered the restaurant and was directed by the headwaiter to Jodie's table. The woman was twelve minutes late. Jodie leaned back and arranged her face into a temporary pleasantness. The stranger was pregnant and was walking with a slightly prideful sway, as if she herself were the china shop. Although she was sporting an attractive watercolor-hued peacock-blue maternity blouse, she was also wearing shorts and sandals, apparently to show off her legs, which were deeply tanned. The ensemble didn't quite fit together, but it compelled attention. Her hair was carefully messed up, as if she had just come from an assignation, and she wore two opal earrings that went with the blouse. She was pretty enough, but it was the sort of prettiness that Jodie distrusted because there was nothing friendly about it, nothing settled or calm. She was the sort of woman whom other women instinctively didn't like. She looked like an aging groupie, a veteran of many beds, and she had the deadest eyes Jodie had ever seen, pale gray and icy.

"You must be Jodie," the woman said, putting one hand over her stomach and thrusting the other hand out. "I'm Gleinya Roberts." She laughed twice, as if her name itself was witty. When she stopped laughing, her mouth stayed open and her face froze momentarily, as more soundless laughter continued to emerge from her. Jodie found everything about her disconcerting, though she couldn't say why. "May I sit down?" the woman asked.

Feeling that she had been indeliberately rude, Jodie nodded and waved her hand toward the chair with the good view. The question had struck her as either preposterous or injured, and because she felt off balance, she didn't remember to introduce herself until the right moment had passed. "I'm Jodie Sklar," she said.

"Well, I know *that*," Gleinya Roberts said, settling herself delicately into her chair. "You must be wondering if this baby is Glaze's. Don't worry. I can assure you that it's not," she said with a frozen half grin, a grin that seemed preserved in ice. The thought of the baby's father hadn't occurred to Jodie until that moment. "I'm in my *fifth* month," the woman continued, "and the Little Furnace is certainly heating me up these days. Bad timing! It's much better to be pregnant in Minnesota in the winter. You can keep yourself warm that way. You don't have any children yourself, Jodie, do you?"

Jodie was so taken aback by the woman's prying and familiarity that she just smiled and shook her head. All the same, she felt it was time to establish some boundaries. "No, not yet," she said, after a moment. "Maybe someday." She paused for a second to take a breath and then said, "You know, I'm pleased to meet you and everything, but you must know that I'm . . . well, I'm really curious about why you're here. Why'd you call me?"

"Oh, don't let's rush it. In a minute, in a minute," Gleinya Roberts said, tipping her head and staring with her dead eyes at Jodie's hair. "I just want to establish a friendly basis." She opened her mouth, and her face froze again as soundless laughter rattled its way in Jodie's direction. "Jodie, I just can't take my eyes off your hair. You have such beautiful black hair. Men must love it. Where do you get it from?"

"From? Where do I get it from? Well, my father had dark hair. It was quite glossy. It shone sometimes."

"Oh," the woman said. "I don't think women get their hair from their fathers. I don't think that's where that gene comes from. It's the mother, I believe. I'm a zoologist, an ornithologist, actually, so I'm not up on hair. But I do know you don't get much from your father except trouble. Sklar. What kind of name is that? Do Sklars have beautiful black hair?"

Before Jodie could answer, the waitress appeared and asked for their order. Gleinya Roberts reached for the menu, and while Jodie ordered a beer, the woman—Jodie was having trouble thinking of her as "Gleinya"—scanned the bill of fare with eyes slitted with skepticism and one eyebrow partially raised. "I'd *like* wine," Gleinya Roberts said, and just as the waitress was about to ask what kind, she continued, "but I can't have any because of the baby. What I *would* like is sparkling water but with no flavoring, no ice, and no sliced lemon or lime, please." The waitress wrote this down. "Are you ordering anything to eat?" Gleinya Roberts asked Jodie. "I am. Perhaps a salad. Do your salads have croutons?" The waitress said that they did. "Well, *please* take them out for me. I can't eat them. They're treated." She asked for the Caesar salad, explaining that she positively lived on Caesar salad these days. "But no additives of any kind, please," she said, after the waitress had already turned to leave. Apparently the waitress hadn't heard, because she didn't stop or turn around. If Jodie had been that waitress, she believed that she wouldn't have turned around, either. "I'm afraid I'm terribly picky," Gleinya Roberts announced. "You have to be, these days. It's the Age of Additives."

"I eat anything," Jodie said, rather aggressively. "I've always eaten anything." Gleinya Roberts patted her stomach and smiled sadly at Jodie but said nothing. "Now, Gleinya," she pressed on, "perhaps you can tell me why we're here."

Gleinya held her left hand out with the fingers straight and examined her wedding ring. It was a quick mean-spirited gesture, but it was not lost on Jodie. "It's about Glaze, of course," she said. "Maybe you can guess that I used to be with him. It ended two years ago, but we still talk from time to time." She took a long sip of her water, and while she did, Jodie allowed herself to wonder who called whom. And when: probably late at night. "Anyway," she went on, "that's how I know about you." She put down her water glass and smiled unpleasantly. "That's how I know about your *sleeping* porch. He's been spending some nights there. He's terribly in love with you," she said. "You're just *all* he talks about."

Jodie moved back in her chair, sat up straight, and said, "He's a wonderful guy."

"Yes," the other woman said, rather slowly, to affirm that Jodie had said what she had in fact said but not to agree to it. Suddenly, and quite unexpectedly, Gleinya Roberts half stood up, then sat down again and settled herself, flinging her elbows out, and before Jodie could ask why she had done so, though at this point the inquiry did seem rather pointless, Gleinya Roberts said, "It's so hard to get comfortable in your second term. All those little infant kicks." She patted her stomach again.

"They don't seem to have hurt you, exactly," Jodie said.

"No, but you have to be careful." She touched the base of her neck with the third finger of her right hand, tapping the skin thoughtfully. "You have to try to keep your looks up. You have to try to keep *yourself* up. Men get fickle. Of course, my husband, Jerry, says I'm still pretty, 'prettier than ever,' he says, a sweet lie, though I don't mind hearing it. He only says that to please me. It's just a love-lie. Still, I try to believe him when he says those things."

I bet you do, Jodie thought. I bet it's no effort at all. "You were going to tell me about Walton."

"Yes, I was," she said. The waitress reappeared, placed Jodie's glass of beer, gowned in frost, in front of her, and Jodie took a long, comforting gulp. All at once Gleinya Roberts's voice changed, going up half an octave. She had leaned forward, and her face was infected with old grudges and hatreds. "Jodie," she said, "I have to warn you. I have to do this, woman to woman. I want you to protect yourself. I know how suspicious this seems, coming from an old girlfriend, and I know that it must sound like sour grapes, but I have to tell you that what I'm saying is true, and I wouldn't say it unless I was worried for your safety. He likes fights. He likes fighting. You've seen how he favors his right foot, haven't you? That old injury?"

Jodie swallowed but could not bring herself to nod.

"He got it in a bar fight. Somebody kicked him in the ankle and shattered the bone. I mean, that's all right, men get into fights, but what you have to know is that he used to beat *me* up—and the girl before me, he beat her up, too. He'd get drunk and coked up and start in on me. Sometimes he did it carefully so it wouldn't show—"

"He doesn't drink," Jodie said, her mouth instantly dry. "He doesn't do drugs."

"Maybe not *now*, he doesn't," Gleinya Roberts said, smiling for a microsecond and patting the tablecloth with little grace-note gestures. "But he has and probably will again. His sweet side is so sweet that it's hard to figure out the other side. He just explodes. He's such a good lover that you don't want to notice it. He's quite the dick artist. But then he just turns, and it's like a nightmare. He waits until you're really, really happy, and then he blows up. Once, months and months and months ago, I told him that someday I wanted to go out to the West Coast and sit on the banks of the Pacific Ocean and go whale watching. You know, see the whales go spouting by, on their migrations. We both had a vacation around the same time—"

"I don't think it's the 'banks' of the Pacific Ocean. That's for rivers. I think you mean 'shore,' " Jodie said.

Gleinya Roberts shrugged. "All *right*. 'Shore.' Anyway, we both had a vacation around the same time, and we drove out there . . . no, we flew . . . and then we rented a car . . ."

She put her hand over her mouth, appearing to remember, but instead her eyes began to fill with dramatic, restaurant-scene tears; and at that moment Jodie felt a conviction that this woman was lying and was still probably in love with Walton.

"We rented a car," she was saying, "and we drove up from San Francisco toward Arcata, along there, along that coast. There are redwood forests a few miles back from the coastline, those big old trees. We'd stay in motels, and I'd make a picnic in the morning, and we'd go out, and Glaze would start drinking after breakfast, and by midafternoon he'd be silent and surly—he'd stop speaking to me—and by the time we got back to our motel, he'd be muttering, and I'd try to talk about what we had seen that day. I mean, usually when you go whale watching *there aren't any whales.* But there *are* always seals. You can hear the seals barking, down there on those rocks. I'd ask him if he didn't think the cliffs were beautiful or the wildflowers or the birds or whatever I had pointed out to him. But I always said something wrong. Something that was like a lighted match, and he'd blow up. And he'd start in on me. You ever been hit in the face?"

Jodie had turned so that she could see the sidewalk through the window. She was getting herself ready. It wasn't going to take much more.

"I didn't think so. It comes out of nowhere," Gleinya Roberts was saying, "and you're not ready for it, and then, boom, he lands the second one on you. The first time he beats you up, it's an initiation, and then he makes love to you to make up for it, but it makes the second one easier to do, because he's already done it. You don't expect it. Why *should* you? Why do you think he got thrown out of medical school? He hurt somebody there. He broke two of my ribs. I had a shoulder separation from him. He got very practiced in the ways of apology and remorse. He has a genius for remorse. And then of course he's a demon under the sheets. The man can fuck, I'll give him that, but, I don't know, after a while great sex is sort of a *gimmick.* It's like a 3-D movie, and you get tired of it. Well, maybe you're not tired of it yet."

Jodie said nothing.

"I don't blame you. I wouldn't say anything, either. I thought he was Prince Charming, too. I've been there. And believe me, I had to kiss a lot of frogs before I found the right guy. I had to kiss them in every damn place they had. But he won't tell you. *He* won't tell you about himself," she repeated. "Ask his father, though. His father will tell you. Well, maybe he'll tell you. You haven't met his father yet, have you?"

She speared a piece of her Caesar salad, chewed thoughtfully, then put down her fork.

"A woman has to tell another woman," she said, "in the case of a man like this. I wanted to help you. I wouldn't want you to be on daytime TV, one of those *afternoon* talk shows, in a body cast onstage, warning other women about men like this. Jodie, you can look in my eyes and see that what I'm telling you is true."

Jodie looked. The eyes she saw were gray and blank, and for a moment they reminded her of the blankness of the surface of the ocean, and then the waters parted, and she saw a seemingly endless landscape of rancor, a desert of gray rocks and black ashy flowers. Demons lived there. Then, just as quickly as it had appeared, the desert was covered over again, and Jodie knew that she had been right not to believe her.

"You're lying to me," Jodie said. She hadn't meant to say it, only to think it, but it had come out, and there it was.

Gleinya Roberts nodded, acknowledging her own implausibility. "You're just denying. You're gaga over him. Just as I was. Taking a cruise on his pleasure ship. But, Jodie, trust me, *that* cruise is going to end. Don't play the fool."

"What?"

"I said, 'Don't play the fool.' "

"I thought that was what you said."

Jodie, her head buzzing, and most of her cells on fire, found herself standing up. "You come in here," she said, "with your trophy wedding ring, and your trophy pregnancy, and your husband who says you're still pretty, and you tell me *this,* about Walton, spoiling the first happiness I've had in I don't know how long? Who the hell *are* you? *What* are you? You don't even look especially human." Gleinya Roberts tilted her head, considering this statement. Her face was unaccountably radiant. "I don't have to listen to you," Jodie said. "I don't have to listen to this nonsensical bullshit."

Her hands shaking, she reached into her purse for some money for the beer, and she heard Gleinya Roberts say, "Oh, I'll pay for it," while Jodie found a ten-dollar bill and flung it on the table. She saw that Gleinya Roberts's face was paralyzed in that attitude of soundless laughter—maybe it was just strain—and Jodie was stricken to see that the woman's teeth were perfect and white and symmetrical, and her tongue—her tongue!—was dark red and sensual as it licked her upper lip. Jodie leaned forward to tip over her beer in Gleinya Roberts's direction, careful to give the action the clear appearance of accident.

What was left of the beer made its dull way over to the other side of the table and dribbled halfheartedly downward.

"He's beautiful," Jodie said quietly, as the other woman gathered up the cloth napkins to sop up the beer, "and he makes sense to me, and I don't have to listen to you now."

"No, you don't," she said. "You go live with Glaze. You do that. But just remember: That man is like the kea. Ever heard of it? I didn't think so. It's a beautiful bright green New Zealand bird. It's known for its playfulness. But it's a sheep killer. It picks out their eyes. Just remember the kea. And take this." From somewhere underneath the table she grasped for and then handed Jodie an audiocassette. "It's a predator tape. Used for attracting hawks and coyotes. It used to be his favorite listening. Just fascinated the hell out of him. It'll surprise you. *Women don't know about men*. Men don't let them."

Jodie had taken the tape, but she was now halfway out of the restaurant. Still, she heard behind her that voice coming after her. "Men don't want us to know. Jodie, they don't!"


In a purely distanced and distracted state, she took a bus over to Minnehaha Creek and walked down the path alongside the flowing waters to the bank of the Mississippi River. The air smelled rotten and dreary. Underneath a bush she found two bottle caps and a tuna fish can. She left them there.


Sitting on the bus toward home, she tried to lean into the love she felt for Walton, and the love he said he felt for her, but instead of solid ground and rock just underneath the soil, and rock cliffs that composed a wall where a human being could prop herself and stand, there was nothing: stone gave way to sand, and sand gave way to water, and the water drained away into darkness and emptiness. Into this emptiness, violence, like an ever-flowing stream, was poured—the violence of the kea, Walton's violence, Gleinya Roberts's violence, and finally her own. She traced every inch of her consciousness for a place on which she might set her foot against doubt, and she could not find it. Inside her was the impulse, as clear as blue sky on a fine summer morning, to acquire a pistol and shoot Gleinya Roberts through the heart. Her mind raced through the maze, back and forth, trying to find an exit.

Gleinya Roberts had lied to her. She was sure of that.

But it didn't matter. She was in fear of being struck. Although she had never been beaten by anyone, ever, in her life, the prospect frightened her so deeply that she felt parts of her psyche and her soul turning to stone. Other women might not be frightened. Other women would fight back, or were beaten and survived. But she was not them. She was herself, a woman mortally afraid of being violated.

Three blocks away from her apartment, she bought, in a drugstore, a radio with a cassette player in it, and she took it with her upstairs; and in the living room she placed it on the coffee table, next to Walton's latest found treasures: a pleasantly shaped rock with streaks of red, probably jasper; a squirt gun; and a little ring through which was placed a ball-point pen.

She dropped the predator tape Gleinya Roberts had given her into the machine, and she pushed the PLAY button.

From the speaker came the scream of a rabbit. Whoever had made this tape had probably snapped the serrated metal jaws of a trap on the rabbit's leg and then turned on the recorder. It wasn't a tape loop: the rabbit's screams were varied, no two alike. Although the screams had a certain sameness, the clarifying monotony of terror, there existed, as in a row of corn, a range of distinctive external variety. Terror gave way to pain, pain made room for terror. The soul of the animal was audibly ripped apart, and out of its mouth came this shrieking. Jodie felt herself getting sick and dizzy. The screams continued. They went on and on. In the forests of the night these screams rose with predictable regularity once darkness fell. Though wordless, they had supreme eloquence and a huge claim upon truth. Jodie was weeping now, the heels of her hands dug into her cheekbones. The screams did not cease. They rose in frequency and intensity. The tape almost academically laid out at disarming length the necessity of terror. All things innocent and forsaken had their moment of expression, as the strong, following their nature, crushed themselves into their prey. Still it went on, this bloody fluting. Apparently it was not to be stopped.

Jodie reached out and pressed the PAUSE button. She was shaking now, shivering. She felt herself falling into shock, and when she looked up, she saw Walton standing near the door—he had a key by now—with Einstein wagging her tail next to him, and he was carrying his daily gift, this time a birdhouse, and he said, "She found you, didn't she? That miserable, crazy woman."


He puts down the birdhouse and squats near her. From this position, he drops to his knees. Kneeling thus before her, he tries to smile, and his eyes have that pleasant fool quality they have always had. This man may never make a fortune. He may never amount to much. That would be fine. His dog pants behind him, like a backup singer emphasizing the vocal line and giving it a harmony. Walton's hands start at her hair and then slowly descend to her shoulders and arms. Before she can stop him, he has taken her into his embrace.

He is murmuring. Yes, he knew Gleinya Roberts, and, yes, they did own a predator tape *she* had found somewhere, but, no, he did not listen to it more than once. Yes, he had lived with her for a while, but she was insane (his father had been dead for a year; she had lied about that, too), and she was insanely jealous, hysterical, actually, and given to lies and lying, habitual lies, crazy bedeviling lies, and casual lies: lies about whether the milk was spoiled, lies about how many stamps were still in the drawer, lies about trivial matters and large ones, a cornucopia of lies, a feast of untruth. Gleinya Roberts was not married, for starters. He could prove that.

*I'm just what I seem,* he says. A modest man who loves you, who will love you forever. Did Gleinya tell you that I beat her up? Do you really think I am what that woman says I am? I used to get into barroom fights, but that's different. I never denied that. She's deluded. If what she said was true, would this dog be here with me?

Jodie looks at Walton and at his dog. Then she says, Raise your hand, fast, above Einstein's head. Look at her and raise your hand.

When he does what he is asked to do, Einstein neither cringes nor cowers. She watches Walton with her usual impassive interest, her tail still wagging. She has what seems to be a dog smile on her face. She approaches him, panting. She wants to play. She sits down next to where he kneels. She is the fool's dog. She looks at Walton—there is no mistaking this look—with straightforward dog love.

Jodie believes this dog. She believes this dog more than the woman.

Let me explain something, Walton is saying. You're beautiful. I started with that the first time I saw you. He does a little inventory: you lick your fingers after opening tin cans, you wear hats at a jaunty angle, you have a quick laugh like a bark, you move like a dancer, you're funny, you're great in bed, you love my dog, you're thoughtful, you have opinions. It's the whole package. How can I not love you?

And if I *ever* do to you what that woman says I did, you can just walk.


One day he will present her with an engagement ring, pretending that he found it in an ashtray at Clara's Country Kitchen Café. The ring will fit her finger, and it will be a seemingly perfect ring, with two tiny sapphires and one tiny diamond, probably all flawed, but flawless to the naked eye. They will be walking under a bridge on the south end of Lake of the Isles, and when they are halfway under the bridge, he will show her the ring and ask her to marry him.

Then she will sit for a few more days on the sleeping porch, considering this man. She won't be able to help it that when he moves suddenly, she will flinch. She will be distracted, but with the new radio on, she will from time to time do her best to read some of the books she never got around to reading before. Literature, however, will not help her in this instance. She will take out her tarot cards and place them in their proper order on the table.

This covers him.

This crosses him.

This crowns him.

This is beneath him.

This is behind him.

But the future will not unveil itself. The newspapers of the future are all blank. She will in exasperation throw all the tarot cards into the Dumpster. She will buy a copy of the Rolling Stones' album *Let It Bleed*.

She will listen to "Gimme Shelter," the song Walton had quoted, but now she hears two lines slurred hysterically and almost inaudibly in the background—lines she had never heard before.

Rape, murder, are just a kiss away,
Kiss away, kiss away, kiss away.

She will throw away the album, also, into the Dumpster.

Once upon a time, happily ever after. She will look occasionally for the hideous fat man at the breakfast counter on Hennepin Avenue, but of course he will have vanished. When you are awarded a wish, you must specify the conditions under which it is granted. Everyone knows that. The fat man could have told her this simple truth, but he did not. Women are supposed to know such things. They are supposed to arm themselves against the infidelities of the future.

She will feel herself getting ready to leap, to say *yes*.

And just before she does, just before she agrees to marry him, she will buy a recording of Granados's piano suite *Goyescas*. Again and again she will listen to the fourth of the pieces, "Quejas ó la Maja y el ruiseñor," the story in music of a maiden singing to her nightingale. Every question the maiden sings, the bird sings back.

One Sunday night around one o'clock she will hear the distant sound of gunshots, or perhaps a car backfiring. She will then hear voices raised in anger and agitation. Sirens, glass breaking, the clatter of a garbage can rolled on pavement: city sounds. But she will fall back to sleep easily, her hands tucked under her pillow, drowsy and calm.

# The Next Building
# I Plan to Bomb

IN THE PARKING LOT next to the bank, Harry Edmonds saw a piece of gray scrap paper the size of a greeting card. It had blown up next to his leg and attached itself to him there. Across the top margin was some scrabby writing in purple ink. He picked it up and examined it. On the upper left-hand corner someone had scrawled the phrase THE NEXT BUILDING I PLAN TO BOMB. Harry unfolded the paper and saw an inked drawing of what appeared to be a sizable train station or some other public structure, perhaps an airport terminal. In the drawing were arched windows and front pillars but very little other supporting detail. The building looked solid, monumental, and difficult to destroy.

He glanced around the parking lot. There he was in Five Oaks, Michigan, where there were no such buildings. In the light wind other pieces of paper floated by in an agitated manner. One yellow flyer was stuck to a fire hydrant. On the street was the daily crowd of bankers, lawyers, shoppers, and students. As usual, no one was watching him or paying much attention to him. He put the piece of paper into his coat pocket.

All afternoon, while he sat at his desk, his hand traveled down to his pocket to touch the drawing. Late in the day, half as a joke, he showed the paper to the office receptionist.

"You've got to take it to the police," she told him. "This is dangerous. This is the work of a maniac. That's LaGuardia there, the airport? In the picture? I was there last month. I'm sure it's LaGuardia, Mr. Edmonds. No kidding. Definitely LaGuardia."

So at the end of the day, before going home, he drove to the main police station on the first floor of City Hall. Driving into the sun, he felt his eyes squinting against the burrowing glare. He had stepped inside the front door when the waxy bureaucratic smell of the building hit him and gave him an immediate headache. A cop in uniform, wearing an impatient expression, sat behind a desk, shuffling through some papers, and at that moment it occurred to Harry Edmonds that if he showed what was in his pocket to the police he himself would become a prime suspect and an object of intense scrutiny, all privacy gone. He turned on his heel and went home.

At dinner, he said to his girlfriend, "Look what I found in a parking lot today." He handed her the drawing.

Lucia examined the soiled paper, her thumb and finger at its corner, and said, " 'The next building I plan to bomb.' " Her tone was light and urbane. She sold computer software and was sensitive to gestures. Then she said, "That's Union Station, in Chicago." She smiled. "Well, Harry, what are you going to do with this? Some nutcase did this, right?"

"Actually, I got as far as the foyer in the police station this afternoon," he said. "Then I turned around. I couldn't show it to them. I thought they'd suspect me or something."

"Oh, that's so melodramatic," she said. "You've never committed a crime in your life. You're a banker, for Chrissake. You're in the trust department. You're harmless."

Harry sat back in his chair and looked at her. "I'm not that harmless."

"Yes, you are." She laughed. "You're quite harmless."

"Lucia," he said, "I wish you wouldn't use that word."

" 'Harmless'? It's a compliment."

"Not in this country, it isn't," he said.

On the table were the blue plates and matching napkins and the yellow candles that Lucia brought out whenever she was proud of what she or Harry had cooked. Today it was Burmese chicken curry. "Well, if you're worried, take it to the cops," Lucia told him. "That's what the cops are there for. Honey," she said, "no one will suspect you of anything. You're handsome and stable and you're my sweetie, and I love you, and what else happened today? Put that awful creepy paper back into your pocket. How do you like the curry?"

"It's delicious," he said.

After Harry had gotten up his nerve sufficiently to enter the police station again, he walked in a determined manner toward the front desk. After looking carefully at the drawing and the inked phrase, and writing down Harry Edmonds's name and address, the officer, whose badge identified him as Sergeant Bursk, asked, "Mr. Edmonds, you got any kids?"

"Kids? No, I don't have kids. Why?"

"Kids did this," Sergeant Bursk told him, waving the paper in front of him as if he were drying it off. "My kids could've done this. Kids do this. Boys do this. They draw torture chambers and they make threats and what-have-you. That's what they do. It's the youth. But they're kids. They don't mean it."

"How do you know?"

"Because I have three of them," Sergeant Bursk said. "I'm not saying that you should have kids, I'm just saying that I have them. I'll keep this drawing, though, if you don't mind."

"Actually," Harry said, "I'd like it back."

"Okay," Sergeant Bursk said, handing it to him, "but if we hear of any major bombings, and, you know, large-scale serious death, maybe we'll give you a call."

"Yeah," Harry said. He had been expecting this. "By the way," he asked, "does this look like any place in particular to you?"

The cop examined the picture. "Sure," he said. "That's Grand Central. In New York, on Forty-second Street, I think. I was there once. You can tell by the clock. See this clock here?" He pointed at a vague circle. "That's Grand Central, and this is the big clock that they've got there on the front."

"The fuck it is," the kid said. The kid was in bed with Harry Edmonds in the Motel 6. They had found each other in a bar downtown and then gone to this motel, and after they were finished, Harry drew the drawing out of his pants pocket on the floor and showed it to him. The kid's long brown hair fell over his eyes and, loosened from its ponytail, spread out on the pillow. "I know this fucking place," the kid said. "I've, like, traveled, you know, all over Europe. This is in Europe, this place, this is fucking Deutschland we're talking about here." The kid got up on his elbows to see better. "Oh, yeah, I remember this place. I was there, two summers ago? Hamburg? This is the Dammtor Bahnhof."

"Never heard of it," Harry Edmonds said.

"You never heard of it 'cause you've never been there, man. You have to fucking be there to know about it." The kid squinched his eyebrows together like a professor making a difficult point. "A *bahnhof,* see, is a train station, and the Dammtor Bahnhof is, like, one of the stations there, and this is the one that the Nazis rounded up the Jews to. And, like, sent them off from. This place, man. Absolutely. It's still standing. This one, it fucking deserves to be bombed. Just blow it totally the fuck away, off the face of the earth. That's just my opinion. It's evil, man."

The kid moved his body around in bed, getting himself comfortable again after stating his opinions. He was slinky and warm, like a cat. The kid even made back-of-the-throat noises, a sort of satisfied purr.


"I thought we were finished with that," Harry's therapist said. "I thought we were finished with the casual sex. I thought, Harry, that we had worked through those fugitive impulses. I must tell you that it troubles me that we haven't. I won't say that we're back to square one, but it is a backward step. And what I'm wondering now is, why did it happen?"

"Lucia said I was harmless, that's why."

"And did that anger you?"

"You bet it angered me." Harry sat back in his chair and looked directly at his therapist. He wished she would get a new pair of eyeglasses. These eyeglasses made her look like one of those movie victims killed within the first ten minutes, right after the opening credits. One of those innocent bystanders. "Bankers are not harmless, I can assure you."

"Then why did you pick up that boy?" She waited. When he didn't say anything, she said, "I can't think of anything more dangerous to do."

"It was the building," Harry said.

"What building?"

"I showed Lucia the building. On the paper. This paper." He took it out of his pocket and handed it to his therapist. By now the paper was becoming soft and wrinkled. While she studied the picture, Harry watched the second hand of the wall clock turn.

"You found this?" she asked. "You didn't draw this."

"Yes, I found it." He waited. "I found it in a parking lot six blocks from here."

"All right. You showed Lucia this picture. And perhaps she called you harmless. Why did you think it so disturbing to be called harmless?"

"Because," Harry said, "in this country, if you're harmless, you get killed and eaten. That's the way things are going these days. That's the current trend. I thought you had noticed. Perhaps not."

"And why do you say that people get killed and eaten? That's an extravagant metaphor. It's a kind of hysterical irony."

"No, it isn't. I work in a bank and I see it happen every day. I mop up the blood."

"I don't see what this has to do with picking up young men and taking them to motels," she said. "That's back in the country of acting out. And what I'm wondering is, what does this mean about your relationship with Lucia? You're endangering her, you know." As if to emphasize the point, she said, "It's wrong, what you did. And very, very dangerous. With all your thinking, did you think about that?"

Harry didn't answer. Then he said, "It's funny. Everybody has a theory about what that building is. You haven't said anything about it. What's your theory?"

"This building?" Harry's therapist examined the paper through her movie-victim glasses. "Oh, it's the Field Museum, in Chicago. And that's not a theory. It is the Field Museum."


On Wednesday, at three a.m., Harry fixed his gaze on the bedroom ceiling. There, as if on a screen, shaped by the light through the curtains luffing in the window, was a public building with front pillars and curved arched windows and perhaps a clock. On the ceiling the projected sun of Harry's mind rose wonderfully, brilliantly gold, one or two mind-wisp cumulus clouds passing from right to left across it, but not so obscured that its light could not penetrate the great public building into which men, women, and children—children in strollers, children hand in hand with their parents—now filed, shadows on the ceiling, lighted shadows, and for a moment Harry saw an explosive flash.

Harry Edmonds lay in his bed without sleeping. Next to him was his girlfriend, whom he had planned to marry, once he ironed out a few items of business in his personal life and got them settled. He had made love to her, to this woman, this Lucia, a few hours earlier, with earnest caresses, but now he seemed to be awake again. He rose from bed and went down to the kitchen. In the harsh fluorescence he ate a cookie and on an impulse turned on the radio. The radio blistered with the economy of call-in hatred and religion revealed to rabid-mouthed men who now gasped and screamed into all available microphones. He adjusted the dial to a call-in station. Speaking from Delaware, a man said, "There's a few places I'd do some trouble to, believe me, starting with the Supreme Court and moving on to a clinic or two." Harry snapped off the radio.

Now he sits in the light of the kitchen. He feels as dazed as it is possible for a sane man to feel at three thirty in the morning. I am not silly, nor am I trivial, Harry says to himself, as he reaches for a pad of paper and a no. 2 pencil. At the top of the pad, Harry writes, "The next place I plan to bomb," and then very slowly, and with great care, begins to draw his own face, its smooth cleanshaven contours, its courteous half smile. When he perceives his eyes beginning to water, he rips off the top sheet with his picture on it and throws it in the wastebasket. The refrigerator seems to be humming some tune to him, some tune without a melody, and he flicks off the overhead light before he recognizes that tune.

It is midday in downtown Five Oaks, Michigan, the time for lunch and rest and conversation, and for a remnant, a lucky few, it may be a time for love, but here before us is Harry Edmonds, an officer in the trust department at Southeastern Michigan Bank and Trust, standing on a street corner in a strong spring wind. The wind pulls at his tie and musses his hair. Nearby, a recycling container appears to have overturned, and sheets of paper, hundreds of them, papers covered with drawings and illustrations and words, have scattered. Like a flock of birds, they have achieved flight. All around Harry Edmonds they are gripped in this whirlwind and flap and snap in circles. Some stick to him. There are glossy papers with perfumed inserts, and there are yellowing papers with four-color superheroes, and there are the papers with attractive unclothed airbrushed bodies, and there are the papers with bills and announcements and loans. Here are the personals, swirling past, and there a flyer for a home theater big-screen TV. Harry Edmonds, a man uncertain of the value of his own life, who at this moment does not know whether his life has, in fact, any importance at all, or any future, lifts his head in the wind, increasing in volume and intensity, and for a moment he imagines himself being blown away. From across the street, the way he raises his head might appear, to an observer, as a posture of prayer. God, it is said, resides in the whirlwind, and certainly Harry Edmonds's eyes are closed and now his head is bowed. He does not move forward or backward, and it is unclear from the expression on his face whether he is making any sort of wish. He remains stationary, on this street corner, while all about him the papers fly first toward him, and then away.

A moment later he is gone from the spot where he stood. No doubt he has returned to his job at the bank, and that is where we must leave him.

# Flood Show

IN LATE MARCH, at its low flood stage, the Chaska River rises up to the benches and the picnic areas in the Eurekaville city park. No one pays much attention to it anymore. Three years ago, Conor and Janet organized a flood lunch for themselves and their three kids. They started their meal perched cross-legged on an oilcloth they had draped over the picnic table. The two adults sat at the ends, and the kids sat in the middle, crowding the food. They had had to walk through water to get there. The water was flowing across the grass directly under the table, past the charcoal grills and the bandstand. It had soaked the swing seats. It had reached the second rung of the ladder on the slide.

After a few minutes, they all took off their shoes, which were wet anyway, and they sat down on the benches. The waters slurred over their feet pleasantly, while the deviled eggs and mustard-ham sandwiches stayed safe in their waxed paper and Tupperware. It was a sunny day, and the flood had a peaceable aspect. The twins yelled and threw some of their food into the water and smiled when it floated off downriver. The picnic tables, bolted into cement, served as anchors and observation platforms. Jeremy, who was thirteen that spring, drew a picture, a pencil sketch, the water suggested by curlicues and subtle smearings of spit.

Every three years or so, Eurekaville gets floods like this. It's the sort of town where floods are welcome. They spill over the top banks, submerge the baseball diamond and the soccer field, soak a basement or two along Island Drive, and then recede. Usually the waters pass by lethargically. On the weekends, people wade out into them and play flood-volleyball and flood-softball. This year the Eurekaville High School junior class has brought bleachers down from the gym and set them up on the paved driveway of the park's northwest slope, close to the river itself, where you can get a good view of the waterlogged trash floating by. Jeremy, who is

Conor's son from his first marriage and who is now sixteen, has been selling popcorn and candy bars to the spectators who want to sit there and chat while they watch the flotsam. He's been joined in this effort by a couple of his classmates. All profits, he claims, will go into the fund for the fall class trip to Washington, D.C.

By late Friday afternoon, with the sun not quite visible, thirty people had turned out to watch the flood—a social event, a way to end the day, a break from domestic chores, especially on a cloudy spring evening. One of Jeremy's friends had brought down a boom box and played Jesus Jones and Biohazard. There was dancing in the bleachers, slowish and tidal, against the music's frantic rhythms.

Conor's dreams these days have been invaded by water. He wakes on Saturday morning and makes quiet closed-door love to his wife. When he holds her, or when they kiss, and his eyes close, he thinks of the river. He thinks of the rivers inside both of them, rivers of blood and water. Lymphatic pools. All the fluids, the carriers of their desires. Odors of sweat, odors of salt. Touching Janet, he almost says, *We're mostly water.* Of course everyone knows that, the body's content of liquid matter. But he can't help it: that's what he thinks.

After his bagel and orange juice, Conor leaves Janet upstairs with the twins, Annah and Joe, who conspire together to dress as slowly as they possibly can, and he bicycles down to the river to take a look. Conor is a large, bearish man with thick brown hair covered by a beret that does not benefit his appearance. He knows the beret makes him a bit strange-looking, and this pleases him. Whenever he bikes anywhere there is something violent in his body motions. Pedaling along, he looks like a trained circus bear. Despite his size, however, Conor is mild and kind-hearted—the sort of man who believes that love and caresses are probably the answer for everything—but you wouldn't know that about him unless you saw his eyes, which are placidly sensual, curious—a photographer's eyes, just this side of sentimental, belonging to someone who quite possibly thinks too much about love for his own good.

The business district of Eurekaville has its habitual sleepy aura, its morning shroud of mist and fog. One still-burning streetlight has its orange pall of settled vaporish dampness around its glass globe. Conor is used to these morning effects; he likes them, in fact. In this town you get accustomed to the hazy glow around everything, and the sleepiness, or you leave.

He stops his bicycle to get a breath. He's in front of the hardware store, and he leans against a parking meter. Looking down a side street, he watches several workmen moving a huge wide-load steel platform truck under a house that has been loosened from its foundation and placed on bricks. Apparently they're going to truck the entire house off somewhere. The thought of moving a house on a truck impresses Conor, technology somehow outsmarting domesticity.

He sees a wren in an elm tree and a grosbeak fluttering overhead.

An hour later, after conversation and coffee in his favorite café, where the waitress tells him that she believes she's seen Merilyn, Conor's ex-wife, around town, and Conor has pretended indifference to this news, he takes up a position down at the park, close to the bleachers. He watches a rattan chair stuck inside some gnarly tree branches swirl slowly past, legs pointing up, followed by a brown broom, swirling, sweeping the water.

Because the Chaska River hasn't flooded badly—destructively—for years, Eurekaville has developed what Conor's son Jeremy describes as a goof attitude about rising waters. According to Jeremy's angle on it, this flooding used to be a disaster thing. The townspeople sandbagged and worried themselves sick. Now it's a spectator thing. The big difference, according to Jeremy, is sales. "It's . . . it's like, well, not a drowning occasion, you know? If it ever was. It's like one of those Prozac disasters, where nothing happens, except publicity? It's cool and stuff, so you can watch it. And eat popcorn? And then you sort of daydream. You're into the river, right? But not?"

As early as it is, Jeremy's already down here, watching the flood and selling popcorn, which at this time of morning no one wants to buy. Actually, he is standing near a card table, flirting with a girl Conor doesn't quite recognize. She's very pretty. It's probably why he's really here. They're laughing. At this hour, not quite midmorning, the boom box on the table is playing old favorites by Led Zeppelin. The music, which sounded sexy and feverish to Conor years ago, now sounds charming and quaint, like a football marching band. Jeremy keeps brushing the girl's arms, bumping against her, and then she bumps against Jeremy and stabilizes herself by reaching for his hip. A morning dance. Jeremy's on the basketball team, and something about this girl makes Conor think of a cheerleader. Her smile goes beyond infectiousness into aggression.

Merilyn is nowhere in sight.

The flood has made everybody feel companionable. Conor waves to his son, who barely acknowledges him with a quick hand flick. Then Conor gets back on his bicycle and heads down to his photography studio, checking the sidewalks and the stores to see if he can spot Merilyn. It's been so long, he's not sure he'd recognize her.

Because it's Saturday, he doesn't have many appointments, just somebody's daughter, and an older couple, who have recently celebrated their fiftieth anniversary and who want a studio photo to commemorate it. The daughter will come first. She's scheduled for nine thirty.

When she and her mother arrive at the appointed time, Conor is wearing his battery-operated lighted derby and has prepared the spring-loaded rabbit on the table behind the tripod. When the rabbit flips up, at the touch of a button, the kids smile, and Conor usually gets the shot.

The girl's mother, who says her name is Romola, has an errand to run. Can she leave her daughter here for ten minutes? She looks harried and beautiful and professionally religious, somehow, with a pendant cross, and Conor says sure.

Her daughter appears to be about ten years old. She has an odd resemblance to Merilyn, who is of course lurking in town somewhere, hiding out. They both have a way of pinching their eyes halfway shut to convey distaste. Seated on a stool in front of the backdrop, the girl asks how long this'll take. Conor's adjusting the lights. He says, "Oh, fifteen minutes. The whole thing takes about fifteen minutes. You could practice your smile for the picture."

She looks at him carefully. "I don't like you," she says triumphantly.

"You don't know me," Conor points out. He checks his camera's film, the f-stop, refocuses, and says, "Seen the flood yet?"

"We're too busy. We go to church," the girl says. Her name is Sarah, he remembers. "It's a nothing flood anyway. In the old days the floods drowned sinners. You've got a beard. I don't like beards. Anyway, we go to church and I go to church school. I'm in fourth grade. The rest of the week is chores."

Conor turns on the little blinking lights in his derby hat, and the girl smiles. Conor tells her to look at the tinfoil star on the wall, and he gets his first group of shots. "Good for you," Conor says. To make conversation, he says, "What do you learn there? At Bible school?"

"We learned that when he was up on the cross Jesus didn't pull at the nails. We learned that last week." She smiles. She doesn't seem accustomed to smiling. Conor gets five more good shots. "Do you think he pulled at the nails?"

"I don't know," Conor says. "I have no opinion." He's working to get the right expression on the girl's face. She's wearing a green dress, the color of shelled peas, that won't photograph well.

"I think maybe he did. I think he pulled at the nails."

"How come?" Conor asks.

"I just do," the girl says. "And I think they came out, because he was God, but not in time." Conor touches the button, the rabbit pops up, and the girl laughs. In five minutes her mother returns, and the session ends; but Conor's mood has soured, and he wouldn't mind having a drink.


The next day, Sunday, Conor stands in the doorway of Jeremy's bedroom. Jeremy is dressing to see Merilyn. "Just keep it light with her," he says, as Jeremy struggles into a sweatshirt at least one size too large for him. "Nothing too serious." The boy's head, with its ponytail and earrings, pokes out into the air with a controlled thrashing motion. His big hands never do emerge fully from the sleeves. Only Jeremy's calloused fingertips are visible. They will come out fully when they are needed. Hands three-quarters hidden: Youthful fashion-irony, Conor thinks.

After putting his glasses back on, Jeremy gives himself a quick appraisal in the mirror. Sweatshirt, exploding-purple Bermuda shorts, sneakers, ponytail, earrings. Conor believes that his son looks weird and athletic, just the right sixteen-year-old pose: menacing, handsome, still under construction. As if to belie his appearance, Jeremy does a pivot and a layup near the doorframe. It's hard for him to pass through the doors in this house without jumping up and tapping the lintels, even in the living room, where he jumps and touches the nail hole—used for mistletoe in December—in the hallway.

Satisfied with himself, Jeremy nods, one of those private gestures of self-approval that Conor isn't supposed to notice but does. "Nothing too earnest, okay?"

"Daad," Jeremy says, giving the word a sitcom delivery. Most of the time he treats his father as if he were a sitcom dad: good-natured, bumbling, basically a fool. Jeremy's right eyebrow is pierced, but out of deference to the occasion he's left the ring out of it. He shakes his head as if he had a sudden neck pain. "Merilyn's just another mom. It's not a big puzzle or anything, being with her. You just take her places. You just talk to her. Remember?"

"Remember what?"

"Well, you were married to her, right? Once? You must've talked and taken her places. That's what you did. Except you guys were young. So that's what I'll do. I'm young. We'll just talk. Stuff will happen. It's cool."

"Right," Conor says. "So where will you take her?"

"I don't know. The flood, maybe. I bet she hasn't seen a flood. This guy I know, he said a cow floated down the river yesterday."

"A cow? In the river? Oh, Merilyn would like that, all right."

"She's my mom. Come on, Dad. Relax. Nothing to it."

Jeremy says he will drive down to the motel where Merilyn is staying. After that, they will do what they are going to do. At the back stairs, playing with the cat's dish with his foot and biting his fingernail, Jeremy hesitates, smiles, and says, "Well, why don't you loosen up and wish me luck?" and Conor does.


Five days before Merilyn left, fourteen years ago, Conor found a grocery list in green ink under the phone in the kitchen. "Grapefruit, yogurt," the list began, then followed with, "cereal, diapers, baby wipes, wheat germ, sadness." And then, the next line: "Sadness, sadness, sadness."


In those days, Merilyn had a shocking physical beauty: startlingly blue eyes, and a sort of compact uneasy voluptuousness. She was fretful about her appearance, didn't like to be looked at—she had never liked being beautiful, didn't like the attention it got her—and wore drab scarves to cover herself.

For weeks she had been maintaining an unsuccessful and debilitating cheerfulness in front of Conor, a stagy display of frozen failed smiles, and most of what she said those last few evenings seemed memorized, as if she didn't trust herself to say anything spontaneously. She half laughed, half coughed after many of her sentences and often raised her fingers to her face and hair as if Conor were staring at them, which he was. He had never known why a beautiful woman had agreed to marry him in the first place. Now he knew he was losing her.

She worked as a nurse, and they had met when he'd gone up to her ward to visit a friend. The first time he ever talked to her, and then the first time they kissed—after a movie they both agreed they disliked—he thought she was the meaning of his life. He would love her, and that would be the point of his being alive. There didn't have to be any other point. When they made love, he had to keep himself from trembling.

Women like her, he thought, didn't usually allow themselves to be loved by a man like him. But there she was.

When, two and a half years later, she said that she was leaving him, and leaving Jeremy behind with him, and that that was the only action she could think of taking that wouldn't destroy her life, because it wasn't his fault but she couldn't stand to be married to anybody, that she could not be a mother, that it wasn't personal, Conor had agreed to let her go and not to follow her. Her desperation impressed him, silenced him.

She had loaded up the Ford and a trailer with everything she wanted to go with her. The rain had turned to sleet, and by the time she had packed the books and the clothes, she had collected small flecks of ice on her blue scarf. She'd been so eager to go that she hadn't turned on the windshield wiper until she was halfway down the block. Conor had watched her from the front porch. From the side, her beautiful face—the meaning of his life—looked somehow both determined and blank. She turned the corner, the tires splashed slush, the front end dipped from the bad shocks, and she was gone.

He had a trunk in the attic filled with photographs he had taken of her. Some of the shots were studio portraits, while others were taken more quickly, outdoors. In them, she is sitting on stumps, leaning against trees, and so on. In the photographs she is trying to look spontaneous and friendly, but the photographs emphasize, through tricks of angle and lighting, her body and its voluptuousness. All of the shots have a painfully thick and willful artistry, as if she had been mortified, in her somewhat involuntary beauty.

She had asked him to destroy these photographs, but he never had.


Now, having seen Jeremy go off to find his mother somewhere in Eurekaville and maybe take her to the flood, Conor wanders into the living room. Janet's sprawled on the floor, reading the Sunday comics to Annah. Annah is picking her nose and laughing. Joe, over in the corner, is staging a war with his plastic mutant men. The forces of good muscle face down evil muscle. Conor sits on the floor next to his wife and daughter, and Annah rumbles herself backward into Conor's lap.

"Jeremy's off?" Janet asks. "To find Merilyn?"

Conor nods. Half consciously, he's bouncing his daughter, who holds on to him by grasping his wrist.

Janet looks back at the paper. "They'll have a good time."

"What does that mean?"

She flicks her hair back. " 'What does that mean?' " she repeats. "I'm not using code here. It means what it says. He'll show her around. He'll be the mayor of Eurekaville. At last he's got Merilyn on his turf. She'll be impressed."

"Nothing," Conor says, "ever impressed Merilyn, ever, in her life."

"Her life isn't over."

"No," Conor says, "it isn't. I mean, nothing has impressed her so far."

"How would you know? You didn't follow her down to Tulsa. There could be all sorts of things in Tulsa that impress Merilyn."

"All right," Conor says. "Maybe the oil wells. Maybe something. Maybe the dust bowl and the shopping malls. All I'm saying is that nothing impressed her here."

A little air pocket of silence opens between them, then shuts again.

"Daddy," Annah says, "tip me."

Conor grasps her and tips her over, and Annah gives out a little pleased shriek. Then he rights her again.

"I wonder," Janet says, "if she isn't getting a little old for that."

"Are you getting too old for this, Annie?" Annah shakes her head. "She's only five." Conor tips her again. Annah shrieks again, and when she does, Janet drops the section of the newspaper that she's reading and lies backward on the floor, until her head is propped on her arm, and she can watch Conor.

"Mom!" Joe shouts from the corner. "The plutonium creatures are winning!"

"Fight back," Janet instructs. "Show 'em what you've got." She reaches out and touches Conor on the thigh. "Honey," she says, "you can't impress everybody. You impress me sometimes. You just didn't impress Merilyn. No one did. Marriage didn't. What's wrong with a beautiful woman wanting to live alone? It's her beauty. She can keep it to herself if she wants to."

Conor shrugs. He's not in the mood to argue about this. "It's funny to think of her in town, that's all."

"No, it's not. It's only funny," Janet says, "to think of her in town if you still love her, and I'd say that if you still love her, after fourteen years, then you're a damn fool, and I don't want to hear about it. It's Jeremy, not you, who could use some attention from Merilyn. It's his to get, being her son and all. She left him more than she left you. But I'll be damned if I'm going to go on with this conversation one further sentence more."

Both Annah and Joe have stopped their playing to listen. They are not watching their parents, but their heads are raised, like forest animals who can smell smoke nearby.

"All I ever wanted from her was a reason," Conor says. "I just got tired of all that enigmatic shit."

"Hey," Janet says, "I told you about that one further sentence." Annah gets out of her father's lap and snuggles next to Janet. "All right," Janet says. "Listen. Listen to this. Here's something I never told you. One night Merilyn and I were working the same station, we were both in pediatrics that night, third floor, it was a quiet night, not many sick kids that week. And, you know, we started talking. Nursing stuff, women stuff. And Merilyn sort of got going."

"About what?"

"About you, dummy, she got going about you. Herself and you. She said you two had gone bowling. You'd dressed in your rags and gone off to Colonial Lanes, the both of you, and you'd been bowling, and she'd thrown the ball down the lane and turned around and you were look-ing at her, appreciating her, and of course all the other men in the bowl-ing alley were looking at her, too, and what was bothering her was that you were looking at her the way they did, sort of a leer, I guess, as if you didn't know her, as if you weren't married to her. Who could blame you? She looked like a cover girl or something. Perfect this, perfect that, she was perfect all over, it would make anybody sweat. So she said she had a sore thumb and wanted to go home. You were staring at your wife the way a man looks at a woman walking by in the street. Boy, how she hated that, that guy stuff. You went back home, it was cold, a cold blister night, she got you into bed, she made love to you, she threw herself into it, and then in the dark you were your usual gladsome self, and you know what you did?"

"No."

"You thanked her. You two made hot love and then you thanked her, and then in the dark you went on staring at her, you couldn't believe how lucky you were. There she was in your arms, the beauteous Merilyn. I bet it never occurred to you at the time that you aren't supposed to thank women after you make love to them and they make love to you, because you know what, sweetie? They're not doing you a favor. They're doing it because they want to. Usually. Anyway, that was the night she got pregnant with Jeremy and it was the same night she decided she would leave you, because you couldn't stop looking at her, and thanking her, and she hated that. For sure she hated it. She lives in Tulsa, that's how much."

Conor is watching Janet say this, focusing on her mouth, watching the lips move. "Son of a bitch," he says.

"So she told me this," Janet says, "one night, at our nursing station. And we laughed and sort of cried when we had coffee later, but you know what I was thinking?" She waits. "Do you? You don't, do you?"

"No."

"I was thinking," Janet says, "that I'm going to get my hands on this guy, I am going to get that man come hell or high water. I am going to get him and he is going to be mine. Mine forever. And do you know why?"

"Give me a clue."

"To hell with clues. I wanted a man who looked at me like that. I wanted a man who would work up a lather with me in bed and then thank me. No one had ever thanked me before, that was for goddamn certain sure. And you know what? That's what happened. You married another nurse. Me, this time. And it was me you looked at, me you thanked. Heaven in a bottle. Are you listening to me? Conor, pay attention. I'm about to do something."

Conor follows her gaze. A living room, newspaper on the floor, Sunday morning, the twins playing, a family, a house, a life, sunlight coming in through the window. Janet walks over to Conor, unties her bathrobe, pulls it open, drops it at his feet, lifts her arms up and pulls her night-gown over her head. In front of her children and her husband, she stands naked. She is beautiful, all right, but he is used to her.

"I'm different from Merilyn," she says. "You can look at me anytime you want."

Now, on Sunday afternoon, Conor cleans out his pickup, throwing out the bank deposit slips. When he's finished, with his binoculars around his neck and his telephoto lens attached to his camera, the 400-millimeter one that he uses for shots of birds, beside him on the seat, he drives down to the river, hoping for a good view of an osprey, or maybe a teal.

He parks near a cottonwood. He is on the opposite side from the park. Above him are scattered the usual sparrows, the usual crows. He gets out his telephoto lens and frames an ugly field sparrow flittering and shiver-ing in the flat light. A grackle, and then a pigeon, follow the sparrow into his viewfinder. It is a parade of the common, the colorless, the dreary. The birds with color do not want to perch anywhere near the Chaska River, not even the swallows or swifts. He puts his camera back in his truck.

He's standing there, searching the sky and the opposite bank with his binoculars, looking for what he thought he saw here last week, a Wilson's snipe, when he lowers the lenses and sees, at some distance, Jeremy and Merilyn. Merilyn is sitting on a bench, watching Jeremy, who has taken off his sweatshirt and is talking to his mother. Merilyn isn't especially pretty anymore. She's gained weight. Conor had heard from Jeremy that she'd gained weight but hadn't seen it for himself. Now, through the binoculars, Merilyn appears to be overweight and rather calm. She has that loaf-of-bread quality. There's a peaceful expression on her face. It's the happy contentment of someone who probably doesn't bother about very much anymore.

Jeremy stands up, throws his hands down on the ground, and begins walking on his hands. He walks in a circle on his hands. He's very strong and can do this for a long time. It's one of his parlor tricks.

Conor moves his binoculars and sees that Jeremy has brought a girl along, the girl he saw yesterday at the flood show, the one who was danc-ing with him. Conor doesn't know this girl's name. She's standing behind the bench and smiling while Jeremy walks on his hands. It's that same aggressive smile.

Goddamn it, Conor thinks, they're lovers, they've been sleeping together, and he didn't tell me.

He moves the binoculars back to Merilyn. She's still watching Jeremy, but she seems only mildly interested in his display. She's not smiling. She's not pretending to be impressed. Apparently that's what she's turned into. That's what all these years have done to her. She doesn't have to look interested in anything if she doesn't want to.

To see better, Conor walks down past his truck to the bank. He lifts the binoculars to his eyes again, and when he gets the group in view, Merilyn turns her head to his side of the river. She sees Conor. Conor's large bearlike body is recognizable anywhere. And what she does is, she raises her hand and seems to wave.

From where he is standing, Conor thinks that Merilyn has invited him over to join their group. Through the binoculars a trace of a smile, Conor believes, has appeared on Merilyn's face. This smile is one that Conor recognizes. In the middle of her pudginess, this smile is the same one that he saw sixteen years ago. It's the smile he lost his heart to. A little crow's-foot of delight in Conor's presence. A merriment.

And this is why Conor believes she is asking him to join them, right this minute, and to be his old self. And this is why he steps into the river, smiling that smile of his. It's not a wide river after all, no more than sixty or seventy feet across. Anyone could swim it. What are a few wet clothes? He will swim across the Chaska to Merilyn and Jeremy and Jeremy's girlfriend, and they will laugh, pleased with his impulsiveness and passion, and that will be that.

He is up to his thighs in water when the shocking coldness of the river registers on him. This is a river of recently melted snow. It isn't flowing past so much as biting him. It feels like cheerful party ice picks, like happy knives. Without meaning to, Conor gasps. But once you start something like this, you have to finish it. Conor wades deeper.

The sun has come out. He looks up. A long-billed marsh wren is in a tree above the bank. He cannot breathe, and he dives in.

Conor is a fair swimmer, but the water is putting his body into shock and he has to remember to move his arms. Having dived, he feels the current taking him downriver, at first slowly, and then with some urgency. He is hopeless with cold. Tiny bells, the size of gnats, ring on every inch of his skin. He thinks, This is crazy. He thinks, It wasn't an invitation, that wave. He thinks, I will die. The river's current, which is now the sleepy hand of his death waking up, reaches into his chest and feels his heart. Conor moves his arms back and forth, but he can't see the bank now and doesn't know which way he's going. Of course, by this time he's choking on water, and the bells on his skin are beginning to ring audibly. He is moving his arms more slowly. Flash-card random pictures pop up in his mind, and he sees the girl in his studio the day before, and she says, "I don't like you."

He doesn't want to die a comic death. It occurs to him that the binoculars are pulling him toward the river bottom, and he reaches for them and takes them off of his neck.

He swirls around like a broom.

He pulls his arms. It seems to him that he is not making any progress. It also seems to him that he cannot breathe at all. But he has always been a large, easygoing man, incapable of panic, and he does not panic now. His sinking will take its time.

The touch of the shore is silt. The graspings of hands on his elbow are almost unfriendly, aggressive. Jeremy is there, pulling, and what Conor hears, through his own coughing and spitting, is Jeremy's voice.

"Dad! What the fuck are you doing? What in the fucking . . . Daddy! Are you okay? Jesus. Are you . . . What the fuck is this? Shit! Jesus. Daddy!"

Conor looks at his son and says, "Watch your language."

"What? What! Get out of there." Conor is being pulled and pushed by his son. Pulled and pushed also, it seems, by his son's girlfriend. Perhaps she is simply trying to help. But the help she is giving him has been salted with violence.

"What do you think?" Conor asks, turning toward her. "Do you think he pulled at the nails?"

Conor's trousers are dripping water on the grass. Water pours out of his shirt. It drains off his hands. Now in the air his ears register their pain; his eardrums are in pain, a complex aching inside the ravine of his head. And Merilyn, the source, the beneficiary of his grand gesture, is simply saying, with her nurse's voice, "He's in shock. Get him into the car."

"Merilyn," he says. He can't see her. She's behind him.

"What?"

"I couldn't help it. I never got over it." He says it more loudly, because he can't see her. He might as well be talking to the air. "I never got over it! I never did."

"Daddy, stop it," Jeremy says. "For God's sake, shut up. Please. Get in the car."

Jeremy opens the door of the old clunker Buick he bought on his six-teenth birthday for four hundred dollars, and Conor, without thinking, gets in. Before he is quite conscious of the sequence of one event after another, the car's engine has started, and the Buick moves slowly away—away from Merilyn: Conor remembers to look. She grows smaller with every foot of distance between them, and Conor, pleased with himself, pleased with his inscribed fate as the unhappy lover, tries to wipe his eyes with his wet shirt.

"I won't tell anybody about this if you don't," Jeremy says.

"Okay."

"I'll tell them you fell into the river. I'll say that you slipped in the mud."

"Thanks."

"That can happen. I mean really." Jeremy is enthusiastic now, creating a cover story for his father. "You were taking pictures and stuff, and you got too close to the river, and, you know, bang, you slipped, and like that. Just don't ever tell Mom, okay? We'll just . . . Holy shit! What's that?"

The car has been climbing a hill, and near the top, where a slight curve to the right banks the road toward the passenger side, there comes into view an amazing sight that has cut Jeremy into silence: an old wooden two-story house on an enormous platform truck, squarely in the middle of the road, blocking them. The house on the truck is moving at five or ten miles an hour. Who knows what its speed is, this white clap-board monument, this parade, a smaller truck in front, and one in back, with flashing lights, and a WIDE LOAD sign? No one would think of measuring its speed. Conor looks up and sees what he knows is a bed-room window. He imagines himself in that bedroom. He is dripping water all over his son's car, and he is beginning now to shiver, as the truck, carrying the burden it was made to carry, struggles up the next hill.

# The Cures for Love

ON THE DAY he left her for good, she put on one of his caps. It fit snugly over her light brown hair. The cap had the manufacturer's name of his pickup truck embossed above the visor in gold letters. She wore the cap backward, the way he once had, while she cooked dinner. Then she kept it on in her bath that evening. When she leaned back in the tub, the visor hitting the tiles, she could smell his sweat from the inside of the headband, even over the smell of the soap. His sweat had always smelled like freshly broiled whitefish.

What he owned, he took. Except for the cap, he hadn't left much else behind in the apartment. He had what he thought was a soulful indifference to material possessions, so he didn't bother saving them. It hadn't occurred to her until later that she might be one of those possessions. He had liked having things—quality durable goods—around for a little while, she thought bitterly, and then he enthusiastically threw them all out. They were there one day—his leather vest, his golf clubs—and then they were gone. She had borrowed one of his gray T-shirts months ago to wear to bed when she had had a cold, and she still had it, a gray tee in her bottom dresser drawer. But she had accidentally washed it, and she couldn't smell him on the fabric anymore, not a trace of him.

Her cat now yowled around five thirty, at exactly the time when he used to come home. She—the cat—had fallen for him the moment she'd seen him, rushing over to him, squirming on her back in his lap, declawed paws waving in the air. The guy had had a gift, a tiny genius for relentless charm, that caused anything—women, men, cats, trees for all she knew—to fall in love with him, and not calmly, either, but at the upper frequencies.

Her clocks ached. Time had congealed. For the last two days, knowing he would go, she had tried to be busy. She had tried reading books, for example. They couldn't preoccupy her. They were just somebody's thoughts. Her wounded imagination included him and herself, but only those two, bone hurtling against bone.

She was not a romantic and did not like the word "romance." They hadn't had a romance, the two of them. Nothing soft or tender, like that. They had just, well, driven into each other like reckless drivers at an intersection, neither one wanting to yield the right-of-way. She was a classicist recently out of graduate school, and for a job she taught Latin and Greek in a Chicago private school, and she understood from her reading of Thucydides and Catullus and Sophocles and Sappho, among others, how people actually fought, and what happened when they actually fell in love and were genuinely and almost immediately incompatible. The old guys told the truth, she believed, about love and warfare, the peculiar combination of attraction and hatred existing together. They had told the truth before Christianity put civilization into a dreamworld.

After she got out of the bathtub, she went to bed without drying herself off first. She removed the baseball cap and rolled around under the covers, dampening the sheets. *It's like this,* she said to herself.

She thought of herself as "she." At home she narrated her actions to herself as she performed them: "Now she is watering the plants." "Now she is feeding the cat." "Now she is staring off into space." "Now she is calling her friend Ticia, who is not at home. She will not leave a message on Ticia's machine. She doesn't do that."

She stood naked in front of the mirror. She thought: I am the sexiest woman who can read Latin and Greek in the state of Illinois. She surveyed her legs and her face, which he had praised many times. I look great and feel like shit and that's that.

The next morning she made breakfast but couldn't eat it. She hated it that she had gotten into this situation, loaded down with humiliating feelings. She wouldn't tell anyone. Pushing the scrambled eggs around on the plate, making a mess of them, the buttered wheat toast, and the strawberry jam, her head down on her arm, she fell into speculation: *Okay, yes, right, it's a mistake to think that infatuation has anything to do with personality, or personal tastes. You don't, uh,* decide *about any of this, do you?* she asked herself, half forming the words on her lips. Love puts anyone in a state outside the realm of thought, like one of those Eleusinian cults where no one ever gets permission to speak of the mysteries. When you're not looking, your mouth gets taped shut. You fall in love with someone not because he's nice to you or can read your mind but because, when he kisses you, your knees weaken, or because you can't stop looking at his skin or at the way his legs, inside his jeans, shape the fabric. His breath meets your breath, and the two breaths either intermingle and create a charge or they don't. Personality comes later; personality, she thought, reaching for the copy of Ovid that was about to fall off the table, is the consolation prize of middle age.

She put the breakfast dishes in the sink. She turned on the radio and noticed after five minutes that she hadn't listened to any of it. She snapped it off and glanced angrily in the direction of the bedroom, where all this trouble had started.

She and he had ridden each other in that bed. She glowered at it, framed in the doorway of the bedroom, sun pouring in the east window and across the yellow bedspread. They had a style, but, well, yes, almost everyone had a style. For starters, they took their time. Nothing for the manuals, nothing for the record books. But the point wasn't the lovemaking, not exactly. What they did started with sex but ended somewhere else. She believed that the sex they had together invoked the old gods, just invited them right in, until, boom, there they were. She wondered over the way the spirit-gods, the ones she lonesomely believed in, descended over them and surrounded them and briefly made them feel like gods themselves. She felt huge and powerful, together with him. It was archaic, this descent, and pleasantly scary. They both felt it happening; at least he said he did. The difference was that, after a while, he didn't care about the descent of the old gods or the spirits or whatever the hell he thought they were. He was from Arizona, and he had a taste for deserts and heat and golf and emptiness. Perhaps that explained it.

He had once blindfolded her with her silk bathrobe belt during their lovemaking and she had still felt the spirit coming down. Blindfolded, she could see it more clearly than ever.

Ovid. At the breakfast table she held on to the book that had almost fallen to the floor. Ovid: an urbane know-it-all with a taste for taking inventories. She had seldom enjoyed reading Ovid. He had a masculine smirking cynicism, and then its opposite, self-pity, which she found offensive.

And this was the *Remedia amoris,* a book she couldn't remember studying in graduate school or anywhere else. The remedies for love. She hadn't realized she even owned it. It was in the back of her edition of the *Ars amatoria.* Funny how books put themselves into your hands when they wanted you to read them.

Because spring had hit Chicago, and sunlight had given this particular Saturday morning a light fever, and because her black mood was making her soul sore, she decided to get on the Chicago Transit Authority bus and read Ovid while she rode to the suburbs and back. Absentmindedly, she found herself crying while she stood at the corner bus stop, next to the graffitied shelter, waiting. She was grateful that no one looked at her.

After the bus arrived in a jovial roar of diesel fumes and she got on, she found a seat near a smudgy semi-clean window. The noise was therapeutic, and the absence on the bus of businessmen with their golf magazines relieved her. No one on this bus on Saturday morning had a clue about how to conduct a life. She gazed at the tattered jackets and gummy spotted clothes of the other passengers. No one with a serious relationship with money rode a bus like this at such a time. It was the fuck-up express. Hollow and stoned and vacant-eyed people like herself sat there, men who worked in car washes, women who worked in diners. They looked as if their rights to their own sufferings had already been revoked months ago.

Over the terrible clatter, trees in blossom rushed past, dogwood and lilacs and like that. The blossoms seemed every bit as noisy as the bus. She shook her head and glanced down at her book.

> *Scripta cave relegas blandae servata puellae:*
> *Constantis animos scripta relecta movent.*
> *Omnia pone feros (pones invitus) in ignes*
> *Et dic 'ardoris sit rogus iste mei.'*

Oh, right. Yeah. Burn the love letters? Throw them all in the flames? And then announce, "This is the pyre of my love"? Hey, thanks a lot.

What love letters? He hadn't left any love letters, just this cap—she was
still wearing it—with CHEVY embossed on it in gold.

*Quisquis amas, loca sola nocent: loca sola caveto;*
  *Quo fugis? in populo tutior esse potes.*
*Non tibi secretis (augent secreta furores)*
  *Est opus; auxilio turba futura tibi est.*

Riding the CTA bus, and now glimpsing Lake Michigan through a
canyon of buildings, she felt herself stepping into an emotional lull, the
eye of the storm that had been knocking her around. In the storm's eye,
everyone spoke Latin. The case endings and the declensions and Ovid's
I-know-it-all syntax and tone remained absolutely stable, however, no
matter what the subject was. They were like formulas recited from a
comfortable sofa by a banker who had never made a dangerous investment. The urbanity and the calm of the poem clawed at her. She decided
to translate the four lines so that they sounded heartbroken and absentminded, jostled around in the aisles.

The lonely places
    are the worst. I tell you,
        when you're heart-
    sick, go
where the pushing and shoving
        crowd gives you
    some nerve. Don't be
        alone, up in your
burning room, burning—
    trust me:
        get knocked
    down in public,
        you'll be helped up.

All right: so it was a free translation. So what? She scribbled it on the
back of a deposit slip from the Harris Bank and put it into her purse. She
wouldn't do any more translating just now. Any advice blew unwelcome
winds into her. Especially advice from Ovid.

Now they were just north of the Loop. This time, when she looked
out of the window, she saw an apartment building on fire: firetrucks

flamesroof waterlights crowdsbluesky smoke-smoke. There, and gone just that rapidly. Suffering, too, probably, experienced by someone, but not immediately visible, not from here, at forty miles per hour. She thought: Well, that's corny, an apartment fire as seen from a bus. Nothing to do about that one. Quickly she smelled smoke, and then, just as quickly, it was gone. To herself, she grinned without realizing what she was doing. Then she looked around. No one had seen her smile. She had always liked fires. She felt ashamed of herself, but momentarily cheerful.

She found herself in Evanston, got out, and took the return bus back. She had observed too much of the lake on the way. Lake Michigan was at its most decorative and bourgeois in the northern suburbs: whitecaps, blue water, waves lapping the shore, abjectly picturesque.

By afternoon she was sitting in O'Hare Airport, at gate 23A, the waiting area for a flight to Memphis. She wasn't going to Memphis—she didn't have a ticket to anywhere—and she wasn't about to meet anyone, but she had decided to take Ovid's advice to go where the crowds were, for the tonic effect. She had always liked the anonymity of airports anyway. A businessman carrying a laptop computer and whose face had a WASPy nondescript pudgy blankness fueled by liquor and avarice was raising his voice at the gate agent, an African-American woman. Men like that raised their voices and made demands as a way of life; it was as automatic and as thoughtless as cement turning and slopping around inside a cement mixer. "I don't think you understand the situation," he was saying. He had a standby ticket but had not been in the gate area when they had called his name, and now, the plane being full, he would have to take a later flight. "You have no understanding of my predicament here. Who is your superior?" His wingtip shoes were scuffed, and his suit was tailored one size too small for him, so that it bulged at the waist. He had combed strands of hair across his sizable bald spot. His forehead was damp with sweat, and his nose sported broken capillaries. He was not quite first-class. She decided to eat a chili dog and find another gate to sit in. Walking away, she heard the gate agent saying, "I'm sorry, sir. I'm sorry."

You couldn't eat a chili dog in this airport sitting down. It was not permitted. You had to stand at the plastic counter of Here's Mr. Chili, trying not to spill on the polyester guy reading *USA Today,* your volume of

Publius Ovidius Naso next to you, your napkin in your other hand, thinking about Ovid's exile to the fringe of the Roman empire, to Tomis, where, broken in spirit, solitary, he wrote the *Tristia*, some of the saddest poems written by anyone anywhere, but a—what?—male sadness about being far from where the action was. There was no action in Tomis, no glamour, no togas—just peasants and plenty of mud labor. On the opposite side of Here's Mr. Chili was another gate where post-frightened passengers were scurrying out of the plane from Minneapolis. A woman in jeans and carrying a backpack fell into the arms of her boyfriend. They had started to kiss, the way people do in airports, in that depressing public style, all hands and tongues. And over here a chunky Scandinavian grandma was grasping her grandchildren in her arms like ships tied up tightly to a dock. You should go where people are happy, Ovid was saying. You should witness the high visibility of joy. You should believe. In . . . ?

> *Si quis amas nec vis, facito contagia vites*
> Right, right: "If you don't
>     want to love,
>         don't expose yourself to
> the sight
>         of love, the contagion."

Evening would be coming on soon; she had to get back.

She was feeling a bit light-headed, the effect of the additives in the chili dog: the Red concourse of O'Hare, with its glacially smooth floors and reflecting surfaces, was, at the hour before twilight, the scariest man-made place she'd ever seen. This airport is really man-made, she thought. They don't get more man-made than this. Of course, she had seen it a hundred times before, she just hadn't bothered looking. If something hadn't been hammered or fired, it wasn't in this airport. Stone, metal, and glass, like the hyperextended surfaces of eternity, across which insect-people moved, briefly, trying before time ran out to find a designated anthill. Here was a gate for Phoenix. There was a gate for Raleigh-Durham. One locale was pretty much like another. People made a big deal of their own geographical differences to give themselves specific details to talk about. Los Angeles, Cedar Rapids, Duluth. What did it matter where anyone lived—Rome, Chicago, or Romania? All she really wanted was to be in the same room with her as-of-yesterday ex. Just being around him had made her happy. It was horrible but true. She had loved him so much it gave her the creeps. He wasn't worthy of her love but so what. Maybe, she thought, she should start doing an inventory of her faults, you know, figure the whole thing out—scars, bad habits, phrases she had used that he hadn't liked. Then she could do an inventory of his faults. She felt some ketchup under her shoe and let herself fall.

She looked up.

Hands gripped her. Random sounds of sympathy. "Hey, lady, are you all right?" "Can you stand?" "Do you need some help?" A man, a woman, a second man: Ovid's public brigade of first-aiders held her, clutched at her where she had sprawled sort of deliberately, here in the Red concourse. Expressions of fake concern like faces painted on flesh-colored balloons lowered themselves to her level. "I just slipped." "You're okay, you're fine?" "Yes." She felt her breast being brushed against, not totally and completely unpleasantly. It felt like the memory of a touch rather than a touch itself, no desire in it, no nothing. There: She was up. Upright. And dragging herself off, Ovid under her arm, to the bus back to the Loop and her apartment. Falling in the airport and being lifted up: okay, so it happened as predicted, but it didn't make you feel wonderful. Comfortably numb was more like it. She dropped the *Remedia amoris* into a trash bin. Then she thought, Uh-oh, big mistake, maybe the advice is all wrong but at least he wants to cheer me up, who else wants to do that? She reached her hand into the trash bin and, looking like a wino grasping for return bottles, she pulled out her soiled book, smeared with mustard and relish.

"Kit?"

A voice.

"Yes?" She turned around. She faced an expression of pleased surprise, on a woman she couldn't remember ever seeing before.

"It's me. Caroline."

"Caroline?" As if she recognized her. Which she didn't. At all.

"What a coincidence! This is too amazing! What are you doing here?"

"I'm, um, I was here. Seeing someone off. You know. To . . . ah, Seattle."

"Seattle." The Caroline-person nodded, in a, well, professional way, one of those therapeutic nods. Her hair had a spiky thickness, like straw or hay. Maybe Caroline would mention the traffic in Seattle. The ferries? Puget Sound? "What's that?" She pointed at the haplessly soiled book.

"Oh, this?" Kit shrugged. "Ovid."

More nodding. Blondish hair spiked here and there, arrows pointing at the ceiling and the light fixtures and the arrival-and-departure screens. The Caroline-person carried—no, actually pulled on wheels—a tan suitcase, and she wore a business suit, account executive attire, a little gold pin in the shape of the Greek lambda on her lapel. Not a very pretty pin, but maybe a clue: lambda, lambda, now what would that . . . possibly mean? Suitcase: This woman *didn't* live here in Chicago. Or else she *did*.

"You were always reading, Kit. All that Greek and Latin!" She stepped back and surveyed. "You look simply fabulous! With the cap? Such a cute retro look, it's so street-smart, like . . . who's that actress?"

"Yeah, well, I have to . . . It's nice to see you, Caroline, but I'm headed back to the Loop, it's late, and I have to—"

"Is your car here?" A hand wave: Caroline-person wedding ring: tasteful diamond, of course, that's the way it goes in the Midwest, wedding rings everyfuckingwhere.

"Uh, no, we took, I mean, he and I took the taxi out." Somehow it seemed important to repeat that. "We took a taxi."

"Great! I'll give you a ride back. I'll take you to your place. I'll drop you right at the doorstep. Would you like some company? Come on!"

She felt her elbow being touched.


Down the long corridors of O'Hare Airport shaped like the ever-ballooning hallways of eternity, the Caroline-person pulled her suitcase, its tiny wheels humming behind her high-heeled businesslike stride; and easily keeping up in her jogging shoes, in which she jogged when the mood struck her, Kit tried to remember where on this planet, and in this life, she'd met this person. Graduate school? College? She wasn't a parent of one of her students, that was certain. *You were always reading.* Must've been college. "It's been so long," the woman was saying. "Must be . . . what?" They edged out of the way of a beeping handicap cart.

Kit shook her head as if equally exasperated by their mutual ignorance.

"Well, I don't know either," Caroline-person said. "So, who'd you see off?"

"What?"

"To Seattle."

"Oh," Kit said.

"Something the matter?"

"It was Billy," Kit said. "It was Billy I put on the plane."

"Kit," she said, "I haven't seen you in years. Who's this Billy?" She gave her a sly girlish smile. "Must be somebody special."

Kit nodded. "Yeah. Must be."

"Oh," Caroline said, "you can tell me."

"Actually, I can't."

"Why not?"

"Oh, I'd just rather not."

A smile took over Caroline's face like the moon taking over the sun during an eclipse. "But you can. You can tell me."

"No, I can't."

"Why?"

"Because I don't remember you, Caroline. I don't remember the first thing about you. I know a person's not supposed to admit that, but it's been a bad couple of days, and I just don't know who you are. Probably we went to college together or something, classics majors and all that, but I can't remember." People rushed past them and around them. "I don't remember you at all."

"You're kidding," the woman said.

"No," Kit said, "I'm not. I can't remember seeing you before."

The woman who said her name was Caroline put her hand on her forehead and stared at Kit with a what-have-we-here? shocked look. Kit knew she was supposed to feel humiliated and embarrassed, but instead she felt shiny and new and fine for the first time all day. She didn't like to be tactless, but that seemed to be the direction, at least right now, this weekend, where her freedom lay. She'd been so good for so long, she thought, so loving and sweet and agreeable, and look where it had gotten her. "You're telling me," the woman said, "that you don't remember our—"

"Stop," Kit said. "Don't tell me."

"Wait. You don't even want to be reminded? You're . . . But why? Now I'm offended," the woman told her. "Let's start over. Let's begin again. Kit, I feel very hurt."

"I know," Kit said. "It's been a really strange afternoon."

"I just don't think . . . ," the woman said, but then she was unable to finish the sentence. "Our ride into the city . . ."

"Oh, that's all right," Kit said. "I couldn't take up your offer. I'll ride the bus back. They have good buses here," she added.

"No," she said. "Go with me."

"I can't, Caroline. I don't remember you. We're strangers."

"Well, uh, good-bye then," the woman muttered. "You certainly have changed."

"I certainly have. But I'm almost never like this. It's Billy who did this to me." She gazed in Caroline's direction. "And my vocabulary," she said, not quite knowing what she meant. But she liked it, so she repeated it. "My vocabulary did this to me."

"It's that bad?" the woman said.

Standing in O'Hare Airport, where she had gone for no good reason except that she could not stand to be alone in her apartment, she felt, for about ten seconds, tiny and scaled-down, like a model person in a model airport as viewed from above, and she reached out and balanced herself on the driver's-side door handle and then shook her head and closed her eyes. If she accepted compassion from this woman, there would be nothing left of her in the morning. Sympathy would give her chills and fever, and she would start shaking, and the shaking would move her out of the hurricane's eye into the hurricane itself, and it would batter her, and then wear her away to the zero. Nothing in life had ever hurt her more than sympathy.

"I have to go now," Kit said, turning away. She walked fast, and then ran, in the opposite direction.


Of course I remember you. We were both in a calculus class. We had hamburgers after the class sometimes in the college greasy spoon, and we talked about boys and the future and your dog at home, Brutus, in New Buffalo, Minnesota, where your mother bred cairn terriers. In the back-yard there was fencing for a kennel, and that's where Brutus stayed. He sometimes climbed to the top of his little pile of stones to survey what there was to survey of the fields around your house. He barked at hawks and skunks. Thunderstorms scared him, and he was so lazy, he hated to take walks. When he was inside, he'd hide under the bed, where he thought no one could see him, with his telltale leash visible, trailing out on the bedroom floor. You told that story back then. You were pretty in those days. You still are. You wear a pin in the shape of the Greek letter lambda and a diamond wedding ring. In those days, I recited poetry. I can remember you. I just can't do it in front of you. I can't remember you when you're there.

She gazed out the window of the bus. She didn't feel all right but she could feel all right approaching her, somewhere off there in the distance.

She had felt it lifting when she had said his name was Billy. It wasn't Billy. It was Ben. Billy hadn't left her; Ben had. There never had been a Billy, but maybe now there was. She was saying good-bye to him; he wasn't saying good-bye to her. She turned on the overhead light as the bus sped through Des Plaines, and she tried to read some Ovid, but she immediately dozed off.

Roaring through the traffic on the Kennedy Expressway, the bus lurched and rocked, and Kit's head on the headrest turned from side to side, an irregular rhythm, but a rhythm all the same: enjambments, caesuras, strophes.

> *My darling girl,* (he said, thinner
> than she'd ever thought he'd be,
>         mostly bald, a few sprout curls,
> and sad-but-cheerful, certainly,
>     Roman and wryly unfeminist, unhumanist,
> unliving), child of gall and wormwood (he pointed his
> thin malnourished finger at her,
>         soil inside the nail),
>     what on earth
>     brought you to that unlikely place?
> An airport! Didn't I tell you,
>                 clearly,
> to shun such spots? A city park on a warm
> Sunday afternoon wouldn't be as bad. People fall
> into one another's arms out there all the time.
>     Hundreds of them! (He seemed exasperated.)
>         Thank you (he said)
>             for reading me, but for the sake

of your own well-being, don't go there
    again without a ticket. It seems
      you have found me out. (He
shrugged.) Advice? I don't have any
          worth passing on. It's easier
to give advice when you're alive
          than when you're not,
    and besides, I swore it off. Oh I liked
what you did with Caroline, the lambda-girl
    who wears that pin because her husband
      gave it to her on her birthday,
March twenty-first—now that
    I'm dead, I know everything
but it does me not a particle of good—
      but naturally she thinks it has no
special meaning, and that's the way
      she conducts her life. Him, too. He
bought it at a jewelry store next to a shoe
        shop in the mall at 2 p.m.
  March 13, a Thursday—but I digress—
    and the salesgirl,
cute thing, hair done in a short cut
    style, flirted with him
      showing him no mercy,
touching his coat sleeve,
    thin wool, because she was on commission. Her
          name was
    Eleanor, she had green eyes.
  The pin cost him $175, plus tax.
    She took him, I mean, took him for a ride,
    as you would say,
then went out for coffee. By herself, that is,
      thinking of her true
and best beloved, Claire, an obstetrician
  with lovely hands. I always did admire
Sapphic love. But I'm
    still digressing. (He smirked.)


The distant failed humor of the dead.
Our timing's bad,

the jokes are dusty,
and we can't concentrate
         on just
               one thing. I'm as interested
in Eleanor as I am
               in you. Lambda. Who cares? Lambda: I suppose
         I mean, I *know,*
he thought the eleventh letter, that uncompleted triangle,
         looked like his wife's legs. Look:
               I can't help it,
I'm—what is the word?—salacious, that's
         the way I always was,
      the bard of breasts and puberty, I was
exiled for it, I turned to powder
six feet under all the topsoil
         in Romania. Sweetheart, what on earth
               are you *doing* on
this bus? Wake up, kiddo, that guy
      Ben is gone, good riddance
is my verdict from two thousand
               years ago, to you.
         Listen: I have a present for you.


He took her hand.
      His hand didn't feel like much,
            it felt like water when you're reaching
         down for a stone or shell
under the water, something you don't
         have, but want, and your fingers
               strain toward it.
      Here, he said, this is the one stunt
I can do: look up, sweetie, check out
               this:
(he raised his arm in ceremony)
         See? he said proudly. It's raining.
I made it rain. I can do that.
         The rain is falling, only
               it's not water, it's
this other thing. It's the other thing
         that's raining, soaking you. Good-bye.

———

When she awoke, at the sound of the air brakes, the bus driver announced that they had arrived at their first stop, the Palmer House. It wasn't quite her stop, but Kit decided to get out. The driver stood at the curb as the passengers stepped down, and the streetlight gave his cap an odd bluish glow. His teeth were so discolored they looked like pencil erasers. He asked her if she had any luggage, and Kit said no, she hadn't brought any luggage with her.

The El clattered overhead. She was in front of a restaurant with thick glass windows. On the other side of the glass, a man with a soiled unpressed tie was talking and eating prime rib. On the sidewalk, just down the block, under an orange neon light, an old woman was shouting curses at the moon and Mayor Daley. She wore a paper hat and her glasses had only one lens in them, on the left side, and her curses were so interesting, so incoherently articulate, uttered in that voice, which was like sandpaper worried across a brick, that Kit forgot that she was supposed to be unhappy, she was listening so hard, and watching the way the orange was reflected in that one lens.

# Poor Devil

MY EX-WIFE AND I are sitting on the floor of what was once our living room. The room stands empty now except for us. This place is the site of our marital decline and we are performing a ritual cleansing on it. I've been washing the hardwood with a soapy disinfectant solution, using a soft brush and an old mop, working toward the front window, which has a view of the street. My hands smell of soap and bleach. We're trying to freshen the place up for the new owners. The terms of sale do not require this kind of scouring, but somehow we have brought ourselves here to perform it.

We're both bruised from the work: Emily fell off a kitchen stool this morning while washing the upstairs windows, and I banged my head against a drainpipe when I was cleaning under the bathroom sink. When I heard her drop to the floor, I yelled upstairs to ask if she was okay, and she yelled back down to say that she was, but I didn't run up there to check.

When my wife and I were in the process of splitting up, the house itself participated. Lamps dismounted from their tables at the slightest touch, pictures plummeted from the wall and their frames shattered whenever anyone walked past them. Destruction abounded. You couldn't touch anything in here without breaking it. The air in the living room acquired a poisonous residue from the things we had said to each other. I sometimes thought I could discern a malignant green mist, invisible to everyone else, floating just above the coffee table. We excreted malice, the two of us. The house was haunted with pain. You felt it the minute you walked in the door.

Therefore this cleaning. We both like the young couple who have bought the house—smiling, just-out-of-school types with one toddler and another child on the way. We want to give them a decent chance. During our eight years together, Emily and I never had any kids ourselves—luckily, or: unluckily, who can say.

Anyway, now that we've been cleaning it, our former dwelling seems to have calmed down. The air in the living room has achieved a settled stale quietude. It's as if we'd never lived here. The unhappiness has seeped out of it.

Emily is sitting on the floor over in the other corner now, a stain in the shape of a Y on her T-shirt. She's taking a breather. I can smell her sweat, a vinegary sweetness, and quite pleasant. She's drinking a beer, though it's only two in the afternoon. She's barefoot, little traces of polish on her toenails. Her pretty brown hair, always one of her best features, hangs fixed back by a rubber band in the sort of ponytail women sometimes make when they're housecleaning. Her face is pink from her exertions, and on her forehead is a bruise from where she fell.

She's saying that it's strange, but the very sight of me causes her sadness, a *complicated* sadness, she informs me, inflecting the adjective, though she's smiling when she says it, a half smile, some grudges mixed in there with this late-term affability. She takes a swig of the beer. I can see that she's trying to make our troubles into a manageable comedy. I was Laurel; she was Hardy. I was Abbott; she was Costello. We failed together at the job we had been given, our marriage. But I don't think this comedic version of us will work out, even in retrospect. She tells me that one of my mistakes was that I thought I knew her, but, in fact, no, I never really knew her, and she can prove it. This is old ground, but I let her talk. She's not speaking to me so much as she's meditating aloud in the direction of the wall a few feet above my head. It's as if I've become a problem in linear algebra.

My general ignorance of her character causes her *sorrow,* she now admits. She wonders whether I was deluded about women in general and her in particular. To illustrate what I don't know about her, she begins to tell me a story.

But before she can really get started, I interrupt her. " 'Sorrow,' " I say. "Now there's a noun from our grandparents' generation. Nobody our age uses words like that anymore except you. Or 'weary.' You're the only person I know who ever used that word. *I'm weary,* you'd say, when you didn't look weary at all, just irritable. And 'forbearance.' I don't even fucking know what forbearance *is.* 'Show some forbearance'—that was a line you used. Where did you find those words, anyway?"

"Are you done?" she asks me. We're like a couple of tired fighters in the fifteenth round.

"What's wrong with saying 'I'm bummed'?" I ask her. "Everyone *else* says that. 'I'm bummed.' 'I'm down.' 'I'm depressed.' 'I'm blue.' But you—you have a gift for the . . . archaic." I am trying to amuse her and irritate her at the same time, so I wink.

"I wasn't depressed back then," she says. "I was sad. There's a difference." I scuttle over to where she is sitting and take a swig from the beer can she's been clutching. Only there's no beer left. I take a swig of air. Okay: we may be divorced, but we're still married.

Before I met her, but after she had dropped out of college, Emily had moved to the Bay Area, quite a few summers after the Summers of Love, which she had missed, both the summers and the love. She had rented a cheap basement apartment in the Noe Valley, one of those ground-floor places with a view of the sidewalk and of passing shoes, and during the day she was working in a department store, the Emporium, in the luggage department.

I interrupt her. "I know this," I say. "I know this entire story."

"No, you don't," Emily tells me. "Not this one." One of her coworkers was a guy named Jeffrey, a pleasant fellow most of the time, tall and handsome, though with an occasional stammer, and, as it happens, gay. He proved himself an effective salesman, one of those cheerful and witty and charming characters you buy expensive items from, big-ticket items, out of sheer delight in their company.

This coworker, Jeffrey, had befriended Emily soon after she had moved to San Francisco. He had shown her around the city, taken her to the wharf and the Tenderloin, an amateur guide and historian to the tourist spots and the dives. He loved the city; he had had his first real taste of a possible future life there, a potential hereafter of happiness. My wife-to-be and this Jeffrey rode BART over to Berkeley once and had a sidewalk vegetarian lunch, mock duck tacos, she says, at a seedy little restaurant devoted to higher consciousness. On another day he drove her to Mount Tam in his rattly old blue VW. He'd brought sandwiches and wine and some pastry concoction he had made himself, as a picnic offering. They ate their picnic in the shade of a tree with the FM radio in the car serenading them with Glenn Gould. Why had he gone to all this trouble? Emily says he was just being a friend, and then she pauses. "His boyfriend had left him a month before," she says, looking at her bare feet on the floor of our empty living room. "So he was lonely. And he was one of those gay men who have a latent hetero-thing going on." How does she know this? She shrugs. She could tell by the way he looked at her, sometimes. On a few rare occasions he looked at her the way a man looks at a woman.

It's true, I haven't heard this story. "So?" I ask.

So one day Jeffrey didn't show up for work. Or the next day or the day after that. He was sick, of course, with pneumonia, and after he recovered, he came back to work for a few days and then disappeared again for another two weeks. But everyone knew he had the plague, and this is before all the antiretroviral drugs broke through to the population at large, so at work everyone avoided the subject of Jeffrey, whom they had all liked.

By this time I am looking out the front window at our street. It's a nondescript neighborhood of similarly designed brick semi-colonials like ours, and as I'm watching, I see a guy in a Santa Claus suit jogging by.

"Look," I say. "It's Rolf, from down the block. He's wearing that goddamn Santa Claus suit again."

Emily glances out, bending upward, lifting herself halfway. "He must not be taking his meds."

"It's not that," I tell her. "He thinks it's better for visibility than a running outfit. Drivers see him right away. 'You don't accidentally hit Santa,' he told me once. At least he hasn't tied on the white beard. At least he's not wearing the cap."

"Who're you kidding?" Emily asks me. "The guy's bipolar. The Santa comes out in him whenever he gets manic."

"You could do worse," I say to her. "*You've* done worse."

We sit there, looking at each other for a moment, unsmilingly. Neither of us says anything, and I hear the furnace come on. The light flaring through the window has that burnished autumnal warmth. The furnace creates this low hum. Outside in the yard, the leaves could be raked, but I'm not going to do that now.

"What happened to Jeffrey?" I ask, after another long pause. "He died, right?"

No, he hadn't died, but he *was* in one of the Kaiser hospitals when Emily went to see him. He didn't look good. "Wasted" is probably the right word here. She tried to cheer him up, but he resisted her efforts. Still, he had one request. He wanted her to take some pictures of him, as a keepsake of how handsome he was despite his illness. He thought his looks had trumped the virus, somehow; beauty had staged its victory over infirmity, he thought. So she did it: she bought a camera at Castro Photo and took some pictures of her friend sitting up in the chair next to the hospital bed, out of his hospital clothes and into his best black jeans and a leather jacket, etc. "You probably didn't know it," he said, as she took his picture, "but I'm an aristocrat." He posed as if he were a rake and a bit of a snob, smiling an old-money smile.

But once the film was developed, the pictures were unshowable: his skin wasn't just sallow, but waxlike. His face seemed rigid, a staring mask. She didn't know what to do with these pictures. Ten years ago, retouching photographs digitally wasn't as easy as it is now. But if the guy could tell lies to himself when looking into the mirror, she thought, maybe he could tell himself the same lies when he saw these photographs.

She arrived at his apartment—he was convalescing at home—and sat down next to him at the dinette table. One by one the pictures were laid out, like playing cards, like the hand he'd been dealt. With his reading glasses on, Jeffrey looked at these images of himself. As it happened, the pneumonia had hung on for a while and he had lost a considerable amount of muscle tone, and in the photos his cheekbones were garishly visible, and his eyes, despite his smile, had that peering-into-the-void anguish—there, I used that word—that you see on the faces of the near-dead. So Jeffrey was sitting there, looking down at these photographs of his death sentence, and he began crying.

Emily tried to console him, but he turned away from her, shaking his head. He went into his bedroom, got dressed, and told her that they were going for a car ride in the blue VW. He asked her to drive. He said that he had to have his hands free.

He directed her down toward the Presidio and then across the Golden Gate Bridge, and when they were about midway across the bridge, he took the packet of photographs and held up the photos of himself one by one outside the window. The wind seized these portraits of him—some of them fluttered over the side of the bridge into the bay and some of them just lay there on the gridded pavement for the other cars to drive over. Emily told him that he could be ticketed for littering, but he didn't listen to her; he was too busy getting rid of these snapshots. "They won't arrest me," he shouted over the road noise. "Not after they get a good look at me."

Then he instructed Emily to drive up the coast so that they could go whale watching. However, it was the wrong season: no whales that time of year. After a couple of hours, they pulled over at a roadside rest area in sight of the Pacific. The two of them got out of the car. Though no whales were visible, Jeffrey, leaning against his car and staring out at the water, said he saw some. For the next half hour, he described the whales swimming by, all the shapes and sizes and varieties of them, whale after whale under the surface. He was like an encyclopedia entry: here were the humpback whales, and there the bottle-nosed, and the pilot, and the beluga, the right whales, and the blue. When he was done with this harmless hallucinatory description, he got back into the car, and my wife, that is, then my wife-to-be and now my ex-wife, drove him back home, to his apartment on Clement. When they got back to his place, he was distracted and confused, so she undressed him and put him to bed, Good Samaritan that she is. And then, and this is the part I couldn't have imagined, she got into bed with him and put her arms around him until he fell asleep.

She's still sitting there in the living room, looking at me in silence, still unsmilingly. The point of this story is that she loved this man, loved him, I think the phrase is, to death.

"No," I say, "you're absolutely right, you never told me that story." My heart is pounding slightly, and I have to work to sound calm. "So you loved him. What happened to this Jeffrey?" I ask her.

She looks at me. "Duh," she says. She removes her foot from my grasp. I hadn't realized I was holding on to it. I wonder what else she might have done for him that she hasn't told me, but I don't ask. "The thing is," she says, "I often dream about him. And these dreams, I often wake up from them, and they're terrible dreams, no comfort at all." She looks at me and waits. "They're really insane dreams," she says.

"How are they insane?"

"Oh," she says, "let's not spoil it with words." But I know my wife, and what she means is that in these dreams she is still lying down next to him. She glances out the window. "There goes Santa again." She laughs. It's not a good laugh, more like a fun-house laugh. I get up, make my way to the kitchen, open the refrigerator, take out two beers—we've cleaned out the refrigerator except for a twelve-pack of low-carb Budweiser—and I bring one of them back to her. I open the other one and gaze out the window, but Santa has turned the corner and is no longer visible, to my great disappointment. It's getting to be late afternoon, the time of day when you could use some Santa and aren't going to get it.

I take a good slug of the beer before I say, "No, you never told me that story. My God. Maybe it's true. Maybe we *didn't* know each other. Can you imagine that? We were married, and we never knew the first thing."

"Spare me your irony," she says.

"I'm not being ironic. I'm telling you what you told me. But the thing is, your story isn't about you, except on the sides, by comparison. You're a minor saintly character in that story. You're just the affable friend," I say, which isn't true, because that's not what the story has been about. I'm feeling a little competitive now, in this singing contest we're having. "After all, I've known plenty of people I've never described to you."

"I've heard that before," she says.

"Well, no, you haven't," I say. "Not exactly."


I am not an admirable man, and my character, or lack of character, accounts for my presence on that living-room floor on that particular day. If I am unadmirable, however, I am not actually bad, in the sense that evil people are bad; if I were genuinely and truly bad, my ex-wife wouldn't have been sitting there on the floor with me, her ex-husband, after we had cleaned the house for the next occupants.

My trouble was that after our first two years together, I couldn't concentrate on her anymore. I was distracted by what life was throwing at me. I couldn't be, what is the word, faithful, but actually that was the least of it, because unfaithfulness is a secondary manifestation of something we don't have a word for.

When I met Emily, I was a clerk in a lighting store; I sold lighting fixtures. I suppose this is a pretty good job for someone who majored in studio art during college. I know something about light. My little atelier was filled with life-study drawings and rolled-up canvases of nakedness. That was pretty much what I did: nudes, the human body, the place where most artists start, though I never got past it.

There was this woman I was always drawing and always painting, and it wasn't Emily. It was never Emily. She was a woman I had seen for about two minutes waiting in line for coffee at one of those bookstore cafés. She had an ankle bracelet, and I could describe her to you top to bottom, every inch, I could do that, trust me—just take my obsession on faith. She had come into my life for two minutes, and when, that afternoon, I couldn't forget her, I began to draw her. The next day I drew her again, and the next week I began a painting of her, and a month after that, I did another painting of her, and so on and so on.

One afternoon—this was about two years after we had been married—Emily came into my studio, sometime in midafternoon, a Saturday. I had college football playing on the radio. Once again, I was painting the woman I had seen standing in line at this bookstore café. Emily asked me again who this person was and I told her again that it was just someone I caught a glimpse of, once; it didn't matter who she was, she was just this person. Which is, of course, untrue. She wasn't just a person. Emily stared at what I was doing with the canvas and then she unbuttoned her blouse and hung it on a clothes hook near the door. She took off her shoes and socks and stood there with her bra and jeans still on, and then she unclasped the jeans and the bra and off they went, onto the littered floor. Finally the underpants went, and she was in the altogether, standing in my studio just under the skylight, the smell of turpentine in the room. I interrupted what I was doing and eventually went over to her and took her in my arms, but that turned out to be the wrong response, so wrong that I can date the decline of our marriage from that moment. What I was supposed to do was look at her. I was supposed to draw her, I was supposed to be obsessed by her, and, finally, I was supposed to be inspired by her.

But that's not how everyday love works. "I want to be your everything," Emily once said to me, and I cringed.

The next time we made love, she was crying. "Please draw me," she says. "Dennis, please please please draw me."

"I can't," I said, because she didn't inspire me and never had, and although I might not have been a great artist, I wasn't going to draw her just because she asked me to. She was my companion. We were getting through this life day by day, the two of us. I loved her, I'm sure, and she loved me, and I'm sure of that, too, but she has never inspired me and she has never obsessed me, and because I couldn't draw her in good faith, everything followed from there, including the affairs, both hers and mine, which were small potatoes, compared to that.

At night I would hug her and kiss her and tell her that I loved her, my flesh pressed against her flesh, and it just made her cry all the more. I never struck her or hit her, but the poisons in the house grew. Emily was not my everything, and not my muse and inspiration; I never knew why she wanted that role, but she did, and because she wanted it and I couldn't lie to her about how she could never be what she said she wanted to be, I could fold my arms around her as we stood or lay quietly together, and it was never enough, and because it was never enough, it was hateful.

We were like two becalmed sailing ships, with sailors from different countries shouting curses at each other, as we drifted farther and farther away.

"No, right, sure, of course," she says, standing up and stretching. "Two ships." She turns toward me and loosens her hair, so that it falls lightly over her shoulders and so I can see her do it. Her eyes are glittery with a momentary thrill of distaste for me. No more housework today. "Right. You just told me stories and listened to the radio and painted your dream girl." She looks at me. "If you had been Picasso, everyone would have forgiven you."

Now, late in the afternoon, we go walking toward the park, a way of recovering our equilibrium before we get into our separate cars and drive off toward our separate residences. Anyone seeing us strolling past the piles of bright leaves on the sidewalk, the last light of the sun in our eyes, might think that we're still a couple. Emily's wearing a little knitted red cap and a snug brown jacket, and she's squinting against the sun's rays, and because we are also facing a cool breeze from the west, her eyes fill with water—I refuse at this moment to think of them as tears—that she must wipe away before she says anything to me.

"It's true," she says. "Sometimes I forget the nicest things you did for me. Like that time you bought me flowers for my birthday."

"Which birthday was this?" I ask. The sun is in my eyes, too.

"It doesn't matter," she says. "What matters is that you walked into the house with these six red roses clutched in your hand, and I smiled, and I saw, from the puzzlement on your face, that in your absentminded way you had forgotten that you had bought roses for me and that you were holding them in your hand at that very moment. Imagine! Imagine a guy who buys roses for his wife and then carries them into the house and still forgets that that's what he's doing. Imagine being so fucking absentminded. It's a form of male hysteria."

"Watch your language," I say, kidding her. "It's true," I say. "I was presenting you with roses that I had forgotten about."

"And what it meant," Emily tells me, as if I hadn't said anything, "was that your instincts, your . . . I don't know what you would call it, your unconscious, still loved me, even if your conscious mind didn't. I thought, My husband, Dennis, still loves me. Despite everything. You could absentmindedly get me roses on my birthday without knowing what you were doing. Somewhere in there, you were still kindly disposed toward me. Your little love light still was shining, before its last flickerings."

We arrive at the park. On this side of it is a small playground with a slide, a climbing structure, swings, and one little boy is still playing while his mother sits on a bench and reads the paper, but now that it's getting to be dusk, she's squinting, bending down in order to make out the print. She calls to her son, but he won't return to her quite yet. He won't follow her orders. Emily sits down in one of the swings, and I sit down next to her. She puts her shoes in the pocketed dirt and slowly begins to swing herself back and forth. Behind us, the woods seem to be breathing in and out.

"I liked childhood," Emily says to me, softly. "I liked being a kid. A lot of the other girls wanted to grow up, but *I* didn't. They wanted to go out on dates, the excitement of all that—boys, cars, sex, the whole scene. But not me. I didn't want to launch my ship into adolescence, I didn't want my periods to start, I didn't want what was about to happen, to happen. I had this dread of it. I wanted to stay a kid forever. I thought being an adult was the awful afterlife of childhood."

I can't remember ever being afraid of growing up, so I don't say anything in response. Even at this late date, Emily can still surprise me with what she says.

"And it was awful, I mean, it *is* awful. It's terrible, but of course you can learn to live with it, and it's okay after a while even if it's terrible, and besides, what choice do you have?"

"No choice," I say to her. The woman on the bench calls to her son again, and this time he comes down to where she's sitting, and he stands by her side and put his hand on her arm as a signal that he's ready. She nods, briefly looking at him, then folds her paper, stands up, and takes his hand. These gestures are of such gentle, subtle sweetness that they feel like a private language to me, and my mind clouds up, given the weight of the day, given my own situation.

"You know," I say to Emily, as I swing back and forth in my swing, "I've been getting postcards. Anonymous postcards."

"Dennis," Emily tells me, "I don't have time for another story. I have to get home. I have a date tonight, if you can believe it."

"No, *listen*," I say. "They've been arriving in the mail every few days. They're anonymous, I don't know who's sending them. Not to work, but to my home address, the apartment. And they have these picture postcard photographs on the flip side—Miami Beach, the Bahamas, the Empire State Building, the usual. But on the message side, it's something else."

"Dennis, really," she says, "I have to go." But she's still sitting there, in the playground, on her swing. "I have to get ready," she says, in a flat, neutral tone.

But I'm going to finish, and I say, "And what it is, these messages— they're always handwritten, always in blue ink, always in large letters, uppercase, all of them. Short, punchy sentences. Condemnations, against me. Judgments." I hold up my hand to suggest a headline, even though the words have to fit on postcards. *'Your work has come to nothing.' 'Your life is a disaster.' 'Someone is watching you.' 'Aren't you ashamed of yourself?'* Now who do you suppose would send postcard messages like that?"

She looks over at me, in the gathering dusk, a genuine expression of surprise, and I understand at the moment that I see her face that it's not she, it's not Emily who has been sending me these postcards. All along I had thought it would be her idea of retribution, these insane postcards. But she hasn't been sending them, and this sends a brief shudder through me. But really, perhaps I had known all along. After all, I would know what her handwriting was like even if she tried to disguise it. We're almost twins that way.

"If you're thinking it was me," Emily says, "think again. It wasn't."

"And last week, I got one that said, '*Have you no remorse?*' "

"Well," Emily says, after a pause, "whoever is sending them must know you. That's a good word, 'remorse.' I could have used that word on you. A flea-market word. Maybe I actually did. It would've been one of my grandparent words. *You* never used a word like that. Must be one of your little girlfriends sending these messages. Somebody who's a little obsessed with you, Dennis."

"Some poor devil," I say.

"Yes," she says, "a poor devil, that sounds about right." She gets up out of the swing and goes over to the climbing structure. "Which one do you suppose it is?"

"Well," I say, "I don't know." But actually I think I do know. Once this woman and I were at dinner together, a woman who in her day had done a lot of drugs, the ones that give you those dimestore visions, and out of nowhere, she said, "I can see all your thoughts, you know. I can see them, and you don't even have to say them aloud, because I know what they are." She was holding her wineglass, this woman, and it had been a good evening until then, but when she said she could see my thoughts, it seemed time to get out of there. She sat up straight. "God and his archangels have taken a real dislike to you," she said, as I was motioning to the waiter. "They have a gun pointed at your head. I just think I should tell you that."

"She really said that?" Emily asks, coming down from the play structure. "That God and his archangels had a gun pointed at your head?"

"Yeah," I say. "Those were her exact words. But I can't imagine anyone being obsessed with me. I have such a . . ." But I can't think of the phrase.

"Where did you find these girls, Dennis?" she asks.

"The place where everybody finds them. In the street, and so on."

"You should look in different places."

"There are no different places." It suddenly occurs to me that I don't know what Emily and I are talking about. I've completely lost the thread.

"No," she says, "there aren't." She waits. "Did you see that woman and her little boy? Did you see how . . . I don't know, how calm they were with each other? God, I loved seeing that. That calm. It makes you want to be a kid again. Of course, I always want that anyway."

I take her hand and we walk back.

When we get to the house, my ex-wife is about to unlock her car and drive away, but she's left her purse and wallet in the kitchen. So, together, the two of us go in the front door, and we step into the foyer and the living room. They're completely dark—it's night by now—and only the streetlight is spraying a little bit of illumination into the room, barely enough to see by.

"Close your eyes," Emily says. "Could you find your way around in this place with your eyes closed? I bet you could."

"Of course," I say.

So I close my eyes and hold my arms out in the dark, and I walk all around the room where the lamps and tables and chairs were, where Em and I once lived, and I go into the dining room, still with my eyes closed, and I walk into the kitchen, past the counter and the dishwasher and then back out, taking my steps one at a time through these spaces I've come to know so intimately. It's just as well that my eyes are closed as I'm walking through this dark house where Emily and I tried to stage our marriage, because I have this image of Santa jogging—no, sprinting— away from me, and I probably have a grim look.

It's right about then that I'm back in the living room and I bump up against Emily, whose arms also have been out, in this game we're playing. In the story that I don't tell, we excuse ourselves, but then, very slowly and tenderly, we are inspired by each other at last, and we take each other in our arms, and all the bad times fall away, and we kiss, and we mutter our apologies, our long-standing whispered complicated remorse, and perhaps we sink to the floor, and we make love together in the dark empty living room, on the floor, understanding that maybe it will not be the last time, after all. And as we make love, Emily makes her utterly familiar trembling cry when she comes.

That's the story that I don't tell, because it doesn't happen, and couldn't, and would not, because I am unforgivable, and so is she. Two poor devils: what we don't feel is remorse, the word on that postcard. We bump into each other, two blind staggerers, two solitudes, and then, yes, we apologize. And that's when Emily goes into the kitchen, her eyes open, but still in the dark house that she knows, as they say, by heart, and she picks up her purse from where she has left it, and she comes out, sailing past me, and she maybe half turns in the dark, and blows me a kiss, but probably she doesn't.

She closes the front door behind her, absentmindedly locking it, locking me into the house. And it's then, and only then, that I speak up. "Good-bye, honey," I say.

# Ghosts

———◆◆◆———

OUT ON THE FRONT LAWN, Melinda was weeding her father's garden with a birdlike metal claw when a car drifted up to the curb. A man with brown hair highlighted with blond streaks got out on the driver's side. He stood still for a moment, staring at the house as if he owned it and was mulling over possible improvements. In his left hand he held an apple with teeth marks in it, though the apple was still whole. Melinda had never laid eyes on the guy before. Her father's house was located in an affordable but slightly run-down city neighborhood with its share of characters. They either gawked at you or wouldn't meet your gaze. Many of them were mutterers who deadwalked their way past other pedestrians in pursuit of their oddball destinations. She returned to her weeding.

"Hot day," the man said loudly, as if comments on the weather might interest her. Melinda glanced at him again. With a narrow Eric Clapton-ish face, and dressed in blue jeans and a plain white shirt, he was on his way to handsomeness without quite arriving there. The apple was probably an accessory for nerves, like a chewed pencil behind the ear.

The baby monitor on the ground beside her began to squawk.

"I have to go inside," Melinda said, half to herself. She dropped her metal claw, rubbed her hands to get some of the topsoil off, and hurried into the house, taking the steps two at a time. Upstairs, her nine-month-old son, Eric, lay fussing in his crib. With dirt still under her fingernails, she picked him up to kiss him and caught a whiff of wet diaper. At the changing table, she raised her son's legs with one hand and removed the diaper with the other while she observed the stranger advancing up the front walk toward the entryway. The doorbell rang, startling the baby and making his arms quiver. Melinda called over to her father, whose bedroom was across the hall, to alert him about the stranger. Her father didn't answer. Sleep often captured him these days and absented him for hours.

She pinned the clean diaper together, and with slow tenderness brought Eric to her shoulder. She smoothed his hair, the same shade of brown as her own, and at that moment the man who had been standing outside appeared in front of her in the bedroom doorway, smiling dreamily, still holding the bitten apple.

"I used to live here," the man said quietly, "when I was little. This was my room when I was small." After emphasizing the last word with a strange vehemence, he seemed to be surveying the walls and the ceilings and the floors and the windows until at last his gaze fell on Eric. The baby saw him and instead of screaming held out his arm.

"Jesus. Who are you?" Melinda said. "What the hell are you doing up here?"

"Yes, I'm sorry," the man said. "Old habits die hard." The baby was now tugging downward at Melinda's blouse buttons, one after the other, which he did whenever he was hungry. "I heard him crying," the man said. "I thought I might help. Is that your father?" He pointed toward the second bedroom, where Melinda's father dozed, his head slumped forward, a magazine in his lap.

"Yes, it is. *He* is," Melinda said. "Now please leave. I don't know you. You're a trespasser. You have serious boundary issues. You have no right to be here. Please get the fuck out. Now." The baby was staring at the man. "I've said 'please' twice, and I won't say it again."

"Quite correct," the man said, apparently thinking this over. "I really *don't* have any right to be here." He made a noise in his throat like a sheep cough. He had the unbudging calm of a practiced intruder. "Truly I didn't mean to scare you. It's just that I used to live here. I used to *be* here." With the hand not holding the apple, he held out his index finger to Eric, and the baby, distracted from the button project, grabbed it. The man loosened the baby's grip, turned around, and began to walk down the stairs. "If I told you everything about this house," he said as he was leaving, "and all the things in it, you wouldn't live here. I'm sorry if I frightened you."

She followed him. From the landing she watched him until he had crossed the threshold and was halfway back to his car. Then he stopped, turned around, and said in a loud voice, a half shout, "Are you desperate? You look kind of desperate to me." He waited in the same stock-still posture she had seen on him earlier. He seemed to be in a state of absolute concentration on something that was not there. People were getting into this style nowadays; really, nothing could outdo the urban zombie affect. It was post-anxiety. It promised a kind of death you could live with. He was waiting eternally for her to answer and wouldn't move until she replied.

"Yes. No," she called through the screen door. "But that's no business of yours."

"My name's Augenblick," the man said, just before he got into his car. "Edward Augenblick. Everyone calls me Ted. And I won't bother you again. I left a business card in the living room, though, if you're curious about this house." He turned one last time toward her front screen door, behind which she was now standing. "I'm not dangerous," he said, holding his apple. "And the other thing is, I *know* you."

The car started—it purred expensively, making a sound like a diesel sedan, but Melinda had never known one brand of car from another, they were all just assemblages of metal to her, and he, this semi-handsome person who said he was Edward Augenblick, whoever that was, and the car, the two of them, the human machine and the actual machine, proceeded down the block in a low chuckling putter, turned right, and disappeared.

Picking up the baby, she went out to gather up her trowel and the bird-like metallic weeder. She would leave the weeds where they were, for now. Doing another sort of chore might conceivably restore her calm.

After taking the tools back to the garage, she surveyed her father's things scattered on the garage's left-hand side, which now served mostly as a shed. You could get a car in there on the right-hand side if you were very careful. Cast-off fishing poles, broken flashlights, back issues of *American Record Guide* and *Fanfare,* operas and chamber music on worn-out vinyl, and more lawn and garden implements that gave off a smell of soil and fertilizer—everything her father didn't have the heart to throw away had been dumped here into a memory pile in the space where the other car, her mother's, used to be. Melinda put her gardening implements on a tool shelf next to a can of motor oil for the lawn mower, and she bowed her head. When she did, the baby grabbed at her hair.

She wasn't desperate. The almost-handsome stranger had got that particular detail wrong. A man given to generalizations might launch into nonsense about desperation, seeing a single mom with a baby boy, the

two of them living in her father's house, temporarily. Eric pulled hard at
her bangs. She was trembling. Her hands shook. The visitation felt
like . . . like what? Like a little big thing—a micro-rape.

She had grown up in this house; he hadn't. It was that simple.

As if taking an inventory to restore herself, she thought of the tasks
she had to perform: her property taxes would come due very soon and
she would have to pay them on her own house across town, where she
would be residing this very minute if her father weren't in recovery from
his stroke. She imagined it: her Arts and Crafts home stood empty (of
her and of Eric) on its beautiful wooded lot, with a decorative rose arbor
in the backyard, climbing in spite of her, in her absence. She missed the
orderly clean lines of her own house and its nursery and its mostly empty
spaces and what it required of her.

"Desperate"—the nerve of the guy.

Over there, at her own house, she would not be susceptible to the vis-
itations of strangers. Over there, she would be within walking distance
of the local college where she taught Spanish literature of the nineteenth
century—her specialty being the novels of Pérez Galdós. Over there, she
was on leave just now, during her father's convalescence, while she lived
here, the house of her childhood.

Looking at her father's ragtag accumulations in the garage, she worried at a pile of books with her foot. The books leaned away from her,
and the top three volumes (*Gatsby*, Edith Wharton, and Lloyd C. Doug-
las) fell over and scattered. The baby laughed.

These garage accumulations exemplified a characteristic weakness of
the late-middle-aged, the broken estate planning of all the doddering
Lear-like fathers. Still holding her son, she sorted her father's books and
restacked them.

Melinda's ex-husband had been a great fan of *Gatsby*. He loved fak-
ery. He had even owned a pair of spats and a top hat that he had purchased at an antique-clothing store. He had been the catalyst for a brief
trivial marriage Melinda had committed herself to during graduate
school. A month or so ago at a party where, slightly drunk on the
Chardonnay—she shouldn't have been drinking, she knew, she was still
nursing the baby—she was telling funny stories about herself, and for a
few moments, she hadn't been able to remember her ex-husband's name.
Anyway, he was just an ex-husband. Now that she had the baby, solitude
and its difficulties no longer troubled her. Her child had put an end to

selfish longings. And besides—she was gazing at her father's old *National Geographic*—she had the languages. She spoke four of them, including Catalan, which no one over here in the States spoke, ever; most Americans didn't seem to have heard of it. And of course they didn't know where it was spoken. Or why.

Her languages were a charm against loneliness; they gave her a kind of imaginary community. The benevolent spirits came to her in dreams and spoke in Catalan.

During her junior year abroad she had lived in Madrid for a few months and then in Barcelona, where she had acquired a Catalan boyfriend who had taught her the language during the times when he prepared meals for her in his small apartment kitchen—standard fare, paella or fried sausage and onions, which in his absentminded ardor he often burned. He gave her little drills in syntax and the names of kitchen appliances. He took her around Barcelona and lectured her about its history, the civil war, the causes for the bullet holes still visible in certain exterior walls.

He had told her that anyone could learn Spanish, but that she, a stupendously unique and beautiful American girl, must learn Catalan, so she did. What a charming liar he'd been.

Time passed, she returned to the States, got her degrees, and then eighteen months ago, when she had taken a college group to Barcelona for a week, she had met up again with him, this ex-lover, this Jordi, and they had gone out to a tapas bar where she had spoken Catalan (with her uncertain grammar, she sounded, Jordi said, like a pig farmer's wife). At least with her long legs, her sensitive face, and her Catalan, she wouldn't be taken for a typical American, recognizable for innocence and obesity. Then she and Jordi went back to his apartment, a different apartment by now, larger than the one they had spent time in as students, this one near the Gaudí cathedral. Jordi's wife was away on a business trip to Madrid. Melinda and Jordi made love in the living room so as not to defile his marriage bed. Out of the purity of their nostalgia, they came at the same time. He had used a condom but something happened, and that had been the night when her son was conceived.

She had never told Jordi about her pregnancy. He possessed a certain hysterical formality and would have been scandalized. As the father, he would never have permitted a Scandia-American name like "Eric" to be affixed to his child. God, he would think, had intervened. Sperm penetrating the condom would be so much like the immaculate conception that Jordi, a Catholic, would have trouble explaining it away. And because he wept easily, he would first weep and then talk, the talk accompanied by his endearing operatic gestures. The sanctity of life! The whatever of parenthood. He had a tendency to make pronouncements, like the pope. Or was this Spanish in nature? A Catalan tendency? A male thing? Or just Jordi? Melinda sometimes got her stereotypes confused.

Anyway, her news about the baby would in all likelihood have destroyed his marriage, an arrangement that Melinda supposed was undoubtedly steady, in a relaxed Euro sort of way, despite Jordi's one-off infidelity that particular night, with her.

Maybe he was habitually unfaithful. What was a married man doing with a condom in the drawer of the bedside table? Hidden but in plain view? Did husbands use condoms when making love to their wives? It seemed defeatist.

It was what it was. Still, she had loved Jordi once. She would say to her Catalan friends, "Have you seen his eyes, and those eyelashes?"—the most beautiful brown eyes she had ever seen on a man. He had other qualities difficult to summarize. All the same, men, at least the ones she had known, including Jordi, were a long-term nuisance, a drain on human resources. Whenever intimacy threatened, they often seemed unexpectedly obtuse. If you were going to couple with straight men— and what choice did you have?—you often had to deal with their strange semi-comic fogs afterward. Jordi snored and after lovemaking clipped his toenails. As Hemingway, another man, once wrote: the bill always came.

Anyway, she was not desperate. Melinda roused herself from her reverie. Augenblick! The stranger had got that part wrong, about the desperation.


She went back upstairs. She put Eric into his crib. The baby occupied himself by listening to a white-throated sparrow singing outside the window. Across the hall, her father sat staring at his dresser. It had been positioned beneath family pictures—Melinda, her brother, her mother, and her father—hung in a photo cluster where he could see them as he made his heroic post-stroke efforts to dress and to greet the morning. Behind the pictures was the ancient wallpaper with green horizontal stripes. He turned toward her, and the right side of his face smiled at her.

"Do you hear it?" he asked.

She waited. Hear what? The sparrow? He wouldn't be asking about that. "No," she said; the room was quite silent. Lately her father had been suffering from music hallucinations, what he called "ear worms," and she wasn't sure whether to grant him his hallucinations or not. Did the pink elephant problem grow larger whenever, being affable, you agreed that there was indeed a pink elephant right outside the door, or shambling about in the street? "What is it? What do you hear?"

"Somebody far away, practicing," he told her. "A violinist. She's doing trills and double-stops. She's practicing someone-or-other's concerto in D. You really don't hear it?" Her father had not been a professional musician, but he had always had perfect pitch. If he heard music in D major, then that was the key signature, hallucination or not.

In the silent room, Melinda gazed down at her father, at his thinning gray hair, the food stains scattered on his shirt, the sleepy, half-withdrawn look in his eyes, the magazine now on the floor, the untied shoelaces, the trouser zipper imperfectly closed, the mismatched socks, the shirt with the buttons in the wrong buttonholes, the precancerous blotches on his face, the half-eaten muffin spread with margarine nearby on the side table, and she was so overcome with a lifelong affection for this calm, decent man that she felt faint for a moment. Her soul left her body and then came back in an instant. "Oh, wait," she said suddenly. "Yup. I do hear it. It's very soft. From across the street. You know, it's who, that scary brilliant teenager, that Asian girl, what's her name, Maria Chang. And I know who wrote that music, too."

"You do?"

"Sure," Melinda said. "It's Glazunov. Alexander Glazunov. It's the Glazunov concerto for violin in D major." She was making it all up as she went along.

"Yes," her father said. "Glazunov. The teacher of Shostakovich. That must be right." He smiled again at her. "But that concerto is in A, baby doll." Turning his head to face her at a strange angle, he asked, "Who was that person who j-j-j-j-just came to the door? Did he come upstairs? Did he watch me? Did he come for me? Was it death? I was half asleep."

"An intruder," she said. "Somebody who said his name was Augen-blick."

"Well, that's almost like death. What'd he want?"

"He said he used to live here. As a baby or something."

"Impossible. I know who I bought this house from thirty-five years ago, and it wasn't anybody by that name. Besides, that's not his real name. It's German. It means . . ."

"Blink of an eye," Melinda said. "An instant."

"Right. But he's lying to you. I never heard of any German person named Augenblick. It's a fiction, that name. There's no such name in German. It's total bullshit." He waved his hand dismissively. Since his stroke, her father had started to employ gutterisms in his day-to-day speech. His new degraded vocabulary was disconcerting. His mind had suffered depreciation. She didn't like obscenity from him; it didn't match his character, or what remained of it.

Her father's potted plant in the corner needed watering—its leaves were shriveling. Lately she had become a caretaker: Eric, and her father, and the lawn and garden out in front, and her father's house, and the plants in it—and if she weren't careful, that caretaking condition might become permanent, she would move into permanent stewardship, they would be her accumulations, and they would pile up and surround her. The present would dry up and disappear, except for the baby, and there would be nothing else around her except the past.

Downstairs on a side table was a business card.

*Edward Augenblick*
INVESTMENT COUNSELOR
"Fortune Favors the Few"
e-mail: eyeblink@droopingleaf.com

Anger spat up from somewhere near her stomach. "Fortune favors the few"! Damn him. And this zealotry from an intruder. At once, the languages roused themselves, spewing out their local-color bile. First, the Catalan. ¡Malparit. Fot el camp de casa meva ara mateix! And then the Spanish. ¡Me cago en tu madre, hijo de puta! What a relief it was to have other languages available for your obscenities. They pitched in.

A day later, she and her friend Germaine were walking in Minnehaha Creek, their pants rolled up, shoes in hand, Eric babypacked on Melinda.

They were searching the creek for vegetative wonders as they bird-watched and conversed. Melinda liked Germaine's witty impatience and had befriended her for it. They had bumped into each other in a bookstore a year ago, and Germaine had grumbled at her amiably. Melinda was bowled over by her wit and asked her out for coffee, an invitation that Germaine accepted. Germaine, a teacher and poet, was now back from New York, where she had toured the restaurants.

"There's a blue jay," Melinda said, pointing. She splashed her feet in the water, being careful not to slip on the rocks.

"Did I tell you how all the staff at one place spoke with accents? Did I mention that?" Germaine asked. " 'Ladies and gentle, let me know eef I can help you in any how.' They sounded worse during the wine-tasting session. 'Yooou like theeese vine? Have a zip.' " She walked up to Eric and kissed him on the ear. The baby giggled. " 'Hold theeese vine to the liiiight to determinate the lascivity.' "

"You should be more tolerant of foreigners," Melinda murmured, turning to face her.

"Why should I? I'm not like you. I put salt in my coffee." She looked at her friend. "You take that beautiful baby of yours around on your back just to flaunt him in front of nature."

"No, I don't. Your leg is cut," Melinda said, pointing. "Where'd you get that mess of scabs?"

"Roses. I was staring at the clematis vine. Its growth habits were unpleasing. I held the ideal in my head so firmly that I obliterated awareness of the rest of the garden, especially the very large, known-to-be-violent rosebush between the clematis and me. I must have lunged at the vine. The rosebush grabbed at my leg, which continued to move. Seconds later I realized that the whole front of my leg had been savagely torn."

"Savagely torn? That's awful."

" 'Laceration' is what the form said, when I finally got out of the ER. I looked the word up, from *lacerate, distress deeply, torn, mangled.* Then I had a drug reaction to the prophylactic antibiotic. It sent me back to the ER. I couldn't walk."

"What's that?" Melinda nodded toward something growing in the creek.

"Watercress?" Germaine said. Her black hair fell downward as she bent to see it, and for a moment Melinda thought of Persephone on her way back from the underworld. Germaine had the wildly intelligent eyes of a genius. "No, it's just an unknown, anonymous weed. By the way, how close are we to the Mississippi? I have an appointment. Well, *I* think of it as an appointment. You might not."

Melinda stood up straight, feeling the baby's weight shift. He was making sucking sounds. "I had a visitor yesterday. Well, not a visitor. A man, an intruder. He looked like Eric Clapton. He walked right into the house. He said he used to live there. But he didn't. He couldn't have. His name was Augenblick."

"You call the cops?"

"No."

"I would have," Germaine told her. "I'd have the law scurrying right over, with the cuffs and the beaters out."

"He said Eric's nursery had once been his own room. He said he knew things about the house, bad things. He said, this stranger, that I was *desperate.* Can you imagine?"

"He got the wrong address," Germaine said. "He meant me."

"Damn him anyway," said Melinda. She pointed to an opening of the creek where the Mississippi River was visible. "There it is. There's the river. We made it."

"Yeah." Germaine slapped at a mosquito on her forearm, leaving a little smear of blood just above her wristwatch. "Is this about your mother?" she asked. Her tone was studiously neutral. "This is about your mother, isn't it? Maybe this guy lived in the neighborhood when you were growing up. Maybe your mother was known to him."

Melinda stopped and looked at her friend. Seedpods from a cotton-wood overhead drifted down onto her hair and into the water. "Oh, well," she said, as if something had been settled. Melinda's mother had been in and out of institutions. Melinda refused to come to terms with it, now or ever; a mad parent could not be rescued or reasoned with. Things were getting dark all of a sudden. "I'm, um, feeling a bit light-headed." She felt her knees weakening, and she made her way to the side of the creek, where she sat down abruptly on the wet sands.

"Are you fainting?" she heard Germaine say, in front of, or behind, a crow cawing. "Here. Let me take your hand. . . ." The force of her friend's voice drifted into her consciousness, as did her voice, someone turning the volume knob back and forth, as she held her own nausea at bay, her head down between her knees. Creek water was suddenly splashed on her face, thrown by her friend, to rouse her.

At certain times, usually in the afternoons, her father would ride the buses, but Melinda had no idea where he went, and he himself could not always remember. He said that he visited the markets, but one time he came back and said that he had knocked at the Gates of Heaven. He would not elaborate. Where were these gates? He had forgotten. Perhaps downtown? Many people were going in, all at once. He felt he wasn't ready, and took the bus home.

This traveling around was a habit he had picked up from his wife, whose wandering had started right after the death of their first child, Melinda's older sister, Sarah, who had died of a blood infection at the age of two. Her mother gave birth to Melinda and then went into a very long, slow, discreetly managed and genteel decline. One day, when Melinda was eleven, her mother, unable to keep up appearances anymore, drove away and disappeared altogether. She was spotted in Madison before she evaporated.

Back in her father's house, Melinda went straight from the phone to her computer. She typed in Augenblick's e-mail address and then wrote a note.

```
hi. i don't know who you are, but you're not who you
say you are, and my father has never heard of you or
your family. i shouldn't be writing to you and i
wouldn't be except i didn't like it that you said you
knew me. from where? we've never met. you don't know
me. i hardly know myself. kidding. i mean, i've met
you and i still haven't met you. you're a ghost, for
all i know.
```

She deleted the last three sentences—too baroque—both for their meaning and her responsibility for writing them. The joking tone might be mistaken for friendliness. She ducked her head, hearing Eric staying quiet (she didn't want to breast-feed him again tonight, her nipples were sore—but it was odd, she also had suffered a sudden brokenhearted need for sex, for friendly nakedness), and then she continued writing.

as far as i know, the previous owners of this house
were named anderson. that's who my mom and dad bought
it from. "augenblick" isn't even a name. it's just a
german noun.
   so, my question is: who are you? where are you from?
what were you doing in my house?
   —melinda everson, ph.d.


She deleted the reference to the doctoral degree, then put it back, then
deleted it again, then put it back in, before touching the SEND button.

Half an hour later, a new letter appeared in the electronic in-box,
from eyeblink@droopingleaf.com.


THINK OF ME AS THE RAGE OVER THE LOST PENNY. BUT
LIKE I TOLD YOU IM ACTUALLY VERY HARMLESS. W/R/T
YOUR QUESTIONS, I CAN DROP BY AGAIN. INFORMATION
IS ALL I WANT TO GIVE YOU. eye two LIVED THERE.
   HA HA.—TED


The school year would be starting soon, and she needed to prepare her
classes. She needed to study Peréz Galdós's *Miau* again, for the ump-
teenth time, for its story of a man lost in a mazelike bureaucracy—her
lecture notes were getting mazelike themselves, Kafkaesque. And worse:
bland. She would get to that. But for now she was waiting. She knew
without knowing how she knew that when Augenblick came back, he
would show himself at night, when both her father and her son were
asleep; that he would come at the end of a week of hot, dry late-summer
weather orchestrated by crickets, that he would show up as a polite
intruder again, halfway handsome, early-middle-aged semi-degraded-
Clapton, well dressed, like a piano tuner, and that he would say, as soon
as he was out of the driver's-side door of his unidentifiable car, perhaps
handmade, and had advanced so that he stood there on the other side of
the screen door, "You look very nice tonight. I got your letter. Thanks for
inviting me over."

These events occurred because she was living in her father's house.

"And I got yours," she said, from behind the screen. The screen provided scanning lines; his face was high-definition. "You're the rage over
the lost penny. But I didn't invite you over. You're *not* invited. It wasn't an
invitation." She hesitated. "Shit. Well, come in anyway."

This time, once inside, he approached her and shook her hand, and in removing his hand, rubbed hers, as if this were the custom somewhere upon greeting someone whom you didn't know but with whom you wanted a relationship. It was a failed tentative caress but so bizarre that she let it happen.

"My father is upstairs," she said. "And my son, too. Maybe you could explain who you are?"

"This is the living room," he told her, as if he hadn't heard her question, "and over there we once had a baby grand piano in that corner, by the stairs." He pointed. "A Mason and Hamlin. I was never any good at playing it, but my sister was. She's the real musician in the family."

"What does she play?" she asked, testing him. "What's her specialty?"

"Scriabin études," he said. "Chopin and Schumann, too, and Schubert, the B-minor."

"She didn't play the violin, did she?"

"No. The piano. She still does. She's a pediatric endocrinologist now. Doctors like music, you know. It's a professional thing." He waited. "Ours was the only piano on the block." He glanced toward the dining room. "In the dining room we used to have another chandelier, it was cut glass—"

"Mr. Augenblick, uh, maybe you could tell me why you're here? And why you're lying to me?" She scooped a bit of perspiration off her forehead and gazed into his game face. "Why all these stories about this locality? Scriabin, Schubert: every house has a story. The truth is, I'm not actually interested in who did what, where, here." She saw him glance down at her body, then at the baby toys scattered across the living-room floor. Her breasts were swollen, and she had always been pretty. She was a bit disheveled now, though still a beauty. "I'm a mother. New life is going on here these days. My son is here, my father, too, upstairs, recuperating from a stroke. I don't have time for a personal history. For all I know, you're an intruder. A dangerous maniac."

"No," he said, "I've noticed that. No one has time for a history." Augenblick stood in the living room for a moment, apparently pondering what to say next. At last he looked up, as if struck by a sudden thought, and asked, "May I have a glass of iced tea?"

"No." She folded her arms. "If you were a guest, I would provide the iced tea. But, as I said, I didn't invite you here. I don't mean to be rude, but—"

"Actually," he said, "you *are* rude. You wrote back to me, and that was, well, an invitation. Wasn't it? At least that's how I took it, it's how any man would have taken it." He pasted onto his face a momentarily wounded look. "So all right. So there's to be no iced tea, no water, no hospitality of any kind. No stories, either, about the house. All right. You want to know why I'm here? You really want to know why I'm here? My life hasn't been going so well. I was doing a bit of that living-in-the-past thing. I was driving around, in this neighborhood, *my* former neighborhood, and I saw a really attractive woman working in her garden, weeding, and I thought: Well, maybe she isn't married or attached, maybe I have a chance, maybe I can strike up a conversation with that woman working there in that garden. I wasn't out on the prowl, exactly, but I *did* see you. And then I discovered that you had a baby. A beautiful boy. You know, I'm actually a nice guy, though you'd never know it. I'm a landscape architect. I have a college degree. All I wanted was to meet you."

"You said I was desperate. You said you knew me. That was unkind. No. It was wicked."

"You *are* desperate. I do know you. Desperation is knowable."

"That's a funny way of courting a woman, saying things like that."

"We have the same soul, you and I," he said. He said it awkwardly. Still, she was moved, beside or despite herself. The sovereign power of nonsensical compliments: a woman never had any defenses against them.

"I don't know," she said. "Come back in a few days and tell me about the house."

"It's just an ordinary house," he told her, glaring critically at its corners. "Anyway, you're right, I never lived here. I lived a few blocks away."

"So make it up," she said. "You were going to make it up anyway. Do what you can with it. Impress me."


The next time Augenblick came by, he brought a bottle of wine, a kind of lubricant for his narrative, Melinda thought.

They drank half the bottle, and then he began with the medical details about the house and what had happened in its rooms. There had been a little girl with polio who lived in the house in the 1950s, encased in an iron lung, with the result that her parents had been the first on the block to buy a TV set, in those days a low-class forgetfulness machine. In those days only two stations broadcast programs, a few hours in the morning, then off the air during the afternoons until four p.m., when *The Howdy Doody Show, Superman,* and *Beulah* came on.

He touched Melinda's hand. From somewhere he poured her another glass of wine, a glass that she had taken down from her kitchen shelf an hour or two ago, and she took it. He did an inventory of ghosts. Every house had them. He told her that the living room had once been an organizing center for Farmer-Labor Party socials of the Scandinavian variety, and that they had planned their strikes there, including the truckers' strike in the 1930s.

"Any violence?" she asked, taking the wine for her second glass.

"None," he said. As a little boy, he said, he had heard that there had once been a murder in these environs, and maybe it had been in this house. He wasn't sure. The body of the murder victim, it was said, had been propped up on the freezer, sitting there, and the police had come in to investigate after the neighbors had called in with reports of screaming, and one of the cops looked directly at the body of the murdered woman, her hair down over her face, and he hadn't seen it, and the police had left.

"Who are you?" Melinda asked Augenblick after they had finished the wine and he had concluded his story. Now they sat on the back porch in discount-store foldout chairs, and through the screens they could see her father's garage with the car on one side and her father's discards, his memory pile, on the other. "Because, right here, there's quite a bit about you that's completely wrong. You tell me a story, the absolutely wrong story, about happiness and a murder, and you say you know me and you say I'm desperate, and I think you said that you and I have the same souls, and your card claimed that you were an investment counselor, and then you informed me that you were a landscape architect." Melinda put her tongue inside her wineglass and licked at the dew of wine still affixed there. "None of it adds up. Because," she said, "what I think it is, what I think you are, sitting here beside me, is a devil." She waited. "Not one of the major ones, in fact really minor, but one all the same."

Through the air pocket of dead silence the crickets chirped. Augenblick did not immediately reply. "Um, okay," he said.

" 'Okay'?"

"Yeah, okay. I used to be an investment counselor until I went broke. I couldn't part with the business cards. So then I went into planting things, landscaping. Not much income, but some. The life I have is modest. I have a kind of ability to, you know, hit the wrong note. And sometimes I tell stories that aren't quite true. It passes the time. Untruths are what I learned how to do in high school and never quite shook off."

"You should work at it," she said.

"I should work at it," he repeated.

"Was there anything, anywhere, you said that was true?"

"Yes," he said. "My name's really Augenblick. You and I have the same souls. I believe that. I still sort of believe that you're desperate. I used to live in this neighborhood. You had a mother once. I remember her. And actually, from the first moment I saw you, weeding out there in the garden, I haven't been able to stop thinking about you."

She waited. "Could we go back to the topic sentence?"

He leaned sideways in her direction. She could smell the wine on his breath. "About devils, you mean?"

"Yeah, that part."

"There are no devils anymore," he said. "There are only people who are messed up and have to spread it around. And they're everywhere. See, what you have to do is, if you're going to get it, you have to imagine a devil who is also maybe a nice guy." And he leaned over farther, so that he almost lost his balance in his chair, and he gave her a peck on each cheek, a devil's kiss.

Making love to him (which she would never, ever do) would be like taking a long journey to a foreign locale you didn't exactly want to visit, like Tangier, a place built on the slopes of a chalky limestone hill. The sun's intensity would be unpleasant, and the general poverty would get in the way of everything. He would make love like a man who didn't quite know what he was doing and who would press that ignorance, hard, on someone else, specifically on her, on her flesh. Still, he would be careful with her, as if he remembered that she was still nursing a child. In the middle of the bed, she would suddenly recall that when she had first seen him, she had thought that there was nothing to him, and she would wonder if there was still nothing to him now. Whether he was actually named Augenblick, despite his claims, whether he did anything actual for a living, whether he would ever hurt her, whether he really might be a devil, though devils didn't exist. Because if they did, times would change and the devils would take new forms. If the name of God is changing in our time, then so are the other names. Then she would come, rapidly, and would forget her questions the way you forget dreams. But it would never happen, not that way.


"You made love to him?" Germaine was outraged. The cell phone itself seemed to be outraged with her anger; even the plastic seemed annoyed. Melinda had called her friend in the middle of the night to consult.

"No, I didn't," Melinda said. "No. No love. But I did fuck him. I was lonely. I wanted to get naked with somebody."

"How was it?"

"Okay."

"Well, in the immortal words of the great Albert Einstein, 'Don't do that again.' "


She wondered if he would disappear. Everything about him suggested a vanishing act. He would not invite her to his house, wherever that was, nor would he ever give her an address. Like everyone else, though, he did have a cell phone, and he gave her the number to that. One night when he told her (she was lying in her bed, and he was lying in his bed, across town, and the phone call had gone on for over an hour), "I lived in your soul before you owned it," she decided that he was one of those crazy people who gets by from day to day, but just barely—he was what he said he was, a failed borderline personality. She resolved to tell him that she would not see him anymore, under any circumstances, but then he invited her to dinner at a pricey downtown restaurant, so she located a babysitter both for the baby and for her father, and when Edward Augenblick arrived to pick her up, she felt ready for whatever was going to happen, accessorized for it, with a bracelet of beautiful tiny gold spikes.

But in the restaurant, he played the gentleman: he talked about land-scape architecture, landscaping generally, so that the conversation took a lackadaisical turn toward the work of Frederick Law Olmsted, and she talked about her work and her scholarship, about Pérez Galdós, the polite chitchat of two people who possibly want to get to know each other, post-sex, and she wondered whether they would ever talk about anything that mattered to them, and whether all his talk about souls was just a bluff, a conversational shell game. She was about to ask him where

he had grown up, where he had been educated, what his parents had
been like, when he said, "Let's take a walk. Let's go down to the river."
The bill for the dinner came, a considerable sum, and he paid in cash,
drawing out a mass of twenty-dollar bills from his wallet, a monotonous
and mountainous pile of twenties, all the cash looking like novelty items,
and Melinda thought, This man has no usable credit.

Across the Mississippi River near St. Anthony Falls stands the Stone
Arch Bridge, built of limestone in the nineteenth century for the railroad
traffic of lumber and grain and coal in and out of Minneapolis. After the
railroad traffic ceased, the bridge had been converted to a tourist pedestrian walkway, and he took her hand in his as they strolled over the Mississippi River, looking at the abandoned mills on either side, and the
rapids and the locks directly below.

"They don't manufacture anything here anymore, you know," he said
to her, close to a whisper.

"The buildings are still here."

"Yes," he said, "but they're ghosts. They're all ghosts. They're shells."

"But look at the lights," she said. "Lofts and condos."

"They don't make anything in there anymore," he said. "Except
babies, sometimes, the thirtysomethings. Otherwise, it's all a museum.
American cities are all becoming museums." He said this with a wild,
incongruous cheer, as a devil would. "Okay," he said. "I'll tell you one
true thing. Listen up."

"What's that?"

"When I was a little boy, I lived three or four blocks down from where
you lived. I've told you this. You don't remember me. That's all. You
don't remember. I remember you, but you don't remember me. No one
ever remembers me. One night I was playing in the living room, with my
toy armies, and your mother came to our door. I think she was drunk.
But I didn't know that. She rang the bell and she entered our house. My
parents were upstairs, or somewhere. Your mother came into the house
and looked at me playing with my soldiers, and she looked and looked
and looked. She smiled and nodded. And then she asked me if I would
like to go away with her, said that she had always wanted to take a boy
like me with her on her travels."

"How did you know it was my mother?" Melinda asked, between shivers.

"I was eight years old. Maybe nine. Everyone knew about your mother. Everyone. I had been warned. You knew that. Everyone knew that. But she had a nice face."

"Where did she say she wanted to take you away to?"

"She had this look in her eyes, I still remember it," Augenblick said. "You have it, too. She wanted to disappear and to take someone along with her. That night, it was going to be me. Your mother was famous in this neighborhood. But everybody thought she was harmless."

"Well, she was a success," Melinda said, the shivers taking her over, so that she had to clutch a guardrail. "In disappearing." She leaned toward him and kissed him on the cheek, a show of bravery. "Death is such a cliché," she said. "She disappeared into a cliché."

"Is it?" He wasn't looking at her. "That's news to me. She grabbed me by the hand and she took me for a walk and then she tried to get me into the car, but I broke her hold on me and I ran back to my house."

"Yeah," she said, dreamily. "Death. It's so retro. It's for kids and old people. It's an adolescent thing. You can do better than dying. *You're tired. But everyone's tired. But no one is tired enough,*" she quoted from somewhere. "Anyway, she disappeared, and so what?" It occurred to her at that moment that Augenblick might have leapt off the bridge to his death but that he had, just then, changed his mind, because she had said that death was a cliché. That was it: he looked like a failed suicide. He was one of those.

"She gave me the scare of my life," he said. "Your harmless mother. She scared everybody until she was gone. Shall we go back now?" he asked. "Should we go somewhere?"

"No," she said. "Not again. Not this time." She waited. "We're going to stay right here for a while."

He eventually dropped her off at the front door of her father's house, thanked her, and drove off in his car, which, he had explained, was a Sterling, a nonsense car. She guessed that the license plates on the car had been stolen so that he could not be traced. Whoever he was— Augenblick! what a name!—he would not return. She wondered for a moment or two what his name actually had been, where he had worked, and whether any of it, that is, the actual, mattered, now or ever.

She paid the babysitter and then went upstairs to check on Eric.

The ghosts of the house, she imagined, were gathered around her son. The couples who had lived here from one generation to the next, the solitaries, the happy and unhappy, the gay and the straight and the young and the old: she felt them grouped behind her as a community corralled in the room, touching her questioningly as she bent over the crib and watched her boy, her perfection, breathe in and out, his Catalan-American breaths.

She tiptoed into her father's room. He was still sitting up, carefully studying the wallpaper.

"Hey, Daddy," she said.

"Hey, sugar," he replied, tilting his head in his characteristically odd way. "How did it go? Your date with this Augenblick?"

"Oh, fine," she said, shunning the narrative of what had happened, how she had fought off his information with a little kiss. Her father wouldn't be interested—especially about her mother.

"I didn't like him. He wasn't out of the top drawer."

"More like the middle drawer. But that's all right," Melinda said. "I won't see him again."

"Good," her father said. "I thought he was a fortune-hunter, after your millions." He laughed hoarsely. "Heh heh. He looked very unsuccessful, I must say, with that dyed hair." He tilted his head the other way. "I went to the Gates of Heaven today," he said, "on the bus. The number eight bus."

"How did it look?" she asked. "The gates?"

"Tarnished," he said. "They could use a shine. No one ever seems to do maintenance anymore. The bus was empty. Even though I was the thing riding on it." He tilted his head the other way. "Completely empty, with me at a window seat. That was how I knew I was almost gone. Honey, you should have more friends, better friends. Someone who doesn't make you groan."

It didn't shock her, somehow, that he had heard them. "I have friends. Just not here. I'm moving back home," she said. "To my house. Where I live. I can't stay here anymore, Daddy. I can't take care of you anymore. I love you, Daddy, but I can't do it. I'll arrange for somebody to watch you and to cook." She leaned down to kiss the top of his head.

"I know," he said. "Oh, I know, honey. Staying here makes you a child, doesn't it?"

"Yes." She could feel the goddamn tears flooding over her. And she could feel the ghosts of the house gathering around *him,* now, easing his way into the next world that awaited him. And somewhere on the planet, her mother, too, drove toward the horizon, forever. "I'll watch out for you, though. I'll drop in. I'll check on you."

"No, you probably won't," he said. "No one does. But that's all right. That's how it happens. By the way, do you hear that violin? That girl is practicing as if her life depended on it."

Melinda bent her ear to the silence. "Yes," she agreed. "I do hear it. All the time. Morning and night. It never stops."

# Royal Blue

AFTER CALLING IT QUITS with being a model and actor—his eyes were a bit too close together for the big time—Nicholas went into the business of acquiring and selling folk art. He and Daphne lived in Brooklyn, where she worked as a real estate agent, and in early autumn he had been up in New Paltz, at the country house of one of his clients, Mrs. Andriessen. Daphne referred to Mrs. Andriessen as "the Adult."

The Adult, a childless woman of a certain age, owned a largish wood-stone-and-glass house with a lap pool, along with views of trees and a lake. She had a crush on Nicholas, which evened things out slightly between them. Every month they ate lunch together in either New Paltz or one of the neighboring restaurants near her city place on East Eighty-sixth, where she spent the weekdays during the winter. On weekends, and during much of the spring, summer, and fall, she stayed put in the country, filling her days with gardening, reading, and bird-watching. The Adult had two degrees from Princeton, one in art history and another in Slavic languages, and she sat on top of several million dollars that she shared with her husband, who resided most of the year in Shanghai. He spoke fluent Mandarin and had a business that the Adult never referred to, because, she said, she was ashamed of it. His income allowed her a measure of indolence. Various accommodations had been made.

She was a tall, brown-haired woman who walked with the deliberation and poise of a former dancer. She laughed easily, but her beauty was complicated by her eyes, which were deep and haunted, and by her distracting habit of falling into thoughtful silences.

When you entered the Adult's house, period-instrument Baroque music would usually be making its way out of the audio system in the living room, and in the foyer you would be confronted with a signboard painted in red on oak slats.

𝕿𝖍𝖊 𝖈𝖍𝖆𝖗𝖎𝖔𝖙𝖘 𝖗𝖆𝖌𝖊 𝖎𝖓 𝖙𝖍𝖊 𝖘𝖙𝖗𝖊𝖊𝖙𝖘, 𝖙𝖍𝖊𝖞 𝖗𝖚𝖘𝖍 𝖙𝖔 𝖆𝖓𝖉 𝖋𝖗𝖔 𝖎𝖓 𝖙𝖍𝖊 𝖘𝖖𝖚𝖆𝖗𝖊𝖘, 𝖙𝖍𝖊𝖞 𝖌𝖑𝖊𝖆𝖒 𝖑𝖎𝖐𝖊 𝖙𝖔𝖗𝖈𝖍𝖊𝖘, 𝖙𝖍𝖊𝖞 𝖉𝖆𝖗𝖙 𝖑𝖎𝖐𝖊 𝖑𝖎𝖌𝖍𝖙𝖓𝖎𝖓𝖌, 𝖙𝖍𝖊𝖞 𝖆𝖗𝖊 𝖙𝖍𝖊 𝖒𝖊𝖘𝖘𝖊𝖓𝖌𝖊𝖗𝖘, 𝖙𝖍𝖊𝖞 𝖆𝖗𝖊 𝖑𝖎𝖐𝖊 𝖘𝖙𝖔𝖓𝖊𝖘 𝖙𝖍𝖗𝖔𝖜𝖓 𝖋𝖗𝖔𝖒 𝖙𝖍𝖊 𝖋𝖎𝖊𝖑𝖉 𝖋𝖔𝖗 𝖙𝖍𝖊 𝖕𝖑𝖔𝖜𝖘 𝖘𝖙𝖗𝖆𝖎𝖌𝖍𝖙 𝖕𝖆𝖙𝖍. 𝖂𝖍𝖔 𝖘𝖍𝖆𝖑𝖑 𝖙𝖊𝖑𝖑 𝖙𝖍𝖊 𝖙𝖗𝖚𝖙𝖍 𝖔𝖋 𝖙𝖍𝖊 𝖑𝖆𝖜 𝖆𝖓𝖉 𝖔𝖋 𝖗𝖎𝖌𝖍𝖙𝖊𝖔𝖚𝖘𝖓𝖊𝖘𝖘? 𝕺𝖓𝖑𝖞 𝕴, 𝖘𝖆𝖎𝖙𝖍 𝕿𝕳𝕰 𝕷𝕺𝕽𝕯.

Nicholas had found this signboard in Kansas a year or so after he had started up a private dealership. A retired dairy farmer, Nahum Fester Cobb, who had put up this sign and others alongside the dirt road leading to his cow barn, had painted it. Nicholas knew that the Adult, his best client, would like it, although "like" was not quite the correct word for the way she responded to these artifacts. He had once asked her if she wanted folk art around the house because it was cutting-edge, and she had scowled.

"The 'cutting edge,' " she said, "has cut its way right out of what I'm interested in. I wish you wouldn't use clichés like that, Nicholas."

"What *are* you interested in?" Nicholas inquired.

"Terror and prophecy," the Adult said quietly, taking a sip of her iced tea. Scattered around her house were little Mexican Day of the Dead skeletons riding their bicycles in processions with grinning voodoo dolls behind them, along with handmade coaches with spectral mad dogs and cats in the passenger seats, followed by more skeletons. Several signboards, with horrifying warnings and predictions printed on them, were hanging on the walls right above the beautiful expensive furniture. She had passed through irony a long time ago and had made a stop somewhere else.

Nicholas hadn't heard about the Twin Towers until he got back into his car, after his lunch with the Adult, and had been driving back home when he had turned on the radio and listened to people being suddenly hysterical. Still on the freeway, he called Daphne to see if she was okay (she was), and then he had called Mrs. Andriessen.

"Yes," she said. Her voice was strange, with an odd stillness. "I just heard. Someone else, a friend, called to tell me."

"Isn't it terrible?" Nicholas asked. "My God."

"Yes, it is," she said calmly. "Quite terrible."

"I don't know what to think," Nicholas said, imagining the smoke and the piles of the dead.

"Oh, you don't?" the Adult asked him. "I do."

Two weeks later, on the day that Nicholas flew up to Alaska, the airplane had so few passengers in economy class that the flight attendants were handing out free meals—this, from an airline known internationally for its stinginess. Nicholas himself had taken a seat in first class, suspecting (correctly) that no one would question his right to be there. The anxious, unattractive people clumping down the aisle toward steerage stared at him helplessly.

Once airborne, after eating the broiled chicken, green beans, muddy mashed potatoes, and brownie, and gulping back the last of his scotch, he turned off the reading light, expecting to see from his window the empty black familiar nothingness of space and the Yukon Territories. Instead, he gazed outward at a vast velvety array of northern lights folding and unfolding. Shimmering with color, purple and blue, as hideously majestic as a floor show in heaven, they kept up with the plane, not underneath or above but *beside* it, and beside him, somehow. He closed his book and for a moment felt deranged by humility.


In Fairbanks he checked into a Holiday Inn near the airport. The next morning, he decided to take a walk after breakfast. The sky had acquired a peculiar royal blue, and when he returned to the hotel lobby, an airline pilot told him that the sky looked that way thanks to the ban on airplane travel that had been in effect for the past two weeks. The upper atmospheres had cleared themselves. Deep colors had returned overhead, at least for now.

The trees around Fairbanks were in full autumnal display. Leaf gold was everywhere. There were no maples up here, so all the usual reds had gone permanently missing. Nicholas drove north of Fairbanks to the house of Granny Westerby, one of his regular suppliers. Like Nahum Fester Cobb, Granny W. was a bit of a graphomaniac, and like him— like all of them—she imagined up for herself Blakean angels, devils, and end-times. A retired cleaning lady whose husband had worked for the Alaska Railroad, Granny painted words on the sides of jug lamps and bottles, though she also made the occasional message board. Her specialty was visionary Eros.

I AM COME INTO HIS GARDEN WHERE MY LOVE HAS BREATHED
MY NAME. MY LOVE IS LIKE UNTO THE CLIMBING VINES, FOR HIS
LUNGS INSPIRE THE FAIREST WINDS AND HE BLOWS HIS GOD-
BREATH AGAINST MY CHEEKS. I AM FAINTED FOR HIM & XIST. I
AM HIS LILY SECRET, I AM PLANTED AS A SEAL UPON HIS LIPS, HE
WATERS ME. G.W.

The sources for these feelings, the words themselves, stumped him. Nevertheless, that blue love-craziness on a painted closet door happened to be the first piece of folk art Nicholas had bought from her. Shipping it down to the lower forty-eight had cost him hours of trouble. A client of his in Connecticut, a lawyer, had bought it and used it as the door to her guest room. When Nicholas had paid out the sum Granny W. had demanded in cash, he had asked her who the lucky guy had been she was referring to on the door. Was it Grandpa Westerby, rest his soul?

Granny Westerby had given Nicholas a look. "Nicholas," she had said, "don't be that way. The blessèd words are there for all to see, *these* words." Occasionally she treated him like a schoolboy. He was used to this treatment from women, who doted on him.

Of course, she didn't really want to sell her art. None of these proletarian folk artists did, and they wouldn't have parted with their signboards and dolls and little sculptures, their private expressive outbursts, if they hadn't needed the money, usually for advanced—that is, optional—medical procedures, or if they had owned personal computers hooked up to the Internet and a blogosphere on which they could have editorialized. The art they made was dying out, as they were. Most working-class oldsters had cancer and diabetes and heart troubles from lifetimes of labor-intensive work and carbo-overloaded diets. Sometimes the income from their art rescued them from the crowds at the outpatient clinics and got them some form of private care. Anyway, he liked to think so.

Granny Westerby was out in her backyard, seated on a bench in front of what looked like a picnic table scattered with brushes, paints, bottles, brake drums, and turpentine, when Nicholas arrived in his rental car. A radio playing rural white gospel was blasting away from inside the house. The old lady's gray hair was pulled back in a bun, and she had one eye shut as she finished painting a phrase on the side of a wine bottle. Beside her, her golden retriever, Roscoe, eyed Nicholas as he approached. But the dog did not get up; he seemed to lack manners in this respect. Everyone in Alaska had at least one dog, Nicholas had noticed. The dogs seemed to be instrumental in getting their owners through the winter. On the Alaska license plates, Nicholas thought, the state motto should have been "The Dog State." Granny W. looked up from her work.

"Oh, good," she said. "It's you."

"Well, I told you I was coming. Hi, Granny," Nicholas said, presenting her, suitor-style, with a clump of cut flowers he had bought at the florist's on the way out. She glanced at them, grinned briefly, and nodded. "Thank you kindly. Would you please put them in water?" she said. "Inside?" With the slightest movement of her head, she indicated the back door of her house. Like her dog, Granny W. lacked conventional hospitality. Nicholas scritched Roscoe on the head before going inside. The dog continued to ignore him.

In the kitchen he found himself surrounded by a welter of antique kitchen equipment: a bread box, flour sifters, rolling pins, popover trays, a flyswatter, a manual toaster. A soiled teddy bear looked down from one of the cabinets. He found a flower vase in a heavily painted blue cupboard above the radio, from whose loudspeaker the gospel music had concluded and some maniac was now shouting rubbishy doomsday predictions. Nicholas cut the stems of the flowers with a steak knife, filled the vase with water, and dropped them in before noticing that, on the side of the glass, Granny had written, in her characteristic royal blue lettering, MY GOD WILL HEAVE ME.

"Heave"? Granny W. sometimes had the diction of a rustic religio-ecstatic prophet. Maybe she meant "heare."

Okay. So be it. He saw an unplugged TV set in the corner of the kitchen, next to the dog dish. Across the glass face of the picture tube, Granny had painted, DO NOT GIVE OVER YOUR HEART TO IGNORANCE. The set would not be turned on again anytime soon, not with this lettering on it. It was like a personal admonitory test pattern. Nicholas loved it; the altered TV would be worth quite a sum on the open market.

Back outside, he sat down next to her and waited while she finished decorating the wine bottle with words. "I used to like autumn," she said, without looking up. "I always loved the spiritual requirements. Not anymore. How about you?"

"Oh, actually, no," he said. "I've never thought that. I like warmth better than cold."

"Of course you do," she said, with a crone's smirk. "You belong in the tropics. Do you know where I get this blue paint? This hue?"

"No," Nicholas admitted. "I don't."

"From the sky," she said, pointing upward. She was an old tease. "I paint with sky." She finished inscribing the sentence on the side of the bottle and gave it a hard professional look. FEAR AND LOVE HIS LOINS, the bottle instructed. It was perfect: wacky lovelorn profundity written in beautiful blue lettering. The Adult might want this one. Finally Granny W. sat back and looked directly at Nicholas. "You can't have this," she said. "The paint's all wet."

"I can wait," he said. "I can just sit here patiently."

"Only if I let you," she said. She put her elbows on the table and her head in her hands. "You'll have to learn about patience, Nicholas. Everybody has to learn about that. I was beautiful and short-tempered, once, if you can imagine it. You take this backyard here. I've always lived here. I was birthed here. I died here and then I came back, and that's why I'm so patient. Do you ever sit quietly? Do you ever contemplate the mountains?" she asked, nodding in their direction. "They say that He lives in the hills."

"There aren't any mountains where I live," he told her. "As you know."

"I expect you're right. Too bad," she said, smiling. "You do realize," she said, after a lengthy pause, "what a pleasure it is for me to see you? I like to sit here and stare at you. Do you mind that?" She rubbed her forehead as if she were embarrassed. "You make me girlish."

"No, I don't mind." Vanity constituted his central spiritual problem. He was ball-and-chained to his good looks. "You know I love you, Granny," he told her. "You know I love what you do. By the way, is the kitchen TV set for sale?"

"The TV? No. The only show I watch is those words," she said, shaking her head and clearing her throat with a bleating sound. She gave off a perfume of turpentine. "So many are giving their hearts over to foolishness that I thought I'd better remind myself not to do the same. It's a little sermon I give myself, up here. A few words are all I need. What do you need, Nicholas?"

"A correction. And doors," Nicholas said, without thinking.

"Beautiful Nicholas," she said, smiling at him. "Stuck forever in the foyer, stuck in the mudroom." Then she gestured at the wine bottle with the message about loins and love and fear on it. She named a price, Nicholas made a counteroffer, which Granny accepted, and which Nicholas had conveniently brought along in cash. This was their routine. She always sermonized in his direction, often about his appearance or his lifestyle, until she named her price. Then she was all business. When the wine bottle's paint was dry, he wrapped it up in newspapers, inquired again about the TV set, received a firm response, said good-bye, and went off to his next appointment.

In Seattle, on the connecting flight back, his plane was stuck on the ground at the gate. Several Arab-American men had boarded and had been seated at different scattered locations. An alarmed passenger, hearing the men speaking Arabic in the waiting area, had alerted the flight attendant; the flight attendant had alerted the gate agent; and the gate agent had called the FBI and the Seattle Bomb Squad. Nicholas, up in first class, finished his first scotch and asked for a second. A voice came on the public-address system: "Please do not pat the bomb dog. This is a working dog. Please do not pat the bomb dog." A big grinning yellow Labrador wearing a police department scarf, obviously happy with his job and his authority, padded up the aisle, then back and forth in the plane, sniffing in a show-offy way for bomb materials. He passed right by Nicholas without noticing him. Dogs did not seem to care for him anymore.

In due course, the Arab-American men were escorted off the airplane to some dim destination. The Airbus door was shut and latched, and the flight took off. The flight attendant, sitting in her forward jump seat, stared at Nicholas and licked her lips as he read his magazine. He had that effect on people.

Hours earlier, when he had boarded, he had told Daphne by cell phone that the airport looked so empty that the terminal might as well have been the Museum of Transportation, there were so few people in it. Forlorn little passengers could be seen scurrying down there at the ends of the corridors, on their errands. The vendors of hot dogs and newspapers presented the public with expressions of end-of-the-world nihilism. From the TV sets hanging from the ceiling came the unreassuring voice of the president of the United States, encouraging the terrified citizenry to help the economy by buying things. It was all very grungy and Amtrak-ish.

" 'Fear and love his loins'?" Daphne asked. "What's that about?"

They were eating in their favorite Brooklyn sushi restaurant, and Daphne, sitting next to an orange window curtain, delicately nibbled at her California roll, held like a prized specimen at the tip of her chopsticks. Beside her, the curtain's folds blew in lightly, ruffled by a mild breeze, and, watching the fabric, Nicholas thought of the northern lights he had seen from the airplane window, and of how Daphne's hair sometimes looked like that, too, a magical electric shivering beyond anyone's descriptive powers. Thinking of his girlfriend's hair, he himself shivered.

"What?" He had lost track of the topic.

"The thing she wrote," Daphne said, noting his inattention. The curtain brushed against her arm. "On the wine bottle." She pointed her chopsticks at him. "Do I even know what loins are? I don't think I do. Why should I fear them?"

"They're down here, I think," Nicholas said, glancing in the general direction of his waist and crotch. "In French I think it's '*reins*' or something like that."

"Oh," Daphne said. "Those." She chewed thoughtfully. "Loins. Like a cut of meat. I wonder if she was ever assaulted. Well, probably not."

Following a respectful pause, Nicholas said, "I don't think so. I don't think it's about that. It's about her husband, or God, or maybe her husband-as-God, or God-as-her-husband, one of those messed-up dirt-road deals. Beats me."

Daphne scowled at her sushi plate, while she fiddled with a piece of raw salmon. "Hey, guess what? I'm pregnant again," she announced with the flat apologetic tone she always employed for big declarations. "What do you think of that?" She tried on a quick, blissful expression for him. "I threw up this morning," she said, trying to disguise her happiness. "But I knew a few days ago."

The calamari in Nicholas's mouth went a little dry as he leaned forward to kiss her. They had been through this whole business a couple of years ago, so in a sense he was prepared, and he remembered to resume chewing. Somehow, they both had been negligent when it came to reproductive issues down through the years, and they had slipped up before. They had known each other since high school and had a devotion to each other that neither of them could quite accept. The last time Daphne had found herself in the family way, the problem had been disposed of rapidly and efficiently, and they had—or at least Nicholas had—chalked it up to one of those unexpected outcomes of sex. Love was one; babies were another. Something told Nicholas it would not go that way this time around. Easefulness, ever so gently, was slipping out of his grasp. He gazed at her hair again. Somewhat against his will, he felt the voltage of his love for her pass through him.

"Wow," he said. "That's *great.* I'm . . . happy, I guess. Oh, honey. It's so . . ." He searched for an adjective. *"Decisive."* He gave her one of his great grins, out of his arsenal of grins and smiles. "I hadn't expected."

"Me, neither. Well, listen, Nickie. We can talk about this more later. You know? We don't have to talk about it now. Not over sushi. I didn't mean to stop the conversation. I didn't mean to drop a bombshell. Well, of course, I guess it *is* a bombshell, but I didn't mean it that way."

"Daph, it's *not* a bombshell," he said, speaking out of his one general principle that a man should never appear to be fazed by anything a woman does. "We'll deal with it. I love you, right? Everything fixes itself when two people love each other. Which we do."

"Speaking of loins and money," she said, "when are you next going to be seeing the Adult?" She had a way of changing the topic when Nicholas didn't expect her to. Even the fact of her pregnancy didn't have a long conversational shelf life with her. Happiness made her shy.

"In a few days. I've called her. I'm taking that wine bottle to her. It strikes the right note. She'll love it. I'll drive up on Tuesday."

"It's you she loves," Daphne said, looking at Nicholas tenderly, as the gangster's wife might look at the gangster. Next to their table, another couple glanced over at them, and Nicholas realized that Daphne had been speaking more loudly than she usually did. "You and that face of yours! It's *mean,* actually, what you do to her—making her all . . . I don't know, gooey. And then you take her money and go home. It's not cruel, but it *is* mean." She used her bad-girl tone on him. "You're *such* a rascal. She just pines and sighs for you. Poor Mrs. Andriessen. Poor Adult."

"Yeah," Nicholas said. "Well, that's life, honey. It's what people expect of me. It pays various bills."

"I pay the bills, too," she said, her voice modulating, and as the curtains continued to blow inward, Nicholas thought of a piece Daphne used to play occasionally on the flute, when she had thought that in order to be hired as a session musician, just out of Juilliard, she'd have to be versatile. She'd sit in the apartment's bathroom, because she liked the acoustics in there, on the edge of the tub, wearing her flowered pajamas, and this miraculous music would come out, the most beautiful music Nicholas had ever heard up to that point in his life, Debussy's "Syrinx," about a girl turned into a reed. "They buy from *me,* too," she said, spearing something white on the plate. She smiled at him. "You and me, we just can't be resisted."

An hour or so after he had arrived in New Paltz and had shown her the Granny-inscribed wine bottle, the Adult asked Nicholas to do a favor for her. She wanted him to clamber up into her backyard apple tree and cut off one of its dead branches. He gave her a skeptical look. Didn't she realize that he was an art dealer, not a tree service? He was miffed. And he wasn't dressed for the job, the sort of chore you'd ask your husband or boyfriend to do. But some complicated subtext had probably attached itself to her request, and he felt a roiling of curiosity. By the time she mentioned the dead branch, they had already had lunch and had talked about the relationship between Granny W.'s work and the famous road signs of Jesse Smith, now on display in several museums, and he wanted to close the deal and get home. Still, there was that gleam in her eye. The Adult had studied Granny W.'s bottle as if she were unsure whether she would purchase it—as if she were waiting for him to do this favor as an act of friendship, or masculine graciousness.

He unbuttoned his white shirt and took off his shoes and socks. The Adult stood on the perfectly mown grass in her running shoes and slacks and blouse, observing him with precise attention. As a boy, he had been an avid tree climber. What had happened to that prehistoric skill, now that he lived in Brooklyn? The proficiency had gone dormant, like all his other childhood aptitudes. Holding on to the handsaw, he made his way up into the tree, and he heard the Adult say, "Be careful."

The dead branch, scaly and virus-ridden, was located about halfway up. The tree branches felt pleasantly rough on the soles of his bare feet, and when he reached the dead branch, after an easy climb past ripe autumnal apples about to fall, he realized that sawing through the dead wood would be effortless. He glanced down at Mrs. Andriessen, and then up at the sky. He began to work.

He had almost finished when he heard the Adult say, "Nicholas, I really do appreciate what you're doing, believe me."

Maybe he was tired, or feverish, but he heard her utter the sentence *in blue,* royal blue, the color of the northern lights and Granny W.'s inscriptions, and he felt himself spiral into light-headedness. The blue words, having entered his brain, had a sky-feeling to them, a spirit of clarity. But that was crazy. Spoken words had no color to them and never would, in this world. The first words spoken by God had been in color, according to the ancient texts, but who believed in that now? He gripped a branch in order to stabilize himself, to keep himself from swaying. The dizziness left him, but the blue, somehow, remained. . . .

He dropped the handsaw. The Adult hopped out of the way of it, though it had landed nowhere near her feet. Nicholas clutched a branch to keep himself from falling.

By the time he came out of the shower and had dressed, Mrs. Andriessen had brewed some espresso and was sitting in her living room reading Edith Wharton's stories. "Want some?" she asked, glancing at him and holding up her cup.

"Espresso? In the afternoon? No, thanks," he said, shaking his hands to dry them. He was still barefoot, because one of his socks had a hole in it, which he did not care to display.

She put her book aside, having placed a marker on the page where she had stopped, and rubbed rather violently at her forehead. "I shouldn't have done that," she said. "I shouldn't have asked you to climb up in that tree to cut that branch. But a few weeks ago, I had a dream about you, Nicholas. In this particular dream, you were aloft in an apple tree, and you were surveying the countryside. God knows how you got up there, but then you were sawing away at a dead branch, and I was down below, and when I woke, I thought: Well, maybe I should see to it that the dream is . . . I don't know, enacted." She said the last word with a slightly embarrassed inflection. "A person rarely gets that chance."

"I used to climb trees," Nicholas said. "When I was a boy."

"Yes, I know," the Adult said. "You once told me. Perhaps that's what led to the dream." She gazed at him quickly, as if a longer gaze would incriminate her. Mrs. Andriessen had a spooky way of suffering silently in Nicholas's presence, but her reticence appeared to be impregnable. Now she looked over at Granny Westerby's wine bottle. " 'Fear and love his loins,' " she read. "That's a royal blue she used."

"She told me that she painted it with the sky," Nicholas offered.

"Did she actually say that? That she painted it with sky?"

"Yes. And it was strange, just now, when I was up in that tree, you said something—about how you appreciated what I was doing, and when I heard those words, when I heard you say them, they were . . . I can't explain it. They were blue. I heard them in color. I heard them in blue."

The Adult leaned back and closed her eyes. "I'm not surprised. Do you know the origin of the phrase 'royal blue'?" He shook his head, but she didn't open her eyes to see. She seemed to know perfectly well where the gaps in his knowledge lay. She knew what he didn't know. "It was a particular tint used in the fabrics set out to greet the visiting heads of state, royalty—in the decorative regalia, the canopies, for example. Royal blue was a color associated with the aristocracy and with hospitality. I don't know if it's related to the phrase 'blue blood,' but I doubt it. That particular phrase, as I remember, is from the Spanish. Do you know how a person would demonstrate blue blood?"

"No," Nicholas said. Outside, the wind was coming up, and the trees beyond the yard swayed gracefully.

"By staying indoors," she told him, turning toward him and speaking urgently. "By not getting a tan in the fields doing fieldwork, so the skin would stay white and the veins would remain visible. Also, the phrase refers to purity, freedom from . . . Arabic bloodlines. Which would have been considered an infection, in those days. In Spain. You know: the Moors." She seemed bored by her knowledge, the length and breadth of it. "Isn't that interesting? Considering recent events? Free of Arabic blood? Blue blood?"

"Daphne is pregnant," Nicholas told Mrs. Andriessen. He stood up to pace for a moment. "She told me a few days ago." He sat down again. Their conversations had, over the past year, acquired a stream-of-consciousness effect, two people thinking as one, although Nicholas knew that the Adult was usually thinking for both of them. Most of the time, he didn't really know what Mrs. Andriessen thought, except when she cast her glances on him.

"Is she? Lucky you," the Adult said. "Daphne pregnant again. She won't have an abortion this time, will she? Will you? Of course not. You'll have the most beautiful child, the two of you. Just a glorious thing. But everything changes now. Love is tested. Can't go on as before. You'll have weight, my dear."

"Weight? I don't—"

"No, no, I don't mean that. You shouldn't take me literally." She reached out and touched his knee. "I meant 'weight' in the other sense."

"Yes, I know."

She leaned back. The Adult often gave the impression that she was both excited and dismayed by Nicholas. "Do you? Well. Here's a little story. When I was a girl, we lived close by a Swedish immigrant family, the Petersons. They were the neighborhood laborers and lived in a coach house. He worked as a caretaker and she took in laundry. She also acted as everyone's part-time nursemaid, if you know what I mean."

Nicholas nodded, bewildered.

"They had a son, about my age, an angelic type, beautiful, and a prodigy, or so everyone said, though I don't remember in what—maybe in everything. A terrible fate. Children like that catch the attention of the gods. He could draw and remember word for word whatever you said, and he had every athletic gift you could imagine: running, balls and bats, the works. Terrible! Also, he was manifestly smarter and more alert than his parents, and they were so proud of him, and he could sit down at the piano and play short Bach and Chopin pieces by ear, and no one even knew in that environment where he had heard them. Gustav, this boy's name was. And then when he was ten years old, he developed a brain tumor, fate being what it is, and when he died of it, his father became so blind with rage and grief that he began to throw all their worldly goods, everything they owned that could be picked up, out of the coach house window. He'd throw out the coffeepot and the lamp, and his wife would calm him down, but the next day his grief would return, and he'd break up a kitchen chair and throw it out the window, poor man, and then the radio and the kitchen blender and the telephone. Whatever he could get his hands on, anything that could be mobilized, he threw out that window. You'd see this little heap of household objects on the driveway. Some languages have a term for grief madness, but English doesn't. Isn't that a shame?"

Nicholas nodded again. What on earth was she talking about?

"When those airplanes hit those buildings," she said, "on that day when you were up here a month ago, do you know what I did?" She didn't stop to look at him or to wait for his response. "After you left, I took the mower out and mowed the back lawn, by myself. It didn't require mowing. The grass had been cut two days before. But I had to do an ordinary task. I had to anchor myself to daily life. To make a routine, to recapture what I love about banality. Then I drove into town, late afternoon, and I gave blood. And what did you do, my darling friend?"

"I drove home, as you know," he said. "It took a long time."

"Ah, Nicholas," she said. "Your foot is bleeding." She reached out and took his foot in her hand and gave him an expression of sweet concern. From a pocket, she drew out a piece of cloth and daubed at a small bloody scratch on his instep.

She was beautiful enough to sleep with, he thought, and it wouldn't exactly be demeaning or patronizing, but he wasn't going to make that particular pass at her and take her into the bedroom and undress her and sleep with her underneath one of Granny W.'s signs. Another blue motto. It had been hung above the bed, a cryptic sentence: SORROW ABIDETH BESIDE MY JOYOUS HEART. He wouldn't willingly give the Adult the Nicholas-treatment in that bed no matter what, even if there were no possible unforeseen complications—and there *were* always unforeseen complications. If he made her momentarily happy, she would no longer be herself. And if Mrs. Andriessen were no longer herself, she would not be interesting; she would no longer be the Adult but just like the rest of them, and he himself would lose his bargaining chips. Besides, some women simply required suffering. She was, Nicholas thought, one of those.

"Patricia," Nicholas said, "I should really go."

"Should you?" she asked, releasing his foot. "All right. I suppose you should."

He and Daphne were walking around the Great Lawn in Central Park when the thought occurred to Nicholas that the woman he was holding hands with should marry him. Or—what was the wording?—*he should marry her.* "Make it official," as they used to say. "Make an honest woman of her," they also said. Most of the leaves had changed color and fallen by now, but a few clung to their branches, and he could feel a rough cooling in the air. He didn't quite know why he and Daphne needed to be married; he just felt that they should be. They had known each other forever, almost since they were kids. What he felt for her was as close to love as he was ever going to get. Something stood between him and the full blast of it, but nothing he had ever done for anybody had brought him closer.

On the baseball diamonds, the groups of boys who were playing softball yelled and smiled and pantomime-slugged each other, coached and encouraged by their parents, mostly the fathers. It was getting too late in autumn to play baseball, but apparently no one wanted to give it up. One team, the Slickers, was wearing white uniforms with green letters, and the other team, the Backpackers, wore white uniforms with blue letters. One of the Backpackers stood at the plate, wearing his batting helmet. He swung at a pitch and missed.

He seemed to be about ten or eleven years old. Nicholas thought of Gustav, the story the Adult had told of him, and of the piles of household items lying in the driveway.

The boy swung again and missed. "Strike two," announced the umpire.

"Something is wrong," Daphne said to Nicholas. She reached for his arm.

"That boy isn't watching the ball," Nicholas told her. "He's distracted."

"Something is wrong," Daphne said again.

The pitcher stood on the mound and studied the batter. Daphne's hand dug into his biceps. "Ow," he said. "That hurts."

All at once Daphne bent over, winced, and then began screaming softly. "Oh god oh god," she said, between deep breaths, and at first Nicholas thought she might fall to the ground in pain, but, no: she had sufficient resources to take his arm and to stagger to Fifth Avenue, where he flagged down a cab to take them both to the emergency room.


"We lost it," Nicholas said to the Adult.

Mrs. Andriessen let the pause go on for a long moment until Nicholas found himself able to say something else into his telephone. "She had a miscarriage," he said. "She miscarried."

"No, not quite," the Adult told him, rather firmly. "You both did, didn't you? You both miscarried."

What did she mean this time? What did she ever mean? "Daphne's still in the hospital, Patricia. She'll be there overnight. She's going to be there overnight. She's very weak. She lost a lot of blood." How rare for him to repeat himself, he thought. He felt more of his composure slipping away, following the composure he had already lost. "I'm going right back over there."

"Why aren't you there now? In the hospital? Why are you in Brooklyn?" the Adult asked him. "Why are you at home?"

"I had to feed the cat," Nicholas told her. "I had to feed Plankton."

"The cat can live. You should be with Daphne now. You should be sitting next to her in the hospital and you should be holding her hand and kissing her on the forehead and on both cheeks. You should try to revive her. Poor thing, she's lying in bed with no one with her, and she's kissing the air. Desperate women kiss the air, did you know that, Nicholas? When they're alone, they kiss the air."

"They do?"

"Yes. Or you could always pray to Saint Anthony. He's the saint of lost things. I was raised Catholic, did you know?" Another pause. " 'Dear Saint Anthony, please look around: something is lost that must be found.' That's the Saint Anthony prayer. It works. It's the only thing in Catholicism that still works for me, that prayer."

"It can't be found," Nicholas said. "It's not lost. It's gone."

"They kiss the air, Nicholas," she repeated. "My darling friend, you are such a dilettante with us. You have just watched us, all your life. You have watched us as we fell in your direction."

"Us?" It was a habit, this repetition. Of course she was right.

"You should go over there right now, where Daphne is." Outside the apartment something was stirring, perhaps just down the block.


At the foot of Daphne's bed, Nicholas stood gazing at the pale green wall behind where she lay. He stared at the wall because it was so hard to keep his eyes on her. Inside and within the room were tubes and pipes and expensive stainless-steel machines, some of which were breathing softly, while outside the room, many floors down, Manhattan traffic beeped on

like the errant sounds of children playing with toy cars and plastic noise-
makers. Daphne, for the moment, was unwatchable: on her face had
been placed an expression he had never seen before. Her skin had taken
on a terrible pallor. He couldn't stand to see it there. It hurt him every
time his eyes swept across her. Every time he took her in, he felt as if he
aged another year.

He approached her and tried to do as the Adult had advised: he kissed
Daphne on the forehead and tried to bend over the sides of the bed so he
could kiss her. When he bent over, he thought he would pass out.

Daphne did not open her eyes. "The next time you go to Alaska," she
whispered, "you can tell Granny Westerby about us."

"I wouldn't do that."

"Yes, but we have a story now." She opened her eyes to look at him.
She did it slowly, as if it were a great effort—a terrible amount of work—
to do so. "Oh, Nicholas," she said tenderly, almost with pride, "you look
awful."

"Do I?" he asked.

"You look all broken and sideways," she said disconnectedly. The
medications had started to affect her speech. Still, no one had ever used
those adjectives about him before. Rather desperately, he turned toward
the window, but there was no refuge there, either, not for him. He felt
himself fading toward Daphne in an effort to comfort her. He lowered
himself again and touched his lips to her cheek.

# The Old Murderer

AN OLD MAN, a murderer, had moved in next door to Ellickson. The murderer appeared to be a gardener and student of history. Prison had seemingly turned him into a reader. Putting out spring-loaded traps for the moles, Ellickson would sometimes glance over and see his neighbor, the murderer, sprawled out on a patio recliner as he made his way through a lengthy biography of General Robert E. Lee. At other times he saw the murderer spreading bone ash at the base of his backyard lilacs. The murderer's uncombed gray hair stood up in sprouts at the back and the sides of his head, and he would wave from time to time at Ellickson, who had delayed introducing himself. Ellickson would wave back half-heartedly. The murderer did not seem to care that he was being snubbed. He kept busy. Bags of topsoil weighed down the back of his rusting yellow truck. He unloaded them and carried them over to the garden beds. Ellickson liked the idea of having a murderer on the same street where he himself lived. A paroled murderer's problems put his own into perspective.

Ellickson had been sober for forty-three and a half days, but he still had the shakes. Just filling the coffeepot required maximum concentration. If his concentration lapsed, the coffee grounds sprayed themselves all over the kitchen floor and had to be cleaned up with a whisk broom and a dustpan. Everything, even the drinking of tap water, called for discipline and tenacity.

All day Ellickson endured. The sun rattled violently in the sky. After the passing hours had presented their trials by fire and ice, he would go to bed feeling that his skin was layered with sandpaper. The post-alcohol world contained no welcoming surfaces, and the interiors of things did not bear much looking into, either. Although God might have supplied a solution, He was in a permanent sulk. A determined Christian, Ellickson had put his faith in the Almighty to get him through this episode and through the rest of his life, but God had declined the honor so far and was keeping up a chilly silence.

The world was glass, and Ellickson felt himself skittering over its surface.

Ellickson, drunk, had lashed out at his family one night and done something unforgivable. Nightfall had always brought his devils out. His wife had therefore taken the two kids, Alex and Barbara, and had driven 150 miles to her mother's. His family hated him now for good reason, and although he could live with his wife's hatred—he was sort of used to it—he couldn't bear the idea that he had become a monster to his children. Ellickson's shame felt so intense that when he contemplated his actions, he groaned aloud.

Patiently and without hope, he went to the twelve-step meetings.


He had maintained the drinking for years in a careful program of adjustments and stealth. His job as a supervisor of hospital cleaning personnel had been so undemanding that he could work steadily under the influence and no one ever noticed. Drunk before breakfast, his mind regulated by alcohol, he'd been as steady as a bronze statue. The vodka had kept his breath clean and his hands strong. Now that he was sober, no one seemed to like him anymore, and his judgment flew away from him in little clouds. The real Ellickson, without the gleaming varnish of the booze, seemed to constitute an offense.

Desperate, unable to move, faced with the frightfulness and tedium of Saturday afternoon, he called his friend Lester, the ex-doctor.

"Lester," he said, "I'm in trouble."

"Hey, buddy. What sort of help d'you need? How's the day so far?" Lester asked, blithely. The man's usual speech was somewhat formal, but Lester was all right. He would cross a minefield without hesitation if you needed him to.

"I'm barely hanging on," Ellickson said. "The sky's falling again."

"It does that. Yes?" He waited. "Go on."

Ellickson tried to speak. But even speech seemed difficult. "It's all creeping up, every bit of it. Do you know the word 'heartsick'?" Ellickson waited for his next thought, and, on the other end of the line, Lester waited, too. "Boy, is that a good word. I'm glad we have that word. So, here's the thing. I can't do it anymore." Ellickson knew that he did not have to define "it" to Lester. "I'm sitting in a chair and I can't do it."

"I can come over." Lester had once been a surgeon—until drinking had led him ungently out of medicine. He couldn't go back. Now he volunteered at a science museum, explaining the fossils to children. "Tell me what to do now. I can be over there in ten minutes. Say the word."

"Maybe. No. It actually isn't that. I just can't live this way anymore."

"No. That's wrong, my friend. You can live any old way," Lester said, "except drunk. We all can. Remember this will pass. Everything passes." Then he said some of the usual admonitory phrases, complete with elaboration into belief and faith. They sounded correct but feeble at two thirty-six in the afternoon. "You can be proud of yourself. This is the hardest thing you've ever done in your life. We're in this together, pal. People love you. Never doubt it."

"Right, right. People. Ha. *What* people? The stars hate me. The moon hates me. The entire creation is opposed to my existence. What I need is a drink."

"No, that's what you *don't* need. Ease up. What about the bus cure?"

The bus cure involved getting on a city bus and riding around until the urge to have a drink had passed. It only worked, however, if Ellickson took the number 13 route, which did not go down the streets where the bars were located. Also, he had to take a book or a newspaper along with him for the bus cure to work.

"I feel all the time as if . . ."Ellickson feared boring his friend and did not complete his sentence. "By the way. I haven't told you: a murderer moved in next door."

"What are you talking about?" Lester asked. "He's murdering people now?" Lester laughed. Murder was easy compared to sobriety.

"No, no, he's paroled or something. A lady up the street told me. I haven't introduced myself to this guy yet."

"Well, you should go do that." Lester waited. "It's Saturday afternoon. Go right over there. Tell the guy that you're an alcoholic. Be up front about it. Provide a basis for friendship. He's a murderer, and you're a drunk. This friendship needs a basis to keep it solid, and you have one."

"So okay. Maybe."

"Not maybe," Lester said firmly. "Definitely. Introduce yourself to the murderer." He laughed at how upbeat the conversation had become. A murderer next door was good luck and great news. "Think of him," Lester said, "as the next stop for your welcome wagon."

Other murderers were probably somewhere in the city, but they weren't in close proximity, at least that he knew about. Ellickson didn't much care whether the murderer had paid his debt to society, because once you had committed a murder, you would always be a murderer. You would never be anything else. Nevertheless, Ellickson managed to get off the sofa. He went to the bathroom and combed his hair, hoping to look convivial. Then he strolled over to the murderer's back patio, where his neighbor was pruning a rosebush with a pair of clippers.

"I was wondering when you'd get over here," the old man said, straightening up and adjusting his glasses to take a look at Ellickson. "You're not alarmed by my yardwork?" He laughed heartily, and his mouth showed uneven gray teeth with a prominent gap near the back. He wore a floppy blue hat, and a stained red handkerchief stuck out of his back pocket. "These roses are blighted."

"No, I can't say that I'm alarmed," Ellickson said. "No, I can't say that. Sorry I haven't come over to introduce myself. I've just been through a spell of difficulties, that's all."

"Well, then," the murderer said, "we've got something in common." He slid off his gardening glove and extended his right hand, wincing as if his shoulder hurt him. "Name's Macfadden Eward," he said, shaking Ellickson's hand. It sounded like a made-up name. "Call me Mac."

"Eric Ellickson."

"Pleased to meet you, Mr. Ellickson."

"Oh, no. Make it Eric."

"First names? Fine. You know, in Germany," the old man said, hawking and then spitting to the side of his rosebush, "they spend a lot of time negotiating with each other about whether they'll use their first names. Before that, it's always 'Herr Ellickson' and 'Herr Eward.' They believe in the formalities. Did you know that?"

"No," Ellickson said. "I can't say that I did."

"Interesting country, Germany," he said, bending over to rub his knee. "They have themselves *quite* a history. Well, now, I'd invite you into my house except I gotta tell you that my place isn't shipshape just yet. The boxes won't unpack themselves, you know what I mean?" The old man leaned back and roared with humorless laughter. All this laughing made Ellickson uneasy. Then Macfadden Eward's laughter suddenly stopped, and he gazed solemnly at Ellickson as he pointed his pruning shears at him. "So you can't come in."

"Well," said Ellickson, feeling somewhat off balance himself, "I wasn't looking for an invite from you. In fact," he said, realizing before the words came out of his mouth that he would now have to invite the murderer over to his house, "I wanted to see if you'd like some iced tea or a cool drink."

"That I would, that I would," Macfadden Eward said, "but not just this minute. It's very kind of you to invite me, Mr. Ellickson. Maybe later. Tomorrow or the day after that." He cut off another dead part of the bush with the clippers. "So I'll just take a rain check, if you don't mind."

"I can't offer you a drink," Ellickson said quickly, remembering what Lester had told him to say. "I'm on the wagon, you know." He tried to smile. "Can't touch the stuff."

"I didn't know, but that's fine," the old man said, with a horsey smile, displaying his teeth again. "There's some things I don't do myself. I can drink, but I can see now that you can't. But that particular discussion'll have to wait until next time." He smiled again and waved in the direction of his house. "One of these days, you can come down to my basement, and I'll show you the spaceship I'm building down there."

"A spaceship?"

"Shh." The old man put his finger to his lips. "Mum's the word." Then he jabbed Ellickson in the ribs. "Maybe I'm kidding! Maybe there's no spaceship!"

Ellickson returned to his house, uncertain about the nature of the conversation he had just had.

For his daughter, Barbara, Ellickson had been putting together a dollhouse, and now, for his son, Alex, he was writing a letter. He hadn't been able to get past "My dear son" despite many attempts. It was as if his heart had suffered a blockage, and the language of feeling that other parents drew upon effortlessly had been denied him. He loved his son, but to say so in so many words seemed unthinkable. If you just put it like that, with the love right out on the table, the words would lack force.

They would sound fatuous. Nothing would stand behind such a state-ment, especially after a father's drunken misbehavior, and besides, the kid might be spoiled if you said it flat-out like that.

Ellickson felt that he had had to earn every single bit of love that he himself had ever received, and that if he hadn't tried to satisfy everyone's expectations for him, he would have been promptly thrown out into the street to die in the gutter like a dog. He still might suffer that fate. He sat at his desk, pen in hand, staring out the window at his neighbor, who was now putting in a bed of petunias.

"Fourteen years ago," Ellickson finally wrote to his son, "I met your mother at a rock concert. Maybe we told you this story. We were stand-ing together in the aisle of this big converted bus terminal downtown that had been turned into a club, and then we both started to dance at almost the same time, and before long, we introduced ourselves." The place had been thick with cigarette smoke and the smell of weed, and the band, Town Dump, had only an approximate sense of how they should be playing, but somehow, despite their ineptitude, or because of it, the musicians lit up the audience, and Ellickson had found himself dancing with this beautiful young woman who had appeared magically in front of him. "Your mother," Ellickson wrote, "was wearing a speckled-green T-shirt with a little pin on it, and plain blue jeans, and she was the pret-tiest woman who had ever looked me in the eye and taken me by the hand." This confession was not quite the appropriate history for him to be laying out for his son, he realized, but he couldn't think of what else to write, or what other route to take toward an apology. "I started to fall in love with your mother right there," Ellickson wrote. "We talked for hours that following week."

Ellickson had had many girlfriends and one ex-wife by that time. He was ready for love to strike. On their first real date, when he had taken the girl he had met at the rock concert out for a spaghetti dinner and a movie, he knew this one, this Laura, would be serious. "And then what happened, what really did it for me, was that your mom took me over to where she lived and played the guitar for me and sang a song she had written herself." She had had a sweet voice. The song was about how things pass and how you have to reach for the moment. Ellickson had always carried a torch for women who raised their voices in song.

"What I'm saying is that I'm not a bad person. My dad used to take me deer hunting in the woods up north," Ellickson continued, in a new paragraph, not wanting to write about how everything had gone wrong with Laura. The letter to his son was growing a bit disconnected, he knew, but this wasn't an English composition, this was a soul statement. "When you're older, I'll take you deer hunting if you want to go up to the woods with me. I haven't really done any hunting since you were born. I don't know why that is. Maybe there hasn't been time. I'm a pretty good shot, and I can teach you how to kill and dress a deer. We should go fishing, too, up north. Have you ever pulled in a fighting trout? It's a great experience. I would love to do that with you."

Ellickson watched his neighbor water his petunias. When he glanced at his watch, he saw that several hours had passed. A miracle. He had almost made it through another day. The phone rang.

"How'd it go?" Lester asked. "With the murderer? Did you talk to him?"

"It went pretty well," Ellickson said. "He's a little strange, though."

"Well, he's a murderer."

"No," Ellickson said. "It's not that. It's like he's a master of ceremonies of some TV show that no one's watching. He told me he's building a spaceship in his basement. Then he said maybe he was just kidding about the spaceship."

"A spaceship, huh? I know the feeling," Lester said. "Did you tell him you're an alcoholic?"

"Yeah," Ellickson said. "I did that."

"Good," Lester said. "Next time you're over there, check out the spaceship and then report back to me."


That night, Ellickson went to his sister's house for dinner. She lived with her partner, a sizable Russian immigrant woman named Irena, in a ramshackle colonial on the better side of town. He continued to get invitations from them, he believed, because he performed small electrical and plumbing repairs whenever he visited and because he had offered to be the godfather if they ever had children. Also, his sister never asked him about how he was, so he never had to explain.

Kate, his sister, met him at the door, her hand at her forehead and her face flushed. The smoke alarm at the back of the house was shrieking. "We've had a little disaster in the kitchen," Kate told him. "A sort of disaster-ette. I was on the phone to the goddamn airline and they put me on hold and I burned the chicken. Well, come in." In the back, the smoke detector wailed on and on, and the dog, Ludmilla, was barking straight up at it.

"Where's Irena?"

"H-h-h-here I am." Irena's h-sounds came out of her throat in the Russian manner. They sounded like gargling. She appeared very suddenly from the living room and, in the entryway, took Ellickson's face in both hands and kissed him on the cheeks, first the left, then the right, as if he were about to go off to a firing squad. Irena's passion for everything, including Ellickson's sister and himself as Kate's brother, was disconcerting. Family feeling was fine, but hers seemed a bit excessive for the American context. She stood an inch taller than Ellickson, and he was terribly fond of her—everything about her was outsized, close to bursting, including her emotions. She had russet hair, large dimpled hands, and her breath always smelled heavily of peppermints, as if she herself were a piece of candy. He could see why Kate and Irena were a couple; anyone could see their complementary mixture of similarities and differences. "We have burned you the chicken," Irena said happily. "This will be dinner, which you can eat after repairing upstairs, where a faucet leaks." She pointed toward the second floor. "I have bought faucet washer at hardware store. Tools are already up there. Please do this?"

"Irena," Ellickson said, "it's a simple job. I could teach you how." The smoke alarm was still screaming, and Kate was cursing it.

"I do not agree," she said, waving her hand dismissively. "As human being, I am uninterested in plumbing." She gave him another kiss, then retreated in her house slippers to the back hallway and lugged in a stepladder. Ellickson watched her climb it and then yank the battery brutally out of the smoke detector, which fell silent. Well, Ellickson thought, why *should* she be interested in plumbing? She taught mathematics at a local college; her theoretical interests were so complex, having to do with the bending of topological surfaces in different dimensions, that they could not be explained to ordinary people like himself.

After Ellickson had fixed the dripping faucet, Kate and Irena sat him down at the dinner table, where they ate the edible parts of the burned chicken, along with veggie-everything pizza, which had just been delivered as the second course. Bent over the pizza, Irena picked up each slice with both hands, rammed it into her mouth, and chewed with her mouth full while Kate daintily cut her pieces with a fork and knife. Following the dinner, they played cards for a penny a point, and Ellickson won two dollars. The conversation mostly dealt with the weather and current political conditions. Personal matters were discreetly avoided. As he was about to leave, Ellickson said, "You know, I love you girls."

Irena nodded. Kate lowered her eyes. " 'Women,' " she reminded her brother. "We are *women*." This was their old familiar routine. "So." She drew breath. "Has Laura called you?"

"No."

"Have you called her?"

"I will. Just not yet."

"Soon?"

"Not yet." She looked at him. "Yes, I promise," he said. "Oh, I forgot to tell you. A paroled murderer has moved in next door to me."

"Is he nice?" Kate asked.

"I don't know," Ellickson told her. "I can't tell yet. He works all day in his garden and then he disappears."

"A murderer next door?" Irena said, putting away the deck of cards. "In Russia, this is not unusual."

Eventually Macfadden Eward invited Ellickson into his house, where Ellickson found himself amid a welter of decaying furniture, chipped and dented Victorian relics, stained and soiled Salvation Army tables and chairs, lamps with three-masted schooners or seabirds painted on the lampshades. On the floor were odds and ends of kitchen gadgets, including a potato peeler and a coffee grinder still in their shipping boxes. Near the unwashed windows sat bookcases with sports memorabilia scattered on their shelves. Everything had been located and partitioned according to no visible plan in the living room and dining room. None of the dining-room chairs matched, and the big living-room easy chair sported dingy antimacassars and a red velvet cushion. The white lace curtains were clean but threadbare. A cheerful chaos dominated these interior spaces, a bachelor-apartment playroom clutter. His relatives had donated most of this stuff to him, the old man claimed. The rest of it he had bought secondhand.

That Saturday, he made Ellickson a lettuce-and-turkey sandwich and then put him to work helping him clean the gutters. It was a dirty job; goop stuck to Ellickson's work gloves. The second time the old man invited him over, he asked Ellickson for aid in washing his pickup truck. "My back's out today," Macfadden Eward said. "So I can't bend over with the hose and such." Ellickson did the work and watched the soapsuds run toward the storm drain where, he imagined, they weren't supposed to go. All over the city, the storm drains were painted with little outlines of fish, along with warnings: FLOWS TO RIVER. Well, what would the cops do? Revoke the old man's parole because of soapsuds?

The third time he dropped by his neighbor's house, Macfadden Eward told him that they had to go somewhere.

"Where?" Ellickson asked.

"That's for me to know and for you to find out," the old man said.

"Are you playing games with me?" Ellickson asked quietly. "Because if you're playing games with me, go fuck yourself." Along with the alcoholism, Ellickson had anger issues.

"Sorry, sorry. Didn't mean anything by it. My apologies."

Ellickson got into the truck reluctantly. After starting the engine, the old man turned on the radio softly to the Twins baseball game. With the play-by-play serving as a soothing white-noise background, Macfadden Eward said, "How much you know about me? You know anything?"

"Not much," Ellickson said. "Actually, no. Nothing."

"Didn't think so." He opened his window and leaned his arm on the sill. "You're okay, Ellickson. I like you all right. You don't ask questions of me. I appreciate that. So let's get one thing straight. I'll tell you this once, but that's it, and no details after I tell you because I don't want to talk about it. All right?"

Ellickson shrugged.

"It's part of my life I can't get back." He picked at his thumbnail. "It happened."

Ellickson nodded.

"It was my wife, and it was twenty-five years ago, when I was still almost your age. Okay. She was younger than me. That's a mistake, right there. She was a kid, real frisky, and she had a pretty face and a nice shape but a mean streak. She had a mouth on her. And she had the soul of a crocodile, that woman. She was reptilian. Reptiles shouldn't drink, and we both *liked* to drink, speaking of alcohol. We'd go at it. No dignity about it whatsoever. We went to bars, and this one time on the way home she swerved and hit a tree. Cop comes to rescue us, EMI and what-have-you, and they do the breath tests, and on the spot my wife falls in love *with the cop*. Officer Wallace, a *cop*! Can you imagine such a thing? Maybe it was the uniform, maybe it was the holster or how he carried himself or the . . . I *don't* know what it was. After all these years, I can't say that I care. I don't think about it. So after we settle the DUI charge with the court, later, she starts calling the cop and then . . . you know. Hoopla. He wasn't married, just a young buck in a blue uniform. She and I had been hitched for five years. No kids. Between my wife and me, whose fault was that? Not mine, I guarantee. But anyway, she starts stepping out on me with this guy, a brawny type, so I can't exactly take him down in a fistfight. When I ask her, finally, about what the hell she's doing, a married woman, with her loverboy cop, she says, 'I want to feel his testosterone between my legs.' That's a direct quote! 'I want to feel his testosterone between my legs.' Spare me honesty like that. What you have to understand is, I loved her. *I really loved her.* If I hadn't loved her, I wouldn't have shot her. And," he added, "if I had it to do over again, I'd still do it."

Ellickson nodded. "You could have shot the cop. I would have. By the way, where are we going?" he asked.

"Cops don't like it when you kill their girlfriends. In prison," the old man said, ignoring Ellickson's question as if it were nonsensical, "I had time on my hands. The day stretches out. A week, ten weeks, who cares? A civilian can't imagine. You just sit there. Your brain gets empty. *You* get empty. No one gives two fucks about you. And you have this big problem. The big problem is the days and hours you're alone with your mind on idle. You don't see the sky, and your mind races. You start to spook yourself up. Crazy stuff. You see the isles of madness, just over there. Ever seen them? The trees are all dead, and there's caves. Archfiends wearing bow ties live in there. The mind is underemployed. It sits there and won't quit. So I gave my mind a job."

They were headed downtown, toward a seedy section. They passed a business called Toyland, with sex toys in the display window. "What job was that?" Ellickson asked.

"I needed to keep my dignity, you know? So I imagined a spaceship. Not like a movie spaceship, but something realistic, a real spaceship to take me away. Out of the world I was in. This world. See, the spaceship had to have rooms, it had to have hallways, it needed a *shape*. So I imagined the flight deck. I imagined the chairs and the seating, the exact kind of leather—Spanish, the best—then the compartments where people slept and ate. The dishes. The flatware. That sort of thing. I figured the materials, shape and quantity. This much aluminum, that much alloy. I designed the doorknobs. The computers, the readouts. I even imagined the jet engines, and I don't know anything about jet engines, so I invented how it'd have to be done. I imagined a workable propulsion system. I had to. Everything required a design, even the bathrooms." The murderer laughed his mirthless laugh. At that moment he did not seem to Ellickson ever to have been a kind man. All he had ever been was a maniac. "Those years I was behind bars, I built my spaceship in my mind, and more important, I built it in my heart." He turned and looked directly at Ellickson, as he pulled into a parking space on the street. "When I was done, I named the spaceship."

"What did you call it?" Ellickson asked.

"Yeah, I thought about the name for a long time. Finally I settled on one. I called it *Queen Juliana*." Macfadden Eward smiled at the memory. "It was the name of someone I knew. It was a tribute to her. Now that I'm an old man, I don't name things anymore."

"What are we doing here?" Ellickson asked.

"I gotta talk to my parole officer," the old man said, getting out of the truck. "I'll be back in two shakes." He crossed the street and entered a side door of a brick building that might have once been a warehouse. Upstairs, one lightbulb burned behind a cracked wire-mesh window. Ellickson doubted that a parole officer would work in such a place.

He opened the door of the murderer's truck and stepped down onto the sidewalk. At the end of the block was a business with bars across the front windows. A sign across the front said MONTE CARLO in neon, and then, in smaller letters, A GENTLEMAN'S CLUB. Ellickson did not see any gentlemen going in or out, and for relief from the sight of the shabby shadow-creatures he did see, he glanced down the length of First Avenue.

What had happened to the downtown area? The city seemed to have been abandoned and appeared to be as unloved and uncared-for as the begrimed men going into the Monte Carlo. He eyed a corner telephone pole and saw a video camera aimed in his general direction. Full of exuberant good humor, he gave it the finger. A young woman with green hair and a pierced lower lip, and carrying a large backpack, approached him on the sidewalk and walked past him, gazing at him fearfully as if he were one of the feral gentlemen going into the Monte Carlo. Had he, Ellickson, turned into a person whom others feared? He had once thought of himself as a handsome, genial man who frightened nobody and attracted companionable attention. Soon people would make the sign of the cross upon seeing him to ensure their own safety.

A customer about Ellickson's age, glancing over his shoulder, slunk into the gentleman's club wearing a leering owlish expression behind thick glasses. He was followed by another scowling man with the general appearance of a Hells Angel: wide face, long hair and beard, strong but portly, black leather regalia, an expression of perpetual hostile evaluation as he surveyed the sidewalk. Inside, they would present their money to the dancers and be given a carefully choreographed imitation of reciprocal desire. They wouldn't get any favors, nor would they expect any.

Where was the murderer? What was his real mission? The midday sun beat down on Ellickson, and suddenly, in the midst of this despoliation and desolation, he felt happy for no reason.

Continuing his letter to his son, Ellickson imagined some words that he intended to write down eventually. "You got to be tough in this life. They'll come at you from everywhere. My dad, your grandfather, would knock me around to toughen me up. We once took a car trip to Monument Valley, and when we arrived there, he was so excited that he punched me in the stomach." Ellickson flinched involuntarily, remembering how he had fallen to the ground after his father had said, "Come here, Eric," and had hit him. In his father, as in some other men, joy expressed itself in high-spirited violence. "I guess I disappointed him. On the high-school football team, I was a wide receiver. I spent quite a bit of time on the bench, and my dad nicknamed me 'Second-stringer' after that." He thought for a moment. " 'Stringer,' as a nickname. I had to bear it. It's too bad he died of lung cancer before you could meet him, I guess. When he was sick, he said he would be glad to die. 'I'll be among the happy dead,' he told the nurses, and the nurses told me, and then he died."

The old man came staggering out of the building. He had a disordered appearance, and his eyes didn't seem to be focusing anywhere. Ellickson crossed the street and took hold of him.

"I don't care what they say," Macfadden Eward muttered. "Men and women are incompatible."

"Come on," Ellickson said, holding on to him and piloting him across the street to the truck. When they got there, Ellickson asked, "Can you drive?"

"I cannot," the old man said. His breath smelled of clam sauce.

"What did they do to you in there?" Ellickson asked, opening the passenger-side door of the truck and easing the murderer inside. "Where were you? Was that another entrance to the gentleman's club?"

"No," Macfadden Eward said. "There weren't any gentlemen in there."

Ellickson realized that he had been tricked. "That wasn't your parole officer you were meeting," Ellickson said. "You lied to me."

Macfadden Eward leaned back on the passenger side. He did not engage in any conversational effort. Behind the wheel, Ellickson started the truck and drove down First Avenue, past the former bus station where he had first met the mother of his children and then south toward his own neighborhood. On the passenger side of the truck, the old man's mouth hung open, and his eyes were half shut as if in repose. Whenever the truck turned a corner, his head tilted to the side. This guy is just another piece of human debris, Ellickson thought, and then another thought hit him: *And he's all I have.*

"Was that a drug deal?" Ellickson asked.

Macfadden Eward did not answer, but his eyes opened slightly. He was nodding off.

"I'm very far away," the old man said in a slur. "You're unimportant to me."

"Come on," Ellickson said. "Don't bullshit me. I'm driving your truck. Was that a drug deal? A fix?"

"I . . . wouldn't . . . describe . . . it . . . that . . . way."

"How would you describe it?"

"Over and out," the old man said. He shut his eyes, and his head lolled back.

When they reached the murderer's house, Ellickson parked the man's truck in his driveway, and, hurriedly, he opened the door on the passenger side and took the old man's arm and threw it around his own neck in a fireman's carry. Macfadden Eward grunted, and Ellickson took this as a good sign. He removed the old man from the truck and walked Eward down his own driveway out onto the sidewalk. The old man's feet stumbled and shuffled beside Ellickson's while his breath came in and went out in punchy oldster bursts. Ellickson headed down the street, the old man clinging to him, and he turned the corner to walk around the block, parading past the houses of all the neighbors.

"What're we doin'?" the old man asked, waking up slightly from his nod.

"We're walking it off," Ellickson said. "In front of the neighbors." They passed a house with a large front porch with a swing suspended from the ceiling; Ellickson thought of it as "the little girls' house" because two little girls lived there with their parents, Republicans who put out lawn signs, and, sure enough, both girls were out on the porch with their rag dolls, their mother sitting in the swing reading a book, as Ellickson and the old man walked by. The girls looked at the two men, and Ellickson heard one of them asking her mother a question, and her mother answering in a low, lawyerly tone. They walked past the house of a widow, Mrs. Sherman, said to be a skinflint, who had told Ellickson about the murderer in the first place. They advanced in front of a duplex with a sharp peaked roof. Two young married couples lived there. Ellickson didn't know who resided in the stucco Tudor beyond, but at the corner they turned again, and Ellickson and the old man stumbled past 1769 Caroline Street, where a boy was out front selling lemonade at a lemonade stand.

"I'd like some lemonade," Ellickson said, fishing in his left pocket for some change.

The boy did not say anything. He looked frightened at the sorry spectacle that Ellickson and the old man, hanging on to Ellickson in a fireman's carry, presented.

"Here," Ellickson said, handing the boy two quarters. "*We'd* like some lemonade." He waited for a moment. "My friend here is a little sleepy." The boy poured pink lemonade with a shaky hand into a Dixie cup and handed it to Ellickson.

"This is for you, old-timer," Ellickson said, reaching over and putting the paper cup to his lips.

"Stop that," Macfadden Eward said with sudden lucid clarity, straightening up slightly and coming out of his stupor. He reached for the cup and took a drink with his left hand. When he had completed the task, he took his right arm from around Ellickson's neck. He stood a bit unsteadily, then handed the Dixie cup back to the boy, who had still said nothing and whose eyebrow was trembling. "Nice day," the old man said. "Can't beat it with a stick."

"Guess so," the boy replied in a quaver.

Macfadden Eward threw back his shoulders and walked forward.

Ellickson followed him. "I'm headed homeward," he slurred to anyone in the vicinity. Then he fell to his knees and gazed at the ground. Ellickson hoisted him up again and walked him back to his house. He took the old man upstairs and deposited him, clothes and all, in the tub and turned the cold shower water on him. Macfadden Eward began to sputter. "What's this? What's this?" he shouted. "Turn that off!"

Ellickson returned to his own house. What had just happened made him feel fitfully justified in his own eyes. His neighbor would live, but someday he might overdose, and everyone would feel contempt for him, and if he didn't OD, there was a good chance he would end up in the gutter that beckoned toward all single men, the gutter that Ellickson believed in more strongly than he did in his God.

At his sister's house a few days later, Ellickson was repairing an overhead light fixture while Irena steadied the ladder and handed him the electrical tape and aimed the flashlight at the wiring.

"Have you called Laura? Your wife?" Irena asked.

"No."

"And why not is this?"

"I can't."

"Why not, I ask again?"

He looked down at her. "Shame."

"No. *Stoltz,*" she said. "In German. Not shame, but pride. In Russia, everyone is like you. Everyone is a shameful drunk full of pride. But they . . . manage. You must call Laura. I shall bully you. Like sister-in-law. Bully bully bully." She nodded. "I am relentless. I am dictator." When Ellickson looked down at her, he saw her grimly smiling Asiatic face, like Stalin's.

The following weekend, Macfadden Eward arrived at Ellickson's front door carrying an apple pie. He appeared to be loaded down with rage and spite. "Here, take this," the old man said, shoving the pie in Ellickson's general direction without a trace of generosity.

"Did you bake it yourself?" Ellickson asked.

"Of course not," Macfadden Eward said. "I just bought the goddamn thing." His glance took in Ellickson's living room. "So, can I come in? You've never invited me in, you cheap bastard. I've been the one who's had to show all the hospitality."

"All right," Ellickson said. "But you're interrupting me. I've been writing a letter to my son."

"Let's hear it," the murderer said, forcing his way past Ellickson, through the foyer, and into the living room. He sat down on Ellickson's sofa. "It's kind of a mess in here," the man said, pointing at a newspaper on the floor. "So. Read me the letter."

"It's not for you, it's for my son."

"Try it out on me."

"Don't be a damn fool," Ellickson said. "This is private."

"Are you kidding? Nothing is private anymore," Macfadden Eward said. "Not when you parade a disabled old man with diabetes in the street in front of his neighbors. Here. Take this apple pie." He plopped it down next to where he was sitting on the sofa.

"When you came out of that place, you were in a—"

"Don't say it," the old man interrupted.

"Diabetes?" A silence followed.

"Well, maybe I was and maybe I wasn't." He made a rude noise with his mouth. "Let's hear that letter. Otherwise, I'm going back home and I'll go back to work on the spaceship."

"To hell with your spaceship," Ellickson said. "Fly to the moon, for all I care."

"Just read me the letter. I need to hear it," the murderer said. "I have to hear it right now."

"No," Ellickson said. "It's not for you. I told you this already. I explained. This letter is for my boy."

"All right, then," the murderer said. "Tell me about your boy."

"His name's Alex."

"Tell me about him. Be the proud poppa."

"I can't do that," Ellickson said. Everything, traveling at sixty miles an hour, was about to hit him.

"Okay. Start with this: How old is he?"

"He's ten."

"Well, that's a good age. Anyway, that's what they tell me. Never had kids myself. Never was blessed with children."

"Would you please leave me alone?" Ellickson asked.

"No. Tell me what's going on. At least tell me what you did. Tell me why your family isn't here with you."

Ellickson began to weep. "Why should I tell you?" he asked, enraged. "You're nothing." Dead trees and caverns yawned open for him, and the devils in bow ties stood ready, and he couldn't stop himself. The sobs broke out of him in a storm. "I was drunk," he said. "And I . . . was angry at him. At Alex. My *kid*. I can't even remember the reason. It can't have been anything. And I . . . I don't know why, but . . . I hit him."

"You hit him," the murderer repeated, sitting next to the gift apple pie. "What's so bad about that? People sometimes hit their kids."

"Not if they love them," Ellickson said, still weeping. "I hit him in the face. With a book."

The old man stood up, gazing at Ellickson. "Eric, you poor guy, you're as bad off as I am," he said. "Yes, after all. Thank you. I needed to hear that. I'll be going now."

Ellickson stared at the murderer's back. "Go back to your spaceship. But I'm still sober! Goddamn it, I'm sober now! Sober and proud!"

"Look where it's gotten you," the old man said gently, letting the screen door slam.


Two days later, Ellickson called his mother-in-law's so that he could talk to his wife, and Laura answered. "Laura? Honey, babe?" he began, speaking with his eyes shut and his hands shaking. "Don't hang up, please? It's me. We have to talk. Really, we have to talk. You know I'm sober now—you know that, don't you? These days? And the effort it's costing me? It's all for you. I know you want to hang up—"

"I'm pregnant," Laura said, interrupting him. "Can you believe that?"

"Oh, Jesus," Ellickson said, "can't you—"

"We should talk soon. But not now."

She had broken the connection.


Ellickson put down the receiver and walked into the kitchen, where he removed a carton of orange juice from the refrigerator and poured a small glass for himself. He swished the orange juice around in his mouth as if it were mouthwash; then he swallowed it. Opening the refrigerator again, he did an inventory of its contents: eggs, milk, salad greens, English muffins, spreadable butter, strawberry jam, leftover chili, salad dressing, yogurt, biryani paste, and a bottle of root beer. The contents constituted the most hopeless array of objects the world had presented to him in some time, and he shut the door against it with a shudder. One of Alex's drawings of a dinosaur and a vampire was still stuck with magnets to the refrigerator door.

He took two deep breaths before leaving the kitchen, exiting through the back, crossing the driveway, and knocking at the murderer's front door. No one answered, Ellickson rang again, and still no one appeared. He tried the doorknob, and the door opened with a slight squeak. Ellickson entered the old man's living room.

"Macfadden?" he called out. "Are you here? Mac?"

Ellickson walked into the kitchen. The phone was off the hook, as if the old man had gone to get something or had left in a hurry. Ellickson went down the back stairs to the basement. He wanted to see the spaceship.

Macfadden Eward sat in a reading chair next to a lamp, the history of Robert E. Lee in his lap. He was listening to music through headphones. "Oh," he said, taking the earphones out, "it's you."

"I rang the bell."

"Well, I didn't hear it." He waited. "I'm sorry. My hearing's not so good."

"The phone was off the hook."

"Yes," the old man said. "I don't like to be bothered when I'm down here."

"Where's the spaceship?" Ellickson asked. "I don't see any spaceship down here."

"That's because you're not looking. I tell you what it is, Eric," the murderer said, "and you should listen to me. When you're in prison, you get used to prison. When you're in the desert, you get used to the desert. You get interested in cactus, you know what I mean? And what I'm saying to you is, inside those four walls, I got used to the four walls. Sometimes I just can't stand being upstairs and the daylight and everything that goes with daylight." The ghost of a smile appeared on his face. "And that's why I'm down here."

"And the spaceship?"

"You're in it," Macfadden Eward said.

———

An hour later, Ellickson found himself back on the phone to his friend Lester. "Lester," he said, "I think you need to come over here. Pronto. I'm in trouble again. I talked to my wife and I'm in serious trouble."

"All right," Lester said. "But I'm in the middle of something."

"And could I ask you for a favor?" Ellickson asked. "Would you please bring your stethoscope?"

"It's pretty rusty," Lester told him. "I don't practice medicine now, as you know."

"Bring it anyway," Ellickson said.

Fifteen minutes later, Lester pulled up in the driveway in his Buick. He came into Ellickson's living room without knocking or ringing the bell, with his stethoscope flapping against his chest. He was a small compact man, with a full and slightly unruly head of hair, and a face on which great intelligence and comical sadness were usually visible—the expression of quizzical wit seemed to animate everything. But Lester also had a distinctive overbite, the attribute of a character actor who will always be left out at the end of the show.

He rushed forward and shook Ellickson's hand, pulling him forward into a tentative hug. "So. What's happened?"

"Lester," Ellickson said, "my chest feels like it's going to explode."

"Pain? Chest pain?"

"No, it's more like a weight."

"Well, you know, we should get you to an emergency room. I'm not really a practicing M.D. anymore."

"I want you to examine me. Please."

Lester gazed at Ellickson with his comically sad chipmunk expression. "Me? Okay," he said. "Take off your shirt. I want to listen to your heart."

Ellickson did as he was told. Lester put the earpieces in and pressed the stethoscope against Ellickson's chest.

"Lester, my wife's pregnant."

"Shh."

"She won't let me talk to Alex."

"Shh. I'm listening to your heart."

"The guy next door is a murderer who lives in a spaceship. And all I want in this life is to have a drink."

"Would you please shut up?"

Finally Lester lowered the stethoscope. Outside the screen door, a cardinal sang in the linden. The air smelled of moisture, of a thunderstorm brewing just out of sight underneath the line of the horizon, and despite the sunlight, Ellickson thought he heard the rumble of thunder. "Well," Lester said, smiling. "There's good news and bad news."

"Tell me the bad news first," Ellickson said.

"You're still alive," the doctor told him.

"And what's the good news?" Ellickson asked.

Lester shrugged. "Same thing," he said.

# Mr. Scary

FOR RICHARD BAUSCH

THERE WAS SOME SORT of commotion at the end of the checkout line. Words had been exchanged, and now two men, one tall and wide-shouldered, the other squat and beefy, were squaring off against each other and raising their voices. Their shoes squeaked on the linoleum. The short one, who had hair from his back sprouting up underneath his shirt collar, was saying a four-letter word. The other man, the tall one, shook his head angrily and raised his fist. An elderly security guard was rushing toward them. He didn't seem up to the task, Estelle thought. He was just a minimum-wage retiree they had hired for show.

"Good God," Estelle said to her grandson, "there's going to be a fist-fight."

The boy didn't glance up from his phone gadget. He held it in his palm and was rapidly clicking the letters. "They're just zombies," the boy said quietly and dismissively after a glance.

"Well, how do you know that?" the grandmother asked, trying for conversation. "I've never met a zombie." The men seemed to have calmed down a bit. They were just rumbling at each other now.

"Zombies *like* discount stores," the boy, whose name was Frederick, said patiently, as if he had to explain everything. He still wasn't looking at the two men. "They eat plastic when they can't get brains." The boy glanced up, showing his grandmother his bright blue eyes. "Just look around if you don't believe me," he said. "This junk? It's all *theirs*." The fight between the two men seemed to bore him, before the fact. Almost everything bored him.

Another security guard had arrived, a red-faced fellow with a crew cut. He would put a stop to things. Together with the older security guard, he herded the two men toward the service area. So: that had happened.

Now it was over. Estelle handed the baseball bat she was buying for Frederick to the checkout clerk, who scanned it and who then held out her palm for money.

"You don't see *that* every day," Estelle said to the clerk, who was frowning.

"Ain't none of my business," the clerk said with a shrug.

Estelle handed the bat to her grandson, who took hold of it in his left hand while keeping up his writing with his right.

"You're giving this to me because *why*?" the boy asked, glancing up.

Estelle sighed. She no longer waited for thanks for anything from him. Gratitude was simply beyond his abilities.

"For your baseball games," she said, over her shoulder.

"What baseball games? I don't play baseball."

"*Thank* you," the checkout clerk said behind her, belatedly, as if prompting Frederick. He followed his grandmother, his eyes downward again, oblivious to her, to the partly cloudy sky outside the automatic doors, to the untied shoelace on his left foot, to his own waddling walk, to the folds of fat under his T-shirt, to the gift of the unthanked aluminum baseball bat. The poor child. He had been so beautiful once, years ago, with a smile to light up the world, and now—well, just look at him.

They drove across Minneapolis and stopped for a red light in front of the Basilica. At the corner traffic island stood a bearded panhandler with a cardboard sign that read: HOMELeSS VetERaN. ANYThING WILL HeLP. GoD BLeSS. The man's face was wreathed in sunburned desolation, and she was reaching into her purse for a dollar when her grandson spoke up from the backseat.

"Grandma, don't give him anything."

"What? Why?" Estelle asked.

"He's a pod," the boy said.

"What?"

"*You* know. A *pod*. A replicant."

Estelle looked in the rearview mirror and saw the boy scowling malevolently at the homeless man.

"No, I don't know. Why do you say such things?"

"See, for starters, he's in the stare-at-you army," the boy said, with his eerie talent for metaphor. "They stare at you. That's the pod game plan. I can always tell. I have *radar.* That guy is garbage." Frederick laughed to himself. "He's the lieutenant colonel of garbage."

"No human is garbage," his grandmother said defiantly, rolling down her window, "and I don't want to hear you talking like that."

"Okay, fine," the boy said, "but I'm just saying . . . How come you *like* these creeps?"

But she had already reached through the car window and placed a dollar bill in the man's palm, and when he said, "Thank you, and God bless you," Estelle felt a small sensation of satisfaction and pride. He might be a bum, but he knew how to be thankful.

"I suppose you think he's a zombie, too," Estelle said, as she rolled the window back up.

"*No,*" the boy replied. "He's a . . . *replicant.* Like I told you. He looks like a human being, but he isn't. Just like this car we're in now *seems* like a real car." Frederick smiled at his grandmother, a private smile, but the smile seemed to be poisoned somehow by the baby fat on his twelve-year-old face and by the boy's customary malice, a thin screen for his unhappiness. Often his face was unreadable—it was as if he had trained his facial expressions to be ungrammatical. The poor child: he even had a double chin, making him look like a preteen Rotarian. Curled into himself, having returned to his phone gadget, Frederick radiated waves of unsociability and ill will. His being hummed with animosity toward the world for having staged the enactment of his various miseries. His revulsion at life had a kind of purity, Estelle thought.

Really, all she wanted to do was to take him into her arms and hold him. But he was too old for that now. What had worked once, all that love she had given him, no longer did.


"Mass times force equals velocity," the boy said, just before his grandmother dropped him off at Community day camp. "It's true. Did you know that?"

"No, I didn't. But actually, Freddie, that doesn't sound quite right."

"Well, it's true. *Absolutely.* I've been studying physics. And mass times force equals velocity. That's why a baseball travels faster if you hit it hard. You're forcing the ball to, like, accelerate." He waited for his words to sink in. "To escape inertia. You want to hear something else? This is even more amazing. *Gravity equals weight times voltage.* That's Yardley's Theorem."

"Yes. Well, okay. We're here," Estelle said, pulling to a stop in front of the Community day camp building, a grim yellow concrete-block affair with a flagpole hoisting a limp flag just inside the turning circle. During the winter, the building served as a community center. During the summer, they offered activities for kids from ages eight to twelve, with trips to spots of local interest. Last week the boys and girls had visited an institution for assisted living, giving each old person a gift of their own devising. Frederick had given his own old person an African violet. The day camp counselors also staged sports activities on the playground in back. Frederick hated all of it and performed his sullen silence with great majesty whenever Estelle picked him up.

"Do I have to go in there?" the boy asked, once she had stopped.

"Well, I *did* drive you over here. Kiddo, give it the old college try."

"I've done that all summer."

"So do it again."

"They all hate me," Frederick said. "They throw their lunch food at me."

"Throw it back."

"Yeah, *that'll* work. They throw sandwiches. Which *explode.*"

"Well, can't you—"

"I got a cupcake in my hair yesterday."

"Make an effort—"

"All right, all *right*," he said.

"To go in there—"

"I said *all right.*"

There was a brief air pocket of dead silence.

"See you in a few hours," Estelle muttered, as her grandson heaved himself out of the car. He was still writing something on his phone. He also had words penned on his arm.

"Don't bother coming back. Just call the coroner," the boy shouted, closing the car door and causing the baseball bat to roll again on the floor.

Her husband, Randall, down on his knees in the garden, waved to Estelle absentmindedly with his trowel as she pulled up on the driveway. "Not enough fertilizer for the pansies," he said to her once she was out of the car and behind him, leaning on him. Using his customary tone of comic despair, he said, "And I've been overwatering the snaps, damn it. Look at them." He stood up, shaking his head before turning and giving Estelle a quick kiss on the lips. When he did, the brim of his sun hat poked against her forehead. "Drop him off okay?" Randall asked.

"So I bought him a baseball bat," Estelle said, putting her hand on her husband's shoulder. "It was a hopeful gesture." She straightened her husband and dusted him off. "But he stayed grumpy. Oh, and this is interesting: there was a fight in the checkout line at the discount store."

Randall nodded, gazing at her carefully. "Sure. Of course there was," he said. As always, she was taken aback by his capacity for understanding her, for knowing her least little mood. "Stel," he said, "I've made some lemonade, and . . . Freddie's disposition isn't your fault, you know."

"I know," she said. "I know." She whistled to the dog, who regarded her with indifference from his shade under the crab apple tree. "I just wish sometimes that Freddie were, oh, I don't know, more . . . *normal,* and I hate myself for wanting that. Who wants normal?"

"You do," he said. "Well, let's have a softball game on the vacant lot when he gets home. Us and a few normal neighbors. With his new baseball bat."

"A softball game?"

"Yes. With Freddie. Or maybe we should just *let him be.*" He gave her hand another squeeze and preceded her into the house, holding the door open behind him. How considerate! Randall had always been considerate: he was one of those easygoing people—affable, graceful, thoughtful—on whom the sturdy world depended, and although her little secret was that she was fatigued with him and felt almost no passion for him, she still needed to have his calm presence around. He was like a preservative, and she would fight to keep him if she had to. He played poker once a week with his chums; he drank one beer per evening; he was semi-retired from his veterinarian practice; he never raised his voice. He was even a graceful and attentive lover. What a paragon of virtue Randall was! Nothing to excess, this husband. But he had never been wild, and Estelle couldn't help herself: she was bored by people like him. Secretly, men who started fistfights attracted her. They had sap. But it was boredom that had the staying power.

"Here," Randall said, handing her a lemonade in a Dixie cup.

"Thank you," she said, leaning forward into him again. His skin had a kind of slippery silkiness, an odd texture for the exterior of a middle-aged man. Her first husband, the dreaded Matthew, whose nickname had been Squirrel—winsome womanizer, alcoholic, self-centered bum, gate crasher, liar, charmer, deadbeat, and cheat—had felt like hair and sandpaper. Sex with him had always been burningly raw and fecund. Children came from it, three of them. Where was Squirrel Van Dusen now? Pittsburgh? Or was it Tucson he had recently called from, yes, somewhere in the Southwest, that sunny haven for bums, asking for a tide-over loan for his newest harebrained scheme? It was hard to keep track of him: Randall had taken the most recent call and kept her from whatever Squirrel had asked for. She still had a soft spot for the guy. The flame could not quite be extinguished. Human wreckage *had* always attracted her. "The Bad Samaritan," Randall had called her once, in that not-quite-teasing way of his.

"It's a stage he's going through," Randall said, sitting down at the dinette. "Frederick's going through a stage. All boys go through a stage. They have to practice at being bad before they become men."

"*You* were never bad."

"Well, okay. I guess I never was," Randall said thoughtfully, nodding his head once and turning away from her. "Not like that."

"You always got up at five o'clock. To pray. With the birds. Like Saint Francis. You were a boy scout," she said, knowing she was being petty. "You still are."

"That's unkind. And I never *prayed,* not like that. I prayed to someday meet someone like you. Actually, Estelle," he said, fixing her with a look, "what *are* we talking about? This isn't about me, is it? Or Frederick?"

"No, I don't suppose so."

"Well, my dear, what is it about?"

She looked at him. Behind her, she could hear the leaves of the ash tree stirring in the dry summer wind. She could even hear the electric clock in the stove, which gave off a dull but thoughtful hum, as if it were planning something.

"It's about the usual," she said. Of course he knew what it was about. He always knew.

They'd run off together as teenagers forty-five years ago, Estelle and Squirrel, and when their kids were still toddlers, they'd crisscrossed the country in the Haunted Buick. What fun it was, being young, rootless, those hours of driving when music would start up for no apparent reason underneath the car's dashboard and then stop a few minutes later. There was a short in the radio, but Squirrel liked to say that the Buick was haunted. An announcer would begin speaking in midsentence from that same place under the dashboard, and Squirrel would say, "Where did *he* come from?" You couldn't switch the radio off: the dial didn't work. The Buick was beyond all that.

In those days, Estelle and Squirrel never stopped anywhere for longer than a few months. They would cross the border into yet another state they hadn't yet ravaged looking for opportunities, surefire moneymaking projects to *put them on the map,* as Squirrel liked to say. That was the expression he used after dark in bed with Estelle in one motel or another, whispering to her about what and where they would be, someday. They'd be settled; and happy; and rich. They'd be *on the map.* The children, the two boys and Isabel, the youngest, whom they called Izzy, slept in the other bedroom, a clutch of little snorers and bed wetters.

All the trouble had been manageable at first. In Maine, there had been midnight phone calls from a girlfriend Squirrel had acquired some-where, and a day later they were treated to her sudden arrival on the doorstep of their rented duplex. She'd been coarsely attractive, this girl-friend, furiously chewing bubble gum, and her waitress name tag was still pinned to her blouse over (Estelle could not help noticing) her plump right breast. *Cheryl.* She was pregnant, this waitress, this Cheryl, said. She wanted satisfaction. *Satisfaction!* What a word. Or else. Or else what? She would be back, she said, with a court order. Estelle and Squir-rel packed the car that night and were gone the next morning, the kids still asleep in the backseat by the time the sun came up. Estelle didn't speak to Squirrel, except about necessities, for a month after that.

In Montana, Squirrel's partner-in-business threatened them all— another midnight call!—with a court suit and, if that didn't work out, personal revenge Western style with a semiautomatic. By the time they had relocated in northern Minnesota, as temporary managers of the Trout Inn on Ninemile Lake, Estelle thought they were finally free of adventures. They'd come to the calm expository part of the movie, the part after the big opening attention-getting mayhem. Squirrel's mischief-making had been all used up, she thought, just flushed right out of him, and she was relieved.

And then one night Estelle had awakened to find that Squirrel had entered her while she'd been sleeping and was thrusting into her with a wild look on his face, with his hands around her neck as if he planned to strangle her, and she screamed at him and shook him off. She loaded the still-sleeping kids into the Buick, against Squirrel's pleading, and took off for Minneapolis. She remembered to take what money there was, and the credit cards, Squirrel pleading with her but not stopping her, and the children crying.

That was Part One of her life. Now she was in Part Two. There would never be a Part Three. Of that she was sure.

Midafternoon, Estelle pulled her car into the turning circle for Community day camp. Of course, Freddie was already there out in front, staring up into the sky as if he were waiting for helicopter rescue. He lumbered toward the car, opened the front passenger-side door, and poured himself in. He aimed the air-conditioning vents toward his face.

"How was it today?" Estelle asked, too brightly.

Freddie sat silently as if the question were much too complicated to be answered. Finally, he said, "We're going to put on a play."

"Yes, I think you told me that," Estelle said. "What is it? What's the play?"

"We're all writing it. Or *they* are. The kids and the counselors." He gave her his best sour look. "It's called *Wonderful World.*"

"And who do you play?" Estelle asked.

"Me? I play Mr. Scary."

"Mr. Scary? Who's that? And what do you do?"

"I stand up at the beginning of the play and I recite my fear monologue and scare everybody."

"Well, that's nice," Estelle said, trying to put the best face on things. "Do you have it? The monologue? Could you read it to me?"

"Yeah," Freddie said. "I got it right here with me." He heaved himself upward, trying to get his hand into his trouser pocket. After much poking, he pulled out a grimy sheet of paper. Her grandson unfolded the paper and began to read. His delivery sounded like a voice-over in a horror movie. "*Fear,*" Freddie intoned. "What *is* fear? You and I live with, interact with, fear. We know fear, but we *shun* it. But what if one were to *embrace* fear? Not to *live* with it, but to *be* it, to *become* fear. In our everyday lives we *divorce* ourselves from *fear.* We tell ourselves it is *distant,* it is *unreal,* it is *abstract.* But this is *not* so. Fear is *tangible,* more tangible than you or I. What if a man *became* fear? Where would fear *live?* He would dwell among us, *hidden* but not unseen. *Who* would fear be? For *what* would fear strive? What would be the *face of fear?* Ha ha ha ha."

"Very good, Freddie. But, well, that's a strange monologue to give to a twelve-year-old," Estelle said, after recovering herself. "The words are awfully big. What does it have to do with a wonderful world?"

"It's like what you have to get out of the way? *Before* the world is wonderful? And yeah, well, that's what they gave me," Freddie said, slumping down in the car. "The counselors wrote it. That's what Mr. Scary says. I've got to memorize it. Also we made T-shirts today. I mean, we wrote words on T-shirts. So they became ours."

"What did you write?"

Freddie held his shirt up. With laundry marker, he had written GOT HERPES? on his. "Well," Estelle said, "that's not very nice."

"It's supposed to be a public health warning," Freddie said. "A wake-up call."

"And the other kids, did they throw food at you?" Estelle asked.

"Not today," Freddie said. "Today was a good day. They liked how I did the Mr. Scary monologue."

"Freddie," Estelle asked, "do you really have to laugh at the end of that? It's a little corny."

"The ha ha ha ha part? I added that," her grandson told her. "That's my contribution." He took out his phone gadget and began tapping letters.

"Are you texting someone?"

"No," Freddie said. "I'm writing a story."

"Oh, good," Estelle said. "What's it about?"

"The underworld," he told her.


Sometimes, on certain days when Estelle had found herself sitting on the front stoop of the house, her coffee cup cooling between her palms, and the morning breeze riffling her hair, Freddie still eating his breakfast cereal inside, she would imagine that the way her grandson had turned out, with his sorrow and obesity and malice, had its own logic. But then at other times, particularly when the breeze stopped, time halted as well.

And when that happened, Estelle was no longer sitting on the front stoop with her coffee but was back *there,* in time, in Part One, taking her daughter, Isabel, to a guidance counselor, and then to that killingly expensive, pill-dispensing psychiatrist in the circular building with curved interior walls that made Estelle think of a gigantic brain, and they, all of them, the brilliant professionals and Estelle herself, were trying to *talk* Izzy out of the sullen and then manic rages—shoplifting, a stolen car, drug-taking, car wrecks, God knows what kinds of sex, and with whom—that had overtaken her and turned her into this oblivious bingeing adolescent force-of-nature who'd actually driven once into a parked fire truck. Well, at those moments nothing had its own logic, or it had the wrong kind of logic, because you couldn't *talk* anybody out of anything, could you? No. How many young women had managed to do what her daughter had accomplished? Had smashed a stolen car into a fire truck? An achievement. Her teenage accomplices had fled, but Isabel had stayed there, dazed behind the wheel but boldly confident that such an excellent accident gave her special monster status. Who else, among Estelle's acquaintances, had also hit, though not very hard, a pedestrian in a parking lot? Her daughter, Isabel, had, and had been unrepentant. *He shouldn't have been there,* she had said of her victim, a retired dentist. In her taste for mayhem, Isabel had truly been Squirrel's child. So there *was* a logic to her actions, of a sort.

Estelle thought that her own life had veered between long patches of drudgery, weeks and months filing claims in an insurance office during the day and then racing home to cook dinner for her children and to put them to bed, typical single-mom scheduling, and then, the next job, working in the front office at the veterinarian hospital where she'd met Randall, accompanied by a choral background of barking. Yes, all that domesticity. And classes taken at the community college, including art history, her new passion. Then other stretches of time superimposed themselves on the dull ones, the moments of high drama, first the ones staged by Squirrel and then the ones staged by her daughter. Her two sons, Carl and Robert, seemed frightened by their little sister and had landed jobs after school at grocery and hardware stores; poor souls, solid citizens before their time, they almost didn't count, those boys.

But Isabel! Even on medications, she drank anything, she took anything, she went anywhere at night; she seemed to have no home place except the deep nothingness that she sought out. In Squirrel, those traits

had been charming, for a while—they looked good on a boy—but with
Isabel they were as charmless as her scowling face. There was really something demonic about her, almost bestial. Estelle imagined her as she saw
her back then: twisted up with injuries, avoiding eye contact, the blond
hair matted and unwashed, her jeans caked with dirt, her fierce young
woman's sexuality attracting the worst of the boys who gleefully hovered
around her waiting for her next bold move.

One night, one of many late nights, Isabel had come home at three in
the morning. Estelle had awakened out of a shallow and dream-infected
sleep and gone into Isabel's room, where Isabel had thrown herself on the
bed in the dark. She was muttering, and after Estelle switched on the
lamp, she noticed that the pillow where her daughter rested her head had
turned gray at the indentation. Isabel never showered anymore, and she
smelled like a feral child.

"Where have you been?" Estelle asked her, trying not to yell.

"I've been inside and outside," Isabel said. "I've covered the world."
She giggled. "Like that paint? That covers the world? I've done that."

"Jesus. What am I going to do with you?" Estelle said to herself, to
the walls. "At least get undressed. At least get some sleep. And you're
grounded," she said, automatically.

"Undressed?" Isabel asked. Every facial expression she gave her mother
indicated that any and all requests were, at that moment, preposterous.
"You want me undressed, Mom? Like those nine-to-five people who are
undressed? Who go to sleep?"

"Yes," Estelle said. "Like those people."

Isabel glanced up at her mother. Picking herself up, she stood next to
the bed, then lowered her jeans. "See?" she said. "I can do this." She
swayed and laughed at herself. "Wanna see something?" She laughed
again. "I'm a magician. I can do this amazing trick. Just watch. You've
*never seen this before in your life.* I can make my panties stick to the
ceiling."

"What?" Estelle said.

After stomping her blue jeans to the floor, Isabel lowered her underwear and clumsily stepped free. She bent down and picked up her
underpants—pink, Estelle noticed, her heart breaking—and then threw
them up at the ceiling. They fluttered back down to the floor.

Isabel gazed upward and said wonderingly, "I thought it would work.
I had such a good time."

Estelle was staring, too. Her mind moved slowly. "What are you talking about?"

"Oh, poor Mom," Isabel said. "You're so sheltered. Can't you guess?"

"No."

"Well," Isabel said, putting her hand on her mother's shoulder to keep herself from swaying, "I was with a boy tonight. And we . . . you know. And, Mommy, did you know that after you do it, I mean when you do it with a boy, it drains out of you? Later? Onto what you're wearing? And it makes your clothes . . . sticky. And that's why I thought my underwear would be up there on the ceiling!" she concluded, triumphantly. "Except it isn't."

Of course Isabel would become pregnant. There was no such thing as safe sex with Isabel. Of course she would have a baby and give it to her mother to raise after naming the baby Frederick (who came out of his mother brown, so his father must have been African-American, or something), and of course she would disappear quickly afterward, leaving no known address.

Poor crazy Isabel. Poor Freddie, her son. It wasn't about individuals anymore; it was about the generations, and what they handed down. The courtrooms, the hospitals, the doctor's offices, the classrooms, the jails where they had put Izzy overnight: sometimes, sitting on the back stoop with her coffee cup, Estelle felt all those places descending over her, as if another person had lived that part of her life and had *not* yet survived it but now was inhabiting her own body. Clouds would cross the sky, cumulus clouds puffy with their own complacency.

In the car, with Freddie explaining about his hero, Argo, and his descent into the underworld, Estelle turned toward Lake Calhoun. When she parked near the beach, Freddie sat up and said, "What're we doing here?"

"I thought it would be nice to go outside," Estelle said. "Just a stroll. It's summer, Freddie. We've got a little time before dinner."

"Of course it's summer. I mean, what are we *doing* here?"

"Well, look at the swimmers." Outside the car, she walked ahead of him in the midafternoon glare on a sidewalk that ran parallel to the beach. At some distance from them, young men and women were playing volleyball. Out on the lake she could see swimmers splashing each other, and, beyond them, hazed in the hot Impressionist light, the sailboats. The air smelled of suntan oil and lake vegetation. People were bicycling past on the bike paths, and everywhere men and women, children and dogs were enjoying themselves. Pop music floated on the air from some radio.

"I hate it here," Freddie said, from behind her. Estelle could hear the shuffling of his shoes on the sidewalk. "I need to practice my Mr. Scary monologue."

"We should have brought your swimming trunks."

"I can't swim."

"You could learn."

"Not if I don't want to, I can't," he said. "I'd rather sleep with the fishes."

"The fish. Not fishes. *Fish*. You shouldn't be so negative," Estelle told him.

"You mean I'm supposed to be *happy*?" He inflected the word with scorn. "Happiness sucks."

"Well, you could try," his grandmother said, feeling a wingfeather of hopelessness. Just to her right, a boy about Freddie's age, maybe a bit older, bronzed with the sun, a kid who obviously lived outdoors, was tossing a football to a friend. The wingfeather beat against Estelle as she watched him. Happiness came only to those who never asked for it.

"I'd rather be Mr. Scary," Freddie said. One of the boys close to them threw his football unsteadily, and it landed near the sidewalk. Freddie stared at it before kicking it out of the way. One of the boys said, "Throw it here!" while Freddie continued on.

Estelle raised her head, closed her eyes, and breathed in. "You could have thrown that ball," she said. "Couldn't you?"

"No," Freddie said. "It's just a trick. They're trying to mess with us."

"Incidentally, I think," Estelle said, "that Randall is organizing a softball game for after dinner. We'll use your new bat!"

"Oh, that's great. That's just great."

"Don't you want to try it?"

He treated her to his silence.


Well, at least there was the Bakken Electrical Museum. After they had returned to the car, Estelle drove Freddie to his favorite place on the southwest side of the lake, the museum where they had a working

Theremin installed. Freddie had been here half a dozen times, and each time he would push impatiently past the exhibits near the front door to the Theremin in the middle of the museum's stairwell. He'd turn on the old instrument and raise his hands in the air between the two antennae.

Here, he was in his element. His hands raised like a conductor, with his fingers out, Freddie would tap and poke the air in front of him, and from the old Theremin came pitched noises that sounded like music but really *weren't* music, Estelle thought, any more than screaming was like singing. According to the information on the explanatory wall plaque, other Theremins had been used for the Beach Boys' "Good Vibrations" and the movie scores for *Spellbound* and *The Day the Earth Stood Still.* Freddie, when he played this thing, had a beatific smile on his face, as if he were summoning his monsters from the deep. Once he had played "Jingle Bells" for her on it, and Estelle thought she would jump out of her skin with revulsion. He had learned through trial and error where to poke the air for certain pitches. Apparently he had a musical ear. He was getting good at it. Soon he would be playing "My Funny Valentine" on this thing and scaring away everybody.

But you couldn't take a kid down to the MacPhail Center for Music for Theremin lessons, and you couldn't bring out your grandson in front of the guests to have him play his Theremin, causing the other grandmothers to applaud, because Freddie wasn't really *presentable,* and neither was this music, which sounded like the groans of the dying, oscillating at sixty cycles per second.

Still, she watched him, poking and prodding the air and producing the hellish glissandos, with something like admiration. Her own sons were not like that. There was no other boy like him.


"There's no one else like him," Estelle said to Randall, who was bending over the grill, the left side for the hot dogs, the right side for hamburgers. He had put on his chef's apron and was worrying the hamburger buns on the edge of the grill with a spatula. Freddie sat writing his story on a picnic bench, on the other side of the back deck. He was concentrating with fierce inward energy.

Late summer evening, and Estelle sat watching Randall cooking the hamburgers and Freddie working on his story. Somewhere in back, the cicadas, harbingers of autumn, were chirring away. Their neighbor Jerry

Harponyi, who played cello in the city orchestra, was watering his garden, and when he saw Estelle across his back fence, he raised his hand, still holding the garden hose, to wave. The water gubbled, airborne, in a snakelike line, before falling.

"No, there isn't," Randall said. "But let's not talk about this now. By the way, I've drafted about seven of the neighbors to play softball in the park in an hour. And Freddie said he'd join us."

"Freddie said that?"

"Yes. I used all my persuasive skills."

"What did you say?" Estelle asked.

"I said it'd be nice if he played."

"He didn't object?"

"I just said that it'd be a nice gesture." Well, Estelle thought, that was Randall, all right: the King of Nice Gestures. "After all, you bought him that baseball bat. And he loves you, you know."

"Who?"

"Freddie, your grandson."

"No, he—"

"Of course he does, Stel. Please. You're the only thing in this world holding him on." He looked at her with a smile, his face disfigured momentarily by smoke from the grill. "I can't do it the way you can. You're his lifeline. Don't you know that? Can't you see it?"

Harponyi waved again. "Looking forward to the game!" he shouted, and the water from his hose flung itself out again in patterns in the air.

"Me?"

"Yes, my dear. You. You're a rock, an anchor. You're all he's got. I love you, too, you know, but I'm not desperate. Anyway, you know what position you should play?"

"No," she said. "First base?" She always liked it when Randall told her he loved her.

"No," Randall said. "Outfield. You need a rest. You can just stand out there and wait for balls to fall into your glove. Like a nun. Like a little sister of mercy."

"I'd enjoy that, I think," Estelle said.


Standing in the outfield, with the sun setting below the park's trees to the west, Estelle felt the early-evening breezes blowing across her forehead, the same breezes that blew Randall's hair backward on the pitcher's mound, so that he looked surprised, or like one of the Three Stooges, she couldn't remember which one. With grown children of his own, and his own sorrows—his wife had pitched herself through a window eight stories up two months after learning that she had inoperable cancer—Randall had every right to be moody, or grumpy at times. Or just sour. But, no: he was relentless in his cheerfulness. And tiresome, if you didn't share it. Somehow the tragedies he had lived through hadn't altered him. They had no relevance to him. There he was. In the fading light, he still gleamed a little.

Randall had just struck out Harponyi, the cellist. The first baseman, a fifteen-year-old from across the street, whistled and cheered. His name was Tommy. He was already chunky with muscle, a real athlete who in a year or two would be playing high-school football, and for a moment Estelle wondered whether it wasn't a bit unfair to have boys like that playing on their side. But it all balanced out: their second baseman was an office temp who lived down the block and who was, at this very moment, talking on her cell phone, and their shortstop was old Mr. Flannery, a retired social studies teacher who lived on the corner and who looked a bit like Morgan Freeman. He was old but wiry. Freddie, when he came to bat, wouldn't have a chance if the ball went toward Mr. Flannery.

These are my people, Estelle thought, and bless them all, here in Part Two. Strange how one's heart could lift sometimes for no particular reason. On the other side of the park, the sounds of the soccer players, their outcries, rose into the air and made their way toward her. A fly buzzed around her head, and she smelled the strangely green smell of the outfield grass. She pounded her fist into the baseball glove, a spare that Randall had found somewhere in the basement.

Freddie was up. He was practice-swinging the bat that Estelle had bought for him that morning. His swings were slow, and even without a ball anywhere near them, they seemed inaccurate, approximate.

Stepping up to the plate, Freddie took one hand off the bat to shade his eyes against the sun. When he saw his grandmother, he waved. Estelle waved back.

Randall's first pitch hit the ground a few feet in front of Freddie and rolled to the catcher, Tommy's brother, who threw it back to Randall. "Good eye," Estelle shouted, and people laughed.

The next pitch went into the strike zone, and Freddie swung at it and missed, by a considerable margin. His physical movements were like those of an underground creature rarely exposed to the light. The umpire, an insurance adjuster who lived with Harponyi, called the first strike.

Freddie took another practice swing.

When Randall threw the next pitch, Estelle could see that it would go into the strike zone and that Freddie would swing at it and connect with it, and when he did, the ball soared up, a high fly, slowly ascending, and as it rose into the air, Freddie headed toward first base, not really looking at where he was going but watching the ball instead and then glancing at his grandmother underneath it. For a brief moment they exchanged glances, Estelle and Freddie, and he seemed to grin; and then the ball began its descent, as Freddie, watching it again, headed toward Tommy, the first baseman, a boy as solid as he, Freddie, was soft. Tommy had taken up a stance and had braced himself with his elbow out, and Estelle saw that when Freddie got there, he would slam into Tommy like an egg thrown into a wall. Estelle tried to shout to Freddie to look where he was going, but her shout caught in her throat out of fear or terror, just before the ball dropped in its leisurely way, with perfect justice, into her out-stretched glove.

# The Cousins

MY COUSIN BRANTFORD was named for our grandfather, who had made a fortune from a device used in aircraft navigation. I suppose it saved lives. A bad-tempered man with a scar above his cheekbone, my grandfather believed that the rich were rewarded for their merits and the poor deserved what they got. He did not care for his own grandchildren and referred to my cousin as "the little prince." In all fairness, he didn't like me, either.

Brantford had roared through his college fund so rapidly that by the age of twenty-three, he was down to pocket change. One bright spring day when I was visiting New York City and had called him up, he insisted on taking me to lunch at a midtown restaurant where the cost of the entrées was so high that a respectful noonday hush hung over the restaurant's skeletal postmodern interior. Muttering oligarchs with monogrammed shirt cuffs gazed at entering patrons with a languid alertness. The maître d' wore one of those dark blue restaurant suits, and the wine list had been printed on velvety pages set in a stainless-steel three-ring binder.

By the time my cousin arrived, I had read the menu four times. He was late. You had to know Brantford to get used to him. A friend of mine said that my cousin looked like the mayor of a ruined city. Appearances mattered a great deal to Brantford, but his own were on a gradual slide. His face had a permanent alcoholic flush. His brownish-blond hair was parted on the right side and was too long by a few millimeters, trailing over his collar. Although he was dressed well, in flannel trousers and cordovan shoes, you could see the telltale food stains on his shirt, and the expression underneath his blond mustache had something subtly wrong with it—he smiled with a strangely discouraged affability.

"Bunny," he said to me, sitting down with an audible expunging of air. He still used my childhood name. No one else did. He didn't give me a hug because we don't do that. "I see you've gotten started. You're having a martini?"

I nodded. "Morning tune-up," I said.

"Brave choice." Brantford grinned, simultaneously waving down the server. "Waitress," he said, pointing at my drink, "I'll have one of those. Very dry, please, no olive." The server nodded before giving Brantford a thin professional smile and gliding over to the bar.

We had a kind of solidarity, Brantford and I. I had two decades on him, but we were oddly similar, more like brothers than cousins. I had always seen in him some better qualities than those I actually possessed. For example, he was one of those people who always make you happier the moment you see them.

Before his drink arrived, we caught ourselves up. Brantford's mother, Aunt Margaret, had by that time been married to several different husbands, including a three-star army general, and she currently resided in a small apartment cluttered with knickknacks near the corner of Ninety-second and Broadway.

Having spent herself in a wild youth and at all times given to manias, Brantford's mother had started taking a new medication called Elysium-Max, which seemed to be keeping her on a steady course where life was concerned. Brantford instructed me to please phone her while I was in town, and I said I would. As for Brantford's two half sisters, they were doing fine.

With this information out of the way, I asked Brantford how he was.

"I don't know. It's strange. Sometimes at night I have the feeling that I've murdered somebody." He stopped and glanced down at the tableware. "Someone's dead. Only I don't know who or what, or *when* I did it. I must've killed *somebody*. I'm sure of it. Thank you," he said with his first real smile of the day, as the server placed a martini in front of him.

"Well, that's just crazy," I said. "You haven't killed anyone."

"Doesn't matter if I have or haven't," he said, "if it feels that way. Maybe I should take a vacation."

"Brantford," I said, "you *can't* take a vacation. You don't work." I waited for a moment. "Do you?"

"Well," he said, "I'd *like* to. Besides, I work, in my way," he claimed, taking a sip of the martini. "And don't forget that I can be anything I want to be." This sentence was enunciated carefully and with precise despair, as if it had served as one of those lifelong mottoes that he no longer believed in.

What year was this? 1994? When someone begins to carry on as my cousin did, I'm never sure what to say. Tact is required. As a teenager, Brantford had told me that he aspired to be a concert pianist, and I was the one who had to remind him that he wasn't a musician and didn't play the piano. But he had seen a fiery angel somewhere in the sky and thought it might descend on him. I hate those angels. I haven't always behaved well when people open their hearts to me.

"Well, what about the animals?" I asked. Brantford was always caring for damaged animals and had done so from the time he was a boy. He found them in streets and alleys and nursed them back to health and then let them go. But they tended to fall in with him and to get crushes on him. Wherever he lived you would find recovering cats, mutts, and sparrows barking and chirping and mewling in response to him.

"No, not that," he said. "I would never make a living off those critters," he said. "That's a sideline. I love them too much."

"Veterinary school?" I asked.

"No, I couldn't. Absolutely not. I don't want to practice that kind of medicine with them," he said, as if he were speaking of family members. "If I made money off those little guys, I'd lose the gift. Besides, I don't have the discipline to get through another school. Willpower is not my strong suit. The world is made out of willpower," he said, as if perplexed. He put his head back into his hands. "Willpower! Anyhow, would you please explain to me why it feels as if I've committed a murder?"


When I had first come to New York in the 1970s as an aspiring actor, I rode the subways everywhere, particularly the number 6, which in those days was still the Lexington IRT line. Sitting on that train one afternoon, squeezed between my fellow passengers as I helped one of them, a schoolboy, with a nosebleed, I felt pleased with myself. I had assimilated. Having come to New York from the Midwest, I was anticipating my big break and meanwhile waited tables at a little bistro near Astor Place. Mine was a familiar story, one of those drabby little tales of ideals and artistic high-mindedness that wouldn't bear repeating if it weren't for the woman with whom I was then involved.

She had a quietly insubstantial quality. When you looked away from her, you couldn't be sure that she'd still be there when you looked back again. She knew how to vanish quickly from scenes she didn't like. Her ability to dematerialize was purposeful and was complicated by her appearance: day and night, she wore dark glasses. She had sensitivity to light, a photophobia, which she had acquired as a result of a corneal infection. In those days, her casual friends thought that the dark glasses constituted a praiseworthy affectation. "She looks very cool," they would say.

Even her name—Giulietta, spelled in the Italian manner—seemed like an affectation. But Giulietta it was, the name with which, as a Catholic, she had been baptized. We'd met at the bistro where I carried menus and trays laden with food back and forth. Dining alone, cornered under a light fixture, she was reading a book by Bruno Bettelheim, and I deliberately served her a risotto entrée that she hadn't ordered. I wanted to provoke her to conversation, even if it was hostile. I couldn't see her eyes behind those dark glasses, but I wanted to. Self-possession in any form attracts me, especially at night, in cities. Anyway, my studied incompetence as a waiter amused her. Eventually she gave me her phone number.

She worked in Brooklyn at a special school for mildly autistic and emotionally impaired little kids. The first time we slept together we had to move the teddy bears and the copies of the *New Yorker* off her bed. Sophistication and a certain childlike guilelessness lived side by side in her behavior. On Sunday morning she watched cartoons and *Meet the Press,* and in the afternoon she listened to the Bartók quartets while smoking marijuana, which she claimed was good for her eyesight. In her bathtub was a rubber duck, and in the living room a copy of *Anna Karenina,* which she had read three times.

We were inventive and energetic in our lovemaking, Giulietta and I, but her eyes stayed hidden no matter how dark it was. From her, I knew nothing of the look of recognition a woman can give to a man. All the same, I was beginning to love her. She comforted me and sustained me by attaching me to ordinary things: reading the Sunday paper in bed, making bad jokes—the rewards of plain everyday life.

One night I took her uptown for a party near Columbia, at the apartment of another actor, Freddy Avery, who also happened to be a poet. Like many actors, Freddy enjoyed performing and was good at mimicry, and his parties tended to be raucous. You could easily commit an error in tone at those parties. You'd expose yourself as a hayseed if you were too sincere about anything. There was an Iron Law of Irony at Freddy's parties, so I was worried that if Giulietta and I arrived too early, we'd be mocked. No one was ever prompt at Freddy's parties (they always began at their midpoint, if I could put it that way), so we ducked into a bar to waste a bit of time before going up.

Under a leaded-glass, greenish lamp hanging down over our booth, Giulietta took my hand. "We don't have to go to this . . . thing," she said. "We could just escape to a movie and then head home."

"No," I said. "We have to do this. Anyway, all the movies have started."

"What's the big deal with this party, Benjamin?" she asked me. I couldn't see her eyes behind her dark glasses, but I knew they were trained on me. She wore a dark blue blouse, and her hair had been pinned back with a rainbow-colored barrette. The fingers of her hands, now on the table, had a long, aristocratic delicacy, but she bit her nails; the tips of her fingers had a raggedy appearance.

"Oh, interesting people will be there," I said. "Other actors. And literary types, you know, and dancers. They'll make you laugh."

"No," she said. "They'll make *you* laugh." She took a sip of her beer. She lit up a cigarette and blew the smoke toward the ceiling. "Dancers can't converse anyway. They're all autoerotic. If we go to this, I'm only doing it because of you. I want you to know that."

"Thank you," I said. "Listen, could you do me a favor?"

"Anything," she nodded.

"Well, it's one of those parties where the guests . . ."

"What?"

"It's like this. Those people are clever. You know, it's one of those uptown crowds. So what I'm asking is . . . do you think you could be clever tonight, please? As a favor to me? I know you can be like that. You can be funny; I know you, Giulietta. I've seen you sparkle. So could you be amusing? That's really all I ask."

This was years ago. Men were still asking women—or telling them—how to behave in public. I flinch, now, thinking about that request, but it didn't seem like much of anything to me back then. Giulietta leaned back and took her hand away from mine. Then she cleared her throat.

"You are so funny." She wasn't smiling. She seemed to be evaluating me. "Yes," she said. "Yes, all right." She dug her right index fingernail into the wood of the table, as if making a calculation. "I can be clever if you want me to be."


After buzzing us up, Freddy Avery met us at the door of his apartment with an expression of jovial melancholy. "Hey hey hey," he said, ushering us in. "Ah. And this is Giulietta," he continued, staring at her dark glasses and her rainbow barrette. "Howdy do. You look like that character in the movie where the flowers started singing. Wasn't that sort of freaky and great?" He didn't wait for our answer. "It was a special effect. Flowers don't actually know *how* to sing. So it was sentimental. Well," he said, "now that you're both here, you brave kids should get something to drink. Help yourselves. Welcome, like I said." Even Freddy's bad grammar was between quotation marks.

Giulietta drifted away from me, and I found myself near the refrigerator listening to a tall, strikingly attractive brunette. She didn't introduce herself. With a vaguely French accent, she launched into a little speech. "I have something you must explain," she said. "I can't make good sense of who I am now. And so, what am I? First I am a candidate for one me, and then I am another. I am blown about. Just a little leaf—that is my self. What do you think I will be?" She didn't wait for me to answer. "I ask, 'Who am I, Renée?' I cannot sleep, wondering. Is life like this, in America? Full of such puzzles? Do you believe it is like this?"

I nodded. I said, "That's a very good accent you have there." She began to forage around in her purse as if she hadn't heard me. I hurried toward the living room and found myself in a corner next to another guest, the famous Pulitzer prize–winning poet Burroughs Hammond, who was sitting in the only available chair. Freddy had befriended him, I had heard, at a literary gathering and had taught him how to modulate his voice during readings. At the present moment, Burroughs Hammond was gripping a bottle of ginger ale and was smoking an unfiltered mentholated cigarette. No one seemed to be engaging him in conversation. Apparently, he had intimidated the other guests, all of whom had wandered away from his corner.

I knew who he was. Everyone did. He was built like a linebacker—he had played high-school football in Ohio—but he had a perpetually oversensitive expression on his wide face. "The hothouse flower inside the

Mack truck" was one phrase I had heard to describe him. He had survived bouts of alcoholism, two broken marriages, and losing custody of
his children, and had finally moved to New York, where he had sobered
up. His poems, some of which I knew by heart, typically dealt with the
sudden explosion of the inner life in the midst of an almost fatal loneliness. I particularly liked the concluding lines of "Poem with Several
Birds," about a moment of resigned spiritual radiance.

> Some god or other must be tracing, now,
> its way, *this* way, and the blossoms
> like the god are suspended in midair,
> and seeing shivers in the face of all this brilliance.

I had repeated those lines to myself as I waited tables and took orders
for salads. The fierce delicacy of Burroughs Hammond's poetry! On
those nights when I had despaired and had waited for a god, any one of
them, to arrive, his poetry had kept me sane. So when I spotted him at
Freddy Avery's, I introduced myself and told him that I knew his poems
and loved them. Gazing up at me through his thick horn-rim glasses, he
asked politely what I did for a living. I said I waited tables, was an unemployed actor, and was working on a screenplay. He asked me what my
screenplay was about and what it was called. I told him that it was a horror film and was entitled *Planet of Bugs.*

My screenplay had little chance of intriguing the poet, and at that
moment I remembered something that Lorca had once said to Neruda. I
thought it might get Burroughs Hammond's attention. " 'The greatest
poet of the age,' " I said, "to quote Lorca, 'is Mickey Mouse.' So my
ambition is to get great poetry up on the screen, just as Walt Disney did.
Comic poetry. And horror poetry, too. Horror has a kind of poetry up
on the screen. But I think most poets just don't get it. But you do. I
mean, Yeats didn't understand. He couldn't even write a single play with
actual human beings in it. His Irish peasants—! And T. S. Eliot's plays!
All those Christian zombies. Zombie poetry written for other zombies.
They were both such rotten playwrights—they thought they knew the
vernacular, but they didn't. That's a real failing. Their time is past. You're
a better poet, and when critics in the future start to evaluate—"

"You," he said. He lifted his right arm and pointed at me. Suddenly I
felt that I was in the presence of an Old Testament prophet who wasn't

kidding and had never been kidding about anything. "You are the scum of the earth," he said calmly. I backed away from him. He continued to point at me. "You are the scum of the earth," he repeated.

Everyone was looking at him, and when that job had been completed, everyone was looking at me. Some Charles Mingus riffs thudded out of the record player. Then the other guests started laughing at the show of my embarrassment. I glanced around to see if I could detect where Giulietta had gone to, because I needed to make a rapid escape from that party and I needed her to help me demonstrate a certain mindfulness. But she wasn't anywhere now that I needed her, not in the living room, not in the kitchen, or the hallway, or the bathroom. After searching for her, I descended the stairs from the apartment as quickly as I could and found myself back out on the street.

Now, years later, I no longer remember which one of the nearby subway stops I found that night. I can remember the consoling smell of New York City air, the feeling that perhaps anonymity might provide me with some relief. I shouted at a light pole. I walked a few blocks, brushed against several pedestrians, descended another set of stairs, reached into my pocket, and pulled out a subway token. In my right hand, I discovered that I was still holding on to a plastic cup with beer in it.

Only one other man stood on the subway platform that night. The express came speeding through on the middle tracks. The trains were all spray-painted with graffiti in those days, and they'd rattle into the stations looking like giant multicolored mechanical caterpillars—amusement park rides scrawled over with beautifully creepy hieroglyphs preceded by a tornado-like racket and a blast of salty fetid air.

The other man standing on the platform looked like the winos that Burroughs Hammond had written about in his fragmentary hymns to life following those nights he had spent in the drunk tank. *No other life could be as precious to me / as this one,* he had written. If only I could experience some kindly feeling for a stranger, I thought, possibly I might find myself redeemed by the fates who were quietly ordering my humiliations, one after the other.

Therefore, I did what you never do on a subway platform. I exchanged a glance with the other man.

He approached me. On his face there appeared for a moment an expression of the deepest lucidity. He raised his eyelids as if flabbergasted by my very existence. I noticed that he was wearing over his torn shirt a leather vest stained with dark red blotches—blood or wine, I suppose now. He wore no socks. For the second time that evening, someone pointed at me. "That's a beer you have," he said, his voice burbling up as if through clogged plumbing. "Is there extra?"

I handed over the plastic cup to him. He took a swig. Then, his eyes deep in mad concentration, he yanked down his trousers' zipper and urinated into the beer. He handed the cup back to me.

I took the cup out of this poor madman's grasp, put it down on the subway platform, and then I hauled back and slugged him in the face. He fell immediately. My knuckles stung. He began to crawl toward the subway tracks, and I heard distantly the local train rumbling toward the station, approaching us. With the studied calm of an accomplished actor who has had one or two early successes, I left that subway station and ascended the stairs two at a time to the street. Then, conscience-crippled and heartsick, I went back. I couldn't see the man I had hit. Finally I returned to the street and flagged down a taxi and rode to my apartment.

For the next few days, I checked the newspapers for reports of an accidental death in the subway of a drunk who had crawled into the path of a train, and when I didn't find any such story, I began to feel as if I had dreamed up the entire evening from start to finish, or, rather, that someone else had dreamed it up for me and put me as the lead actor into it— this cautionary tale whose moral was that I had no gift for the life I'd been leading. I took to bed the way you do when you have to think something out. My identity having overtaken me, I called in sick to the restaurant and didn't manage to get to an audition I had scheduled. A lethargy thrummed through me, and I dreamed that someone pointed at my body stretched out on the floor and said, "It's dead." What frightened me was not my death, but that pronoun. "I" had become an "it."

There's no profit in dwelling on the foolishness of one's youth. Everyone's past is a mess. And I wouldn't have thought of my days as an actor if it weren't for my cousin Brantford's having told me twenty years later over lunch in an expensive restaurant that he felt as if he had killed someone, and if my cousin and I hadn't had a kind of solidarity. By that time, Giulietta and I had children of our own, two boys, Elijah and Jacob, and the guttering seediness that was the New York of the 1970s was distant history, and I only came to the city to visit my cousin and my aunt. By then, I was a visitor from Minnesota, where we had moved and where I was a partner in the firm of Wilwersheid and Lampe. I was no longer an inhabitant of New York. I had become a family man and a tourist.

Do I need to prove that I love my wife and children, or that my existence has become terribly precious to me? Once, back then in my twenties, all I wanted to do was to throw my life away. But then, somehow, usually by accident, you experience joy. And the problem with joy is that it binds you to life; it makes you greedy for more happiness. You experience avarice. You hope it will go on forever.

A day or so after having lunch with Brantford, I went up to visit Aunt Margaret. She had started to bend over from the osteoporosis that would cripple her, or maybe it was the calcium-reducing effects of her anti-depressant and the diet of kung pao chicken, vodka, and cigarettes that she lived on. She was terrifyingly lucid, as always. The vodka merely seemed to have sharpened her wits. She was so unblurred, I hoped she wasn't about to go into one of her tailspins. Copies of *Foreign Affairs* lay around her apartment near the porcelain figurines. NPR drifted in from a radio on the windowsill. She had been reading Tacitus, she told me. "*The Annals of Imperial Rome.* Have you ever read it, Benjamin?"

"No," I said. I sank back on the sofa, irritating one of the cats, who leapt up away from me before taking up a position on the windowsill.

"You should. I can't read the Latin anymore, but I can read it in English. Frighteningly relevant. During the reign of Tiberius, Sejanus's daughter is arrested and led away. 'What did I do? Where are you taking me? I won't do it again,' this girl says. My God. Think of all the thousands who have said those very words in this century. I've said them myself. I used to say them to my father."

"Your father?"

"Of course. He could be cruel. He would lead me away, and he punished me. He probably had his reasons. He knew me. Well, I *was* a terrible girl," she said dreamily. "I was willful. Always getting into situations. I was . . . forward. *There's* an antiquated adjective. Well. These days, if I were young again, I could come into my own, no one would even be paying the slightest attention to me. I'd go from boy to boy like a bee sampling flowers, but in those days, they called us 'wild' and they hid us away. Thank god for progress. Have you seen Brantford, by the way?"

I told her that I had had lunch with him and that he had said that he felt as if he had killed somebody.

"Really. I wonder what he's thinking. He must be all worn out. Is he still drinking? Did he tell you about his girlfriend? That child of his?"

"What child? No, he didn't tell me. Who's this?"

"Funny that he didn't tell you." She stood up and went over to a miniature grandfather clock, only eight inches high, on the mantel. "Heavens," she said, "where are my manners? I should offer you some tea. Or maybe a sandwich." This customary politeness sounded odd coming from her.

"No, thank you." I shook my head. "Aunt Margaret, what child are you talking about?"

"It's not a baby, not yet. Don't misunderstand me. They haven't had a baby, those two. But Brantford's found a girlfriend, and she might as well be a baby, she's so young. Eighteen years old, for heaven's sake. He discovered her in a department store, selling clothes behind the counter. Shirts and things. She's another one of his strays. And of course he doesn't have a dime to his name anymore, and he takes her everywhere on his credit cards when he's not living off of her, and he still doesn't have a clue what to do with himself. Animals all over the place, but no job. He spends all day teaching dogs how to walk and birds how to fly. I suppose it's my fault. They'll blame me. They blame me for everything."

"What's her name? This girl?" I asked. "He didn't mention her to me."

"Camille," Aunt Margaret told me. "And of course she's beautiful— they *all* are, at that age—but so what? A nineteenth-century name and a beautiful face and figure and no personality at all and no money. They think love is everything, and they get sentimental, but love really isn't much. Just a little girl, this Camille. She likes the animals, of course, but she doesn't know what she's getting into with him." She looked at me slyly. "Do you still envy him? You mustn't envy or pity him, you know. And how is Giulietta?" Aunt Margaret had never approved of Giulietta and thought my marriage to her had been ill-advised. "And your darling children? Those boys? How are they, Benjamin?"


Aunt Margaret turned out to be wrong about Camille, who was not a sentimentalist after all. I met her for the first time at the memorial service five years after she and my cousin Brantford had become a couple.

By then, she and Brantford had had a son, Robert, and my cousin had ended his life by stepping out into an intersection into the path of an oncoming taxi at the corner of Park Avenue and Eighty-second Street. If he couldn't live in that neighborhood, he could at least die there. He suffered a ruptured spleen, and his heart stopped before they admitted him to the ER. He had entered that intersection against a red light—it was unclear whether he had been careless or suicidal, but it was midday and my cousin *was* accustomed to city traffic. Well. You always want to reserve judgment, but the blood analysis showed that he had been sober. I wish he had been drunk. We could have blamed it on that, and it would have been a kind of consolation.

One witness reported that Brantford had rushed onto Park Avenue to rescue a dog that had been running south. Maybe that was it.

In the months before his death, he had found a job working in the produce department at a grocery. When he couldn't manage the tasks that he considered beneath him—stacking the pears and lining up the tomatoes—he took a position as a clerk behind the counter at a pet food store on Avenue B. A name tag dangled from his shirt. He told me by telephone that he hated that anyone coming into the store could find out his first name and then use it. That offended him. But he loved that store and could have worked there forever if it hadn't gone out of business. After that, he worked briefly at a collection agency making phone calls to deadbeats. He edited one issue of a humorous Web literary magazine entitled *The Potboiler*. What Brantford had expected from life and what it had actually given him must have been so distinct and so dissonant that he probably felt his dignity dropping away little by little until he simply wasn't himself anymore. He didn't seem to be anybody and he had no resources of humility to turn that nothingness into a refuge. He and Camille lived in a cluttered little walk-up in Brooklyn. I think he must have felt quietly panic-stricken, him and his animals. Time was going to run out on all of them. There would be no more fixes.

I wanted to help him—he was almost a model for me, but not quite—but I didn't know how to exercise compassion with him, or how to express the pity that Aunt Margaret said I shouldn't feel. I think my example sometimes goaded him into despair, as did his furred and feathered patients, who couldn't stand life without him.

At the memorial service, Camille carried the baby in a front pack, and she walked through the doors of the church in a blast of sunlight that seemed to cascade around her and then to advance before her as she proceeded up the aisle. Sunlight from the stained-glass windows caught her in momentary droplets and parallelograms of blues and reds. When she reached the first pew, she projected the tender, brave dignity of a woman on whom too many burdens have been placed too quickly.

Afterward, following the eulogies and the hymns, Camille and I stood out on the lawn. Aunt Margaret, with whom I had been sitting, had gone back to her apartment in a hired car. Camille had seemed surprised by me and had given me an astonished look when I approached her, my hand out.

"Ah, it's you," she said. "The cousin. I wondered if you'd come."

I gave her a hug.

"Sorry," she said, tearfully grinning. "You startled me. You're family, and your face is a little like Branty's. You have the same cheerful scowl, you two." She lifted baby Robert, who had been crying, out of the front pack, opened her blouse, drew back her bra, and set the baby there to nurse. "Why didn't you ever come to see us?" she asked me, fixing me with a steady expression of wonderment as she nursed the baby. "He loved you. He said so. He called you Bunny. Just like one of his animals."

"Yes. I didn't think . . . I don't think that Brantford wanted me to see him," I said. "And it was always like a zoo, wherever he was."

"That's unkind. We had to give the animals away, back to the official rescuers. It was *not* like a zoo. Zoos are noisy. The inmates don't want to be there. Brantford's creatures loved him and kept still if he wanted them to be. Why'd you say that? I'm sure he invited you over whenever you were in town."

She looked at me with an expression of honesty, solemn and accusing. I said, "Isn't it a beautiful day?"

"Yes. It's always a beautiful day. That's not the subject."

I had the feeling that I would never have a normal conversation with this woman. "You were so *good* for him," I blurted out, and her expression did not change. "But you should have seen through him. He must have wanted to keep you for himself and his birds and cats and dogs. You were his last precious possession. And, no, he really *didn't* invite me to meet you. Something happened to him," I said, a bit manically. "He turned into something he hadn't been. Maybe that was it. Being poor."

"Oh," she said, after turning back toward me and sizing me up, "*poor.* Well. We liked being poor. It was sort of Buddhist. It was harder for him than for me. We lived as a family, I'll say that. And I loved him. He was a sweetie, and very devoted to me and Robert and his animals." She hoisted the baby and burped him. "He had a very old soul. He wasn't a suicide, if that's what you're thinking. Are you all right?"

"Why?"

"You look like you're going to faint."

"Oh, I'm managing," I said. In truth, my head felt as if the late-afternoon sunlight were going right through the skull bones with ease, soaking the gray matter with photons. "Listen," I asked her, "do you want to go for a drink?"

"I can't drink," she said. "I'm nursing. And you're married, and you have children." How old-fashioned she was! I decided to press forward anyway.

"All right, then," I said. "Let's have coffee."


There is a peculiar lull that takes over New York in early afternoon, around two thirty. In the neighborhood coffee shops, the city's initial morning energy drains out and a pleasant tedium, a trance, holds sway for a few minutes. In any other civilized urban setting, the people would be taking siestas. Here, voices grow subdued and gestures remain incomplete. You lean back in your chair to watch the vapor trails aimed toward LaGuardia or Newark, and for once no one calls you, there is nothing to do. Radios are tuned to baseball, and conversations stop as you drift off to imagine the runner on second, edging toward third. Camille and I went into a little greasy spoon called Here to Eat and sat down at a table near the front window. The cook stared out at the blurring sidewalk, his eyelids heavy. He seemed massively indifferent to our presence and our general needs. The server barely noticed that we were there. She sat at one of the counter stools working on a crossword. No one even looked up.

Eventually the server brought us two cups of stale, burned coffee.

"At last," I said. "I thought it'd never come."

The baby was asleep in the crook of Camille's right arm. After a few minutes of pleasantries, Camille asked me, "So. Why are you here?"

"Why am I here? I'm here because of Brantford. For his memory. We were always close."

"You were?" she said.

"I thought so," I replied.

Her face, I now noticed, had the roundedness that women's faces acquire after childbirth. Errant bangs fell over her forehead, and she blew a stream of air upward toward them. She gave me a straight look. "He talked about you as his long-lost brother, the one who never came to see him."

"Please. I—"

She wasn't finished. "You look alike," she said, "but that doesn't mean that you were close. You could have been his identical twin and you wouldn't have been any closer to him than you are now. Anyway, what was I asking? Oh, yes. Why are you *here*? With me? Now."

"For coffee. To talk. To get to know you." I straightened my necktie. "After all, he was my cousin." I thought for a moment. "I loved him. He was better than me. I need to talk about him, and you didn't plan a reception. Isn't that unusual?"

"No, it isn't. You wanted to get to know me?" She leaned back and licked her chapped lips.

"Yes."

"Kind of belated, isn't it?" She sipped the hot coffee and then set it down. "The *mom*. A little chitchat over coffee with *the mom*."

"Belated?"

"It's a bit sudden, isn't it? That desire? Given the circumstances?" She gazed out the window, then lifted the baby to her shoulder again. "For the personal intimacies? For the details?" Her sudden modulation in tone was very pure. So was her irony. She had a kind of emotional Puritanism that despised the parade of shadows on the wall, of which I was the current one.

"Okay. Why do you think I'm here?" I asked her, taken aback by her behavior. The inside of my mouth had turned to cotton; rudeness does that to me.

"You're here to exercise your compassion," she said quickly. "And to serve up some awful belated charity. And, finally, to patronize me." She smiled at me. "*La belle pauvre.* How's that? Think that sounds about right?"

"You're a tough one," I said. "I wasn't going to patronize you at all."

She squirmed in the booth as if her physical discomfort could be shed from her skin and dropped on the floor. "Well, you probably weren't planning on it, I'll give you credit for that." She poured more cream into her coffee. My heart was thumping away in my chest. "Look at you," she said. "God damn it, you have a crush on me. I can tell. I can always tell about things like that." She started humming "In a Sentimental Mood." After a moment, she said, "You men. You're really something, you guys." She bit at a fingernail. "At least Branty had his animals. They'll escort him into heaven."

"I don't know why you're talking this way to me," I said. "You're being unnecessarily cruel."

"It's my generation," she said. "We get to the point. But I went a bit too far. It's been a hard day. I was crying all morning. I can't think straight. My apologies."

"Actually," I said, "I don't get you at all." This wasn't quite true.

"Good. At last."

We sat there for a while.

"You're a lawyer, aren't you?"

"Yes," I said. She stirred her coffee. Her spoon clicked against the cup.

"Big firm?"

"Yes." Outside the diner, traffic passed on Lexington. The moon was visible in the sky. I could see it.

"Well, do me a favor, all right? Don't ask me about Brantford's debts." She settled back in the booth, while the server came and poured more burned coffee into her cup. "I don't need any professional advice just now."

I stared at her.

"Actually," she said, "I *could* use some money. To tide me over, et cetera. Your aunt Margaret said that you would generously donate something for the cause." She gave me a vague look. " 'Benjamin will come to your aid,' she said. And, yes, I can see that you will." She smiled. "Think of me as a wounded bird."

"How much do you need?" I asked.

"You really love this, don't you?" She gave me another careless smile. "You're in your element."

"No," I said. "I'm not sure I've ever had a conversation like this before."

"Well, you've had it now. Okay," she said. "I'll tell you what. You have my address. Send me a check. You'll enjoy sending the check, and then more checks after that. So that's your assignment. You're one of those guys who loves to exercise his pity, his empathy. You're one of those rare, sensitive men with a big bank account. Just send that check."

"And in return?"

"In return," she said, "I'll like you. I'll have a nice meal with you whenever you're in town. I'll give you a grateful little kiss on the cheek." She began to cry and then, abruptly, stopped. She pulled out a handkerchief from her purse and blew her nose.

"No, you won't. Why on earth do you say that?"

"You're absolutely right, I won't. I wanted to see how you'd react. I thought I'd rattle your cage. I'm grief-stricken. And I'm giddy." She laughed merrily, and the baby startled and lifted his little hands. "Poor guy, you'll never figure out any of this."

"Exactly right," I said. "You think I'm oblivious to things, don't you?"

"I have no idea, but if I do think so," she said thoughtfully, "I'll let you know. I didn't fifteen minutes ago."

"It seems," I said, "that you want to keep me in a posture of perpetual contrition." I was suddenly proud of that phrase. It summed everything up.

"Ha. 'Perpetual contrition.' Well, that'd be a start. You really *don't* know what Brantford thought of you, do you? Look: call your wife. Tell her about me. It'd be good for you, good for you both. Because you're . . ."

I reached out and took her hand before she could pronounce the condemning adjective or the noun she had picked out. It was a preemptive move. "That's quite enough," I said. I held on to her hand for dear life. The skin was warm and damp, and she didn't pull it away. For five minutes we sat there holding hands in silence. Then I dropped some money on the table for the coffee. Her baby began to cry. I identified with that sound. As I stood up, she said, "You shouldn't have been afraid."

She was capable of therapeutic misrepresentation. I knew I would indeed start sending her those checks before very long—thousands of dollars every year. It would go on and on. I would be paying this particular bill forever. I owed them that.

"I'm a storm at sea," she said. "A basket case. Who knows? We might become friends after all." She laughed again, inappropriately (I thought), and I saw on her arm a tattoo of a chickadee, and on the other arm, a tattoo of a smiling dog.

Back in the hotel, I called Giulietta, and I told her everything that Camille had ordered me to say.

———

That night, I walked down a few blocks to a small neighborhood market, where I stole a Gala apple—I put it into my jacket pocket—and a bunch of flowers, which I carried out onto the street, holding them ostentatiously in front of me. If you have the right expression on your face, you can shoplift anything. I had learned that from my acting classes. More than enough money resided in my wallet for purchases, but shoplifting apparently was called for. It was an emotional necessity. I packed the apple in my suitcase and took the flowers into the hotel bathroom and put them into the sink before filling the sink with water. But I realized belatedly that there was no way I would be able to get them back home before they wilted.

So after I had arrived in the Minneapolis airport the next day, I bought another spray of flowers from one of those airport florists. Out on the street, I found a cab.

The driver smiled at the flowers I was carrying. "Very nice. You are surely a gentleman," he said, with a clear, clipped accent. I asked him where he was from, and he said he was Ethiopian. I told him that at first I had thought that perhaps he was a Somali, since so many cabdrivers in Minneapolis were from there.

He made an odd guttural noise. "Oh, no, not Somali," he said. "*Extremely* not. I am Ethiopian . . . very different," he said. "We do not look the same, either," he said crossly.

I complimented him on his excellent English. "Yes, yes," he said impatiently, wanting to get back to the subject of Ethiopians and Somalis. "We Ethiopians went into their country, you know. Americans do not always realize this. The Somalis should have been grateful to us, but they were not. They never are. We made an effort to stop their civil war. But they *like* war, the Somalis. And they do not respect the law, so it is *all* war, to them. A Somali does not respect the law. He does not have it in him."

I said that I didn't know that.

"For who are those flowers?" he asked. "Your wife?"

"Yes," I told him.

"They are pretty except for the lilies." He drove onto the entry ramp on the freeway. The turn signal in the cab sounded like a heart monitor. "Myself, I do not care for lilies. Do you know what we say about Somalis, what we Ethiopians say? We say, 'The Somali has nine hearts.' This means: a Somali will not reveal his heart to you. He will reveal a false heart, not his true one. But you get past that, in time, and you get to the second heart. This heart is also and once again false. In repetition you will be shown and told the thing which is not. You will never get to the ninth heart, which is the true one, the door to the soul. The Somali keeps that heart to himself."

"The thing which is not?" I asked him. Outside, the sun had set.

"You do not understand this?" He looked at me in the rearview mirror. "This very important matter?"

"Well, maybe I do," I said. "You know, my wife works with Somali children."

The cabdriver did not say anything, but he tugged at his ear.

"Somali children in Minneapolis have a very high rate of autism," I said. "It's strange. No one seems to knows why. Some say it's the diet, some say that they don't get enough sunlight. Anyway, my wife works with Somali children."

"Trying to make them normal?" the cabdriver asked. "Oh, well. You are a good man, to give her flowers." He gazed out at the night. "Look at this dark air," he said. "It will snow soon."


With my suitcase, my apple, and my flowers, I stood waiting on the front porch of our house. Instead of unlocking the door as I normally would have, I thought I would ring the bell just as a stranger might, someone hoping to be welcomed and taken in. I always enjoyed surprising Giulietta and the boys whenever I returned from trips, and with that male pride in homecoming from a battle, large or small, I was eager to tell them tales about where I had been and what I had done and whom I had defeated and the trophies with which I had returned. Standing on the welcome mat, I looked inside through the windows into the entry-way and beyond into the living room, and I saw my son Jacob lying on the floor reading from his history textbook. His class had been studying the American Revolution. He ran his hand through his hair. He needed a haircut. He had a sweet, studious look on his face, and I felt proud of him beyond measure. I rang the bell. They would all rush to greet me.

The bell apparently wasn't working, and Jacob didn't move from his settled position. I would have to fix that bell. Again I rang and again no one answered. If it had made a noise, I couldn't hear it. So I went around to the back, brushing past the hateful peonies, stepping over a broken sidewalk stone, and I took up a spot in the grassy yard, still carrying my spray of flowers. Behind me, I could smell a skunk, and I heard a car alarm in the distance. If I had been Brantford, all the yard animals would have approached me. But if I had been Brantford, I wouldn't be living in this house. I wouldn't be here.

Giulietta sat in the back den. I could see her through the windows. She was home-tutoring a little Somali girl along a floor balance beam, and when that task was finished, they began to toss a beanbag back and forth to each other, practicing midline exercises. Her parents sat on two chairs by the wall, watching her, the mother dressed in a flowing robe.

I felt the presence of my cousin next to me out there in the yard, and in that contagious silence I was reminded of my beautiful wife and children who were stubbornly not coming to the door in response to my little joke with the doorbell. So I rapped on the window, expecting to startle Giulietta, but when she looked up, I could not see through her dark glasses to where she was looking, nor could I tell whether she saw me.

I have loved this life so much. I was prepared to wait out there forever.

# The Winner

IN THE HILLS BORDERING Lake Superior's northern shore, Krumholtz was lost. Behind the wheel, searching for a landmark, he had not seen a road sign or any other indication of a human presence for miles. The surface on which he had been driving had altered from asphalt pavement to rutted dirt, and the route appeared to be undecided about its direction. It had been headed north, but after a sharp curve, it had angled south again. The rotting telephone poles, without wires, had been listing down toward the ground and now had disappeared entirely, swallowed up by forest-matter.

Having advanced for the last half hour feeling that he had moved back into an era of primeval undergrowth, Krumholtz found himself in a thick wooded area of spruce and maple trees. They were edging closer to the road as one mile followed another. He had lost sight of the lake and was getting anxious about the time. He pulled his rental car over— there was no shoulder, just a patch of weedy grass—to consult his directions, which appeared to be contradictory. The rental car's GPS system wasn't working. Having little idea of where he was, exactly, he turned off the engine and got out of the car.

The sharp raw pine scent made him think of his childhood in rural Oregon. He noticed a hawk circling above him. Nearby to the right, a sumac bush displayed deep autumnal red leaves. When he looked at it, the leaves trembled, as if his gazing had caused the bush to shiver.

He took in a deep breath, then coughed. Slowly and with careful deliberation over word choices, he began cursing.

Krumholtz was a freelance journalist and had been assigned by *Success* magazine to interview the subject of February's cover story. Just as *Playboy* always had a foldout, *Success* always had a Winner. The title always appeared in uppercase format. February's Winner, James Mallard, lived back in this forest somewhere in a large compound of his own design, Krumholtz had been informed. His article on Mallard was to include a combination of background information and personal narrative—the rise to fortune, lifestyle choices, opinions, etc.—along with anecdotes about the winner's current well-being. To deserve a place in *Success,* the subject had to have made a significant mark measured in dollars. These feature articles, celebratory but not effusive or craven, would have as their subtext an understanding of the *complexity* of achieving great wealth. Seasonings of wit and irony were acceptable if dropped knowingly here and there throughout the article, but even a hint of skepticism in the face of affluence would be ruthlessly blue-penciled. "*Vogue* does not mock fashion, and *we* do not mock riches," Krumholtz's editor had told him. "The amassing of a large fortune is to the readers of our magazine a sweetly solemn thought."

James Mallard, pronounced Mall*ard,* British style, accent on the second syllable, had been difficult to research. The biography was paltry. He was almost an unknown. The Wikipedia article on him was "under revision," and several other Web articles on him had been withdrawn or were impossible to access. The print media had mostly ignored him. Mallard appeared to have lived and worked in the shadows. He "valued his privacy," according to one source. Colleagues of his had been reluctant to discuss anything about him over the phone. Voices dropped melodramatically when Mallard's name was mentioned. "I haven't talked to you, and you haven't made this call," one of Krumholtz's interviewees said to him.

A photographer, a stringer, would supposedly be sent out to do portraits-and-poolsides a few days after Krumholtz's interview, but that prospect now seemed unlikely, even preposterous, given the remoteness and isolation of Mallard's compound.

Krumholtz had never heard of Mallard before getting his assignment but was glad to have the work. Given the current economic climate, feature-article jobs like this one were drying up, as subscription levels plunged and newsstand sales declined. Even *Success* itself had experienced its first red-ink quarter, as if the act of reading about fortunes had become too laborious for the average would-be winner to master.

He checked his watch: two thirty. The hawk was still circling above him, and from the west a breeze touched his face. He heard a distant songbird, a melancholy warbling. He felt as if the song might be directed to him or against him.

According to the bits and pieces of information that Krumholtz had cobbled together, his subject, James Mallard, had been born on a farm in Iowa. The young man had lettered in football and had quarterbacked the hometown team in his senior year to a conference championship. He had been named prom king and class valedictorian before attending Dartmouth on a full scholarship, where he had participated in intramural sports including water polo and rugby. He had graduated cum laude with honors in economics. His nicknames had been "Duck" and "the Duckster." After having dropped out of business school at Northwestern, Mallard had attended Columbia Law (graduating in '93, specialty: patent law). Soon after receiving his law degree and passing the bar exam, he had married the former Jane Estes (Columbia, Class of 1992), with whom he had had two children, James "Jiminy" Mallard Jr. and Mary Stuart "Gubbie" Mallard. His hobbies were listed as mountain climbing and art collecting. Using finance capital borrowed from a fellow student at Dartmouth, Mallard had bought several apartment buildings in Lincoln, Nebraska, and Ann Arbor, Michigan. He had fixed them up, converted them to condos, sold them for a good profit, and then had escaped from the real estate market before the bottom fell out of it. As a consequence, he had won the annual King Midas Award from the Omaha Chamber of Commerce. A year later, with an electrical engineer as partner, he had founded a privately held medical tech start-up; this company, InnovoMedic, had formulated a proton-based imaging device now commonly used for diagnoses in hospitals worldwide, the financial rewards for which—Mallard owned the patent; he had bought out his partner—were in the high nine figures. After acquiring these great riches, Mallard had divorced Jane Estes, and in 2004 had married Eleanor "Ellie" Bacon-Starhope, no college degree listed, and had fathered two more children, the twins, Angus and Gretel, both homeschooled. He owned several houses, including a brownstone on the Upper West Side in New York, another one in the desert Southwest, and this one, near Lake Superior and the city of D———. Mallard also owned a freshwater yacht, the *Temps Perdu,* which apparently he rarely sailed. He was noted as a fund-raiser for the Democratic Party. He served on the boards of several hospitals and charities; however, he had not appeared in public for eighteen months.

Krumholtz's typical procedure was to research the winner and then to do follow-ups after the face-to-face interview. Most winners left behind them a slime trail of ex-wives and embittered business partners. But neither Mallard's ex-wife nor his business partners would agree to speak to Krumholtz.

He was watching the hawk, circling slowly above him. Aloud, Krumholtz said, "I am lost. I am *nowhere.*" He took out his cell phone to check the time. No signal.

Several hours before, sitting in an airport lounge before his flight to D———, attended by a pleasantly overweight server with ketchup stains on her apron, Krumholtz had searched through his fact sheet for an angle. Certainly the medical device. Perhaps the art collection? The trophy wife with the preposterous name? The failed ambition to be a business-school student? The trick of buying out his partner before the medical device began to spout gobbets of cash? The rural Iowa upbringing? The liberalism? The house outside of D———? None of it seemed particularly promising. In fact the entire biography was anti-promising. Mallard might fall into that dangerous category of rich people who were non-narratable, who were story-unworthy: invisible, bland Olympians with no apparent personality and no social graces and no worldly interests of any kind apart from the amassing of treasure. Hearing the announcement of his plane's departure, Krumholtz had tossed back his scotch, taken one last bite of his veggie-everything pizza, signaled to the server for the check, and, after having paid with the company's credit card, had made his way down to the gate, stumbling against a refuse container near a water fountain.

Nervously he had combed his hair on the jetway before getting on board. This ritual had kept all his airplanes aloft.

Seated in row 27, wedged in between a manufacturer's rep and a dozing matron, Krumholtz had felt an aurora of pain around his heart. He took two antacids from a roll in his pocket. After chewing and swallowing the tablets, which tasted of drywall, he felt the aurora diminish for a few moments before it returned with greater force, burning down his arm. He groaned inwardly as the plane hit an area of turbulence and the passengers were instructed to fasten their seat belts. The matron sitting next to him woke up and screamed once, quietly.

In D————, Krumholtz had picked up the keys for the rental car from an agent wearing rainbow suspenders. As soon as he found himself in traffic, he knew he had been misdirected. His goal had been Happy Valley Road, which led north out of the city in the general direction of Mallard's compound, but somehow he had detoured onto a collection of chain restaurants and stores on Sam Wallis Boulevard, which was not actually a boulevard but a narrow two-way street with left-turn lanes that appeared out of nowhere and traffic lights that turned red almost without warning. On both sides Krumholtz saw slumped drivers, their faces shadowed with glumly placid Christian resignation. He was used to the honking of defiant urban car horns, but here in D————, traffic proceeded within an ominous defeated silence. The GPS in the rental car had been disabled, but Krumholtz decided he wouldn't have been able to use it anyway. After stopping at a FirePower gas station for directions, he asked the kid behind the inside counter where Happy Valley Road was.

"You from here?" the kid asked. He did not make eye contact with Krumholtz.

"No."

"You want to get to Happy Valley Road?"

"Yes."

"Business?" The kid unwrapped a Charm Skool candy bar, then bit into it.

"Yeah. I'm going to see James Mallard."

The kid whistled between lips browned by milk chocolate. "You're going to see *him*? No one sees *him*. He's like Baron von Dracula or somebody. Also I heard he's blind."

"That's not what I heard," Krumholtz said.

"Huh. Reason I ask about Happy Valley," the kid said, "is that it's hard for outsiders to find." He took another bite of the candy bar and chewed thoughtfully. "You gotta turn around, go past the Señor Big Cheese and the On Spec! Glasses place, then angle past the curve where the U-Store-It thing is, and then you have to watch carefully, because Happy Valley Road is just past the Au Secours MegaDrug, there on the right."

"Thanks," Krumholtz said. "Thanks a lot. By the way, you've got a bit of chocolate, right there, on your chin."

"That's what I meant to do," the kid said. He turned around and opened the till, counting the singles, giving his back to Krumholtz.

Once out of D——— and headed up Happy Valley Drive, Krumholtz had consulted his directions. He was supposed to turn off Happy Valley onto Eitel Avenue, which would take him to County Road M, and then to Valhalla Road, where Mallard lived. But now, having twisted and turned on the roads that seemed to have no destination at all in mind, that wandered through swampy areas and then back up to rocky plateaus before descending again, he had found himself in this post-wilderness spot that looked as if the first-growth trees had been cut years ago before the spruce and maples had replaced them. He had never been in northern Minnesota before, but the manufacturer's rep on the airplane headed toward D——— had told him that there were still wolves up here. He could believe it. "Wolves," his fellow passenger had said. "And moose." The passenger sat back. "Oh, and the bears. I forgot to mention the bears. And they all eat things."

How many places could you find in the world where a cell phone wouldn't work? Krumholtz checked his watch again, a cheap drugstore brand, and noticed that it had stopped. The time was still two thirty and would be two thirty from now on. He was very late. Folding himself back into his car—he was a big man, and the top of his head had almost continual bruises and bumps from lintels and beams and overhead luggage racks and doorframes—he started the engine and edged forward back onto the road. Overhead, the hawk circled away.

Ahead of him the road began another series of indecisive twists and turns, heading into a forest so dense that a desolate canopy of branches blocked the sky and shielded the road from the sun. He felt as if he were drifting into a tunnel of vegetation where the usual norms had been reversed. Here the trees were permanent, but the route was temporary and subject to disappearance. At almost exactly the moment when Krumholtz thought he should turn the car around and head back, he came upon a long expanse of hurricane fencing with razor wire at its top. He saw a driveway on the right-hand side, and a high gated barrier with the word MALLARDHOF carved in wood at the top. The driveway, behind the fencing, angled up to a high bluff. A sign in front of the gate announced VALHALLA DRIVE. The hurricane fence stretched away in both directions, north and south.

An intercom with a white button stood in front of the gate. Krumholtz drove up in front of it and pressed the button.

"Yes?" A woman's voice.

"It's Jerry Krumholtz." He waited. The silence continued for five seconds, ten seconds, almost half a minute. "From *Success* magazine. I have an appointment? With James Mallard?"

Now he might have a story: Mallard, perhaps emulating Howard Hughes, feared the world's toxicity.

"It's been arranged. I'm here *to interview James Mallard.*"

From the forest came an insucking breath of wind.

"This interview was set up *a long time ago.* And . . . and a photographer will be here in a few days for the artwork."

He waited. The engine of the rental car hummed quietly.

"This *has all been arranged.* It's been agreed to."

"You don't have to plead," the voice on the intercom said. "Do you believe in angels?"

"Excuse me?"

"It's a simple question."

"Well, it may be simple, but I don't know."

"You don't know if you believe in angels?" Just then, the gate lifted as if on invisible wires, and Krumholtz drove in. He had the impression that video surveillance cameras were trained on him as his car made its way up a switchback dirt road around the bowl of a valley to the crest of the bluff, where he saw the house splayed out lengthwise across the top.

The house, Mallardhof, built of concrete and glass, commanded a distant view of Lake Superior in one direction and the forest in another. A green Jeep speckled with dried mud sat in the driveway along with a car whose make Krumholtz didn't recognize. A small perennial garden had been planted to the right of the garage. From where he had parked, Krumholtz could not quite see where the house ended; it just went on and on. It was in Martian Embassy style: ostentatiously inhuman. Near the front door was a display area consisting of a fragile-seeming pile of rocks, like a cairn, possibly a sculpture of some kind, encircled by bricks. The austere lavishness of the house presented the viewer with showy neutrality, as if the old styles of grandiose display—Italian palazzos,

Tudor palaces, and castles—had given way to a nondecorative fortress brutalism of glass and stone. How the floor-to-ceiling glass supported the concrete roof was a mystery, unless the glass was thicker than it appeared to be and was load-bearing, as required by law. Krumholtz did not feel like getting out of his rental car, but when he saw a woman emerging from the front door, he thought he had better get to work.

"Hello hello *hello*!" she said, smiling with what must have been forced cheer, but the smile was so dazzling that Krumholtz thought for a moment that she might actually be happy to see him. She wore beige capri pants and a simple gray blouse, and she looked, as the wives of the rich usually did, like a professional beauty. In fact she was terribly beautiful, so much so that he could hardly keep his eyes on her. Beautiful women had always made him shy, and gazing at this one was like looking at the sun. After a few seconds, he had to turn away. "Mr. Krumholtz," she said, holding out her hand. "I'm Ellie Mallard."

"Jerry," he said. "Please call me Jerry."

"I shall call you Mr. Krumholtz," she said, holding her ground. "For the sake of your *dignity.*" Her skin, which at first he had assumed to be deeply tanned, he now saw had a permanent attractive darkness to it. Did she have an African-American mother or grandmother? Or was her family Persian? How to ask such a question? Her black tangled hair fell down to her shoulders, and gold hoop earrings sparkled against her skin in the fading light. "Please come in," she said, holding the door open for him. "You must be tired out."

"Well, I got lost," he said.

"Everyone does. Absolutely *nobody* knows how to get here. I still get lost myself sometimes, when I'm not paying attention. But anyway you're here now, and welcome to Mallardhof."

"Why is it called Mallardhof?" he asked.

"No reason at all!" she said with a practiced dry humor. She moved fluidly, like the perfect beauty she was. "We just decided that it needed a name and that's the name we gave it. Maybe we should find another name. It's so German. What would *you* call it? Did you like the sculpture out in front? It's a Rocco Steiner."

"Very impressive," Krumholtz said absentmindedly. He was looking down the front hallway into the depths of the house: the corridor disappeared in the distance as if replicating the geometry of infinity. "My goodness," he said, under his breath.

"Goodness had nothing to do with it," she said, quoting Mae West, "but it *is* rather stupendous, I'll grant you that." The diamond on her finger was the size of a grape. "Of course we love it, but sometimes it's simply white-elephant time around here, especially on cleaning days and wash days."

"Yes. I'll bet. So. How many square feet *is* this house, anyway?" he asked, feeling her hand on his back as she guided him toward a living room—which he imagined to be the first of many—down the front hallway.

"No idea," she said. "Quite a few, but we never counted them up. Would you like a drink? Something to eat?" From invisible speakers came the sound of music: Bach, or Handel. Baroque something, performed on the original instruments: court music, yes, *The Water Music,* that was it. "You must be starving."

"No, thank you." On the wall, a flat-panel video screen showed a man's face contorting in agony, relaxing, smiling, then contorting in agony again. Hung next to it was another screen showing a woman who appeared to be shouting soundlessly for help. "What's that?"

"Oh, that diptych? That's an installation by Herb Cello, the video artist. He's a wonderful guy, do you know him? He's become *such* a good friend. It's called *Agony #6.* It's a poor title. I begged Herb to change it, but I do love his work, and after all Herb's a thoughtful guy even with his irony, and he has the right to name his pieces, because he's the artist. But, you know, there never was an *Agony #5.* Isn't that odd? Maybe it was the wrong kind of agony." The face on the video screen began to smile and then froze into that genial expression, as if shocked suddenly by open displays of sodomy. The effect was terrifying. "You see? It's *not* agony at all. You have to think about it. You're sure you wouldn't like something to drink? The sun's almost past the yardarm."

"No, really. I should start my interview with Mr. Mallard."

"Well, I could be mistaken, but I think Jimmy's in the tub. Earlier today he was outside making furniture, and I think he probably worked up quite a sweat. He was expecting you, you know, and after waiting for a while for you, and you didn't come, he went outside, and now he's back. He didn't expect you to be late."

"Yes," Krumholtz said. "I'm very sorry about that." Had she really just touched him on the cheek with the tips of her fingers? Why would she do such a thing?

"Why don't I show you around the house first?"

"All right. But if you don't mind my asking, what did you do before you met Mr. Mallard?"

"Me? Oh, that." She laughed humorlessly. "The past life. That's over, that life. I was a model. And I did some acting. Some TV movies and whatnot." The interior walls consisted of poured concrete, and now, when she touched part of the wall, it gave way under her hand—it was actually a door, invisibly hinged—and they stepped into another entryway, and then into a classroom, where two rather beautiful children were sitting at a long table, writing under the eye of a young Asian woman with straight black hair and reading glasses. Beyond them, the window, from floor to ceiling, gave a view of the woods. The young woman, the teacher, was also a great beauty. "That's our hired tutor, Ping," she said under her breath. "The children are homeschooled. Bonjour, Ping!"

"Bonjour, madame."

"Ping is from Beijing by way of Paris," Ellie Mallard said to Krumholtz. The children, Angus and Gretel, glanced up quickly at Krumholtz and, finding nothing in particular that interested them, turned back to their writing. They were dressed in identical shirts, trousers, and shoes. "All their classes are taught in French and Mandarin."

"Except science," Angus said sourly without looking up. "We do science in English. We just learned that when scientists split the atom, God got killed."

"Do you have children, Mr. Krumholtz?" Ellie Mallard asked, gazing directly into his eyes. He forced himself not to look away. What a weapon beauty could be, and only the rich could own it.

"Yes," he said. "I have two daughters."

"Jimmy and I, we believe in public schooling," Ellie Mallard said, waving her hand at the schoolroom and the overhead projector and maps of the world, "but the local school is *much* too far away, and the school bus doesn't even come out here, as you can imagine. So there's no way to get there. We're just lucky to get the *mail*! Besides, I think children should learn foreign languages, don't you? Given the world that they will be entering?"

"Maybe so," Krumholtz said. "But French? I understand the need for Chinese, but French . . ."

"Mandarin for work, French for *play*!" Ellie Mallard said brightly. "Well, we mustn't take up any more of the children's time." She closed the concrete door behind her. Krumholtz heard Gretel saying good-bye as the door silently shut.

"I'd be teaching them Spanish, myself," he said.

"Oh, Spanish is so easy, they can just pick it up along the way. And, what, they're going to live in *Mexico*?" She threw her head back and laughed. "It's just a *hobby* language, don't you think? Or of servitude?" Krumholtz's older daughter was learning Spanish and finding it difficult going. "Now here," she said, returning to the main hallway, "is one of our Bento Schwartz photographs. Do you like it?" She gazed at it thoughtfully. "I think it's *quite* marvelous."

The photograph was large, three feet by about five feet. It appeared to be a photograph of a trash heap. "What is it?" Krumholtz asked.

"Well, it's part of a series called *Disposed*," she said. "This one, by coincidence, since we were just talking about Mexico, this one is of the Mexico City landfill. It's a digital photograph, but Bento has *personally* colorized some of the objects in it, such as that bucket in the foreground. Isn't it a beautiful blue? I think it's ravishing. He paints over certain objects to give them, I don't know, a *feeling*. I always find something new in the photograph to study every time I look at it. It has quite an aura. Because of the colors. And the detail. And the dynamic negative space. Do you know Bento's photographs?"

"No," Krumholtz said. "Bento Schwartz?"

"He's very well known," she said doubtfully. Krumholtz had taken out his small notebook and was writing down the names of the artists he had heard her mention, and he was making an effort to get the details about the photograph. Squatters' shacks rested on the landfill, and Krumholtz could see the squatters, miserable wretches, inside them. Krumholtz felt an old familiar hatred of the rich welling up inside him. They were all obtuse in an almost comical way. He looked down and saw that Mrs. Mallard was barefoot. "Why did you ask me about angels?"

"Excuse me?"

"When I was in the car, at the gate, before you buzzed me in, you asked me whether I believe in angels."

"I did? No, I don't think so. Why would I do that? I didn't buzz you in. It might have been Lorraine. Lorraine is the other woman. Incidentally, I should have asked you whether you'd like to freshen up." She turned and gazed at him again. "The bathroom's right here." She pointed at the opposite wall.

"Oh, okay," he said. "Where is it? I don't see it."

She touched the wall, and the concrete gave way again, and Krumholtz, who now felt like an angry resentful ambassador-without-portfolio from a Third World country, walked in. The lights flickered on automatically, as did the exhaust fan. He was surprised to find an ordinary toilet, humiliated by its functionality, in front of him, but on the wall above the toilet was a small signed pencil drawing by Paul Klee, and near the washstand and toilet was a waist-high table on which were piled several books. At the top was a signed first edition of Kurt Vonnegut's *Mother Night.* Beneath it were other signed editions of James Baldwin's *Go Tell It on the Mountain,* Adrienne Rich's *Selected Poems,* and T. S. Eliot's *Ash Wednesday,* just the book to have around when you were scrubbing your hands. So far, he hadn't seen books anywhere else in the house. Krumholtz washed up, splashing soapy water on his face before soiling the hand towels, and when he returned to the hallway, Ellie Mallard was standing in exactly the same spot where she had been before, smiling pensively, her right foot half raised and planted with the arch on her left leg, a dancer's position. "*Do* you believe in angels?" she asked.

"No," he said.

"Well, neither do I, but I used to," she said, proceeding down the hallway toward an open doorway. Krumholtz followed her and noticed a Bonazzi painting next to a Hockney—no, it wasn't a Hockney, though it looked like one, with a nude male swimmer underwater—and a Dentinger, a Fabian, and a huge Dierking that went all the way up to the ceiling, the dirty-brown and grayish paint mixed in with what looked like rusted metal fragments expressive of terrible agony on an epic scale. When he turned the corner, he found himself in what appeared to be a master bathroom placed in the middle of the hallway with a large whirlpool bath built into the floor. Leaning back in the bathtub, with his eyes fixed on Krumholtz, was the winner, James Mallard.

"Ah, so at last you're here," Mallard said. "We thought you must have been a little lost, being late. As you were. What happened to you?"

"Yes, I'm sorry," Krumholtz said, putting his notebook away.

"Oh, that's all right." Mallard stood up and stepped out of the whirlpool bath. He was quite magnificent, still in possession of a sculpted athlete's body, classically muscled and proportioned. Somewhere else in this house, Krumholtz knew, would be a fully equipped gym and possibly a full-time personal trainer. "We wondered what had gone wrong with you," Mallard muttered flatly, as if Krumholtz's absence actually had been a matter of the greatest indifference. Without a trace of shyness, and still wet, Mallard stepped toward Krumholtz and shook his hand, hard. He had a strong wet grip and large, thick fingers. Having finished with the handshake, Mallard stepped backward toward a grooved section of wall, where he pressed a recessed button. Hot air came blowing out on him from louvers in the wall, drying his body as he pivoted, his arms held slightly up. Krumholtz glanced over at Mallard's wife, who was gazing appreciatively at her husband. Like the gods, these people had no timidity or shame. "Darling," Mallard said to his wife, "would you hand me a towel?"

She reached over for a red bath towel, with a JM monogram, and handed it to her husband, though not before giving him a peck on the cheek. Mallard dried the backs of his legs and his hair, still in full view of Krumholtz, whose hand was now sopping wet. After drying himself, Mallard tossed the bath towel onto the floor.

"Well," he said. "How shall we conduct this interview? This *little* interview?"

"Perhaps in your den?" Krumholtz asked. "I have a digital recorder—"

"Wouldn't you rather be *doing* something?" Mallard asked. "Something physical? Do you hunt? It's deer season, and we could go hunting. Actually, no. Unfortunately for us, the light is going, and it's too late in the day. We could go out tomorrow, if you wish."

"Well, no, I don't hunt," Krumholtz said. Here I am, he thought, talking to this naked man, while his wife looks on.

"We could chop some wood," Mallard said. "There's time. We could do that."

"But you've just washed. And I have to take notes."

"You mean there's a rule?" Mallard laughed. "Didn't know there was a rule." He walked into the bedroom on the other side of the bathroom and put on the worn clothes he had apparently just taken off. "There's never a rule. That's the first thing you have to learn. Come on."


Outside, in the backyard, Mallard, or someone, had set up a small platform of slatted wood and, a few feet away, a sawhorse. Off to the side were axes, hatchets, a steel wedge, and a chain saw neatly arranged inside a wooden holding-frame with pegs at the top from which to hang other tools. A large pile of unsplit logs had been dumped nearby, and now Mallard picked up a log and stood it up on the platform. He took out an ax before stepping away from the log. With one powerful blow, he raised the ax and brought it down on the log, splitting it cleanly in two.

"Is this your hobby?" Krumholtz asked. "Splitting wood?"

"It's not a hobby, no. Hobbies are for others. It's an activity, a physical exertion, that we like to engage in," Mallard said. Again he placed a log vertically on the platform, and again the ax came down in one clean arc. The two parts of the log dropped away on either side. "A few minutes, and then you can take over."

Krumholtz took a long look at Mallard's face, which now, in the diminishing light, seemed to have a rock-jawed solidity, with eyes set far apart and a heavy five-o'clock shadow over a thick neck. Wherever Mallard turned, he gave off an air of command: the velvet glove over the iron fist had grown very thin with him. He split logs with efficiency, Krumholtz thought, but also as if he were in a permanent rage.

"So, you have questions? Ask questions," Mallard said, his breath coming out in snorts. "Ask me questions."

"Why did you move out here? It's a bit remote."

"We didn't want to see any neighbors. So we bought up the entire valley. You can look in any direction, and you won't see anybody. It gives you a . . . freedom, you know?"

"Yes, well. Something else I meant to ask right away. This can be on or off the record, but your wife mentioned something about 'the other woman,' and I think she said her name is Lorraine. When I came to the gate—"

"Lorraine?" The ax came down. "Are you doing a gossip sheet? I thought this was for *Success* magazine. Well. This isn't for publication. Lorraine's my girlfriend. My *mistress,* if you will."

"She's here?"

"Of course she's here. You didn't meet her? Sometimes—" He set up another log, then took off his jacket and rolled up the sleeves of his shirt. "Sometimes Lorraine stays down at her end of the house. Or she's out in back." He waved his arm at the air.

"Your wife doesn't mind? Your having a live-in girlfriend?"

"Off the record? Or on it? Well, write what you please. We don't care. No, she *doesn't* mind. She knows that a man like me needs more than one woman. That's how it happens to be. Always has been. From the start. We simply choose not to lie about it and not to indulge in the usual middling hypocrisies. I could tell you about men who have a different mistress *every month*. If you can afford it, you can do it. Everyone knows and nobody cares. So. Have you met Lorraine?"

"No."

"Why don't you go back into the house and go back toward the other wing and introduce yourself to her and get her version of things, then come back and split some logs? Obviously, you need to get the girlfriend thing out of the way. Then we'll have a drink." Mallard pointed at the door.

Walking down the hallways in a kind of trance, with the artwork appearing to register his presence—here was another video installation, switched on possibly for his benefit, this one by an artist, Frederic Winkelman, whose work he recognized, the flat screen showing a woman staring straight out at the viewer, this same woman wearing a slightly antique stained silk chiffon bridal gown à la Miss Havisham but posed sitting in a folding chair on a busy urban sidewalk (it looked like midtown Manhattan somewhere near Forty-second Street) while all around her the blurry pedestrians parted and then reclustered—walking away from this visual disturbance, and making his way past more artistic plunder perfectly mounted and framed, Krumholtz thought first of his wife, Cathy, working at her desk at the agency, and then of the remote castle in *Beauty and the Beast,* not the Disney version (his daughters' favorite movie, both of them addicted to princess figures), but the Cocteau film with the hallway chandeliers consisting of bare human arms holding candlesticks, and all the other inanimate objects down to the cups and saucers having taken on resentful life as servants, everything under a spell that could be broken only by love, by a kiss. Cathy would be headed home about now, picking up the girls at after-school care, driving them homeward while she tried to quiet them and think of what to serve for dinner, and he wondered if she would have a thought for him out on this assignment, and at that particular moment he turned another corner near an open door and saw a woman, the one who must certainly be the girlfriend, Lorraine, lying back on a fainting couch. She was reading a glossy magazine and glanced up when Krumholtz entered.

"Oh," she said. "You must be that guy."

After a moment Krumholtz realized that this woman, this Lorraine, was wearing flowered pajamas. The roses on the pajamas had a slightly sinister efflorescence. "Yes," he said, "I'm that guy." He examined her. Unlike the wife, she was not particularly beautiful. On her left cheek was a birthmark in the shape of a candle flame. "I'm the guy you asked about angels. You were at the intercom."

"The guy from the magazine? You didn't answer my question."

"No, I suppose not." He pointed at her. "You're wearing pajamas. It's midafternoon. Been napping?"

"What did you say your name was?"

"Krumholtz. Jerry Krumholtz."

"Jerry, did you think Jimmy looked okay?" Lorraine asked. "I'm worried about him. He hasn't been himself lately, and no one knows why."

"He looked all right. What do you think could be bothering him?" Krumholtz asked, getting out his notebook.

"Me? What do I think? It could be anything. He's restless. I think he's run out of worlds to conquer. And that makes him sick." She tossed the glossy magazine onto the floor. "He's got everything. What would you do if you had everything?"

What a preposterous question. Krumholtz took out his pen. "Doesn't Ellie—doesn't the wife—mind that you're here?"

"What did you say your name was?" She was unapologetic about her forgetfulness, apparently.

"Jerry Krumholtz."

"Oh, right. Where did you ever get a name like that?"

A moment passed while he absorbed her question. "My parents gave it to me. I think I was asking about whether the wife minds that you're here."

"Here? In this room, or here in the house? No. Oh, you mean my *existence,* here on earth, taking up the sexual slack? Why should she mind? Maybe you don't understand about men like Jimmy. He's just bigger than other men. Everything about him is bigger and stronger than they are. Those *herd* men. All the little Shmoos. So *unimportant.* He's just richer and smarter and more . . . beautiful than they are. He's at the top of the pyramid. The rules for the little doofuses don't apply to him. Do you understand that? If you don't understand that, Krumholtz, you don't understand anything."

"So this is the harem?"

"Because otherwise," she continued, as if she hadn't heard him, "there's no point in your being here. Or doing this story. He loves both Ellie and me. He has more than enough love for both of us, and the children. And the previous wife and the previous children. He flies to see them. He has a private jet. He's not like ordinary men, is what I'm saying. I satisfy some of his needs, and Ellie satisfies other needs, and that's how it is, and if it isn't bourgeois enough for you, that's too bad."

"What needs do you satisfy?" Krumholtz asked.

"What sort of question is that? Is this going into the article?"

"It might. We'll see."

She stood up and walked over toward him. "You don't get it, do you?"

"Maybe I do. So explain it to me."

"I don't have to explain it," she said. "I can do a demo." She leaned in to him, reaching around his back, and, in what Krumholtz could tell instantly was a cruel practical joke, brought her face close to his and planted a long kiss on his lips, with the slightest suggestion of tongue. The kiss constituted sheer mockery of his unimportance. She might as well have been kissing a lampshade. "That's what I give him," Lorraine said, leaning back. "And that's just for starters. Get it now?"

"Yes, I suppose I get it," Krumholtz said. She was wearing a French perfume, which he recognized as one of the varieties of Plage de Soleil.

"I'm good at what I do," Lorraine said with a fixed smile. "I'm a spell-caster. An energizer. I've got Jimmy in my grip and he has me in his."

"And the wife?" Krumholtz asked. "Ellie?" This woman, Krumholtz thought, is trying to break my soul into little pieces just for fun. Out of sheer boredom.

"If you only believed in angels, Mr. Krumholtz, you might be lifted up now and then out of your pathetic little life." Lorraine had touched him gently on the cheek. "But, sadly, no."

From outside came the sound of a rifle shot.

"No one knows how we live," she said. "And no one's going to." She lifted her head and listened. "Now I wonder what Jimmy's shooting at?"

She stepped backward and dropped onto the fainting couch. Krumholtz saw that she was wearing a small ankle bracelet of brilliant gold. "You can go," she said.

Krumholtz returned to the corridor, again walking past the video of the midtown Miss Havisham, but he could not find the door out to the back terrace. He touched the thick glass in an effort to find the doorway. Night appeared to be descending on trembling batlike wings, and inside Mallardhof the music continued to float down from the invisible built-in speakers. At the moment, they were playing the first book of Debussy *Préludes*. Krumholtz had once been a pianist, playing keyboards in a rock band in high school, and had played in another band, Sweat Stain, in college, but had found no way of making a living from it and after majoring in music had gone into journalism, thinking that he might preserve some elements of artistic work in what he did. He had been a good enough pianist to work in a cocktail lounge to pay for his tuition, but greatness was far beyond him, and he knew it. You had to be a great musician to make a real living at it. He stopped to listen to the music. The sound was slightly smeary: an old recording: Walter Gieseking playing.

Cathy would be sitting the girls down about now, for dinner. They would be gathered under the kitchen light, maybe eating spaghetti together. Cathy made a great sauce. Her spaghetti sauce was one of her little glories. Krumholtz went through a brief shudder of longing for his wife and daughters and home. He had never felt anything but love for Cathy from the moment he had met her. He thought of asking someone in this infernal Olympian household for a telephone, so he could call to check up on her, see how she was doing. Lately he had been a bit worried about her. She had appeared to be distracted and preoccupied and hardly listened to him when he was talking to her. The job at the agency, she had told him, had been getting her down.

All at once he found the door out to the back terrace where Mallard had been chopping firewood. When he saw Mallard now, Krumholtz could make out that the man was covered with blood. He was bent over something with a knife in his hand and was cutting it lengthwise.

"A deer, damn it," Mallard said. "Somehow it got on the property. You know, they eat everything. There must be a hole in the fencing. They can be very aggressive. And destructive." Mallard had in his hand a four-inch field knife and another tool Krumholtz didn't recognize. "Have you ever done this?" he asked. Without waiting for an answer, he said, "Some hunters bleed the deer. They cut its throat. But that's ridiculous, because after all the heart isn't pumping, so you have to hang the damn thing with its head down so the blood drains out. Anyway, we don't do that. So what you do is, you get the deer on its back. Maybe you know. You look like you may be a hunter."

"Yes, I can see what you're doing," Krumholtz said. Would this scene provide him with the opening of his article? "A winner not afraid of blood!"

"And then what you do is, you put your gloves on and then cut with a gut hook—damn, the light should be better—from down here, the genitals, up to the sternum. But you don't cut too deep because if you do, you'll cut into the intestines, and then you've got a god-awful mess on your hands, and you'll smell bad for a week. You cut out the bladder. You *can* skin the deer at this point, pulling the skin back from the meat. Some do, some don't. I usually don't."

"I see."

"After you've cut the diaphragm away, you get the knife up to cut the esophagus out. Once that's cut—maybe you could get us a flashlight— you pull the lungs and the heart out, but that's tricky because they're attached with peritoneum, and if there's anything left of the intestines they just go with them. The heart's good. Always save the heart. You can eat the heart. We do. Skinning comes later. You can help with that. God damn it, the light's bad. We'll have to hang this thing up." He turned around and stood, blood dripping down from his gloves. "What's the matter with you?"

"I'm just watching." He waited. "You said 'we.' Does your wife do this, too?"

He turned around. "Another way to do it is, you get the cutting tool up past the rib cage and just sever the windpipe off as far up as you can. When you perform the action properly the heart and lungs will also just come dropping out. Also, there's the blood, maybe you want to drain the animal. Blood, yes . . . blood. Sausage? If the thing is a male, you cut the reproductive organs and then you also—"

Krumholtz couldn't be sure that he was hearing James Mallard properly. The man's words weren't making any sense. The winner seemed to be slipping into a verbal salad, a garble of ejaculations and non sequiturs as he worked. "You push! Bloody the flashlight, slipcase the meat sauce, bloodstop the tenderloin—and offal! A whitetail—umph!—sealing intestines sausage blood wedding drool! A house marine edible brains! Venison salad pepper cake? Or not?"

Perhaps he had misheard. He hadn't had anything to eat after gulping down that drink in the airport lounge. His heartburn was acting up again. Feeling light-headed, Krumholtz backed away from Mallard and let himself into the house. In what appeared to be a sitting room close to the central hallway, he deposited himself onto a coal-black sofa. On the opposite wall another work of art had been installed, an enormous monochromatic study of what appeared to be human teeth reconsidered in a post-Cubist style, close-up, so that they resembled mountains. Krumholtz, turning his gaze away, looked down at the floor and noticed that he had tracked dirt in from the backyard through the hallway and onto the carpeting in the sitting room. He felt tired and hungry. For a moment, he closed his eyes.

When he opened his eyes again, he saw Angus and Ping standing in front of him, staring at him. "What's the matter with you?" the little boy asked. "You're as white as a sheet."

"I felt faint."

"Sight of blood do that to you?" Ping asked. Who was she? The tutor? Yes, the tutor. She was also possibly, no, *probably*, another one of the mistresses.

"Well, it's just that I haven't eaten since breakfast," Krumholtz said.

"You want something?" Angus asked. He was tossing a tennis ball up in the air and catching it with his right hand. "I could get you a cookie." He didn't move. "In Chinese, it's *bǐng gān,* and in French it's *petit gâteau.*"

"Yeah," Krumholtz said. "I know. Yes. Maybe something to eat."

"You're the person who came to ask us questions. Ask me a question," Angus said. Apparently he wasn't about to get anything for Krumholtz after all. A request for a cookie meant nothing to this child.

"Okay. Here's a question for you. How come you get to be happy?"

"How come? That's a *hard* question," the boy said. "I don't know. I'll go get Mom." When he left the room, Ping went with him, smiling mysteriously. Perhaps she was amused by his question. You weren't supposed to ask such questions of the rich. They would resent such inquiries and find the means to punish you. Krumholtz shut his eyes again, imagining his wife. When he opened them, both James and Ellie Mallard were standing in front of him. Wearing a crisply ironed pair of black slacks and a thick wool sweater, James Mallard was bending toward Krumholtz, a drink in his hand.

"Scotch?"

"No, thanks, not just yet. What happened to all the blood? You were covered in blood, last I saw you."

"You're sure you don't want a scotch? It'll warm you up. Single malt."

"No. That's all right." He took the glass and drank from it. "Thanks."

"His mind rejects it, but his hand accepts it," Ellie Mallard said with delight. "Will you have dinner with us?"

"I really should get back into town. It's time to go. I'll come back tomorrow."

"You'll get lost!" He noticed that she was very exclamatory. "You'll never get back. Weeks later, searchers will find you. Oh, but where are you staying?" Ellie sat down opposite him on a love seat, and James Mallard sat down beside her. She raised her legs so that they were crossed on her husband's lap. He began to massage her feet.

"In D———," Krumholtz said. "I have a reservation at a hotel there."

"You'll never get back. A hotel! Those smoky rooms! Those TV sets!" She pretended to shudder. "Oh, stay with us," Ellie said. "Never go away!"

"Yes," Mallard said, agreeing with his wife, though unsmilingly. "Ask us the questions that you want to have the answers to, and maybe, just maybe," he said, with the ghost of an ironic smile, "we'll answer them someday."

Krumholtz took another slug of the scotch. "All right," he said. "Here's my question." He took out his digital recorder and pretended to turn it on.

"Shoot," Ellie Mallard said pleasantly. As her husband massaged her feet, she closed her eyes in bliss.

"Why do you get to be happy?" Krumholtz asked. "I asked your boy Angus this very same question a minute ago, and he was stumped."

"*Why do we get to be happy?*" Mallard repeated. "What an absurd question. But I'll tell you. We have a lot of money. *Geld macht frei*. We worked for it, we worked very hard, long days and long nights, and then, of course, we were lucky."

"The royal 'we' again?" Krumholtz muttered to himself. More loudly, he said, "Yes, it's the luck I'm interested in. About that 'luck.' The reason I asked is that other people, little people, work long days and long nights, very long days, days that go on for longer than twenty-four hours, days that go for weeks at a time." He felt a sudden lift-over into either joy or rage. "That kind of day, you know, a working day that lasts for weeks. And *they're* not happy, and, well, maybe that's because they're *not* lucky. Also, they have to live with neighbors, you know, that *Rear Window* situation? Just surrounded by mere people with every sort of problem. And I wondered what you thought about that."

Krumholtz heard what sounded like a grandfather clock ticking somewhere down the hallway to his left. In front of him, the teeth opened ever so slightly.

"Is there a question in there somewhere?" Ellie Mallard asked, still not opening her eyes.

"You take me, for example," Krumholtz said, feeling some crucial disconnection. "We, that is, my wife and I, have neighbors. And the two of us, we . . . well, I was once a musician, and she wanted to be a social worker, and she *was* a social worker for a while before they cut the state and federal funding, which they never restored, and then, well, this *thing* happened to us, and this, what I'm about to tell you, this was about eighteen months after we were married, and she became pregnant. And immediately she had complications." He took another swig of the scotch, emptying the glass. "For the last four months of the pregnancy, she was spotting, so they kept her in bed. But she got through it. The baby—it was a breech, so they had to perform a Cesarean, and they didn't give my wife, Cathy, enough anesthetic, so the whole procedure took a bad toll on her, she was in terrible pain there for a while, but our son was born, Michael, and it seemed as if everything would be all right. And we would recover."

Mallard had stopped massaging his wife's feet, and both he and his wife were staring at Krumholtz, their attention fixed on him. Mallard lightly dropped his wife's legs on the floor, rose, and took Krumholtz's glass, refilling it, and then returned it to him. Krumholtz could not stop himself. Where had this story come from? It wasn't untrue, exactly, even though it hadn't happened.

"And Michael seemed to be all right for a while, and he thrived, and by the time he reached his fifth birthday, we thought we were out of the woods. But then, and I wouldn't be telling you this if it weren't the end of the day and I weren't tired out—"

"Go right ahead," Ellie Mallard said. "Disunburden yourself."

"Thank you. He . . . he became sick. It began with coughing, and he lost his appetite, and he was pale, and he never had any energy, which you're not expecting in a child that age, they're animals really, or they *should* be, running and shouting all the time, that's what nature intended, I mean, but instead he, I mean Michael, would sit in a chair morning until night, listlessly, you know, and usually television was all he could do, and we at least gave thanks for that. . . . Well, we couldn't get a diagnosis from the pediatrician, and of course, it was understandable. Who knows how to look? Or where? We did one blood test after another, I mean, *they* did, *they* did one blood test after another, beyond what our insurance could pay for, those ghouls, though I suppose I shouldn't say that, they mean well, those medical professionals, and each time, *each time* we went in, Michael would start crying before they had even taken the blood, which tore at my heart. He'd just see the exterior office door, which was painted this bright terrible frightening red, not comforting at all, and he'd start howling. How can you get used to the suffering of a child? I mean, you can't. You can't get used to it. Or you *shouldn't*. There's nothing there in that situation you should ever accept. And he was bleeding from the nose all the time, and sometimes from his mouth, for no reasons that we knew, and then finally we got a diagnosis."

"What was it?" Ellie Mallard asked in a whisper.

"Chronic thrombocytopenic purpura," Krumholtz said. He had once written an article about the disease and knew something about it. "And there's no cure for it and no treatment and invariably it's fatal. So . . . well, we had a certain amount of time. There was this question we were facing. What should we do? *What should we do with the time we had left with our little boy?* It's such a terrible decision. I mean, no one can make a decision like that. Of course we asked Michael what he wanted to do, we had to ask him, what he wanted to do more than anything else in the world. He didn't want to go to any of those destination places. He said he wanted to sit by the window."

Krumholtz took another swig of the scotch.

"Michael sat by the window, and he would narrate what he saw, almost as if he could imagine what his adulthood might have been like. People going to work in the morning, people coming home in the evening, laboring at their jobs. And the sun, traveling across the sky. And the street. And the birds. And squirrels. There was one particular bird, a sparrow that came by for the bread crumbs that Michael put out on his windowsill. And then, when Michael died, the sparrow came by waiting for him, for the food he had put out there. The bird would hop out on the sill and chirp. Then one night we heard a terrible thump against Michael's window. The next morning we found the sparrow on the lawn. It seemed to have flung itself against his window. When I bent down to pick it up, I discovered that its heart had stopped."

Well, he had his triumph: the winner and his wife were in tears. The damn tears: against the riches of the world, they changed almost nothing. But now Krumholtz felt a power surging through him. No one would dare to move him from his comfortable position on the sofa. He took another swig. "Oh, stop," Ellie Mallard said, touching a hankie to her face. But he wasn't finished. The boy, Angus, had come into the room and was staring wide-eyed at his mother. And now here was Gretel, dressed just like her brother, in the doorway, listening intently, and alarmed by the parental weeping. Krumholz did not intend to budge: he would sit there, with his audience in front of him, elaborating this story of suffering and terror for as long as he pleased. He had just gotten started.